PEACEMAKER
BOOK SIX OF THE
REVELATIONS CYCLE

Kevin Ikenberry

Seventh Seal Press
Virginia Beach, VA

Copyright © 2017 by Kevin Ikenberry.

All rights reserved. No part of this publication may be reproduced, distributed or transmitted in any form or by any means, including photocopying, recording, or other electronic or mechanical methods, without the prior written permission of the publisher, except in the case of brief quotations embodied in critical reviews and certain other noncommercial uses permitted by copyright law. For permission requests, write to the publisher, addressed "Attention: Permissions Coordinator," at the address below.

Chris Kennedy/Seventh Seal Press
2052 Bierce Dr.
Virginia Beach, VA 23454
http://chriskennedypublishing.com/

Publisher's Note: This is a work of fiction. Names, characters, places, and incidents are a product of the author's imagination. Locales and public names are sometimes used for atmospheric purposes. Any resemblance to actual people, living or dead, or to businesses, companies, events, institutions, or locales is completely coincidental.

Ordering Information:
Quantity sales. Special discounts are available on quantity purchases by corporations, associations, and others. For details, contact the "Special Sales Department" at the address above.

Peacemaker/ Kevin Ikenberry. -- 1st ed.
ISBN 978-1942936800

For My Girls

Chapter One

A Peacemaker always honored the threat. Jessica Francis silently released her pistol from the holster on her thigh without looking away from her target's back. Fingers light on the pistol's grip, the Peacemaker trainers' words reverberated in her mind. *Brandish a weapon only when threatened and never to make a point.* The Zuparti trader, Ch'tek, was about to open a cargo container and get one hell of a surprise. Its interior privacy system destroyed, the container doors would slide completely open. The illicit cargo inside, gift-wrapped for the destruction of Earth, secured her provisional appointment as Earth's first Peacemaker. Try as she might, trusting the little Zuparti trader not to become a threat wasn't a chance worth taking.

Ch'tek's claws scraped against the interior mechanism of the control panel she'd carefully damaged with her ex-husband's help. Marc Lemieux had never been a competent commander. Succeeding because of the exploits of his subordinates only managed to get Marc so far. His ego finally managed to get the better of him, and several promising young mercenaries died including one of Jessica's best friends. The recovery of the container had been the only thing to go right during the mission. She blinked the recent, painful memories away.

The door sprang open. Jessica removed the laser pistol deftly and leveled it at Ch'tek's narrow chest as he spun and wiped his dirty little paws. Behind him, a viable Canavar egg, incapable of hatching unless directly breached, rested on a bed of hay.

"What are you—"

"Ch'tek." Jessica kept her voice measured and direct. "By the laws of the Union, you are under arrest for the unlawful removal and possession of a Canavar egg, deceitful employment of a registered mercenary force, and coercion."

"What are you talking about?" Ch'tek laughed. "That's not what's in—"

From her side, Lemieux pointed at the open door. The small Zuparti turned and fell silent. After a moment, he turned back to Jessica and grinned. "How much to forget this unfortunate incident? Commander Lemieux? Miss Francis? You're a bounty hunter and cannot arrest—"

With her free hand, Jessica pulled out a thin black sleeve from a chest pocket. On it was a platinum shield. "That's Peacemaker, not bounty hunter. On my authority, Ch'tek, you're under arrest." She raised her voice. "Bay Control? Authorization Zulu Four Zero."

Large hangar doors opened. A squad of Peacemakers entered the space with their weapons trained on Ch'tek and the Canavar egg. A dozen other officers of varying species filed past them and surrounded the Zuparti trader. Two lumbering Lumari Peacemakers flanked Ch'tek and quickly placed shackles on his arms and legs, leaving the small alien defeated, as Jessica continued. "By Union Laws, you are under arrest. You will be held until such time as you are placed before a Peacemaker tribunal. Your rights of redress and citizenship are suspended until you are released or acquitted. You cannot complete or enter into any contracts with the sole exception of legal representation. You are entitled to obtain said representation, if possible.

Credit will be extended to you if you cannot afford said representation. Do you have any questions?"

Ch'tek shook his head and looked away. His eyes narrowed. Jessica knew Ch'tek's worst nightmare was about to come true. A pair of Buma diplomats, their wide-eyes taking in everything, shuffled into her view. Ch'tek was secured in his chains, and she holstered her pistol without looking.

"Peacemaker Francis?" the nearest one said. "Are these allegations true?"

"Of course, they're true," Ch'tek snarled. "The Union did not need this pathetic species! I demand to see the Zuparti consul at once!"

Jessica looked at two officers standing close by. "Please remove the accused." Ch'tek disappeared behind a group of white-coated scientists rushing to the Canavar egg.

Jessica nodded to the Buma. "Please relay my gratitude to the Besquith, Cael Doontal."

"Well done, Peacemaker." The Buma bowed and retreated from them.

Gods, I love the sound of that!

Lemieux glanced at her, trying to be charming, with a smile on his face she wanted to forcibly remove. He'd always tried to make light of things with inane sayings, as though humor was akin to leadership, and a good laugh moved mountains. For six years, she'd wanted to find him and shut him the hell up. Now, though, she could go one step further.

She stared at him for a long moment and watched the smile drain away from his face almost as fast as the color did. "Marc, you are an accessory to this."

"The hell I am!" Lemieux argued. "My contract was violated. I'm no party to anything. If anyone's an accessory, you are! You took it onboard your ship!"

"I told you that was for evidence, don't you remember?" Jessica smirked. "I'm trying to decide if I should charge you with anything. I'm sure I could find a few things in your records." She'd been his executive officer, his second in command, until their divorce, and she knew the books better than he ever would. Without the help of a substantially talented accountant, all of it could be easily found.

Lemieux snorted. "Bounty hunter was your cover, right?"

Always remain calm. The first tenet of being a Peacemaker held true in every instance. Jessica forced herself to relax her clenching fist and keep her words measured. "I never said I was a bounty hunter, Marc. But, you're getting there."

"And the egg? You knew it was there, didn't you?"

Jessica shook her head. Some things were not for a mediocre mercenary commander to know. "Peacemaker business, Marc. It's classified. Give me Elly and you walk away."

"Fine," Lemieux said. He bent down, carefully unzipped the lower leg pocket of his coveralls, and withdrew a small white gift box. Worn on the corners and held together with yellowing tape, seeing the box made her heart leap in anticipation. "Your mother left explicit instructions."

"That I should never get it?" Jessica chuckled. "I knew she sent it to you. For whatever reason, she went to her grave thinking you were a wonderful man and would try to look out for me. That's code for putting me off to the side and taking me for granted, by the way."

Lemieux flushed. "That's what you think of our time together?"

Gods, yes.

"Pretty much." She took the offered box and opened it. Wrapped in a double layer of white tissue paper was a small, porcelain elephant statuette that easily fit in the palm of her hand. "She's as pretty as I remember."

"I didn't realize she meant that much to you."

"You never realized a lot of things, Marc." She glanced at him with hard, cold eyes. "The guild will pay your fee for this operation on one condition. You are to pay your soldiers and your creditors. With the remaining balance, you are to retire, preferably somewhere far from the trade routes. Stop playing mercenary commander. You're simply not fit for it."

Lemieux sighed. "Fine. I'm retired. Are you happy, Jess?"

"Peacemaker pays better than being a merc or a bounty hunter," she said. Ten years ago, when they'd started the Marauders, she hadn't known anything about war. Being a merc sounded a lot better. The first years were hell, but they'd built something that could have been great, only to see it collapse under poor decision making and judgment. Bounty hunting hadn't been glamorous at all, but the Peacemaker Guild had seen something they liked enough to grant her a provisional candidacy. In order to assume full duties, the standing requirements were completion of the Peacemaker Academy, an arduous three-year commitment, and the completion of one approved operational mission. Given the nature of Ch'tek's capture and the dissolution of his plan to attack Earth, she believed his arrest would easily qualify as her operational mission for commissioning. Her exams and physical trials to complete the Academy were two months behind her. Nothing stood in the way of her full commissioning. Earth's first Peacemaker would make a damned fine epitaph.

"That's not what I meant," Lemieux replied. Color crept up his neck, like it always did when he was mad but defeated. He'd never change, and that was a bad thing. The blame would come next. "You always get what you want! You've taken everything from me since day one—"

Gods. The porcelain elephant's cartoon face smiled up at her as if knowing a secret. It was time to find out what Elly knew.

Make sure she gets Elly! When she's ready!

Her father's voice, almost 20 years in the past, was crystal clear in her memory. The smell of rocket fuel and dust always came with him, mixed in the air with his cheap aftershave. He'd been a shadow leaving in the night when she was 10 years old, never to be seen again. Elly, her most prized possession, knew better, and it was time to learn why. She dropped the elephant to the cold steel deck and watched it shatter into a few dozen pieces.

At her side, Marc gasped but said nothing.

In the center of the debris lay something rectangular and black. Jessica bent down and retrieved it quickly. As she stood, she rotated it in her palm and he could see it was a type of computer chipset with the tiny word "Snowman" printed in bright orange against the dull black surface. Her heart swelled as she closed her fist around the chipset.

"What the hell is that? Why does it have your father's callsign on it?" Lemieux asked.

"Wouldn't you like to know?" Jessica winked and walked away, leaving him behind on the deck. *Good riddance.* She turned around the aft end of a skiff hauling CASPers marked for delivery to Asbaran Solutions and saw her Selector ambling toward her with his long-beaked face curled in an appreciative smile.

The Sidar nodded at her. A few sprigs of silver hair on top of his angular head caught the lights of the high bay. "Peacemaker Francis."

"Selector Hak-chet." Jessica nodded with respect. Hak-Chet had taken her under his wing two years ago and presented her to Rsach, the Peacemaker Guild Master as Earth's first candidate. He'd been with her the entire time as counselor, mentor, and motivator. Until now, her existence as a candidate was a closely-held secret. Once she was commissioned, her identity would be well known across the galaxy.

"Well done, Peacemaker. Save for brandishing your weapon unnecessarily," Hak-Chet's jaw worked under his smile. His eyes, though, were cold and distant. He looked away, side-to-side, as if concerned about eavesdropping. "We should speak privately."

Jessica nodded as the Selector swept past her into a narrow opening between CASPers. The Selector's compliment and criticism erased the adrenaline high threatening to crash through her system, and brought her focus clearly to the moment. His black robe swirled, as the atmosphere fans recycled and churned the stale hangar air. "Is something the matter?"

Hak-Chet turned to her, and one side of his mouth curled under. It was an all-too-human expression that looked positively awkward on the Sidar's face. "You've passed the operational phase of your trials, Jessica. Of that, and you, I am extremely proud. There are others, though, who are not proud of your efforts, successful as they have been."

Jessica frowned. "You said politics would rear its ugly head."

"Its ugly, many-faced head," Hak-Chet chuckled. He waved away whatever thought came next with his clawed hand. "That is not important, nor why I am here now. The Guild Master wants to speak with you."

Jessica felt a bolt of adrenaline course through her system. "Rsach? He wants to speak with me? Personally?"

"With your Selector present, of course." Hak-Chet tilted his long face to one side and studied her for a moment. "I do not know what he might say."

She felt a sudden smile cross her lips. Throughout her training, especially in the dynamics of conversation and persuasion, he would give her a similar look and say a single word that could fluster her instantly. The word came out with a smile she knew was both playful and sarcastic. "Speculation?"

Hak-Chet laughed and raised a hand to the side of his jaw. "I cannot." Another bout of laughter erupted, this much louder than before. Her mentor placed his hands on his belly and shook his head.

Jessica squinted. "Surely there must be something?"

"Oh, there is." Hak-Chet composed himself with a deep, hitching breath. "You are trouble, Jessica Francis. Exactly what I thought you'd be. Others, though, think you must be properly tested. That is what I suspect, not what I speculate."

"Another test?" Jessica frowned. "They thought it was too easy, right? Or that I was using my position to get back at my ex-husband?"

"Perhaps." The Sidar shrugged. "The phrase I heard was diplomatic aplomb. You are an outstanding field commander and operative. You have all the ability in the world to handle yourself in a fight."

Jessica fought the pride swelling up in her. There was a *but* coming. Despite the praise of her Selector, her commission as a Peacemaker hung in the balance. She said it for them both. "But they are worried I cannot negotiate?"

Hak-Chet shook his head. "There are many ways to solve a problem, Jessica. Do you remember what I asked you when we first met?"

She nodded. The interview had been scheduled for six hours in a rundown concrete building that had been a National Guard armory in New Mexico. She'd arrived in sweltering heat and found the building open. Searching for 20 minutes, she'd finally found the Selector staring out a window at Sandia Mountain with his claws clasped behind his back. He hadn't even bothered to look at her.

"You are faced with an obstacle. Do you go over it? Around it? Or through it?"

"Through it," Jessica had said without hesitation. Going over something meant leveraging position or power against an obstacle that might, or might not, require it. Jumping the chain of command was a fast way to unemployment in the mercenary guild. Going around something tended to imply spending more effort and time thinking about how to get around, or out of, a task instead of just doing it. Through it meant doing what was required to get the task done.

Jessica nodded and met Hak-Chet's eyes. "I have to go through it. Whatever they want me to do, don't I?"

"If you want to be a Peacemaker." The Sidar's eyes glistened.

"Yes."

* * *

The Guild Master's yacht was unlike anything Jessica had ever seen. The richly-appointed cabins and open spaces could have easily held the entire Marauder force, yet there were no visible weapons, and the massive supply holds were empty. Boarding at the quarterdeck, trailing her Selector as protocol required, Jessica marveled at the mahogany floors as they crossed into an ornate, very Earthly-appointed conference room. Tri-V pictures of Earth shimmered along the walls. The Great Pyramids of Giza, the Great Wall of China, and the Ceylon Elevator all tugged at her heart. She hadn't been on Earth in more than eighteen months, not since burying her mother along the Missouri River.

"Jessica?"

She turned to Hak-Chet. He'd clearly said her name at least once, maybe twice before. "Sorry, Selector. My mind was elsewhere."

Hak-Chet glanced at the Tri-V displays. "Our Guild Master wants you to feel at home, nothing more."

It's not that, she wanted to say. *Earth is no more my home than a CASPer. You both know this. Why dangle Earth in front of me like a carrot, unless you expect me to fail?*

The far door opened and Rsach entered alone. His body contorted and flowed with multiple pairs of arms waving gently. She'd been up close to a Jeha only once before and none with as much power as her Guild Master. Even standing in his presence was an honor. She bowed her head in respect. "Master Rsach."

"Peacemaker Francis," Rsach replied. "Won't you and Selector Hak-Chet make yourselves comfortable?"

Jessica grabbed a high-backed chair, pulled it away from the table, sidestepped it, and sat down. Hak-Chet sat across from her, and Rsach sat in his position at the head of the table. "Thank you."

"Selector Hak-Chet reported you completed your operational assignment as directed." Rsach clasped two sets of arms on his chair's armrests. "The undertaking, while successful and certainly of grave importance, did lack certain qualities necessary of the Guild's members."

Jessica shifted in her seat but said nothing. When she'd suggested the mission to Hak-Chet, his shocked reaction made her feel she'd struck something unique and different. He'd approved the mission, but it was obvious he'd known something at the time. Aware the Guild Master was looking at her, and not Hak-Chet, she said, "There was nothing in my mission briefing that was inferred to be missing, Master Rsach."

"Miss Francis," he said. "Your operational abilities were never in question. A Peacemaker with Union military and mercenary experience would be expected to excel at the operation you proposed and executed with distinction. Success, however, is not a measure of ability." The Guild Master's face was impassive, and his many arms were still. From her class on species interaction, she remembered it as a sign of resolution. Nothing was going to change his mind.

Her gut twisted in panic and she flinched. Taking a breath, she said, "Are you withdrawing my commission offer?"

Rsach replied, "No. I am concerned you cannot handle a discussion without reaching for the nearest weapon when the Peacemaker's greatest weapon is patience."

Jessica clenched her leg muscles under the table, but tried to keep her face relaxed. "But you're hesitating, Master. Is it because I'm human?"

The Jeha bristled and leaned forward. "Absolutely not! Your species does not matter—it's your performance and bearing when no one is watching, Miss Francis. I do not believe you can handle a diplomatic dispute without violence."

Jessica snorted. "Are you taking away my commission or not?"

Hak-Chet leaned forward. "Peacemaker. Please?"

She looked at him for a moment. He slowly turned his head toward the Guild Master. "Master Rsach, as Jessica's Selector I am empowered to ask what conditions you and the Guild have placed upon her commissioning."

"Article Six, Section Four."

Jessica closed her eyes as she heard Hak-Chet respond. "Any Peacemaker who completes a mission in sub-standard form may be required to complete a second mission prior to the receipt of an Enforcer's commission."

"Indeed," Rsach said from the end of the table. The tone of his voice sounded like the crack of damnation.

"My mission wasn't sub-standard!" Jessica opened her eyes and banged a fist on the table. "I stopped a gods-damned Canavar egg from being transported to Earth and hatched there!"

"And the Galactic Union is thankful for your work, Miss Francis," Rsach said. "What matters is your bearing as a Peacemaker. You are the first candidate from Earth and, as such, you must understand that rigorous testing is required to ensure the Guild, and your planet, are best represented."

"What mission is being proposed?" Hak-Chet said.

Rsach looked at them for a moment before speaking. "Are you familiar, Miss Francis, with the Dream World Consortium?"

* * *

"It's not as bad as it sounds, Jessica." Hak-Chet sat across from her at a small table nursing what the station's main watering hole called cider. The Sidar loved the sweet, strong brews of Earth. He swirled the chilled liquid twice and lowered his chin to get into her line of sight.

"Did you hear what I said?"

"I did," Jessica sighed. "Araf sounds like a beautiful planet, Selector. But a conflict that's gone on for two years? And getting worse? That's where they want to send me?"

"It would appear so."

"They want me to fail!" Jessica bit the inside of her lip. Anger was a waste of time and tears would be a mark against her bearing. Angry tears equaled disaster and there was no way in hell she'd cry in front of Hak-Chet. She took a breath and centered her thoughts. "Stopping that egg wasn't enough for them. All the intelligence I had to gather—working with the Besquith and creeping back to Karma alone? None of that mattered. Why else would they give me a no-win situation that's been lingering for years?"

"Perhaps it's an opportunity." Hak-Chet sipped from his glass and set it down on the dirty table with a clink. "A no-win situation depends greatly on who the players are and what it is they want to win. Understanding all sides is the key."

"You're telling me that like I don't have a choice."

Hak-Chet's eyes widened in surprise. "Of course, you have a choice. Any choice other than acceptance of the mission will relinquish your commission opportunity. This mission, as difficult as it seems, is really dependent upon the Peacemaker assigned."

"They don't believe in me, Selector." Her tone, she knew, was defeatist but she could not help it. Training had been hard enough. To even hold a provisional commission, as a human, was unheard of, and the Guild made her pay for it in lumps and bruises. Through it all, she focused on the platinum shield of a Peacemaker. Being the first human wasn't as much a pride factor as people believed it to be. Ultimately, someone always had to be first. The journey of the second person, or the third, wouldn't be that much different from hers. What would matter was that someone did go first and made things happen. "I don't want to be a mercenary anymore."

Hak-Chet laughed and reached out a clawed hand to touch her arm lightly. He seldom sought any type of physical interaction in the Sidar way, so the gesture's unspoken message was clear. "You stopped being a mercenary when you began your training as a Peacemaker, Jessica. I think it's time you finish it."

She nodded. "And if I fail?"

"You won't," Hak-Chet said. "Under the codicils of the diplomatic code you are entitled to receive a mediation assistant. I've taken the liberty of arranging their passage with you."

"You think I need an assistant?" Jessica fumbled in her pockets for a smoke that she hadn't had in years and mentally slapped herself. "That tells me everything, huh?"

Hak-Chet tossed back the last of his cider and stood. "If you believe that, you're not ready to be a Peacemaker, Jessica. Every advantage you can legally empower is worth the effort. Let me know your decision by midnight."

She sighed. "I will."

"Try to behave yourself, please?"

Jessica looked around the dingy bar. A few merc wannabes nursed shitty beers at the bar. She'd seen them looking at her a few times, behaving like they thought older, tougher mercs did. All sex, guns, and rock and roll. Pathetic. Older mercs never chased anything but a good stiff drink and a steady paycheck.

Gods help me.

"Don't I always behave, Selector Hak-Chet?"

The Sidar smiled at her and nodded. "You do, Peacemaker Francis. Shall I tell the Guild you'll take the mission so I can arrange your transport?"

Fuck it.

"Please," Jessica said and reached for her glass of Jack Daniels. She'd barely touched it for the last hour. The Tennessee whiskey bit through her doubt, as it always did. "I'll take the mission, and thank you for arranging a mediation assistant."

"I want to see you succeed, Jessica," Hak-Chet said. "If not on the Guild's terms, at least on your own." The Sidar bowed gracefully, per his race's customs, and walked slowly out of the bar, leaving Jessica alone with her half-full drink. She played with the glass for a moment, watching the amber liquid swirl. A fresh one appeared.

"I didn't order this," she said and looked up at the robot bartender.

The bartender looked to its right and Jessica followed its wide-lensed eyes. A young blonde woman wearing the olive drab coveralls of an armor crewman raised a glass to her. "Congratulations, Peacemaker."

Jessica nodded a thank you, but didn't speak. She sipped the new drink cautiously but did not look in the woman's direction again. There wasn't time or interest for a conversation or even a casual roll in the hay. That the drink could have been a simple gesture wasn't lost on Jessica, but it was better to be safe than sorry. More so, casual flings went against her plans and aspirations, and nothing got in the way of those since Marc Lemieux did his best to fuck up her life.

Bringing down Ch'tek, with the unwitting help of her ex-husband, had taken nearly six months to plan and execute. For this new mission, she'd have no preparation time beyond the 170-hour transit from Sol to the Araf's emergence point. Even with a mediator to assist with her lack of diplomatic aplomb, the situation couldn't be worse.

Did you expect it to be easy?

She snorted at the thought and tapped the bulge in her breast pocket reassuringly. It had been worth it to finally get Elly and whatever secret her father left behind. Seven years old and cowering in the jamb of her bedroom door, she'd heard her father burst in from a mission two days early and rummage through the house collecting every spare weapon he could find. Her mother argued; her shrill voice rose in volume and pitch until it brought tears to Jessica's eyes. Everyone outside their family called him Snowman. She didn't know until years later it was a callsign.

James Edward Francis had been a decorated starship pilot with more than 2,000 interstellar jumps under his belt. She closed her eyes, every detail of last seeing him as vibrant as it had been 20 years before.

"I love you, bulldog," he'd said. *"You stay tough and I'll be home soon."*

"Where are you going?"

His breath hitched. *"Far away, Jess. And I'll miss you, but I'll be home soon."*

He'd squeezed her one last time. With her face pressed into his neck she could smell his Old Spice aftershave. His skin was always warm, and his beard tickled her ear. "Okay, Daddy."

They separated, and he moved quickly to the door, leveling a finger at his estranged wife. "Make sure she gets Elly! When she's ready!"

Jessica opened her eyes and tossed back a healthy swallow of whiskey. She'd been trying to get ready all her life. Whatever her Daddy left behind in that chipset was enough for her mother to fearfully hide for decades. The technology looked like nothing she'd ever seen.

Her wrist slate beeped. She looked down at it and frowned.

Transport to Araf arranged courtesy of the Dream World Consortium. Departs in four hours. Bay 7.

She watched a football game on the Tri-V for a moment and tried to relax. Ten minutes later, she gave up. Jessica polished off the rest of her drink and laid five credits on the table. The blonde wasn't in the bar anymore so Jessica couldn't say thanks for the drink. Again, it was just as well. She'd have just enough time to shower, pack, and grab a bite to eat. She could have Lucille research her father's mystery gift while she packed, but first she needed to say goodbye to Hex.

* * * * *

Chapter Two

Dawn broke across the arid highlands of Araf. From the high ground of the Li Hills, the orb of the rising Nehra dappled the sandy, brown terrain in reddish gold light. Below the hills to the east lay a wide river valley. In the midst of the glacier-fed river, straddled across a sandbar, lay the wreckage of one of the largest Dusman Raknars, known in the Union's records only as 6C8. The 200-foot-tall mecha last walked more than a century before at the hands of ill-trained Besquith mercenaries. Faulty servo motors were determined to be the cause of the giant's eventual failure. Whatever the reason, its collapse had been a great boon for the Altar. Their continental dispute with two other races began almost from the moment of first landing.

South of the Altar's high desert terrain, the GenSha held millions of acres of fertile grassy plains fed from small dams and aquifers laid just as the Dream World had been colonized. Ten generations of GenSha, though, had grown their colony 400 percent and more dams had been built. The once fertile river valley was narrower than it had been in the last 50 years. As the water receded from the giant Raknar, the Altar found the one thing they needed to grow their brood. Power.

Exposed motors below the Raknar's waist gave them access to the mecha's dwindling, but still capable, power source. The Altar believed wind and solar energy would be enough to power their generators and keep their incubators working year-round, but the weather on Araf had been anything other than what was advertised. Persistent clouds and lower than minimal winds left their solar arrays dormant and their windmills still. No amount of complaint or threat of adjudication could persuade the Consortium to adjust the manufactured planet's weather. Contracts were contracts, the officers of the Consortium said. The Dream World had been offered "as-is" and that was all there was to it.

For 20 years, five whole generations, the Altar used the Raknar's remaining power to fuel their incubators and help provide for their young. As the GenSha lowered the water level, the power plants in the Raknar's wide legs were increasingly exposed. Without the water to cool them, the power source's efficiency decreased with every centimeter of water lost. A meter more, and the power output would decrease enough that the Altar incubators would be unable to work. The less-than-promised Araf climate would decimate the Altar colony within 10 years. But the GenSha's use of the river was only half the problem. Twenty kilometers to the north, at the river's delta into the Great Sea lay a colony of Selroth. By rights, the Selroth had as much space as they wanted in Araf's plentiful seas, but they preferred the freshwater deltas of the major rivers to the depths of Araf's shallow oceans. Like the Altar, they wanted to raise their children in an environment that was more suited for them. The three colonies grew closer and closer to war with every passing day.

Feeling the warmth of the summer sunlight, Klatk sat down on the high spur of rocky ground and watched Nehra rise slowly in the east. Atop the ridge, she could see the Great Sea with the fertile grasslands on the periphery. Like her own colony, the others seemed slow to rise and begin their routines as the long, warm summer wore down. The rocks warmed her abdomen as she watched the day begin. Soon enough, her assistants would rise to look for her and ensure her safety. There had been too many attacks in recent weeks to allow for many unescorted excursions from the colony walls. A few years ago, she'd have roamed from the GenSha colony to the mouth of the river they called Choote without hesitation or risk of injury. The GenSha's mercenary forces, recruited in the name of defense under Dream World policies, often patrolled well north of their lands into Altar property. In recent weeks, they'd fired on the fallen Raknar. Scare tactics, she'd told her council, but they'd called for emergency evacuation planning.

Founding the colony in the ragged ridges west of the Choote gave the Altar a place to mine for precious metals left behind in the terraforming process. The Consortium paid handsomely for gold and platinum pulled from the ground, and the Altar took to the work easily enough. But, as the Consortium wanted to go deeper, the Altar found tragedy. Below 250 meters, the ground grew unstable. Drilling more shafts only resulted in minimal gains of metals and brought the same results. Hundreds of lives were lost and without sustainable incubation, the colony's population dwindled to just over a thousand. Her charter stipulated that a colony strength of 800 or less required evacuation to the Altar homeworld.

This is home. She thought. *We wanted to be nowhere else but here. Returning home in shame is not an option.*

A faint whiff of breeze tickled her antennae and she faced the breeze, looking toward the GenSha plains. A storm system hung over the southern part of the continent instead of over their lands during the summer months as was promised. Precipitation would come, the Consortium said, but the GenSha lands grew drier and the Choote receded even farther. A rising plume of dust caught her eyes, far down by the GenSha colony's walls. Another joined it. As a third one rose, drifting slightly to the east, Klatk stood and moved to the edge of the escarpment. More plumes came up, consistent with vehicles picking up speed.

Half of the dust plumes cut toward the river and a wide sandbar the GenSha used for crossings. Her blood ran cold with realization and she scrambled down from the rocks and tapped the slate on her bandolier. "Raffa? Can you hear me?"

"Klatk? Where are you?"

She hustled down, four of her six legs working hard to maintain her balance as she sped toward the colony. "Sound the alert and get all crews to stations. The GenSha have sent another patrol. I want them stopped before they reach the outer boundaries."

"What about the brood?"

Klatk scrambled over a boulder and onto flatter ground where she picked up speed through the low brush. "Set the defense around the incubators and the usual positions. Moving the brood to the shelters will take too long and leave gaps in the perimeter. Every able body to the perimeter."

"But the council said—"

"I don't care! Sound the alert! Now!"

Klatk moved lower, leaving the sharp-faced escarpment and entering the rolling hills next to the high ridgelines. She tore through a thicket at full speed and heard, at long last, the alarm siren bray from the walls of their colony. Risking a glance at the horizon, she saw the thickening plumes of the GenSha attack racing in from the southeast. Three bright spots of light arced up into long contrails. She slapped her slate again.

"Missiles inbound!"

Through the last of the brush, Klatk broke out onto the clearer terrain and accelerated toward the colony. When she reached the gate, she saw almost every position manned along the northern wall. Alarms continued to bray, and she could hear the chittering announcements in her native tongue.

"Unknown patrols to the southeast. Prepare to defend the colony. Weapons to hold. I repeat, weapons to hold."

Through the gate, she sped into the center of the colony and found her executive officer waiting. "Ma'am! We're at 94 percent defensive strength. The GenSha have employed mercenary forces, unit and designation unknown. The inbound missiles will impact away from the main colony. It's a warning, at best."

Klatk stood on her hind legs and surveyed the scene. The last few Altar scattered from the tunnel complex and took up their assigned defensive positions. A knot in her abdomen twisted. "If they fire again, prepare to defend the brood."

"They'll attack our children?" Tracha recoiled. "They can't!"

Klatk pushed past her second in command. "Those missiles were a show of force. They'll fire again and target us where it hurts."

"Ma'am?"

"Tracha! Missiles don't miss the colony on their own. It was meant to show us the GenSha have given their mercenaries complete control of the tactical situation. They will—"

"Missiles Inbound! Missiles Inbound!"

Klatk scrambled toward the southeast wall, but made it no farther than 100 meters before the first explosion rippled through the colony behind her. Flung to her face in the dust, she closed her eyes and flinched, expecting the worst. As the detonation washed over her, she turned and looked at the damage. A full section of the brood, at least 10 percent of their next generation, was gone. Her abdomen clenched in rage and she fought to maintain her balance on her hind legs in the stress. Through the sudden, blinding loss, a tiny fire burned inside.

"Get the brood below!" she ordered. Looking back at Tracha, she pointed with her forearms. "Run the power couplings from the Raknar to keep the incubators powered throughout. We cannot lose anymore!"

"Every 100 meters of cable results in a loss of delivered power. We could lose 15 percent of the brood." Tracha said.

"We have no choice, Tracha. Get the brood underground!"

"Yes, Klatk," Tracha said and sped away chittering orders as she went.

Klatk watched a full third of her combat power move to the brood and hoist the incubator cells toward the mine openings. "Internal perimeter. Stand-off weapons are free."

"Firing!" one of her gunnery commanders called. His call was stepped on by five others as all six missile batteries roared to life and rained steel over the approaching mercenary forces.

"Sustain your maximum rate of fire," Klatk called. "Keep them away from direct fire range until the brood is below ground!"

She turned and saw the stream of Altar carrying the brood scurry into the mine entrances. *How much longer?* In their best simulations, they'd pushed the brood into viable tunnels within four minutes. She consulted her slate and relayed the information from the security cameras mounted on the main masthead. Scrolling with her clawed hands took a moment, but she had the data she needed in the first swipe. The second was simply confirmation.

Five minutes ETA. We have time!

As soon as the thought crossed her mind, Klatk knew it wasn't enough. Time was subjective—a finite resource that could be manipulated by a bevy of unforeseen consequences. The only way to ensure their tentative victory was audacity. Klatk rushed through the walled compound and mounted the wall just as the first bursts of direct fire crashed into the barriers. Her slate beeped and she blinked up the message.

"Klatk? The brood is 70 percent secured in Level Two tunnels."

"There's no time to move them deeper," she replied. "Standby to return fire. Observers? Report."

"Northeast post, ma'am. No contacts—we're maintaining air guard at this time. No viable targets in range."

"Southeast tower. Approximately 12 vehicles with lasers and direct fire weapons crossed the river and are three kilometers from our forward positions. Estimated time of arrival is one minute, 12 seconds. The other group has slowed southeast of the colony and is at standoff distance. We believe this is where the missiles have come from."

Klatk tapped the side of her jaw with a pincer. *Overwatch position and support by fire. Half of their combat power is waiting for something to happen on the offensive.*

"All stations, standby to attack."

There was silence on the network for 10 seconds. "Ma'am? Say again?"

Klatk looked over the wall and into the advancing prongs of the mercenary attack. The support by fire position was clear. A roll of the terrain protected the paused vehicles from taking direct fire from the colony. A smart move, to be sure, but one that could be nullified by a swift offensive action. She thought for a second, no more, and determined the course of action that would best allow her people to delay the enemy's assaulting their position or destroying their power couplings to the fallen Raknar. The massive mecha essentially protected one half of her perimeter from direct fire, and that further limited the GenSha's mercenary forces.

Her slate beeped with an incoming radio transmission. She routed it to her headset with a twitch. "Klatk."

"Honored Queen, this is Qamm of the Wandering Death with terms for your surrender."

Klatk chuckled. *At least we know what they want.*

"Qamm. Be advised, the Altar do not surrender. Our lands are guaranteed under the Dream World agreements, and we'll defend as necessary." Klatk snapped off the connection and picked up a laser rifle, cleared it, and seated a magazine to fire. "All stations, prepare to charge."

"Klatk? Say again?" Tracha called from the opposite wall. "You want to charge?"

"Secure the colony. Once they're underground, seal the doors and prepare to engage. Pray that our request for a Peacemaker is answered soon."

* * *

Hex sat on the open hold of the *Victory Twelve* as the last of the Peacemakers swept and cleared the ship for any additional evidence. Elbows on his knees, the young man cradled his head in his hands and tousled his short blonde hair.

"We're done. You can collect your gear now and move along." A burly Lumari Peacemaker looked down at him and stepped off the decking. Hex watched the massive alien clomp through the hangar and caught sight of Jessica moving his way. He stood slowly and straightened the gig line of his coveralls, avoiding eye contact with her.

"Hey," she said. "You doing okay?"

No.

He shook off the thought. "I don't have a unit, a job, any friends. Yeah, I think I'm good."

Jessica frowned. "Sorry about the inspection. These guys like to check everything twice."

"It's okay. Not like I have anything but a CASPer to my name," Hex winced. "Will I even get paid my fee?"

"That's up to Hammer," Jessica said. "I'll make sure the Guild follows up and gets him to pay."

"Thank you," Hex said. "Might be enough money for me to rebuild the Marauders."

Jessica looked away. "There's no Marauders, Hex. Marc has been forcibly retired. Go your own way."

"And how am I supposed to do that?"

"You are your father's son," Jessica touched his arm. "You can do anything you choose to do."

Hex flushed. "Jessica, thank you. But I—"

She raised a palm to him. "Yes. You can."

Hex looked away, not wanting his eyes to soften up. Maya often told him the same thing. Being Sergeant Major Robert Alison's son didn't matter to anyone, he would tell her. She would say he was right. That being himself was all the mattered. "I don't know where to start."

"A starting point isn't what you think it is, Hex. You have you and a CASPer. You can build from there," Jessica said. "I had the Guild secure you a room for as many nights as you need to get your shit together. You're in the Grand's inner ring."

Hex felt fresh tears form in his eyes and his vision blurred. "What if I can't get my shit together, Jessica. Then what?"

"You will," Jessica said. "For no other reason than the fact that there will come a day when I need your help, Hex. Whether you have your own crew or not won't matter. We've been through far too much, even before this botched mission. Get your gear and take a break for a few days. Formulate a plan and move forward."

Hex nodded and held back a sob in his throat. "Maya wanted to leave a year ago. I should have let her go. She'd be alive and—"

Jessica stepped forward and put her hands on his shoulders. "Enough, Hex. You can't change the past. Don't try. Don't look for it in the bottom of a glass either. Get some rest, some food, and spend some time getting your head on straight. If you want to lead a team, lead one. If you want to pack it up and go home, go. Nobody is going to judge you."

Hex looked up and saw the intensity in her eyes. "I understand."

"You think you do, but you don't. Not yet." Jessica half-smiled at him then took a breath. "Now, your CASPer is going to be moved back up here and loaded aboard the *Victory Twelve*. I have another mission, and I'm not going to pay for my ship to sit in mothballs collecting dust. I'm loaning it to you."

Hex blinked. "I can't take your ship, Jessica. It costs more than all my assets together."

"I'm loaning her to you. Nothing operational. Use her to find work, if you have to. Go home. Whatever you want."

"Don't you need it?"

Jessica smirked. "The Guild is sending me on another confirmation mission. I'll be gone a few weeks, that's all. I figured you could use a break."

"They're sending you on a second mission? They can do that?"

Jessica shrugged and stepped into the *Victory Twelve's* cargo bay. She pulled something black from her pocket and placed it in an analysis station. "They can and they did."

"Why?"

"They're concerned I am not as diplomatic as a Peacemaker should be."

Hex chuckled. "You do prefer a fight, Jess."

She grinned over her shoulder at him. "Playing to your strengths isn't a bad thing, Hex."

Hex snorted. "I've been running ops for two years straight. Without a unit, I don't know what to do. What are you working on?"

"Seeing if I can access this old chipset," Jessica said. The analyzer panel beeped and chimed. A series of lights flashed green and then turned red—a null report. "Looks like a bust, though. It will have to wait until I get back. I'll have some leave time." Her voice trailed off and for the first time in a while, he could hear fatigue in her voice. She needed time off, and there was none in sight.

A break sounded good. He and Maya spoke often about the Gold Coast of Australia and wanting to see the Great Barrier Reef. Going there didn't seem right, but the thought of going home banged his heart.

Mom would love to see me.

"I might go."

Jessica nodded. "Then take my ship. I'll call Lucille if I need you."

"Lucille? She belongs to Marc." The statement he thought was fact became a question as he saw Jessica's eyebrows raise. "You have her?"

"She's a program, Hex. A very good one, and almost illegal, but she's a program. I scripted her a long time ago—so I've always had her, in a way." Jessica cocked her head to one side. "Marc never understood her true potential anyway. She was built to fly my ship, and he took a copy of her thinking she'd be good in a tank."

"She was good," Hex said.

"Not as good as she could have been." Jessica patted his arm. "I have to get going. Take her. Take a run around the solar system if you have to. Get your head on straight."

Hex nodded, and words failed him. Tears filled his eyes and splashed onto his cheeks, and he let them come. Jessica said nothing, merely stepped forward and wrapped her arms around him. Head buried in his friend and former executive officer's neck, Hex let out the sobs threatening to choke him. There would be a time to go and do exactly what he needed to do. The first step was to let it out. He knew Jessica would stay there as long as he needed her to.

That only made him cry harder.

* * * * *

Chapter Three

Carrying a duffel bag of clothing and another of protective gear and weapons, Jessica strode into the main hangar deck in fresh olive drab coveralls with Peacemaker insignia on both shoulders. She'd never worn them before, and it felt really good. Her freshly trimmed auburn hair was down, brushing her collarbones above her suit's chest pockets. The lack of human facilities on Araf was a consideration to cut off her long, but still regulation, braid, and somehow it felt right. A chapter of her life had closed and another was about to open. She'd had her morphogenic tattoo removed prior to taking the tests for Peacemaker because it hadn't felt right. Her hair was easily changed, too. She wasn't in the business of attracting any attention.

Walking through the main hangar door changed that as more than a few heads turned. The human eyes stayed locked on her, and more than a few had incredulous looks on their faces. It took everything she had not to smile. As she walked with the heavy bags on her shoulders, their weight seemed to evaporate. Back straight and eyes level, she marched through the hangar toward the berth where the Dream World Consortium's yacht waited. She rounded a stack of shipping containers. Selector Hak-Chet stood there with his short arms crossed under his ceremonial cape.

"Peacemaker Francis," he smiled with one corner of his mouth. "I believe you've caused a bit of a sensation in the hangar."

Jessica flushed slightly. "It's an official mission. I thought it was—"

"You misunderstand my tone." The Sidar smiled fully, revealing his craggy teeth. The gesture, while all too human, looked purely evil on her mentor's face. Like most humans, she'd loved dinosaurs as a child. Face to face with an alien that looked much like a pterodactyl capable of killing her in a microsecond, she knew better. "It looks good on you."

"Thank you, Selector."

"I imagine all these good people will be telling a few of their friends what they've seen today," he said. "Earth's first Peacemaker. It does have a nice ring to it."

"As you've said many times," Jessica said. The day they'd met, the Sidar elder statesman looked at her with that same quizzical, amused look on his long face and said she would be the one. Engineering school had only been the start. She'd passed her voluntary off-world assessments with flying colors and, yet, the mercenaries did not come calling. VOWs scores, the dreaded Voluntary Off-World assessments, it turned out, weren't everything the recruiters said they were. So, she'd chosen the most difficult program of study she could and gave it everything she had. Six months after graduation, magna cum laude from Rose-Hulman in electrical engineering, and still without a mercenary appointment, she'd signed up with one of the planetary militaries. Although unsatisfying due to the pitiable quality of her peers, it allowed her to hone her skills and distinguish herself from her competition. She finally made it to the stars when she was hired as an engineer by the Cartography Guild, and that had been a good job. But then she'd met Marc Lemieux.

Their marriage lasted less than three years, and the first year of it had been good enough, but the second she'd seen his faults and inabilities. During the third year, she could not bear it any more and walked away. He'd done the shittiest thing he could and had run off without signing the divorce papers, leaving her in limbo for more than six years before she'd tracked him down. Still, his crappy mercenary unit *was* a mercenary unit and that gave her some credibility to enter the pits on Karma and fend for herself from contract to contract. At least until Hak-Chet found her and thought she could be something more.

"I meant it every single time." Hak-Chet grinned again. "I've come to see you off on your last confirmation mission."

Jessica sighed. "I'd hoped for only one."

"The selection criteria were created to weed out candidates who do not meet the intense qualifications required of a Peacemaker. In some cases, additional missions are required." Hak-Chet shrugged. His amusement with the situation made her feel slightly better. "It is something you must do, and in reality, something only you can do."

I hope you're right.

She nodded. "Thank you for believing in me, Selector."

"You are most welcome," he said. "The Guild and I have many interests in common given your situation. Like me, they do not want you to fail. As such, they've sent you a mediator to assist with the diplomatic effort on Araf. You'll meet him onboard. I cannot tell you much more about him, I'm afraid. I've never met him."

"His name?"

"Taemin," Hak-Chet said. "He is young, but highly recommended."

"I wish you could come along."

"And so do I. But it's not to be. My days as a field operative are long past," Hak-Chet said. He looked past her shoulder and nodded. "It's time I introduce you to the planet's administrator, and for you to be on your way. Many representatives strongly believe in you, Jessica. You do not understand what that means yet, and I believe this mission will teach you the one thing you need to be a Peacemaker."

"And that is?" Jessica fought a grin.

"You've always looked out for yourself. That must change. A Peacemaker's duty is to the citizens of the Union."

She heard a rustle from behind and turned. Hak-Chet swept around her gracefully, his winglets kicked up and back. "Administrator Kenos. The Peacemaker Guild thanks you for your offer of transportation and support."

A gold-furred Cochkala walked up, the approximation of a smirk on his badger-like face, and nodded solemnly at Hak-Chet. "Selector." His ears flickered, and he looked at Jessica with wide, dark eyes.

"You must be Peacemaker Candidate Francis," Kenos said. "I trust you'll be able to help us solve this situation once and for all." He stretched out a forepaw with carefully manicured nails unlike anything she'd ever seen. The resulting handshake was almost effeminate. "Very nice to meet you. I'm afraid I don't know many humans. Forgive any unfortunate slights."

Jessica smiled and nodded, but realized there was nothing gracious in his words. It was a cop out to allow him to say offensive things as often as possible while feigning ignorance. As far as humans were concerned, the game was often played by other species, but reciprocity was considered just short of an act of war. "Of course, Kenos. It is a pleasure to meet you and thank you for your generous offer of transportation."

"It is nothing," Kenos said and waved away the conversation with the flick of a paw. "I was afraid you weren't coming. The *Victory Twelve* filed a flight plan for Mars an hour ago."

Good for Hex.

"I've lent her to a friend for a few weeks; that's all."

Kenos nodded solemnly. "Understandable and for the best. Your mediator is aboard and preparing for our discussions."

Jessica twitched. "Discussions?"

"Of course, Peacemaker," the last word dripped off the Cochkala's maw. "We have 170 hours of transit. I believe none of them should be spared in the effort to bring peace to the colonies on our 'Dream World.' This situation is...troubling. I'm afraid one of our colonies is hoarding resources from the others in clear violation of our by-laws and covenants. We can discuss it more, of course, with your mediator present. Forgive me, I've not even welcomed you aboard my ship."

Hak-Chet turned to Jessica. "I will leave you in Kenos' good hands. I look forward to hearing from you as the negotiation continues, Jessica." He nodded at her and lowered his voice. "I have great faith in you."

"Thank you, Selector." She turned and caught the Cochkala looking at her figure. Managing to suppress a shudder, Jessica nodded. "I believe you were going to show me your ship, Administrator?"

* * *

The yacht had an unpronounceable name despite Jessica's best efforts. Fourteen credit hours in Languages of the Galactic Union failed her, unlike most of her college education. Some things were better learned the hard way by sheer immersion. When she queried her translator, it replied that the transport's name was simply *Tchrt One*. Jessica managed to not roll her eyes as she followed Kenos through the traffic of the main hangar, and he prattled on about the ship's unique design. To Jessica, it looked like a mutant porpoise.

"The curvature? Well, it's designed to ride gravitational disturbances without causing motion sickness in the main cabin," Kenos said. "It's very proprietary in its design. There's a lot I can't tell you, simply because you're not a Cochkala, but we believe it will change interstellar ships design galaxy-wide within the next 10 years. Maybe less."

Jessica realized he expected a response just as he turned to look over his shoulder. "It's certainly impressive, Administrator Kenos."

"Please, just call me Kenos." The Cochkala tried to smile, causing Jessica to shudder involuntarily. The badger-like alien's face contorted into something between a snarl and a roar. There were some human expressions that aliens were better off avoiding.

"I'll try to remember that." Jessica forced herself to smile and nod. The second unwritten rule of being a Peacemaker was that diplomacy was an awful lot like ass-kissing. A successful Peacemaker knew when to stop before getting a face full of shit. "I hope my presence aboard your yacht will not be seen as an inconvenience in any way."

Kenos chittered. "Please, Peacemaker Francis. You are our guest in transit to Araf. Your presence is hardly an imposition. I would hate for you to feel uncomfortable in any way before getting started with your mission."

Like hell you would. Jessica held her eyes level and her head still. Any movement that could be misconstrued as acquiescence would violate her charter. "My mission has already started, Admistrator Kenos. Again, I appreciate your assistance with the transit, and I hope it's not misconstrued as ingratitude if I disagree with your assessment of my duties."

Kenos stared at her for a moment, his eyes narrow and dark as if sizing her up. He nodded. "No offense taken, Peacemaker. Please excuse my insinuation that you were not on duty. A Peacemaker's job never ends."

Jessica nodded. *The saying is that a Peacemaker's duty never ends. Jobs are jobs, but duty is something you can't easily leave behind.* Kenos obviously knew both that saying, and that her duties started when they were officially introduced. Caution wasn't going to be enough when dealing with the administrator. She would have to be on her guard at every turn.

What did you get me into, Hak-Chet?

They kept walking until reaching the yacht's rounded stern where Kenos stopped and reached for her bags. "If I may?"

You could have 200 meters ago, you little shit.

"Certainly. Thank you." Jessica bit the inside of her lip as Kenos struggled with the weight of her equipment bag. A Pendal, complete with robe and covered face, reached down from the cargo hold, hefted the bag with ease, and gestured for Jessica to pass over her personal bag, which she did. The Pendal disappeared into the hold without a word.

"Please excuse him," Kenos said. "He is a competent pilot, but a bit rude."

"Does he have a name?"

Kenos snorted. "If he does, I don't know it. He's never spoken at all, even after being assigned to this yacht. I simply do not understand the Pendal."

Jessica squinted. "It's something he doesn't want to do. Talk, that is. Maybe he doesn't feel there is anything he should say?"

Kenos shrugged. "It doesn't matter. As long as he gets me where I need to be, when I need to be there, that's all I care about. Please, let's board and get this journey underway." Before she could answer, Kenos stomped forward toward the crew hatch. Jessica followed a few paces behind, lingering to look over *Tchrt One's* curved hull. Protrusions that could only be weapons pods appeared in even distances down the spine and matched up with gun ports on the high empennage of the vehicle. Jessica assumed there would be others on the front. For a diplomatic vessel, the *Tchrt One's* armament selection was impressive, if not a bit much.

There was something odd about Kenos, too, beyond the aloof administrator's aura, and his hideous idea of a smile. As much as he wanted to be friendly to her, he did not trust her. That mutual feeling made it easier for her to retain the distance her position defined. He bore watching, to be sure, but his bluster and suitably greasy manner of doing things struck her as odd for a being in his position of authority. The Cochkala were hardly human in any way, but Kenos was an administrator of the Dream World Consortium and an important party to the discussions on the horizon. Kenos ducked through the hatch, and a figure in a red and black jacket with dark trousers stepped out and turned to meet her. If Kenos' reaction to her was troubling, the Caroon's reaction was positively baffling.

"It's about time, Peacemaker. Does your Guild not teach promptness?" His elongated face curled in a sneer, and the Caroon stood with his arms behind his back in a posture of self-importance the likes of which she'd never seen.

Jessica blinked. After a second, she extended a hand. "You must be the mediation assistant. My name is—"

"Mediator. I am the mediator, and you are the Peacemaker." The Caroon's beady eyes narrowed at her. He made no effort to shake her outstretched hand. "My name is Taemin. You are Jessica Francis, and you are not a Peacemaker. You are a candidate. Does that cover everything you wanted to say to me?"

Jessica realized her mouth hung open, and she closed it slowly. "That's how this is going to be?"

The Caroon snorted. "I was merely stating fact, Candidate."

"You were," Jessica said and withdrew her hand. "How about we get aboard and —"

"The codicils of the Peacemaker Guild state that any candidate required to pass multiple assessments has the right to refuse a secondary assessment and stand before the Guild Master to challenge their position as a candidate. Were you aware of this?"

Jessica kept her face straight. Hak-Chet wouldn't have lied to her. If there really was a way out, he would have told her. The Guild determined what missions were confirmation missions. There was no ability for a candidate to change their mission.

Was there?

"I was not aware of this."

Taemin smirked. "I surmised that from the fact you showed your face in this hangar. While humans are good for several things in this Union, I am of the opinion that being a Peacemaker is not one. I do not believe you have the fortitude or strength to handle matters of great importance because your species cannot handle itself in most matters. Before your First Contact, which your people clearly botched, you were little more than squabbling children. You've not done much better in the years since."

Jessica replied and before the words even came out, she knew what her decision was going to be. "Are you done?"

The Caroon blinked. "What did you say?"

"I asked you if you were done." Jessica stepped past the shocked mediator and into the ship's hatch. The ship smelled like cat food and Jessica suppressed an urge to gag. Throwing up all over the Consortium would look bad on her final report.

"You can't speak to me like that," Taemin said. "There are two colonies counting on your ability to peacefully negotiate their terms. If you approach negotiations—"

"You said two colonies." Jessica spun and looked at him. "My briefing said three."

Taemin nodded. "The real dispute is only between two of the colonies. That's where we should focus our efforts."

Jessica stepped through the inner hatch to a lushly-appointed passageway. Kenos stood in the middle blocking their way. His arms were crossed and that awful smile stained his furry face. "Talking strategy already, then?"

Taemin started to speak, but Jessica cut him off. "Taemin was telling me that the real dispute is between two colonies and not the three about which I was briefed. That hardly seems like strategy to me."

"Mediator Taemin is correct in his assessment. The GenSha and the Selroth have a viable dispute for water rights. The Altar are simply caught in the middle and suffering because of it." Kenos shrugged. "Unless you're prepared to conduct our meetings under thrust, here in an unsecured passageway, I suggest you stow your gear and meet in the lounge as we push off and get underway."

Jessica nodded. "If you'd be so kind as to show me where, Kenos."

The Cochkala grinned. "Certainly. Your room is here. Your mediator's is just down the hall past the galley. We'll push off in 10 minutes."

She pushed through door of her room and found her gear bags stowed under the full-size bed built into one wall. The small, cozy room had a very human sink and toilet built into one wall, as well as a closet with actual clothes hangers, and a plush bathrobe with matching fuzzy slippers. An Aethernet terminal and desk took up the corner opposite her bed. Tri-V screens hung over the desk and the wall opposite the bed for entertainment. A small, bright bouquet of wildflowers rested in a crystal vase. Lush carpeting and fresh linens complicated the scents of the room, but all this essentially led to the same conclusion.

"All of this is brand new." Jessica said to herself. "Built just for me."

And more than likely under surveillance and bugged, she heard Hak-Chet's voice say. The mental admonition served its purpose. After they were underway, she'd sweep the room for any devices and frequency monitoring. The chances her primary kit had been tampered with approached virtual certainty, and there weren't any second chances. Her secondary kit, a backup weapon, and a mini-slate in her pockets would be more than enough to protect her during the 170-hour trip to Araf.

Ten minutes wasn't going to be enough time to unpack and check her equipment. Food wasn't the answer, either, and there was no way in hell she was going to "freshen up" or anything like those annoying old movies said. Jessica sat instead on the bed and fought the urge to flop back on it and rest.

The patches on her shoulders said Peacemaker, and while she wasn't fully one yet, it had never been so close and yet so far. The Guild wouldn't have sent her on a mission she could not handle. Constant training in diplomacy and inter-species relations told her that she'd walked into a veritable hornet's nest and the situation on Araf was only going to be much worse. The brand-new cabin nailed the coffin shut.

Kenos did not trust her. Her Guild assigned mediator wanted her to quit. Both of them claimed the crisis was something much simpler than what Hak-Chet had told her it would be. They'd undoubtedly gone through her gear with a fine-toothed comb when she boarded.

You never expected this to be easy, did you Peacemaker?

The instructors loved to say those things during the myriad of tests and challenges she'd performed over the last few years. Every mistake she'd made in training had only helped push her to better handle the situations thrown at her. Walking into the hangar 10 minutes before, she'd felt ready for anything. Situations change, some for the good and some not, her instructors liked to say. She'd proven the negative side of that statement correct in less than 10 minutes.

Jessica stood and smoothed out her coveralls and then the bed itself. The act of wiping away the wrinkles helped straighten out her thoughts in a few quick seconds. She stood and checked her watch-slate. Three minutes to spare. She looked at her room and decided that malicious or not, the intent to provide her a human home for a week was comforting. After she'd given it a proper screening, it could even be a place of rest and relaxation. For the moment, it was a reminder that her game face always needed to be on, especially when she wanted it off.

You can relax after the mission is over, with a Peacemaker shield on your chest.

Now, get out there. Bulldog.

Her father's voice was as clear as the memory that came with it. Third grade basketball. She'd wanted to quit, but was one of the best players on the team. In tears, she'd sat on the school's stage and said she would never play again.

You're better than that. Her father leaned down and whispered in her ear.

Now get out there, Bulldog.

With a deep breath, Jessica activated the door of her cabin and strode down the passageway to the lounge. For a moment, she smiled to herself in exasperation, and then set her face and mind to the task at hand.

* * * * *

Chapter Four

"**G**enSha regular forces are moving on the southern mine entrances!" Raffa called from the command center as Klatk reached the western wall and vaulted over it. "Prepared to charge at your command."

Her slate beeped, and she consulted it. Command and control icons ringed the colony. Clearly marked enemy icons converged at three points. The mercenary forces charged straight at the walls from the south and the east. The GenSha moved slower, but there was no doubt their intention was to avoid any type of contact and enter the mine system from the high ground to the south. A charge wasn't necessary. Mercenaries tended to wilt like cut flowers under decent artillery fire, and Klatk believed hers to be outstanding.

The radio connection buzzed again. "Klatk, this is the Wandering Death. We are two minutes from attacking your position. Discussion is still an option. Your people do not have to suffer."

Klatk ground her mandibles. "We are not people, Qamm. You are about to find out how the Altar fight firsthand."

"Suit yourselves," the mercenary leader called. Klatk maneuvered into her small command center and found Raffa alone, having several animated conversations at once. He turned and looked at her for a moment before realizing who she was. She'd left her ceremonial dress behind. While not a matriarchal queen of her species, Klatk's status as a female colony leader was equal in respect and title. Raffa flinched.

"Queen Klatk." He said. "We are under attack from three sides and outnumbered. The southern mine complex is threatened."

Klatk moved to the console and tapped several icons. "Activate the automated defenses to compliment direct fire on the eastern and southern walls. Lower security on the western wall to standoff weapons only and place a squad in the main shaft. Push out three squads to defend the brood and secure the tunnel complexes in the main mine. Prepare to destroy the mine entrances where the GenSha are attacking."

"What about the north? We leave ourselves open to the Selroth."

Klatk considered the options. "Engage radar and sensors along the river. If something moves out of their colony, we'll know and can shift our defenses."

Raffa pointed at the screen. "We have range on them."

Klatk did not hesitate. "Fire at all targets. Hold off Qamm and her mercenaries at all costs. Once we've stopped them, concentrate on the GenSha infantry at the southern mines. We'll have the advantage there." There were four mine complexes in the Altar colony. The southern ones lay empty and disconnected from the rest of the complexes. Any GenSha there would be trapped easily.

"I'll cut the power and—"

"Not yet," Klatk said. "If we cut it, they'll suspect something and hesitate. We want to draw them deeper and close them off completely. Give them as much access to the southern complex as they want. When their command elements move into the mine, destroy it."

Raffa nodded. "Weapons firing, Excellency."

"Move out to the external command post and monitor the firing systems. Engage the mercenary infantry as necessary. Primary targets are all enemy fast movers and armor." Klatk said. "Who has command in the mines?"

"Goss, Excellency," Raffa said and stepped out of the command post. "Are you moving to the main mine complex? Your protection cell is there and prepared."

"No," Klatk said. "These mercenaries don't scare me, Raffa."

"It's not a matter of fear, Excellency. The colony needs you."

Klatk twitched her antennae. "If there's not a colony left to lead, what good am I, Raffa?"

An alarm sounded, and Klatk checked the display. "The GenSha have hit the southern mines outer defenses and are pressing forward. Stop the mercenaries, Raffa. I'll handle the rest."

Her executive officer left quickly as she tapped controls and connected to Goss deep in the mines near the southern entrances. "Goss, you have inbound GenSha in Sector A."

"Copy, command." The infantry commander whispered. "We are in the auxiliary vent system. We will cut the power to the main shaft once they pass the central junction. Once their command element is 200 meters into the entrance shaft, we'll destroy it as ordered. Will advise on destruction of the vent and return to the colony perimeter."

Well done, Klatk thought. Goss was young, but extremely capable. He tended to think outside the tunnel, meaning he often sought solutions others did not even consider viable. Unpredictability was a strength she needed to exploit.

"Affirmative, Goss. Proceed with your plan and protect the brood."

"They won't get past us, Honored Klatk."

She looked outside just as a fusillade of rockets tore out of the launchers along the southern wall. Qamm's mercenary force scattered, but not quickly enough. Several vehicles and armored infantry went down in the burst of rockets. Her own losses were less than eight percent. The mercenary fire tore into the eastern wall more heavily, and she shifted the automated defenses in response. Again, her rockets tore out a respectable chunk of the assaulting force.

"You'll have to do better than that," Qamm laughed over the radio connection. Klatk attempted to triangulate the simple UHF transmission but could not. It appeared to come from every one of the Wandering Death vehicles at once.

Or none of them at all. Klatk blinked in realization.

"Goss! Prepare for mercenary forces! Destroy your sector and move to the western complex immediately." She switched frequencies to Raffa's private comms. "Raffa, take two squads of infantry and a squad of heavy weapons to the main mines. Secure the far western corridors and recover Goss and his soldiers."

"Moving!"

The distraction had been almost perfect. Wherever Qamm was, she seemed to be a viable foe. The GenSha proved to be slow and methodical attackers and surprise was hardly their strongpoint. They were notoriously hard to kill, though, and proved much hardier fighters than her own Altar soldiers.

"We're under attack!" Goss reported suddenly. In the transmission, she heard a constant stream of laser bolts and missile fire. "Moving toward the western complex. Under heavy fire, repeat heavy fire. Enemy forces in the western high ground."

Klatk froze. The mercenary forces hung back at standoff distances where her weapons were marginally effective. *Daring me to withdraw forces into the mines! Bastards!*

"Slow the rate of fire," she commanded her forces on the walls. The mercs had taken cover behind a slight roll of the terrain about 500 meters from the walls to the south and a craggy mini-ridge between the colony and the river. "If they move from cover, swat them back!"

Raffa's link activated. "We're in the western corridor, Excellency. The mercs have breached the outer containment. We've pushed them back, but they've damaged the automated extraction system and—"

Klatk gripped the command console tight enough that her arms spasmed. "Raffa? What did we lose?"

There was no response so she switched frequencies. "Goss! Report!"

"Taking fire! Taking fire!"

Klatk's head snapped up. The entire southern wall was under intense fire from the mercenary positions. She tapped the slate, brought up the rocket launchers and fired two quick bursts, quelling the incoming fire. Through the vision systems, she watched the mercenaries begin to withdraw with their guns firing—a withdrawal by fire.

"Indirect systems to active. Keep hitting them until they leave our territory." As the Wandering Death continued their retreat, Klatk's command and control systems showed a much smaller force of GenSha leaving the mine complex to the south. Nothing exited the western corridors.

"Honored Queen, you may wish to consider a change in strategy. We got through your defenses and entered your mine complex with little effort. Next time, the damage won't be nearly as contained." Qamm laughed on the radio. "If you want to discuss this, you can—"

She snapped off the conversation, and ran from the command center aware that she was leaving the firing batteries to their own leaders and turning her back on the battle itself. Klatk ran for the central mine entrance. "Goss! Raffa! Report!"

There was nothing but static in the connection. Klatk sprinted as fast as four legs would carry her toward the western main corridor entrance. Three hundred meters outside the colony's security wall, a four-meter-wide hole gaped in the Araf soil. Eyes adjusting instantly to the near darkness, Klatk hardly broke stride for more than two thousand meters until she reached the junction of the southern and western corridors. Ozone seemed to crackle in the air from the weapons fire. A thick haze of smoke hid the upper meter of the mine shaft. Dozens of her soldiers were injured. More than a few were dead.

Among the wounded, she saw Raffa propped against the curved wall. Other soldiers looked up at her, and she tried to comfort them as she moved, but it was difficult to see their faces as she closed the distance to Raffa. His injuries looked grave, and the medical team had essentially abandoned him.

"Raffa?"

His eyes lolled to meet hers, and he struggled to straighten up against the wall but failed. His voice was little more than a whisper. "Excellency."

"What happened?" She leaned down and touched his upper shoulder. "Are you in pain?"

Raffa nodded. "Pain, yes. It will pass soon enough." He moved his upper arms and Klatk saw a ragged, oozing hole in his carapace. Black blood spilled out. "I didn't move fast enough, I guess. The brood was damaged as we moved them."

Klatk leaned closer. "We will take care of the brood, Raffa. Please—"

"Hit them." Raffa coughed once. "They tried to take our children, Klatk. They could have destroyed them but did not. Want to...scare us."

Klatk nodded. "We won't be scared, Raffa."

He twitched once, and the light in his eyes dimmed suddenly. The small belt monitoring his vital signs beeped in alarm. Klatk tapped it twice gently and disengaged the biomonitors. "Rest, Raffa." She touched his face lightly and stood. Goss stood watching her, a laser rifle held across his chest, barrel facing down. Blood caked in a few spots across his dark face, but he looked otherwise unwounded. He nodded once at her.

"Excellency," he said. "Raffa was as good as they come."

Klatk nodded, her mandibles clacking. "You will try to do better, Goss. My need for an executive officer is greater than your need to lead our infantry. Find a suitable replacement and get them started with the engineers. We need to know what damage those bastards did."

"Fifteen percent casualties to the brood, Excellency. Twenty-four killed and twice that wounded. The western corridor sustained heavy damage at the first junction. The southern corridor lost all automatic defensive systems before we destroyed it. The GenSha made it past the first junction and tunneled down to destroy the extraction system. We stopped them on Level Two, but they'd already hit the incubators in that section. We lost 700 young, Excellency."

Klatk stiffened in shock. The loss of 700 young was a priority information demand from the Consortium. Likewise, she'd have to report the loss to the Altar Council as it met their critical reporting criteria. The Altar council could recall the colony.

Which is exactly what the Consortium wants.

"They withdrew as soon as they'd damaged the incubators and the extraction system in the western corridor?" Klatk asked. "Or did they attempt to press the attack?"

Goss shook his head. "They went only to Level Two and hit there. We stopped them at the third section, and they withdrew. None of them found the connection tunnel to the central complex."

Dirt fell from the ceiling and Klatk brushed it away without immediately realizing what it was. Her eyes widened in shock. "We need to evacuate this section! To the surface! Carry the wounded and leave the dead. When the rocks settle, we'll return for them."

The Altar skittered to and fro, gathering their nearest comrades and tossing them across their backs. As she ran for the main tunnel complex, Klatk looked back at Raffa's remains and set her jaws. The GenSha would pay. They'd done more than ensure a war by purposefully attacking the Altar brood. Children were non-combatants and were to be treated as such. The despicable attack was no accident.

Klatk hoisted a wounded soldier to her back and made for the fortified tunnels of the upper levels. The rounded ceilings held as they moved toward the exit, but every rumble from the surface seemed to reverberate throughout the entire mine. Peace, like dependable weather, was increasingly out of the question.

Goss came alongside as they moved. Two wounded soldiers rested on his back. "The mine is holding, Excellency. The lower levels have been evacuated. We still have robots working there and production continues."

"Fine," Klatk barked through sudden anger. Removing the various precious metals from Araf's terraformed soil provided a solid income for the colony, but it was not worth any more loss of life. "Recall the supervisors. Our priority is surface defense and counterattack. The mine systems can go into standby as far as I am concerned."

"Understood. I'll recall them immediately."

They reached the fortified levels and found her medical team waiting. The wounded soldier was lifted from her back as she entered the chamber. Chaos became a systematic process of triage and treatment. As such, there was nothing she could do, so Klatk moved to the side of the chamber and eventually to the door. Goss was already there, and they watched their doctors work. He leaned over and spoke softly in her ear.

"The defenses are re-armed and ready," he said. "Mercenary forces have withdrawn toward the GenSha colony and are out of effective weapons range."

"Stand down the defenses to ready five status." Klatk said. "Initiate a rest plan and prepare to hold the defenses all night."

"Yes, Excellency."

"Anything else?"

"The Consortium has asked for a status report on the mine. They say they're going to look into the attack, but have encouraged us to maintain production at the required rates."

Klatk whirled on him. "You tell them any investigation will wait until the Peacemaker arrives, and that I will not extract another gram of anything in that mine."

"With respect, Excellency, we don't know that a Peacemaker is even coming."

Klatk looked back at her wounded soldiers and those trying to care for them. "Two dozen dead. Seven hundred young lost. Two of our mines inoperative. Was the Raknar damaged?"

"No. Our power couplings remain intact, Excellency. Levels are stable and the damaged sections have been disconnected," Goss reported. "We must find another way to warm the young. We cannot expect the Raknar's power to last forever."

Klatk nodded. "We can't, but this planet does not provide the necessities our colony needs. The Peacemakers will come, and they will help us."

"What if they can't, Excellency? What then?"

Klatk studied the younger male. "The Peacemaker Guild will send the best they have. The Consortium lied to us, and our people are suffering because we need power. We scrounged to find and use it for our benefit when it was promised to us. Three colonies are set against each other, Goss. A Peacemaker will come. And they will defend us."

Goss nodded. "That's a lot to assume. We must do something other than hope."

He was right. They needed to do something besides bolstering their defense and preparing for the inevitable attacks to come. Klatk considered the options and found her thoughts turning to the 700 young ones that would never see the sunrise or know the love of their colony.

"The GenSha protect their children in a central paddock, do they not?"

Goss flinched. "Yes, Excellency. In the center of their colony."

"Can it be reached via tunnel?" Klatk asked.

"Perhaps," Goss said. "I'll check with the engineers and see if we can make it happen. It may take several days to dig, Excellency. You're not considering another response? The GenSha are mostly peaceful and not prone to war. That's why they've brought in the mercenaries."

"I don't care that they are peaceful and not prone to war. They've taken our young!" Klatk looked at him. "If the engineers think it's possible, take a squad and hurt them. Hurt them like they've hurt us."

"Of course," Goss answered. For the moment, he appeared sated with her response to the attack. "Should we prepare the defenses?"

Klatk nodded. "Full perimeter. If there is no attack by sundown, place listening posts in a five-kilometer ring around the colony with set artillery missions from every automatic system. When they come back, I don't want them getting any closer than that."

"You believe they'll be back?"

Klatk watched the receding plumes of dust smear the verdant swathes of the GenSha prairies. "I would, so they have my attention, Goss. When they return, we will be ready for them. If no Peacemaker is sent, we will stand for what is ours."

* * *

The prospect of going home didn't thrill Hex, nor did the idea that he could just run around the solar system with the *Victory Twelve*. Filing a flight plan for Mars gave him the flexibility to visit his sister and her family if he wanted. They were nice people, but oil drilling wasn't like being a mercenary. No matter how nice their estate was, and how well-prepared they were for any type of impending disaster, Hex could not relate to them. Four days was about all he could handle in the presence of any of his family anymore. They didn't understand why he wanted to be a mercenary. His father, they said, made more than enough money to take care of the family for generations. No one else in their family needed to go fight someone else's wars. Hex knew differently. Fighting another's war could be dangerous, but it was lucrative as hell. Depending on where you go and what you do, his father said once, a soldier can live like a king without hearing a shot in anger.

Hex tore at the label on a bottle of Budweiser. Alone at an empty bar, he idly watched a football game on the Tri-V screen and tried to figure out what to do next. There was no unit to go back to. Lemieux's Marauders had been officially disbanded with Marc "Hammer" Lemieux's forced retirement. Only Hex and Lemieux, himself, had survived the Marauders' final mission, except for those aboard the *Trigger Happy* who'd run for Karma when things went south. The Mercenary Guild would deal with them soon enough, but Hex Alison was a soldier without a unit, and it stung.

He did, however, have a ship, even if it was loaned. There would be a time to go back to Karma and re-enter the pits to search for a posting or maybe even create his own unit. It wasn't the right time yet, even though he knew that getting back on the proverbial horse would be both good and bad for him. Maybe he should go visit his sister, play with her kids, and try to be a normal human being again?

"Pardon me? Is this seat taken?"

Hex snorted and gestured to the emptiness of the bar. "I think you have your choice of seats, friend. Why sit next to me?"

"I have my reasons," the voice said.

Just my dumb luck, Hex thought. There were always people who just had to strike up a conversation even if for no reason other than to hear themselves talk. Hex spun and spoke slowly, "Look, I really don't want to..."

The words died on his lips.

A Sidar, his pterodactyl-like visage smirking, stood at Hex's side. His ceremonial robe was dark, and the glint of a Selector's badge shone even in the dim light of the bar. "Mister Alison, I presume?"

"Selector Hak-Chet," Hex sputtered. "I meant no disrespect."

"None was taken," Hak-Chet said. "May I join you?"

Hex nodded and the Sidar spun into the high-backed barstool quickly. The robot bartender appeared and Hak-Chet carefully looked at Hex's beer and frowned. "I'll have a cider, please."

So much for good first impressions, Hex thought. He looked up, met the Selector's eyes, and tried to think of something to say to open the conversation. He'd never been approachable or the kind of person to speak first. The Sidar said nothing, merely drinking from his pint of cider without looking at Hex. Hex licked his lips. "So, what brings you—"

"Mister Alison, I'm afraid this visit must be short and to the point," Hak-Chet said as he downed a solid third of the pint of cider in one swallow. "I've closed the bar to make this meeting possible and must move quickly before people ask questions, do you understand? The Guild has need of your services."

Hex blinked. He'd never considered being a Peacemaker. "I don't know what to say, Selector. I'm honored the Guild would ask me."

Hak-Chet scowled and shook his head. "You are not Peacemaker material, Mister Alison. The Guild, however, has need of your services and is prepared to compensate you for your efforts."

"I don't understand," Hex squinted. "I have a single CASPer and a few million credits to my name. What can I possibly do for your Guild?"

Hak-Chet took another long sip of cider. He wiped his maw with the back of one hand, a completely human gesture that looked totally out of place for an alien, and locked eyes with Hex. "You are a friend of Peacemaker Francis, yes?"

"I am," Hex said. "She saved my life on that last mission. But you already know that, don't you?"

Hak-Chet nodded. "I am aware of that and of your own tactical abilities, that's why I'm here, Mister Alison. You are currently in possession of the Peacemaker's personal vessel and have filed a flight plan to Mars. You were planning on leaving when? Tomorrow? Or when you sober up enough to realize you did nothing wrong on your last mission and people died anyway?"

The words slapped Hex as effectively as if the Selector had punched him in the face. "I was thinking about visiting family."

"Noble, yes. But what if I told you that your friend was going to need help? Would you be willing to go?"

"I'm one guy with a ship." Hex bristled. "What can I do to help her? Besides, she's a Peacemaker now and has way more power and authority than I could ever muster."

"No," Hak-Chet replied as if talking to a child. The effect was not lost on Hex. "You are one guy with a ship. I suggest you start there."

Hex raised his beer and took a deep swig from the bottle. As he swallowed, the tumblers clicked into place. "Jessica is in danger?"

"More specifically, Earth's first Peacemaker is in danger. There are those in and around the Guild that want her to fail. The leadership, and myself, do not. She is about to enter a three-way fight where two of the sides have retained mercenary forces to help achieve their goals. The third side has not. Knowing Miss Francis as well as I do, and as well as you do, I believe that's precisely where she'll align herself based on the situation. When the tactical situation deteriorates, as it inevitably will, she will be in need of assistance. I am prepared to ensure that she has what she needs. Given the resources, her actions will either confirm her place as a Peacemaker or render her another ineffective human candidate for Peacemaker."

Hex turned one side of his mouth down. "She's not the first candidate?"

"No. There have been several. None of her predecessors have passed a single confirmation mission. Jessica did, but the Guild was not ready to declare her a Peacemaker and have ordered her into a dispute that reeks of corporate infringement and proxy aggression. To be fair, Mister Alison, I cannot let her fail. It's time for Earth to play a role in the Galactic Union other than slaughtering human soldiers in other people's wars."

Hex found himself nodding. "You think Jessica can solve this dispute?"

"In her own particular way, yes." Hak-Chet drank again from his pint, nearly draining it. "Now, you are one man with a ship. I believe the tonnage and space inside the *Victory Twelve* will allow you some armor and a few more CASPers, am I right?"

"There's room for a platoon of tanks and two fire teams of CASPers. It would be tight, but doable," Hex said. He set the empty bottle down on the bar and looked up at Hak-Chet. "I don't have the contacts here to create a unit from scratch."

Hak-Chet polished off his cider and stood. "You won't have to. Bay 12, Mister Alison."

"What about the contract? The details?"

Hak-Chet smiled. "Bay 12, Mister Alison. You best hurry. *Tchrt One* is preparing to jump. I expect Peacemaker Francis to arrive in a hot landing zone at the very least. She'll need friends in her corner."

Hex nodded and stood. "I'm taking you at your word, Selector."

"You are, Mister Alison." Hak-Chet turned to walk away, but looked back over his shoulder. "Have you ever known the Peacemaker Guild to not make good on its promises?"

"No," Hex said simply. "But would you go this far for any other Peacemaker, Selector?"

Hak-Chet grinned. "Who says I haven't before, and that I won't again, Mister Alison?"

* * * * *

Chapter Five

The *Victory Twelve's* cargo hatch was open when Hex entered Bay Twelve. Three Mark Five assault tanks were already loaded, with a fourth being backed into position by a ground guide. A platform with six CASPers mounted on it rolled into position. All of it was a coordinated, professional effort that no one seemed to be leading. Hex marched into the center of the action and looked left and right for someone in charge.

"You're Alison, right?" a female wearing green coveralls with red epaulets said. Her blonde hair was tied back in a ponytail at the base of her neck, and her eyes were hard and serious. "We're almost loaded and ready to depart."

"Who the hell are you?" Hex asked. "How did you get the hold open?"

The blonde's brow furrowed. "Didn't Selector Hak-Chet speak with you?"

"I just left him. There's no way he could—" The thought died in Hex's mouth. He'd left the bar not 10 minutes before. There was no way Hak-Chet could have started this process in the time they'd been apart. The Selector had started things well before talking to Hex knowing that the young mercenary would agree.

That sonuvabitch, Hex thought with a grin.

"The Selector gave us the order to move an hour ago." The blonde extended a hand. "I'm Tara Mason. I've got four tanks that used to be part of Death On Tracks with me."

Hex nodded. The armor-heavy mercenary force had attacked a fortified objective held by the Besquith in the Cimaron region. Outnumbered four to one, the mercenary armor commander decided to use nuclear weapons against the Besquith and paid the price. A full regiment of human armor fell in minutes. "You got out just in time?"

"Never deployed," Tara said. "Drop ship couldn't de-orbit. We watched the whole fucking regiment die in place."

"Sorry to hear that," Hex said as sincerely as he could. Human mercenary commanders were a dime a dozen, and there seemed to be more bad ones than good ones in the race for off-world contracts. As bad as Marc Lemieux had been as commander of the Marauders, even he wouldn't have stooped to what that idiot Schwartz had done with Death On Tracks. The largest human mercenary armored force was gone. For a moment, Hex couldn't help but wonder if the woman standing in front of him, or her tanks and crewmen, were lucky or good. He sincerely hoped for the latter. "Where are the CASPer troops?"

Tara shrugged. "On their way. There's two squads straight from the academy from what I understand."

Hex blinked and looked at the Mark Eight suits on the rolling racks. "Newbies?"

"Yeah," Tara said. "At least they'll have some good training."

"There's no time for re-training them." Hex shook his head. "We'll be fighting their bad habits from the schoolhouse the whole time. They always tend to teach the basics just wrong enough that bad things happen in combat."

"You said *we*," Tara curled up one side of her mouth. "You must think I'm experienced. We haven't even played 'where've you been and who do you know' yet."

Hex grinned. "We'll have 170 hours to do that. You may not have made that last jump, but you've made more than your fair share." Telling her that it was obvious she'd "seen the elephant" didn't seem right. The evidence was in her eyes and her mannerisms. She'd taken control of the loading of a vessel she'd never seen before, expertly loaded her tanks and left more than enough room for the CASPers in the *Victory Twelve's* hold. "I want you to be my XO, Tara. That good with you?"

"Absolutely," she nodded. "You need to go to the bridge and change the flight plan. I'll get the CASPers loaded and recall their owners. They're probably all in the Class Six getting what they think they need for the trip."

Hex laughed. A few years before, he'd have been right with the CASPer pilots hitting the base liquor store for liquid courage before heading out on his first mission. "You're probably right."

Tara gestured to the CASPer racks and yelled to someone behind him. "Let's go! Get those things aboard!"

Hex turned and saw mobile racks moving forward. Behind them, through the main hangar door, came 11 fresh-faced kids no more than 20 years old. Five of them were men, the other six women. Women increasingly found their way into CASPers out of the Academy. They were better pilots, everyone knew, but the CASPers had been a man's world for most of the last few decades.

Times are a'changing.

Tara met his eyes, then he turned around and headed for the bridge. She didn't say anything, and she didn't have to. She was all business, and that was just fine with Hex. For a split second, his heart fluttered as he thought of how Maya would have grabbed his arm or said something quick and gentle. He could find that again, but not now and not with Tara Mason. That was as obvious as her combat experience.

The *Victory Twelve's* bridge was two decks above the main hold and roughly amidships on the long, sleek corvette. Hex climbed up the second ladder and stepped into the automated bridge. As his feet passed the bulkhead threshold into the room, a chime sounded from everywhere followed by a woman's voice.

<<Captain on the bridge.>>

Hex smiled at the familiar voice. "Thank you, Lucille."

There was no response. His assumption that the electronic voice on the bridge was Marc Lemieux's nearly perfect, artificially-intelligent counterpart appeared to be inaccurate. That voice was identical to the voice on the *Victory Twelve*, but Lucille would have at least replied. Not that it mattered. Hex could fly the ship on his own. Of course, knowing a key word to activate it would have been nice to know.

Hex ran a hand through his hair. "Bulldog, what did you leave me?"

<<Captain Francis is not aboard, sir. You are in command, and I will respond to Lucille or shipmind, whichever you prefer.>>

So it is Lucille. Weird.

"Lucille it is," Hex said. "Connect me with departure control."

<<Button two.>>

Hex found the communications console by his right hand and pressed the button. "Departure control, this is *Victory Twelve* with a change of flight plan notification."

"Go ahead, *Victory Twelve*." The voice on the other end sounded bored and half-asleep.

"*Victory Twelve* making way to Araf, Jesc arm and Craft region. We are not transiting to Mars, over," Hex said. With a few taps of the control console, he verified the flight parameters that Lucille programmed based on his transmission. While not a conversational interface, the computer knew what it was doing.

Departure Control came back a few seconds later. "*Victory Twelve*, confirmed. You're number six for the gate. Transition is in two point five hours, how copy? Over."

Hex frowned. The *Tchrt One* had at least a two-and-a-half-hour head start on them, so they'd be going through the stargate at the same time, but a number of ships ahead of them. He wanted to make sure they stayed as close as they could to her—if they landed in a hot LZ, it could be an incredibly short mission for Hex and his new team. "Copy, Departure. Two point five hours. *Victory Twelve* standing by. Out."

With time to kill, Hex moved back down to the bay and collected his personal belongings. Two immense duffel bags slung over his shoulders, Hex walked into the drop bay of the ship and saw his CASPer being loaded at the far end. Tara stood there supervising the loading as carefully as she had the other eleven. Hex walked the length of the bay past the four tanks hanging suspended in their drop racks and stopped at Tara's side.

"She's a little beat up, don't you think?" Tara asked. She pointed to the large slash marks across the suit's torso and arms. "That cosmetic or are you leaving it there to attract women?"

Hex shook his head. "It needs repairing. Offloaded it today to get it fixed. Now I'm right back on the ship and headed out again."

"Doesn't look too bad. We'll get the newbies to do the maintenance—they love teaching that stuff in school. Will be good experience for them," Tara said. "Once she's aboard, we're ready to push off."

"We have some time—about two hours." Hex shrugged. "Enough time to get the team together and brief them, I guess."

"I've already scheduled a briefing for right after we hit the gate. As soon as the ship's course is set, we can meet with them and start figuring out how to skin the cat as a group." Tara said. "If we've got the time—I want to go back into the port for a bit and try to find us some air cover."

Hex sighed. "I hadn't even thought of that."

Tara squared her shoulders to him. "I'm not trying to take charge of your mission, Hex. My instructions from Hak-Chet were to make sure Peacemaker Francis has the support she needs, and that you have the support you need. I know about your mission, okay? I'm here to help you as much as we need to help the Peacemaker."

Her words didn't feel that great, but Hex believed he understood. Hak-Chet wanted Jessica protected, but he knew that Hex wouldn't be able to do it on his own. The sinking feeling that whatever waited them at Araf was much worse than Hak-Chet let on grew with every passing moment. "They're going to be ahead of us at the gate, but we'll be close."

Tara answered, "Good. Then we won't have any problems."

Hex didn't believe her for a second.

* * *

Jessica woke in the forced darkness of the ship and pushed herself upright, resting her back against the combination headboard and wall that encircled her bunk. Her wrist slate said the *Tchrt One* was 87 hours into the 170-hour transition from Earth to Araf. The last three days had been some of the worst days of her life. Each day brought a negotiation session, which Jessica immediately objected to because the other parties, specifically the Altar, Selroth, and GenSha, were not present at the table.

"It's not fair to discuss the situation without talking to those on the ground. Especially if they're fighting over it," she said.

Kenos laughed. "Our agreements with the colonies and their home worlds are legally sound. You humans use the term *airtight*. That's certainly what we've done. The Consortium will handle their differences. Your position, Peacemaker, is to force them to come to the table and discuss an end to hostilities." Kenos sat back in his chair and lowered his dark eyes to her. "I can forgive your lack of policy understanding, Miss Francis, but I cannot forgive your inability to see that the Consortium handles its own policy."

Jessica sat forward in her chair. "Then why am I even here, Kenos?"

Taemin cleared his throat and spoke for the first time in two days. As a mediation assistant, she'd assumed he would do the lion's share of the talking instead of remaining virtually silent. "The Altar specifically requested a Peacemaker, as is their right under the Consortium's agreements. They believe the Consortium does not have the best interest of their colony in mind."

Kenos chittered in disagreement. "There are fourteen colonies on Araf. Eleven of them live in peace. We, the Consortium, have all of their best interests in mind with everything we do."

Jessica sat back against the chair, her thoughts racing. "The Altar have a legitimate complaint? About what?"

Taemin looked at Kenos for a long moment and then spoke. "There are three colonies along the Choote River on the largest southern continent. Inland are the GenSha who use the rolling plains for agriculture. The river flows through a desert region where the Altar set up their colony to mine precious metals. Where the Choote meets the Great Sea, the Selroth have a major colony. They take advantage of the fish and other fauna in the freshwater delta. The river's flow rate is lower than promised, a part of the Consortium's concessions regarding their climatological control system, and as such, all three colonies believe they are about to lose this resource because of the actions of the others."

A Tri-V display snapped to life and Jessica could see the layout of the Choote River. Two long and wide sandbars appeared in the winding river as it flowed to the sea. "It's not very deep, is it?"

"It still meets the required criteria," Kenos said.

Taemin tilted his chin at her. "Every system on a Dream World is designed for certain criteria. Climate, hydrology, and soil are manufactured and terraformed to the specifications of the colonies. There are occasional problems. Araf is more problematic than the other worlds by fifteen percent in reported discrepancies."

Kenos bristled. "An entire planet's climate can only be jumpstarted, not controlled. Araf's progress rested inside the 98th percentile for the last 150 Earth years of development. The recent fluctuations in weather and climate are within the projected norms, just at the low end."

Jessica understood. "You have a drought in this area, and the three colonies who need water to survive are fighting over the river."

Taemin shook his head. "The Altar do not need water."

"Then why are they fighting the other two colonies? Or are they stuck in the middle?"

Kenos barked. "Hardly."

"The GenSha want to use the water for agriculture. The Altar and the Selroth believe the wastewater will contaminate the Choote." Taemin said.

"But the Altar do not need water. You just said that. Why would they care what the GenSha do?" Jessica asked.

Taemin sighed. "The Selroth believe the Altar are withholding underground water sources. Repeated efforts on the part of the Consortium have failed to bring the three sides to any agreement. The Altar refuse to give up their territory or the rights to the water found therein."

"Is that allowed under their agreement with the Consortium?"

Kenos barked. "Of course it is! We want our colonies to be successful. We give them the rights to what they find on their lands so they can use it or leverage it as necessary."

"Then we have to have all three parties, plus the three of us, at the table. End of story," Jessica said.

Taemin cleared his throat. "Administrator Kenos? Would you give us a moment?"

"Certainly," the little Cochkala left the table and disappeared through a door.

Jessica turned in her chair to face the Caroon mediator. His longish face curled in a defiant smirk. "You are treading on dangerous ground, Peacemaker Francis."

Her eyebrows rose in surprise. "Really? How so?"

"The Consortium has asked the Altar to give up their colony position and move, with full logistical and financial support. This would free up the water sources for both the GenSha and the Selroth to take advantage of. They have refused and the Consortium asks that they be moved—that is our first task when we reach the planet."

"Our first task?" Jessica squinted at him. "Seems to me that there's a lot of anger and death that should be stopped first. Removing the Altar doesn't solve the problem as you've explained it. The GenSha and the Selroth will still fight over it. The question is why the Altar cannot leave, not how fast you can get them to move."

"You're belittling the importance of this disagreement." Taemin said. "Is it because you have information about your father's disappearance? Are you racing to get home?"

Jessica felt an ice-cold bolt of electricity shoot down her spine, but she kept her calm. "What did you say?"

"You have new information about your father's disappearance. You have many documented instances of violence and poor judgment when it comes to information regarding him."

Nothing since high school. What the fuck is going on here?

As soon as the thought crossed her mind, Jessica knew the quizzical look made its way to her face. While not a mistake, it provoked a twinkle in the Caroon's eyes. He was baiting her, and it was working.

Whose side are you on, Taemin?

"The last instance of violence, as you put it, was in high school and, frankly, she had it coming," Jessica said. "That's beside the point. How did you know about my father's disappearance, and who told you I had new information?"

Taemin's thin mouth smiled. "Your Peacemaker training files were provided to me as a preparatory exercise. Marc Lemieux spoke to investigators from your Guild shortly after Ch'tek's arrest. They believe you were using the situation for personal gain and not to stop Ch'tek's irrational attempt to plant a Canavar egg on Earth."

That's why the second mission.

Godsdamnit.

"I see," Jessica said. "You think the only way I'm going to solve this crisis and earn my Peacemaker commission is to listen to the Consortium. And you believe ordering the evacuation of the Altar will lead to a rational solution between the GenSha and the Selroth?"

Taemin nodded. "I believe that is a wise and viable solution, yes. It doesn't answer my question about your motives."

"My motives, Mediator, are not your concern. Is that clear?"

Taemin bowed his head slightly, enough that Jessica couldn't tell if his mouth moved in a smile or a smirk.

Prick. She took a breath and changed the subject. "What's so important about the Altar's position at the river?"

Taemin frowned. "There is a Raknar lying partially submerged on a sandbar just outside their colony. Both the GenSha and the Selroth are concerned the Altar are trying to find a way to activate its weapons systems."

"It has power?" Only a fraction of the Raknar wreckage in the galaxy had evidence of a viable power source. The Dusman's engineering skills were far above those of most civilizations. Viable power sources gave insights into the inner workings of the Raknar and its ability to defeat the Canavar.

"They believe so, but there has been nothing confirmed," Taemin said. "If they are using power from the Raknar, there is no issue. If they are actively trying to employ it, then the Consortium's fears are merited. It would be best if they were evacuated to another site. I have taken the liberty of finding alternate locations. There are four viable ones..."

Jessica wasn't listening. Her gut railed against the idea of moving anyone. Kenos obviously wanted the Altar moved so he could leverage any remaining power, or weapons, on the Raknar for the gain of the Consortium. For a mediator trained to find the middle ground, Taemin was decidedly behind the Consortium's proposal. His deflection about her father was a calculated move—a poorly played one, too. Yet it left a lingering doubt that, with time, would get worse and fester.

Hak-Chet would have said something. Unless he knew the Guild's real motivation for sending me here.

"Peacemaker?"

The question jostled her back into the present. Taemin stared at her. The accusatory look on his face meant he'd asked the question more than once.

"Is everything okay?" he asked without a trace of interest.

"Fine," Jessica said.

"How do you want to proceed?"

Jessica looked at him for a long moment and realized she could not trust him, or his information. "I need to see the area for myself."

A Peacemaker's senses told the ground truth. Observation and patience were critical to success. While there was little doubt that Taemin would continue to pressure her into a quick solution benefitting the Consortium, something about the whole mess didn't make sense. The GenSha's water processing shouldn't be allowed to affect anything downstream for starters. The Selroth could move their colony more easily than the other two could simply by finding another suitable river delta. The Raknar was a wildcard to the entire situation.

If it was viable, the colony who controlled it would have a serious advantage. Given that the planet barely met the climatic needs of its inhabitants already, persistent drought and unstable weather would either drive the colonies to evacuate at a significant loss to the Consortium, or they'd fight for whatever resources they could scrounge.

"What should I tell Administrator Kenos?"

Jessica stood. "I will apologize for our private conversation and cancel tomorrow's formal session and maybe the next for research purposes. You said you had my file as a preparatory exercise? I want a copy of everything you have on this situation. I will not go into this unprepared and pressured to do something for anyone other than the colonists on that planet. Is that clear, Taemin?"

The Caroon nodded solemnly. "Of course, Peacemaker."

"Very well. I'll expect those files by the evening meal." Jessica walked out of the conference room and hesitated in the passageway for a split second before turning to find Kenos and make her apologies. For two days, they'd briefed her on the situation and, while she'd known it was biased and incomplete, the motive was clear. They wanted to avoid a financial loss. An embarrassing failure of a paradise world would cost them billions of credits at the very least. Then there was the Raknar.

Accessing a powered Raknar was akin to a technological Holy Grail. Spread throughout the galaxy, the abandoned giants once fought off the gigantic Canavar before the Dusman vanished. Their internal systems baffled the top scientists in the Union. Finding one capable of movement was almost unheard of—only a handful of the thousand or so recovered Raknar could move any of their appendages. Finding one with its power source intact was equally rare. However, in each case, the ability to see, decipher, and replicate the intricate technologies was priceless. Kenos wanted the Altar to leave the Raknar; that was clear. What wasn't was why the Altar would risk their colony for the partially submerged mecha.

Jessica shook off the thoughts as she moved forward to make her apologies. She'd not had her head on straight since her meeting with the Guild Master. It was time to change that with good old-fashioned research and intelligence preparation of the battlefield.

Good planning never made up for poor execution, but it would help her get through whatever the next set of challenges would be. The hours ticking past were against her.

* * * * *

Chapter Six

Hex woke five minutes before his alarm, rolled over, and put his feet down on the *Victory Twelve's* cool deck. Using Jessica's suite hadn't been something he planned to do, but everyone on the ship looked to him as their expedient mercenary unit's commander, and such privilege was expected. He'd moved in after the *Victory Twelve* had entered hyperspace. With Lucille in command, there was little he needed to do. While not an artificial intelligence, per se, Lucille's programming and capabilities made her more than a viable pilot and a seriously well-informed leader.

<<Good morning, Hex.>> Lucille's voice came from a speaker built into the headboard of the king-sized bed. <<The unit is awake and preparing for stand-to in 30 minutes. We are slated to arrive at the Araf emergence point in 156 hours, 42 minutes, and 12 seconds.>>

"Thank you, Lucille."

<<You're welcome, Hex. There is coffee in the galley, and the shower is ready for you.>>

Hex grunted and stood. After padding to the wall unit and retrieving a steaming mug of Kona coffee, freshly ground and brewed, he tore off his shirt and sleep shorts and stepped into a steaming shower. Awake and ready, Hex washed quickly and shaved under the almost scalding stream of water before turning it off and donning a fresh pair of coveralls. Without a unit patch or any type of rank, the blank coveralls said nothing about him or where he'd come from. To the untrained eye, he looked like a cadet fresh from the mercenary preparatory schools on Earth.

He laughed. Except for the last several years of missions and actual operations, he could have attended those pinnacles of mercenary education. Instead, he'd earned several degrees under fire. There were plenty of good leaders produced by the schools every year, but just as many tended to die from untrained troops and fratricide than from enemy contact.

* * *

Twenty-four hours into their 170-hour jump, Hex had gathered the team in the main hold, which spun to provide gravity, and laid out his plan to prepare them for what they might find on Araf.

"Now that you've been fed and had a good night's sleep, it's time to get down to business. My name is Hex Alison, and I'm in command. We don't have a unit name or heraldry yet, and honestly, we don't have time to sit around and come up with something. We have about a 155 hours until we arrive at Araf. What we know is that Earth's first peacemaker, Jessica Francis, is headed there on a ship that will arrive just before us. She's probably going to be dropping into a hot LZ and is going to need help. There are three colonies fighting over water rights, and two of them have employed very capable mercenary forces—we're not sure just who they are yet. You'll get the last round of intelligence we were able to pull after this briefing."

Hex took a breath and pointed at Tara. "This is Tara Mason. She's in command of our platoon of tanks. Once we hit the ground, we'll have two squads of CASPers acting like marines out in front of us to secure a position and provide security and overwatch." Hex looked at them and smiled. "All twelve of you are fresh out of CASPer pilot training and that's not as bad as you might think it is. What we have to do is correct your bad habits. I have a pretty good idea how we can start that." He nodded at Tara.

Tara stepped forward. "We didn't have a lot of warning, so we are going in without immediate air support. We've requested any assistance the Peacemaker Guild can give us, but we're likely going to hit the beach alone. Our ability to identify and kill targets in the airspace is critical. Shooting, moving, and communicating are not going to be enough. We have to fight as a unified front."

"Especially because we don't know where the attack might be coming from," Hex said. "To that end, we're going to be training a lot. We've networked the tanks and CASPers into an Aethernet training module, and we're going to mount up and get to that in a few minutes. We've barely gotten to know each other, and none of you know Jessica. I do. She was a part of my last unit for a couple of years and is like my sister. The Peacemaker Guild obviously wants her to succeed, otherwise we wouldn't be here. There's going to be time for us to get to know each other. Right now, though, we have to learn to fight together. That's where we're going to start. The rest of it will come later. We have four tanks and a dozen CASPers. We're outgunned and lack experience, but we have the advantage of surprise. With that, we can afford a little time to make shit up as we go."

The group laughed, and the tension broke a little. They would need time to gel as a team, but Hex could see excitement in the young pilots' eyes, and quiet resilience in the vets from Tara's tanks. It would have to do, and it felt damned good to be in command.

"Okay," Hex said and looked over the collected group with a satisfied grin. "Communications are set. The CASPers are the Angels, one through twelve, and the tanks are the Demons—one through four. I'm commanding the CASPers in Angel One, and my callsign is Boss. I'll need two fire team leaders. We'll set that up after the first series of sims. The tanks are commanded by Tara in Demon One. I'm attached to Alpha Team for movement. Everybody with me so far?"

The murmurs became smiles. Tara nodded approvingly and tapped on a slate in her hands. "Boss, I've got a basic sim loaded for everyone. The tanks will use it for simulated gunnery practice, but the CASPers will have a chance to shoot, move, and communicate as we go. It's a standard firing simulation with infantry attached."

Hex grinned. He'd been thinking the same thing. "Sounds good. Everybody take five and come back prepared to mount up for training."

The group splintered between those looking for a fresh bulb of coffee and those hitting the latrine one last time. Tara walked over with her slate and showed it to Hex. "You've got a couple of promising standouts. I've put them in Angels Two and Seven. The rest of the CASPer pilots don't really strike me as...competent."

"Really?" Hex squinted at her. "What makes you say that?"

Tara shrugged. "Most of them are young and overconfident."

He couldn't help but smile. "Not necessarily unlike any tanker I've ever met."

Tara laughed, and he realized he liked the sound of it. No sooner did the smile on his face widen, then it faltered. Tara's smile did, too.

"Yeah," she smoothed back a stray lock of hair and focused on the slate again. "So, the sim is a movement to contact. The tanks will roll out from a berm complex and proceed south about 300 meters to their first firing point. When that happens, the CASPers will leave from their start point to the west. They'll roll up on my flank, and we'll use them to bound forward and take out some infantry targets before the enemy armor appears. They'll have to stop, wave us in, and keep bounding forward. We can see how they do."

"Great," Hex said with a nod. But, it wasn't great. Standing close to Tara, he felt guilty for smiling at her as if he sullied Maya's memory. Less than two weeks had passed since her death. It was too fresh and painful. She wouldn't be mad at him for smiling at another woman, especially one he would fight alongside. Still, Maya's loss hung over him like an awkward sheet. "Hey, uh, thanks for figuring out who should do what. I appreciate it."

Tara shrugged. "*De nada.* Get ready to roll, okay?"

"Yeah," Hex said. His eyes followed Tara across the hangar deck as she moved to the right front skirt of a Defender Mark Four tank and climbed aboard with ease. From each of the four tanks, a collection of cables snaked into a central hub. Another set of cables stretched from the hub to ports on each of the CASPers. The Mark Eight mechs could be physically networked for training, which made them invaluable. Between the two racks of fairly new CASPers was his Mark Seven. The armor was scored in a half dozen places from massive Oogar claws, and much of its paint was shredded, and the hulking beast looked ancient next to the gleaming like-new ones Hak-Chet had provided for the newbies. He hadn't been inside it since they'd lost Maya and the rest of the Marauders. It was a matter of time, he'd thought, but the idea of getting into it gave him pause.

You have to get in there.

Hex sighed and walked to the CASPer. The cockpit was open, the clamshell hanging up at an angle from the narrow opening. Inside there was a picture of his parents tucked against one of the multi-function displays. On the other side, where he couldn't see, would be the one of him and Maya on the shore of Kaua'i from a year ago. They'd come back to Earth after a difficult defense mission on Haight Four when she'd knocked on the door of his quarters aboard the *Trigger Happy* with a bottle of wine.

His father would have said something along the lines of never eat and shit in the same place, meaning in his particular lexicon that pursuing a romantic relationship where you work is dangerous and doomed for failure. However, he would also have understood, because the only reason Hex existed was that his parents had done the same thing. His mother retired to raise him and his siblings to alleviate that danger, but they'd come together because they each understood where the other had been. For them, it had worked. With Maya on his arm, Hex never considered the inherent danger of their lifestyle. Maya was simply too good, he believed. They were simply too good. He'd planned to take her back to Kaua'i after Marc Lemieux's milk run mission and propose. All of it seemed so far away now.

He paused to tug himself into the Mark VII's haptic suit and pushed the memories away. With hesitant steps, Hex climbed aboard the CASPer's crew ladder and backed into the seat, dropping his legs into their sleeves and pushing backward against the seat. Hands moved as if on autopilot, attaching the haptic suit's cables by feel alone. As he did, his eyes rested on the photo of him and Maya together. He reached out for it and stopped.

It's okay. Maya's voice was as clear in his memory as if she were standing right there. *I'm here, and it's okay.*

Hex bit the inside of his lip and settled into the cockpit. Scents of old sweat and silicone wafted around him as he brought his arms into the cockpit and began the power-up sequence from memory. With a few keystrokes on the right multi-function display, he deleted the previous mission information and cleared the mecha's memory banks. One by one, the displays powered on, and he felt the vibration as the servos and motors within the CASPer came to life.

With a flick of his wrist, Hex found and flipped the canopy close switch and brought the clamshell down. As it closed and sealed around him, the Tri-V screen came to life and began internal diagnostics. When the camera systems came online, a view of the hangar outside filled his vision. The other CASPers looked to be in various states of checkout.

<<All systems are nominal.>>

Hex flinched and yelped. "Lucille! What in the hell are you doing? You're supposed to be flying the ship!"

<<I am an assistive program, Hex. I can be in more than one place at a time.>>

Hex shook his head. "I don't need you in my CASPer, okay?"

<<I detect an emotional response variant, Hex. Assistance from me could increase your combat readiness and performance by five percent.>>

"Thank you, Lucille, but I'd feel a lot better if you were solely focused on flying the ship."

<<Understood. I am capable of immediate action if necessary. Connection terminated.>>

For a moment, Hex did not move or hardly breathe. Flying the *Victory Twelve* was one thing, but tactically supporting him? The idea of a near-AI performing alongside him seemed too far-fetched to consider. CASPers were capable vehicles in and of themselves, and in the hands of a skilled operator they could do amazing things. He shook off the thought of taking Lucille's offer seriously. There were more important things to do.

Diagnostics completed, Hex powered up the communications suite and turned the simulator mode on. He put the radio and radar sets into the same mode and let the system boot as if the CASPer were on its own and ready to deploy from auxiliary power. Though networked, the radios and other onboard systems would function normally. Hex pressed the transmit button. "Angels and Demons, check in."

One by one, the CASPers checked in followed by the tanks. Tara was last. "Boss, this is Demon One. All vehicles are green on the board and ready for simulation STARTEX."

Hex flexed his fingers and grabbed the CASPer's controls. With a glance at Maya's picture, he replied. "Roger, Demon One. STARTEX, time now." The hangar view faded away to black and came back to a wide, rocky plain under a bright yellow sky. A thousand feral Oogars appeared on the screen and roared as one towards his forces.

Hex froze. *What the fuck?*

"Hex!" The voice was a thousand light years away and still urgent. "Hex! Engage!"

He flinched and grasped for the CASPer's controls. Palms sweaty, he tried to blink away the image, but the simulation continued to run. In that lasting moment, he was there with Maya and

Hammer trying to fight their way out of a purple-furred shitstorm. Shock turned to a quick burst of anger. *Fuck!*

He keyed the radio. "Roger, Boss is moving."

On his command display, the line of CASPers pressed forward more than a thousand meters from his position. Hex jumped forward and accelerated as he bounded toward them. The two squads moved as a single unit in a rough line abreast. Hex selected Angel Two and Angel Seven by voice only. "What in the hell are you doing? Angel Two, set your squad down and lay covering fire. Angel Seven, halt where you are and wait until Alpha Team is laying down fire so you can move."

"Angel Two, roger," a female voice called. He heard a click as she departed the frequency. The squad of CASPers stopped and laid down covering fire as advertised.

"Angel Seven, moving now." As disciplined as the first squad was as they stopped and did what they were told, the second squad was not, moving forward in a ragtag fashion that made his blood boil the more he watched.

"Seven, get your people together! Move in three- to five-second rushes and try to find—"

Two icons in second squad winked out. Angels Nine and Eleven were gone. Hex made for second squad as they finally came to a stop and first squad bounded forward. Oogar fanned out away from them as if to pounce on first squad—sensing weakness. Hex blinked and a flash of memory caused him to stumble as he bounded forward. The Oogar, just two weeks before, turned away from his escape aboard Hammer's tank to pursue the stragglers, including Maya.

The damned things, even in a simulation, could sense it.

"Alpha Team, set." Angel Two called. "Second squad cleared to bound."

"Moving," Hex heard Angel Seven call. The Oogar swarmed them and two more icons winked out, Seven among them.

"Angel Two, this is Angel Eight in command of Bravo Team. Request to join on your left flank."

"Granted, we'll hold position for you." Angel Two replied.

"Boss, this is Angel Eight, can you cover our move?"

Hex smiled. Someone had their shit together. He changed course and bounded into the teeth of the advancing Oogar. With the flick of a wrist, he engaged both external rocket pods on his shoulders and jumped as high as his jets would allow. At the apex of his leap, Hex fired both pods, a full complement of 24 unguided high-explosive rockets, into the mass. The forest canopy erupted around him as the CASPer landed. He pivoted 45 degrees to the right and found the icons for first squad on his display.

"Demon One, this is Boss, moving across your sector in 10 seconds. Clear our six, over."

"Boss, negative. Unable to center fires."

Mid-bound, Hex scanned his tanks and found them in disarray. Demon One and Demon Four were in position to provide supporting fire, but Demons Two and Three were a 100 meters behind them with their gun tubes oriented away from the enemy. "Demon One, Boss. Sitrep. Over."

A private comm message window blinked to life. "Boss, I've got two drivers that can't get their tracks out of a creek we forded."

Hex bit back a laugh. *Tankers.*

Fording a creek wasn't exactly easy in a 100-ton tank, but it was a simple process if the creek was shallow enough. Drop the nose into the creek and let the tank find the bottom on its own—don't press down the accelerator. When the tracks hit the bottom, accelerate gently across the bottom and then push hard up the far side. Accelerate at the wrong time and the front end of the tank plugged into the creek or bounced off. With a strong enough current, the tank would be stuck in the creek, exactly like Demons Two and Three.

"Copy, Tara. We'll get them straightened out. Go ahead and pull the plug on them."

"Done."

Hex looked back at the eight remaining CASPers. They'd formed a wedge with the tip pointed into the Oogar and were attempting withdrawal by fire. Angel Twelve's icon flashed red and blinked out. Angel Eight's did the same three seconds later. The left edge of the wedge collapsed. Hex jumped in that direction, his eyes fixed on the position of his powerless tanks. Unable to oversee any movement in that direction, his worst fear was confirmed. The armored vehicles were essentially worthless and unable to even lob indirect rounds into the attacking Oogar.

Hex jumped again, laser cannons firing as he tried to protect the tip of the wedge, where Angel Two stood mowing down the Oogar with lethal efficiency. Her icon blinked out and a series of caution and warning bells rang in Hex's ears. The simulator displays went dark and he engaged the canopy switch and felt the cooler air of the hangar deck sweep into the hot, cramped space. Across the way, the commander's hatch of Demon One swung up. Hex watched Tara climb up and sit on the cupola. She ran her hands through her hair and shook her head. A thin smile appeared, and Hex knew what it meant. *No one said this was going to be easy, huh?*

"What do you want to do, boss?" she called through his headset.

Hex snorted. "Take 10 and then we do it again. Same scenario, same mission. We run it until we get the basics right."

* * *

Hex decided to end the first day after seven runs. From the third on, the mission parameters were harder, and while they struggled at times, by the end of the last mission there was progress, and all of them could see it. Hex waved Tara over to his CASPer. "Let's call it a night, at least in the sims."

Tara nodded. "They did a lot better that last time."

"They did," Hex agreed. "Angel Two is a solid leader. I think I like Angel Eight in command of the Bravo Team. He's got instincts – let's switch him with Angel Seven. We still need to run a few missions so that everyone has a chance to command, but they're the standouts so far. How are your crews?"

Tara sighed. "Three seems like a good crew, but Demon Two has some issues. I'll rebalance it tonight and see if there is a better lineup. We can keep going tomorrow—maybe get to a full mission set."

"Just no Oogars," Hex said and immediately wished he hadn't.

"Why not?" Tara blinked and looked over at the deep slashes in the armor of his CASPer's left arm. "Oh. That's why you froze up."

Hex clenched his fists and forced himself to relax. It wasn't an accusation. As much as it embarrassed him, it was fact. "Yeah," he conceded. "It was the last thing I expected or wanted to see."

"You want to talk about it?" Tara half-shrugged.

"Not tonight," Hex said. He wanted some food, a beer, and a good night's sleep, even if he had to take a sleeping aid again. Avoiding the nightmares required the small pills.

"You sure? You really look like you should."

"Thanks, but I'm okay," Hex said. "Do you want some help reorganizing your crews?"

Tara shook her head and smiled. "I can handle it. Look, Hex." She paused. "Are you sure you're up for this? You pretty much lost everything two weeks ago. I understand that Jessica Francis is your friend and all, but I don't think this mission is a good idea."

"You think Hak-Chet set me up? Or is setting Jessica up to fail?"

Tara frowned. "I don't think either of those things. I think you're not ready to command this mission, and that puts all of our team at risk. They're clearly not ready for a mission. We've got four more days—that will help. We're only as good as our weakest link, and right now that's you. Not professionally. You handle a suit like a pro. I'm talking about your head, Hex. I need it screwed on tight. You need to get your shit together and brief your team leaders ASAP."

Tara spun on her heel and walked toward the collecting group of soldiers. He heard her telling them it was time for chow, and they'd meet later in the hangar to talk about tomorrow's training plan. The group left in ones and twos, Tara among them. She didn't look back over her shoulder at him. Alone in the hangar, sitting in the tight, familiar cockpit of his CASPer, Hex looked down at the picture of him and Maya on the beaches of Kaua'i. *I miss you.*

Tears sprang to his eyes, and he let them come. Maybe when they stopped, if they ever did, he could find a way to move on.

* * * * *

Chapter Seven

Bukk crept slowly into the main tunnel shaft. Four days of continuous digging through the layers of karst that marked the boundary of the Araf plains had been difficult and exhausting. Under the walls of the GenSha colony they'd moved deeper underground and slowed their pace to avoid detection. The slightest tremor or noise could alert the GenSha to their presence. As the Chief Scout, Bukk understood that the value of surprise far outweighed the need for speed. Klatk's orders were clear. Attack the GenSha compound at its very center, where the young spent their days, without detection. There was no timetable, only the requirement for success.

Crawling forward on all six legs, Bukk reached Kseh at the controls of their tunnel corer and tapped his right rear leg twice. The machine spooled down, quieting the noise in the tunnel, and the dust cleared somewhat as Kseh backed out. He looked at Bukk and twitched his neck from side-to-side as if to stretch. "Moving faster now. We're only 200 meters from the drop point."

Bukk reached for the control in Kseh's front claw. "I'll take it from here. Get some rest and have the others ready to move the moment we plant the device."

"I will," Kseh said but hesitated leaving.

"What is it?" Bukk tried to push past his soldier to get to work, but Kseh didn't move.

Kseh twitched his head backward, gesturing to the central paddock area 30 meters above them. "They're kids."

Bukk grunted. "They killed 700 of our brothers and sisters; lives that will never see the sky or feel the heat from the stars on their skin."

"I understand," Kseh said. "But why attack their children? An eye for an eye?"

Bukk nodded. "Klatk wants them to hurt, Kseh. That's what our orders are, and we're going to follow them."

"Even when we don't want to follow them?"

Bukk whirled on the young soldier. "What did you say?"

"None of us want to kill their kids, Bukk." Kseh stuck out his chest plate and faced his squad leader. "We want to hurt them, but not their kids."

Bukk ground his mandibles. "Our orders are to strike the central paddock."

"We don't have to hit it during their assembly," Kseh said.

"Yes, we do," Bukk said. "The intent was clear. Klatk will not be intimidated, and we will avenge the loss of our young. Is that clear?"

Kseh nodded and lowered his chest toward the ground. "I understand, Bukk. I don't like it, but I understand."

"That's why I'm here to plant the device, Kseh. It's why I'm going to be the one to detonate it. I understand how you feel, but I'm okay with hurting the GenSha just as they hurt us, exactly as our queen ordered." Bukk crept into the tunnel and found the coring device. Within a few seconds, he began drilling toward their target with expert precision, though his mind was on other things.

Leadership was never easy, and it often meant pushing relationships with soldiers and leaders to the very brink of disaster. Kseh's and the other young soldiers' experience in combat seemed almost sheltered compared to the rest of the main army. Granted, the main army was no more than 200 regular soldiers who provided security and protection for the colony walls. The others in the colony received some basic instruction in weapons and defensive protection systems, but they didn't live, eat, and breathe being a soldier like Bukk and his men.

Bukk didn't like the assignment either, and while it would have been easy to say he was privately on the side of Kseh and the others, that would have been wrong. Undermining Klatk's leadership and his own chain of command were one thing, undermining his own leadership and the tight-knit squad were another. He could lead from a place of understanding and sympathy, but there would be a time when lives would be on the line, and he would be unable to lead the men who thought he was their friend and agreed with them. Far easier was the difficult path of keeping his mouth shut and doing the work his queen, and the command, placed upon him. Only twice in his career did he really feel required to say something that differed from their chosen courses of action. In both cases, he'd been wrong. Those above him in rank and authority possessed wisdom he did not, and until he saw the world through eyes like theirs, it was best to shut up and keep moving.

The small slate screen on the tunnel corer showed they were directly underneath the central paddock. Bukk adjusted the tracked vehicle, and set the drill vertical to bore through the 30 meters of rock and soil between them and the completion of the mission. Checking the time, he noted the maximum point of impact, when parents and children assembled on the paddock, would be in an hour. Even drilling slowly to prevent discovery, he could make that distance in 20 to 30 minutes at the most. The GenSha assembly typically lasted 30 minutes or so—some kind of morning devotional according to the Altar intelligence officers. He did the math and decided that while Klatk could live with infanticide, he could not.

Bukk adjusted the speed of the drill and stepped back to avoid the cascade of detritus from the drill head as it filled the tunnel. Two hours would give them enough assurance that they would not be discovered under the paddock and allow time for a majority of the parents and children to leave. There would still be unavoidable casualties. However, he would hit his target as ordered, and be able to live with himself if he survived the run back to the colony.

That was enough for Bukk.

* * *

Jessica woke as the *Tchrt One* decelerated at the Araf emergence point. Her gear lay ready for debarkation at the door. She rolled off the bed, zipped herself into clean Peacemaker blue coveralls, and walked to her weapons case.

"Loss of gravity in one minute. Secure all belongings for yacht departure." The flight deck announcement was toneless and slow.

At the end of one rotating arm of the *Tchrt One* main vessel, the similarly named yacht would detach and transition to normal space operations for the trip from the emergence point to the surface. Thankfully, they'd only have about an hour of microgravity before landing. The Consortium's Dream Worlds all existed exceptionally close to stargates and emergence points. Jessica assumed that any deal with the Cartography Guild to construct each system that way had involved a substantial payoff.

More organizations than the Consortium will get squeezed if this one fails.

At that realization, she paused for a moment as she opened her weapons case. Jessica grabbed her pistol and belt, strapped the belt around her waist and the holster to her left thigh. On her right, she secured a long, black bladed knife and slipped a standard Peacemaker baton through a loop above it. She snapped the weapons case closed and secured her bags to the deck as the yacht disengaged and microgravity returned. Up became down, and down became up as her vestibular system freaked out for a moment. She closed her eyes and focused on her breathing as her body adjusted to the loss of gravity.

When she felt centered, or as centered as she could feel, she opened her eyes and forced herself to see through the walls and spaces of the ship. The nose of the yacht was down and the stern's equipment bays were up. Left and right were the same as ever. With practiced ease, she pushed off her bags and floated to her room's door. The automatic hatch slid open and remained that way as she maneuvered into the main passageway and headed for the bridge.

The doors to Taemin's quarters remained closed, she noted with a grin. Floating through the wide passageway gave her the illusion of flying, and while throwing her arms out in front of her like a superhero would have been fun, she kept a ready position with her legs together, knees flexed, and arms out in a push-up position as she glided silently forward.

Down, she told herself. *Down. Where was that from?*

Ahead, she saw the vertical ladder to the bridge. Using her hands to grasp the bulkhead and slow her movement, she pivoted almost effortlessly into the 90-degree junction and changed direction with a tap on a few of the ladder's rungs.

Not bad. Especially for having failed my first null-gravity movement course.

The last few years had flown by. After leaving the Marauders and Marc behind, she'd tried to find another mercenary unit with human leadership that would take her on, but her experience with the Marauders ruled her out of new contracts. She thought, at first, it was because she was a woman, but she soon realized it was more a distrust of Marc's leadership ability and his integrity. They saw her as damaged or unqualified goods. An inability to make them think differently led her to Selector Hak-Chet and the Peacemaker program. He'd been less than impressed at their first meeting.

"Humans are seldom qualified for work such as this, despite being the perfect beings for it. You may be able to think on your feet and make snap judgments better than any species in the Union, but your self-doubt and paralyzing second-guessing are also second to none."

From that moment, she'd tried to always "switch on" and force every ounce of her being to engage in dealing with the situations around her. During the first three days of the transit to Araf, she'd languished on Hak-Chet's words and suffered a humiliating defeat of reasoning. She'd steadied the course with research and introspection for the last few days. Kenos and Taemin, she was relatively sure, believed she was incompetent. When they arrived at Araf, their most likely course of action would be to ask for a replacement Peacemaker. The least likely was that they'd let her do her job without interference.

The most dangerous course of action, though, was the one she'd spent the most time preparing for. Once they arrived at Araf, they would select a neutral landing site for her to operate from and alienate all three colonies at once. The problem was that a neutral site would take her away hundreds of kilometers from the disputed ground itself. The Consortium would spare nothing to control the negotiations; that was evident. When she made no progress, they would file an injunction against the Peacemaker Guild and allow the mercenary units already on the ground to fight it out. The only problem was that the Altar had no mercenary units to support them and would come to the gunfight with knives instead.

Jessica almost smiled in the passageway. She'd come up with a plan to combat both an injunction and an all-out mercenary war. All she had to do was the impossible—get the Altar to agree with her.

On the bridge, she found Kenos sitting in a chair behind and to one side of the nameless Pendal pilot. He startled. "Peacemaker Francis. You've emerged from hiding. What can we do for you?"

His veiled insult bounced off her smile. "Thank you, Administrator Kenos. Now that I've had the chance to fully review the files and prepare myself accordingly, I'm ready to tackle this negotiation."

A small, slow smile appeared on the Cochkala's face. "I am certainly glad to hear that. What brings you to the bridge? We're preparing for atmospheric interface right now." His tone said it was a bad time, which brightened Jessica's smile all the more.

"I'm aware it's not the best time, but I wanted to request a fly-by."

"Of what?" Kenos asked, his little eyebrows raised comically.

"There is a section of the southern continent about 1,500 kilometers west of the Altar colony that looks like it might work for a relocation effort."

Kenos sat forward. "Relocation? Of whom?"

"The Altar, of course," Jessica said. "It appears to be a simple way to get a handle on the Choote river situation."

Kenos nodded. "We can certainly adjust our course. You're speaking of the Dor'Chak Plateau, correct?"

"That's the one," Jessica grinned. "And since we'll be in the atmosphere, I'd like to swing over the Choote River. The entire length."

The smile on Kenos' face faltered slightly, but he caught it quickly. "Certainly. I believe your full reconnaissance to be a wise choice, Peacemaker."

"Thank you, Administrator."

"Once we've flown over the Choote, I'd like to host you at the main spaceport complex for the negotiations. I'll be happy to send conveyances for the delegations at the Consortium's expense."

You little bastard, Jessica thought approvingly. He'd played almost perfectly to type.

Careful not to nod, Jessica replied. "I'd like to conduct my reconnaissance first, please. We can discuss a neutral site based on what we see on the ground."

Kenos turned to the pilot. "Lay in a course for the Dor'Chak Plateau and a south to north reconnaissance of the Choote River. Alert the colonies to our presence."

The Pendal pilot nodded, saying nothing as always. With its haunting hooded cloak and four arms, the typical Pendal topped the creepy factor. She'd never had one speak to her, not even the one in her Peacemaker class. In fact, she'd never seen him after the first day, and that was just as well.

Kenos turned to her. "I believe you'll see that Araf is a beautiful world created from a lifeless hunk of rock—a technological marvel. We started the process more than a thousand years ago. The only major setback in this planet's development was the Canavar."

Jessica looked out the window at the approaching planet. From a distance, it looked like Earth. On closer inspection, cyclones that should have gathered along the equatorial regions rolled in the higher latitudes. The northern ice cap was immense and easily two or three times the size of the southern one. "It is beautiful, but I can see what Taemin mentioned. About the weather, that is."

Kenos made a dismissive gesture with his paws. "Humans. You bitch about the weather more than any other species in the Union," he laughed. The chittering sound evoked a memory of her mother's fingernails rasping across an Emery board. "I jest, Peacemaker. Araf's climate control system is located at the D'nart Spaceport. You are free to inspect it before the negotiations begin. We expect to have the system calibrated in the next two years. Our colonies...our *clients* will have perfect weather every day—optimum moisture levels and temperatures."

Jessica decided to keep Kenos talking a while longer. "Those are some pretty serious deviations. That cyclone there," she pointed at a gigantic swirling storm in the northern hemisphere, "is at what? Forty or fifty degrees North latitude?"

Kenos frowned. "It is. While the number of cyclones that form and get away from us is much lower now than 10 years ago, we still haven't managed to manipulate the system parameters to get it exactly right."

"We had a saying where I grew up in North America. If you don't like the weather, wait five minutes, and it will change. Weather isn't predictable and maybe, just maybe, can't be controlled."

Kenos studied her for a long moment. "Your point is taken, Peacemaker. However, the Consortium believes that weather manipulation and control is vital to our Dream World initiative, and we will continue our efforts to succeed. Nature merely needs to be stimulated properly. The planet's systems will respond to our efforts in time."

A red light blinked to life on the console in front of them. Jessica slipped into a seat and buckled the five-point harness. "Atmospheric interface burn in 10 seconds," a slow, monotone voice said. Jessica realized it was from the previously silent pilot.

The *Tchrt One* burned and the nose snapped up to allow the keel of the yacht to bite into Araf's upper atmosphere. A tiny vibration rattled through her seat as if the planet reached out to shake her just enough to let her know that gravity was coming.

"Interface."

Jessica watched out the front windows as the first licks of ionized plasma appeared like tiny orange flames dancing around the yacht's blunt nose. She tried to see the speed indicator but could not. The horizon tilted to the left as the yacht began a long, fast turn to the north to bleed off speed. A full minute passed as the pilot held the turn. With an equally measured movement, he turned in the opposite direction. As Jessica watched, the Pendal repeated the maneuver three times. A blink of realization shot through her. *Just like Earth's space shuttle a couple hundred years earlier!* The shuttle, really the orbiter because space shuttle was the name for the whole damned system, would perform a series of high-altitude hypersonic S-turns as it returned to Earth. *Hadn't one disintegrated during re-entry? Discovery?*

Jessica shook her head. *No, Columbia.*

"Everything okay over there, Peacemaker? You look a little concerned."

"Trying to remember a piece of trivia. Nothing important."

Kenos chittered again, and it made Jessica clench her left fist—the one the Cochkala couldn't see from his position. "We're about three minutes from the Dor'Chak."

Jessica nodded and kept looking outside. The feeling of gravity was there now, pulling her naturally down into the seat. Combined with the feeling of speed from the passing terrain and clouds, it was as close as she could get to flying. As the *Tchrt One* continued to slow and turn, Jessica imagined the controls in her hands and let the illusion play out in her mind. As quickly as it began, it was over as the yacht settled fully into Araf's atmosphere and banked toward a wide, high plateau surrounded by ragged mountains running east to west. Geologically, it was perfect for the Altar, albeit without a prevalence of the precious metals the Consortium paid them to mine. There were other alternatives, Jessica believed, but it could be a good home for the Altar, if all else failed.

Kenos leaned over. "What do you think?"

"I think it could work very nicely," Jessica said conspiratorially. "You'll just have to pay them to mine something else."

"I'm sure that something could be arranged."

"Something financially viable and acceptable to the Altar?" Jessica asked.

Kenos chuckled. "Your treading very close to a line where your mediator needs to be involved, Peacemaker."

Jessica leaned back in her chair. "You're right, Administrator. We should table this discussion until Taemin is able to be present."

"The Caroon don't handle microgravity very well," Kenos said. "He should be fine about the time we land at D'nart."

Which means he'll miss most of the flight down the Choote. Perfect. Sarcasm felt right, even if she couldn't overtly express it.

Jessica pointed. "Those are the Wet Mountains, yes?"

Kenos nodded. "Indeed. You have been studying, Peacemaker. On the far side of them is the source of the Choote River. As it winds through the mountains there are some significantly deep gorges impassable at high water. When…" he paused. "*When* we fine-tune the climate systems, there will be significant winter snows in the mountains that will feed the Choote more, raising the water line by 50 percent for most of the downstream colonies."

But that's years away, if ever.

"More water would solve your problems, certainly," Jessica said.

Kenos said nothing. The effect was as significant as throwing down the gauntlet at his feet. His silence meant one of two things: either he wasn't expecting her to place blame for the climatological problems solely on the Consortium and derailed his thoughts, or he'd realized she was onto something and would entertain her effort to move, at least by appearances, the Altar Colony. "And until we get that water, what would you have us do, Peacemaker?"

Option two, Jessica thought.

"Let me see the ground, Administrator. I can evaluate my plan based on what I see."

Kenos tapped the pilot on one shoulder, and the yacht sped toward the Wet Mountains. The rounded, older hills reminded her of Appalachia and the side of her family no one talked about. Her father's family lived there working renewed tobacco farms and making moonshine like they'd done 400 years before. The difference was that alien races loved both exports and paid handsomely for them. Her father's business centered on running tobacco and moonshine through the Earth trade unions and out to interested species at ridiculous payment rates. At least it did until his disappearance.

Her mother never spoke his name after he left that stormy August night. Every effort she'd made since turning 18 to find out what the Union or Earth's governors knew came up empty. The Peacemaker Guild's computer system gave her a little more information. "Snowman" disappeared on a flight to the Outer Rim—what the cartographers called the Mismert region now—carrying a load of unspecified cargo. Nothing more was in the entry, but it was more than even the Cartography Guild would provide. The emergence gate information was blank and invalid, too. He'd vanished into a black hole or something, but no one knew what had actually happened. What mattered, besides the chipset in her pocket, were the things he told her as a child. Things like "seeing is understanding."

The diagrams and Tri-V images from her briefings were worthless until she saw the ground with her own eyes. The yacht soared over the last ridgeline, and the Choote River flowed to the north like a wide blue swath through the high desert plains. In the distance, vast green prairies dominated the horizon.

"That's the GenSha land," Kenos said. "They farm more than 10,000 square miles of land for us, producing everything from potatoes to gm'lisk." Vegetables of all kinds were in high demand throughout the galaxy, even the strange ones that tasted like gunpowder and produced a nasty headache when consumed by humans.

"That much land requires a lot of water. How much do they use daily?"

Kenos shrugged. "Fifteen to twenty million liters."

"And the downstream affect to the Selroth?"

"Unknown." Kenos frowned. "They believe that the processing kills fish in large numbers. We haven't seen this effect and doubt its veracity."

The river widened and bent sharply to the east. A large sandbar appeared in the river and Jessica fought the urge to sit up. Across the northern horizon were dust plumes racing toward the Altar colony. The erratic patterns indicated they were mercenary vehicles. Traditional units tended to move in straight lines with predictable turns. "Mercenaries."

Kenos sat forward. "Mercenary forces are strictly forbidden! The Consortium retains the responsibility to negotiate and settle disputes peacefully!"

Liar.

"Your agreement states that a colony can hire a mercenary force to protect its interests, exploit tactical advantages, and secure contested resources, Administrator. I believe these mercenaries are doing exactly that. The GenSha want the Raknar." Jessica almost added a statement about his real amount of knowledge, but stopped herself. He would tip his hand soon enough. "Can we broadcast a message on all frequencies?"

"Of course," Kenos huffed.

"Good. Transmit the following message." Jessica paused. "This is Peacemaker Francis. Under the Articles of War, you are ordered to cease fire and prepare for negotiation. Stand down from all hostile actions and report your unit, your combat strength, and your commanding officer's name for the record."

The response took a full 30 seconds to arrive, but the delay was worth it. "This is the Wandering Death with 300 personnel. My name is Qamm, Peacemaker. We are standing down and returning to quarters."

The dust plumes reversed course and headed back to the GenSha colony. Jessica watched them for a second. There was no denying it felt great to stop a mercenary force with nothing more than her words. The Wandering Death were new to her. Even after years in the business, she'd never run across them. With more than a thousand mercenary units operating in the galaxy, it wasn't that much of a—

A hot white light blossomed in the center of the GenSha colony.

As soon as it appeared, the light was gone and replaced by a large, dark cloud over the central paddock. Scores of voices filled the radio channels. Mercenary forces reversed course again, turning north for the Altar colony faster and more recklessly than before.

Kenos turned to her. "It would appear that your cease fire has not been followed, Peacemaker."

"Broadcast the message again," Jessica said. When it finished, there was a clear, solitary transmission.

"Peacemaker Francis, this is Tgenn of the GenSha. The Altar have struck children. We cannot let them get away with this."

Jessica hesitated to push the button and another voice came in to the fray. "This is Klatk, Queen of the Altar. Peacemaker, do not listen to the GenSha. They attacked us four days ago and killed 700 of our brood. This is what they deserve."

Jessica looked at Kenos. "Let me talk to them, now."

"The channel is yours," Kenos replied.

"This is Peacemaker Francis. All stations will cease fire and return to your colonies immediately. Failure to comply with this message will result in fines against mercenary forces and diplomatic sanctions against colony leadership under the Articles of War." Jessica paused. "I will hold negotiations in an official setting within 96 hours, as codified by the Articles, at a place of my choosing. Both mercenary forces and contracting officials will respond to this message accordingly. Acknowledge."

Jessica heard each check in. The GenSha and their Wandering Death force and the Altar checked in. There was another click, almost too faint to be heard, but it was there. Someone else had been on the frequency and tried to time their departure from the frequency to coincide with another disconnection and hide their presence, only to fail.

Kenos stared at her. "It appears your message has gotten through. Shall I set course for D'nart?"

The bridge hatch opened and a very green-faced Taemin looked inside. Jessica shook her head. "I will set up the neutral site on neutral ground in the center of the operations area. Land at the Raknar. Under the Articles of War, I declare it a non-combatant neutral site, effective immediately."

* * * * *

Chapter Eight

The gentle flowing Choote made the attack easier than expected. Moderately deep, the clear, cold waters provided ample fish for the downstream Selroth colony. It also provided a direct avenue of approach the Altar could not monitor until it was too late. Six figures swam in a lazy wedge formation into the current, more than two meters below the surface. For Wahl, the team leader, the 10-kilometer warm-water swim approached paradise. Trained to fight, but constantly held back by policy and diplomacy, the chance to get into the water and conduct a clandestine operation freed him and his unit in a way few species understood. The diversion created by the GenSha antagonizing the Altar positions from the south would allow the Selroth a chance for intelligence gathering. The Altar found a way to use the latent power sources aboard the abandoned Raknar; that much the Selroth knew. What precisely the Altar were doing with that power was unknown and troublesome. There was no doubt the Raknar still carried viable ordnance that could be used against an enemy force. Whether the Altar understood the Raknar's systems enough to employ them was of great concern to Ooren, the Selroth colony's leader. Given an opportunity, he'd acted and sent Wahl to determine what had aggravated the GenSha to the point of all-out war.

At the head of the wedge, with two scouts to either side and one immediately to his rear, Wahl held out a webbed hand and motioned them to slow their pace and ground themselves on the river bottom.

The crystal-clear water barely muddied as they did, and Wahl studied the dark, hulking shape of the Raknar's lower extremities a mere 30 meters ahead. Among the dark rocks near the mecha's feet were small round shapes he recognized.

Mines.

Wahl tapped a display on his right wrist and keyed his communications suite. A series of communications buoys every 500 meters behind them would carry the signal to headquarters. "Ooren? They've mined the Raknar."

"You're certain?" the Selroth governor replied.

Of course, I am. Wahl paused. "Yes, I'm certain. I'll get close enough to get confirmation of models and specifications."

"Can you get to the Raknar?"

"Yes," Wahl decided. The minefield was laid out in an irregular pattern obviously intended to defeat a small craft. An experienced swimmer could easily get between the mines and close enough to the Raknar to carry out the mission objectives. "It will take us longer than expected, but we can get there."

"Copy. Proceed at your discretion, Wahl."

The connection clicked back to standby in Wahl's ears. He tapped the display again and opened a channel to his squad. "Remove all your extra gear and leave it here, under a marker. Weapons and basic gear only as we move forward. Once we've identified the mine, load its parameters into your slates. And don't hurry. We'll rendezvous on the Raknar's lower leg armor, as planned. For no reason should you get within a meter of the surface. Any questions?"

The squad's silence meant consent. Wahl nodded and went through specific tasks by squad positions. "One, you've got point. Ensure there are no listening devices. Two and Three, you've got mine recon. Get a solid confirmation on model and relay it directly to Ooren. Four and Five, you're with me through the field. Four, you've got the left, and Five, you've got the right. I'll go up the middle and set the rendezvous point."

Wahl shrugged out of his pack and left his larger rifle next to it on the river bottom. From an external pocket, he retrieved a small fluorescent marker and tied it to the pack so he could find it. With the beacon set in his head-mounted positioning system, Wahl glanced up and saw the squad ready to move, and it almost made him smile.

"Move out," he said and they swam slowly toward the minefield. One moved out in front a dozen meters and glided effortlessly over the sandy bottom. In several places, he hovered and checked the bottom methodically.

"Six, One. There's nothing I can see as far as a monitoring device."

Wahl nodded. The Altar were more about passive defense than they were about doing anything that required effort outside of mining and raising children. "Copy, One. Proceed. Two and Three, follow and type match the nearest mine."

"Copy, Six."

Using his webbed hands and feet, Wahl sculled the water to remain virtually still in the current as his team fanned out to accomplish their missions. One made his way through the minefield on exactly the path Wahl himself would have chosen. The young one's promotion to sergeant would come very soon. Two and Three stopped and examined a mine from a meter's distance with imaging devices and a thermal scanner. With Four and Five at his side, Wahl maintained his position and waited.

"Six, Two. The mine appears to be Besquith-manufactured but a Sidar design. It's designed for small attack craft. We shouldn't cause enough wave motion to set one off inadvertently."

"How long have they been here?"

"Based on the mussel growth on the retaining chains, guessing five years," Two said. "Could be longer. This model is a CA-102 and has a maximum life expectancy of 40 years."

Instability would not be a problem. As long as they were careful and slow, they should be fine. "Copy all. Relay to command and follow One through the field to the rendezvous point."

Wahl and the other two trailing Selroth closed the distance to the first three and weaved through the mines easily. Nothing moved around them as they approached the leg armor of the fallen Raknar. With his squad in position, Wahl looked over the legs and saw no evidence the Altar had connected anything to the Raknar. Fresh water barnacles covered the leg and almost obscured its design features. "I'm going up the body. Five? Follow me."

The young Selroth at his side, Wahl swam gently along the leg armor to the bare knee joint and paused to look inside. There was no evidence the Altar had done anything to the Raknar. Smooth, composite armor grew freshwater barnacles and sweeping tendrils of algae in both directions. Ragged holes in the upper leg suggested intense combat, but no Canavar remains were found. Near the Raknar's waist, 20 meters away, two large black cables snaked across the river bottom.

"Do you see that?" Wahl asked.

"Yes," Five responded. His name was Frool and despite being the youngest and most inexperienced of Wahl's squad, he'd proven to be quite a soldier. "They must attach inside the hull. Going through the waist joint was smart."

Wahl grunted. "The Altar are smart, but they leave too much evidence." As they got closer to the waist joint, Wahl traced the cable's path with his eyes to where it disappeared into the Raknar via a square hatch propped open with a large rock. "Here."

He peered inside and could not see anything, even after turning on the helmet's lighting system. A clear look at the hole suggested he would not be able to get inside, but the smaller Frool might. "Five, can you get inside?"

"I can try."

"Do it." Wahl swam out of the way and watched Frool knife through the open hatch easily. "Engage your cameras and sensors. We need to know where they've accessed the power source."

"Copy," Five said and swam deeper into the Raknar.

Thirty seconds passed and then a minute. Wahl called, "Frool? What do you see?"

"The cables are routed into a reactor of some sort. I can't read the writing on it, but it's clear this is the power source."

Wahl keyed his helmet to see a real-time relay. A control panel rested above two connection points. The cables were stripped and lashed into the panel without a great deal of skill. The amount of power had to be ridiculously low.

"Disengaging the cables," Frool called.

Wahl saw him reach out for the cable and rip one away from the panel. A bright blue arc of electricity shot from the panel. Frool spasmed and thrashed until his life signs faded. In the water, Wahl felt a buzzing noise around him.

An alarm!

He swam straight out from the Raknar's waist, ducking through the mines as he accelerated toward open water. "Go! Go!"

WHAMM!

Wahl spun through the water as the concussion wave thumped his chest hard. Silt flew up, clouding the water and blinding him. Bouncing off the bottom, he looked back in the Raknar's direction and saw a square object enter the water and sink toward the bottom. Two and Three emerged from the minefield near where the object fell. They swam as fast as they could. Wahl whipped the water around him to try and help the gentle current clear the turbidity.

"Come on!" he screamed into the radio. There was a flash and—

WHAMM!

Wahl tumbled through the water. A bright flash of pain exploded in his left shoulder as he ricocheted off a large rock and spun downstream.

"Six, this is Four moving to your—"

WHAMM!

Wahl grasped for a rock and held fast to it. The concussion wave raced past him, but with his body streamlined it did not rip him away from his purchase. Wahl looked up into the river and saw nothing except the faintest outline of the Raknar's legs. The slate on his wrist showed life signs only for One and himself.

"One, where are you?"

A second later, One's voice came back as a scared whisper. "By the Raknar's foot. They're dropping depth charges, Six. If I move from here, they're going to target me."

Wahl kicked his feet and swam forward into the current fifteen meters and stopped. There was too much debris hovering in the water to see where One had managed to hide. "Stay where you're at. I'll try to get to you."

"Copy."

Wahl held his position for two minutes as the current swept much of the cloudy water away and left him a clearer picture of One's position and the Altar response from the surface. He scanned the area and paused. Halfway between his position and One's hiding place, a large black object lay half buried in the river bottom. The dark surface was completely smooth and did not reflect the light from Araf's sun, Zehra, in the bright afternoon.

"One, can you see the object between us?"

"Affirmative, Six."

"Are there any visible markings on your side?"

One hesitated. "Nothing I can see, Six."

Wahl started to swim forward and stopped to initiate a connection to the colony 10 kilometers to the north. "Command? Are you seeing this?"

There was no response. He and One were alone with a host of Altar above them waiting for any movement to drop another depth charge. One would be okay based on his position, but Wahl realized he could not move. The last blast blew him too close to the Altar controlled bank. In the water were a thousand tiny vibrations from the shore. The bastards swarmed above him searching desperately for any remaining infiltrators.

Wahl took a long, slow draft of the fresh water and studied the terrain. There was a chance they could get away after all. Most of the minefield around the Raknar was gone—detonated in the secondary blasts from the depth charges. One could move toward the main channel and potentially provide enough distraction to let him slip down the bank away from the gathered Altar. Try as he might, he could see no other viable alternatives. Making a young soldier bait did not sit well in his stomach. Unless he did it, though, the Altar would eventually find them and kill them.

"One? Can you swim to the west away from the feet?"

"Not without breaking the surface, Six," One replied. "There's a wall of rock and debris here where this thing fell. I'll have to cross it to get away."

It would have to do. "When I count down to null, I want you to break west as fast as you can. Get over that wall and get into the main channel. Head north. If we get separated, relay every bit of intelligence we've gathered. Do you understand?"

"Copy, Six. Ready to move on your mark."

Wahl bared his teeth in a feral grin. "Get ready. Ten seconds." Wahl closed his eyes and tried to visualize the escape. Giving One a five second head start, Wahl moved down the bank and out toward the channel. "Five, four, three, two, one...go."

Wahl tried but could not see One move out. A flurry of bolts tore through the water between them. Two depth charges impacted near the Raknar. Wahl pushed off from the rocks and swam hard toward the center of the channel. Past a line of rocks, he could see a deeper section of river. If he could get there...

WHAMM!

A depth charge fell at the Raknar's feet and Wahl hesitated. One's life signs flashed and disappeared. A burst of static filled his helmet as the radio reconnected to the command frequency.

"Wahl? It's Ooren? You have traffic for us?"

Wahl didn't answer. He looked back over the Raknar and the large object in the river bottom. A depth charge appeared, floating down through the water. Wahl braced himself for the depth charge's detonation. There was no sound, vibration, or concussion wave. The depth charge exploded and in a split second, the object turned white hot and—

* * *

"Detonation!"

Ooren turned to the watch officer. "What class?"

"Unknown, sir. Thermal readings do not suggest nuclear, and there's no evidence of radiation. Likely a high explosive, concussive device."

"Life signs?" Six of his best underwater operators were likely dead. The Altar had illegally mined the river and killed his men.

"None, sir."

Ooren took a breath from the re-breather around his chin. The action gave him time to think through a plan. "I want intelligence to go over the site immediately. I want reconnaissance assets in place and I expect our combat forces ready in one hour."

"Sir? Communications buoys are sending a contamination warning. The water has been polluted by an unknown source."

Damn the Altar! Ooren seethed. "They would contaminate our home and mine our waters!"

The watch officer called. "Incoming transmission from Commander Leeto. He reports the Darkness forces are deployed and ready for combat operations."

Mercenaries. Ooren sucked on his tongue and quelled his own distaste. He'd believed mercenaries were necessary months before, and he'd stationed a battalion of them in the main holds of his underwater city, out of sight of the Dream World Consortium, in the event the GenSha and Altar went to war. While a war would open up opportunities for his colony, the disruption of clean water and the contamination of the ample supply of fish in the lower Choote were something he could not abide.

Ooren reached for the radio handset. "Commander Leeto?"

The Sidar mercenary replied. "Honored Ooren. What are your orders?"

A new voice shattered the connection. "This is Peacemaker Jessica Francis calling the Selroth colony. Put Honored Ooren on this channel immediately."

Ooren flinched. *A Peacemaker. Interesting.*

"Peacemaker Francis, this is Ooren of the Selroth."

"All stations will cease fire and return to your colonies immediately. Failure to comply with this message will result in fines against mercenary forces and diplomatic sanctions against colony leadership under the Articles of War." Jessica paused. "I will hold negotiations in an official setting within 96 hours, as codified by the Articles, at a place of my choosing. Both mercenary forces and contracting officials will respond to this message accordingly. Acknowledge."

"The Altar have killed a fishing party in neutral waters! I cannot—"

"Honored Ooren. Acknowledge my message or prepare to face the consequences."

Ooren almost laughed, but the pause gave him clarity. "Of course, Peacemaker. The Selroth are standing down immediately. We await your orders for negotiations with great enthusiasm."

"My orders stand for all mercenary forces. I will have words with the commanders in the next 24 hours. Is that clear?"

Ooren bit his lip. "Understood, Peacemaker Francis. May I ask where you'll be setting up your negotiation headquarters? We are prepared to send a diplomatic team to D'nart at your discretion."

"I've declared the Raknar's remains neutral ground. The Altar ceded it to my control under the Articles of War. All future negotiations will be done there. I'll be in touch, Honored Ooren. Peacemaker Francis, out."

Ooren stared at the commset for a long second. *This is unexpected.* The Consortium maintained a policy against involving the Union or the Peacemaker Guild in their Dream World dealings. The policy was nothing that could be found in their copious contracts and addenda, but an understanding the humans called a "gentleman's agreement." Internal arbitration gave the Consortium a way to handle larger disputes, even those that involved mercenary forces. A Dream World was not supposed to entertain conflict, but the rule of law was that mercenary forces could be used to handle any matter of dispute. All out warfare was discouraged on a Dream World, so internal arbitration had its advantages. When the Consortium could solve a problem on its own, it saved them millions of credits in litigation which the bastards didn't mind sharing with their allies, often under the proverbial table. The Altar stood to lose everything from their colony position; that was clear. The choice to go straight to the Peacemaker Guild was theirs and theirs alone.

Ooren grinned. The Consortium would be at that table, too. They wanted the Altar gone and the river open for the GenSha to dam and farm. Without the Altar, the Selroth could engage purification systems to cleanse the water and avoid the loss of food sources to the colony. The perfect place lay near the Raknar's remains. The power source in the Raknar would be enough to run the purification systems indefinitely, if they played their cards right.

Ooren stabbed a button on the commset. "Commander Leeto? Are you still there?"

"Standing by for your orders, Ooren."

The Selroth leader set his jaw. "My orders have not changed, Leeto. We will attack the Altar mines and gain entry to the Raknar if not by the river, then through their tunnels."

"Their mines aren't very profitable, Honored Ooren," Leeto said. "At least, not based on what they're reporting to the Consortium."

Ooren nodded. He'd theorized for years that the Altar's reports of their mineral gains did not equal the actual tonnage they'd been able to extract. For a simple species, one so comfortable doing what they were told, it seemed far outside their norms to lie. But, anything was possible in the quest for credits.

"Perhaps. Prepare your forces for multiple scenarios. By law, the Peacemaker has 96 hours to make substantial progress to avoid armed confrontations. Once her time is up, we will attack the Altar positions by land and river."

"What about the GenSha? Will they see our attack as beneficial or as an affront to their own operations?" Leeto asked. "Have you broached a solution with them?"

Ooren snorted. The sound was a choked laugh. "I do not care about the GenSha, Commander Leeto. As far as I am concerned, they are just as much an enemy of the Selroth as the Altar. If they cannot be defeated, the Consortium will broker a cooperative agreement to use the Choote for both colonies. The Altar are the key and they must be removed. If the GenSha, or anyone else, gets in our way, you will destroy them. Is that clear?"

The mercenary commander chuckled. "Affirmative, Ooren. The Darkness will prevail."

Ooren turned away from the commset and peered across the river's delta from the command center. Leeto was bold and a bit reckless, making him a perfect mercenary commander. He also understood that the simplest way to approach the conflict was from a standpoint that everyone was the enemy. A great many credits were on the line. The livelihood of his colony notwithstanding, there was money to be made from the Consortium's goal of keeping the peace through any means possible. That they didn't want a Peacemaker on the ground, he was sure. In the next few hours, the Consortium would undercut the Peacemaker's position and smooth the edges of the conflict from all three sides. A workable solution was there, and all it took was credits and the removal of one colony.

Ooren consulted his order of battle and that of the attached mercenary forces, and saw an opportunity to surprise the Altar and gain the initiative. The moment the Peacemaker failed, and she would fail, an all-out assault on the Altar position would gain the Selroth enough of the river to push back against the GenSha. With control of the lower river country, they could demand the immediate removal of the Altar colony and preserve their colony's position for the foreseeable future.

Ooren picked up a slate and wrote his plan.

* * * * *

Chapter Nine

Klatk entered the command center to find seven somber faces staring at her. The elders ringed the tight space. With its consoles dark and quiet, the room felt like a tight cavern. Klatk understood their mood even before she met any of their eyes or said anything. Goss entered the command center behind her and closed the door. The atmosphere seemed to swell and press against her eyes and abdomen and every part in between. The youngest of the Council, a third-level worker named Erk was the first to make eye contact with her.

"Honored Klatk. The Council feels it is time to seek the protection of the Peacemaker Guild and ask for an escort home."

That didn't take long.

Klatk squared her shoulders and looked at them one by one. Her eyes rested on Erk's for a moment before she looked at Doort, the quiet one who never wavered in his support for her. His calm gaze centered her, and she turned back to Erk and spoke. "I will meet Peacemaker Francis in a few moments. Understanding that the council's guidance is paramount to the performance of my tasks, your recommendation is unanimous?"

Erk nodded. At the edge of her vision, Doort looked away and spoke. "The recommendation is unanimous, Klatk. We feel it is time to either hire a mercenary force to protect us, or ask for an escort home and invoke our contractual evacuation clause. The Consortium's provisions allowed them to manipulate our economic collapse.

Because the colony's recent mining drought drained much of our residual funds, we feel that hiring a mercenary outfit is not the best use of our remaining capital. Nor can we risk the Consortium discovering the bounty below. We believe arrangements should be made to return home."

Klatk clenched her mandibles and forced herself to relax. Mining was never a sure thing, and the colony had lived through significant gains and losses during the previous six months. Her engineer's recommendations to divert from the primary shaft structure and pursue deeper veins to the west found resistance in the very same council. Their requirement for safety outweighed their ability to accept any degree of risk. "I see. I believe you do not think we can win this situation and would rather leave here, disgracing my tenure, to save your own reputations."

Erk stiffened. "You cannot believe that we can win any type of prolonged conflict, Klatk! They attacked our outermost tunnels and killed 700 of our young! The GenSha and their mercenaries can cut through our defenses like a blade through soft dirt."

"They tipped their hand when they went after our young. They know, now, that we can go after them just as easily. We will not allow them to enter our tunnels again. We collapsed the southern complex. All brood units have been moved to the main complex. These mercenaries will have to take the central mine to destroy us."

Doort spoke quietly. "They will simply overwhelm us with their weapons on the surface."

Klatk looked at him and shook her head. "We barely fired our defensive systems."

"We need to find a way to use the Raknar," Goss said from behind her. The gathered councilmen collectively gasped. Goss laughed. "You believe the Raknar's power is absolutely fine, no—necessary for our survival. If it has power, it can fire its weapons! We need to bring them to bear against those who would drive us from our lands."

Erk stepped forward, his forearms raised and waggling. "We cannot attempt to use the Raknar's weapons."

"Why not?" Goss pressed. Klatk placed a hand on his shoulder to hold him back as she turned to Erk. Goss was right. Why not try to use the Raknar against their enemies?

"We need the power to incubate our colony."

Klatk tilted her head toward him. "We can engage solar or geothermal conduits to do that just as easily, Erk, despite the weather problems. We used the Raknar simply because it was there and available to us. It was a matter of speed, not a matter of necessity."

"It will take too long to convert from the Raknar's power, Klatk. You know this," Erk said. "We should ask for the protection of the Guild until our brood hatches, and then we should depart for home immediately thereafter."

"You would give up this home? The one thing we've worked toward for *cycles*—our home on this planet. You would give this away because the GenSha and the Selroth want the water? You hear them say we should leave, and you agree? They cannot use our lands—only the water that flows through it. There is nothing that says we cannot stay here except your unwillingness to stand."

"Why stand when we are certain to lose?" Erk asked.

Klatk laughed. "We are only certain to lose if we do not fight, Erk."

"You cannot believe we can win against two enemies without additional support that we cannot afford." Erk pointed at Doort.

"We've done the numbers. Plec says the brood is four weeks from hatching. The Peacemaker Guild is obligated to help us until the brood is hatched."

Klatk inclined her head to agree. "You're right, Erk. They would be obligated. But we then forfeit our lands and our rights to the Consortium."

"They will protect us! We have a contract!" Erk shouted.

Klatk shook her head. "No, they will not. If anything, the Consortium will want us to go as quickly as we can. Even to the point of enabling the mercenaries on either side of our colony to eradicate us in the process."

Erk rubbed his claws together. "You've overreacting. The Consortium would pay for our way home."

"They would take all of our residual funding, our property, and everything but what we can carry. That is unacceptable."

"Unacceptable to you," Erk smirked.

Klatk reared up on her hind legs. "Our people voted to come here. They chose this land. They knew the risks and the trouble it might cause, but they chose where we stand. I will listen to their hearts. Have you asked them for their support of your plan?"

None of them met her eyes. She knew they had not asked their people and acted solely on their own interests. A sick feeling rolled up through her abdomen, and she resisted the temptation to ask if their needs had been purchased because she already knew they had.

Erk spread his arms in a shrug. "There is no time to conduct a vote of the people. We have barely avoided a vote for emergency action."

There's the threat. Klatk forced herself not to smile. While they couldn't overthrow her governmental responsibility, they could enact rules against her that would place the colony in their hands. As long as she was capable and in control of her armed forces, they could not act on such a threat. She checked her slate and looked at them.

"The Peacemaker is arriving in five minutes. I intend to meet her and discuss our options and your...recommendations," Klatk said. "Once I have done that, I will take the Peacemaker's guidance and consider a course of action. I will share that with you when we meet again tonight."

She turned and Goss opened the door for her. Out in the warm afternoon sunlight, she heard him fall in behind her. "What will the Peacemaker say?"

Klatk looked over her shoulder. "I don't know, Goss. The council's recommendation carries some weight. A Peacemaker must listen to all sides and determine the best course of action. I believe that our lack of need for the water rights to this land will cause the Peacemaker to move us somewhere else. If we do not have the Raknar, our ability to fund a geothermal power source or a viable solar grid falls short. The Trading Guild may have asked the Consortium to assist us, but that would be a loan with interest that would be unbearable over time unless we hit a motherlode of precious metals outside the bounty. The chances of that aren't good."

"What if the Peacemaker doesn't want to move us?" Goss moved alongside her as they descended from the command center toward the colony's main deck. Klatk could see the *Tchrt One* approaching in the distance and considered the question.

There were two courses of action if the Peacemaker did not want to move the colony. The first was for the Peacemaker to declare no contest and let the Consortium deal with the problem. That meant the colony would have to move, or ask for protection and evacuation home. The second course of action was for the Peacemaker to declare a cessation of hostilities until the colony could either appoint or contract a mercenary force. Since the colony could not afford a quality force the second option seemed impossible.

"I don't know, Goss," Klatk said. "I believe the Peacemaker is human."

"Human? They have Peacemakers?"

Klatk met his incredulous eyes. "It would appear so."

"Humans are too presumptuous and unpredictable to be Peacemakers."

Klatk nodded. *Tchrt One* glinted in the sunlight as it pivoted on an axis and landed on the dusty ground between the colony walls and the river's edge. As the sleek yacht settled on its three landing struts, Goss remained behind as protocol demanded. Klatk looked over her shoulder. "That unpredictability may serve us well."

* * *

Klatk waited as the Peacemaker offloaded her bags from *Tchrt One*. Behind her, a Caroon in the typical dark attire they preferred jumped to the ground and gathered his things before standing off to one side with a disinterested look on his elongated face. Administrator Kenos made no effort to help the young human woman with her bags and stood in the boarding hatch with a scowl on his face. Klatk stood 10 meters away completely alone, with the colony's defenses lowered as required. *Tchrt One's* engines spooled up, and the sleek yacht rose from the ground and accelerated to the west before the Peacemaker even grabbed the handles of her two large bags. As she did, Klatk moved forward and grabbed the larger bag easily.

"Peacemaker Francis." Klatk bowed her head. "I am Klatk, the Queen of the Altar Colony and the commander of our armed forces. My colony is grateful for your intervention per our request to the Peacemaker Guild. I am at your service."

The human woman brushed away her auburn hair from her face and reached out a hand. "Honored Klatk, the pleasure is mine."

Klatk looked at the outstretched hand for a long moment before remembering the Galactic Union's comical training holo programs about interaction with human beings. She reached out a clawed forearm and gently took the Peacemaker's hand. "Welcome to Araf, Peacemaker."

"I appreciate your hospitality, Klatk. I'll set up my quarters here at the Raknar," Francis said.

"Will you be in need of provisions?"

Francis nodded. "Administrator Kenos will have a temporary domicile delivered by sundown along with some supplies. I would be grateful for anything you might think I would need."

Klatk nodded. For a human, the Peacemaker seemed very confident and strong. There was nothing the Altar could provide a human besides the only common denominator between them—water. "We'll make sure you have what you need."

Francis squinted at her. "What is it, Klatk? You're hesitating."

Klatk shifted her weight from side to side unconsciously. "I am considering my options, Peacemaker. I want to defend my colony, but I cannot do that and not risk losses. I am prepared to seek the Peacemaker Guild's protection and escort if the situation merits it."

Francis shook her head. "We've not even started negotiations. I cannot recommend you take that opening position, especially in light of the attack you perpetrated against the GenSha central paddock."

Klatk's pincers twitched. "A decision under duress that I regret."

"Do you?" Francis asked. "I don't believe you do, Klatk. I believe you wanted to hurt the GenSha. I believe you don't want to run home with the remnants of your colony. I believe you want to stand and fight."

Klatk looked away. Three of her soldiers approached. "My detail will see to it that you are settled and can begin your work."

"My first work is with you. I can have that conversation right here and right now."

Klatk balked. "I cannot, Peacemaker. I have to tend to my colony right now."

"Forgive my flippancy, Klatk, but your colony needs you to commit to a course of action."

Klatk locked eyes with her detail. The three young soldiers were third-level squad members. They approached rapidly with their heads down as a sign of respect. A glint of sunlight caught her eye. "I cannot—"

The soldier in the rear darted to his right and came up with a rifle in a millisecond. Klatk stepped forward, between the rifle and the Peacemaker, knocking the human to the ground with a shoulder. The young soldier fired once and missed the Peacemaker. She spun and tore the rifle from his claws and made to strike him. He wore a bandolier with its pockets stuffed full. A third-level soldier did not carry a bandolier, and she realized in a millisecond that it was an explosive device. Before he could reach for it, she tore off one of his arms with her claws and rendered the other unusable with her mandibles. The soldier screamed and fell to the ground. Black blood pooled around him.

Klatk roared. "What is the meaning of this?"

The soldier armlessly reared up, anger filling his twisted face. He spoke in a guttural dialect from the deep mines. "She is not here for us! We cannot trust her."

Klatk blinked at the harsh language. Through a universal translator, it would have sounded like gibberish. She knew the Peacemaker would not understand it either. She inflected the same dialect. "Who told you that, drone?"

"The Consortium. They say all we have to do is give up the Raknar..." His eyes rolled back and the soldier collapsed into the dust.

Francis came forward with a large pistol in her hands. "What did it say?"

Klatk spun towards her. "He. Most of my colonists are males. He said you needed to die. That the Peacemakers cannot save us."

Francis kept her pistol trained on the other two soldiers. "Stand them down."

Klatk motioned at the soldiers and they scattered into the colony. "They won't harm you."

"I have to question them! If they are a party to this attack —"

Klatk turned to her. "I will deal with my colony, Peacemaker."

Francis met her gaze for a long moment before holstering her pistol. "You want to take the colony and run, the Consortium wants you gone, and your own men just tried to kill me. I'm tempted to give you exactly what you want even though that gives the Consortium what it wants and sends you home in disgrace."

"I haven't said what I want, merely what I am considering."

Francis looked at the slate on her wrist. "We will meet soon, Klatk. I suggest you have a better idea of where you want to go and what you want to do then."

The Caroon, dressed from head to foot in blacks and reds, bounded up behind the Peacemaker. He spoke without emotion. "Peacemaker? Are you injured?"

Francis turned. "No, I'm fine, Taemin."

"I must protest your decision to stay here, Peacemaker. This colony is clearly agitated by your very presence. I must insist upon setting the neutral site at D'Nart."

Klatk saw Francis study the Caroon's face for a long moment. The human female looked back at her and then at the Caroon. "My command post is the Raknar, Taemin. Ensure that Kenos places the promised supplies near the mecha's head. I want a housing unit, too, not a tent or anything of the sort. A second one would be best for the negotiation site. Please radio the *Tchrt One* and do that before Kenos attempts to leave us here without anything."

The Caroon actually smiled a bit. "Indeed, Peacemaker."

Francis gestured to Klatk. "Taemin, this is Klatk. She is the colony Queen. Taemin is my mediator."

They bowed toward each other, but said nothing. She'd never met a Caroon mediator, and while it didn't seem likely that one would enter the practice of Union Law, she'd seen stranger things over the course of her life. "Well met, Taemin."

"Honored Klatk."

Their eyes locked for a long moment, and Klatk saw nothing at all in the mediator's coal black pupils. Most species had a glint of something there, and the Altar could see it. After a thousand years of unmoving faces and facial tics characterized by clicking mandibles, the Altar had developed an uncanny ability to read the eyes. Things like anger or malice were easy to see, as were love and patience. There was no life in the Caroon's eyes.

Taemin moved back to their stack of supplies, leaving her and the Peacemaker together for a moment. The young human's eyes followed her mediator. The Caroon withdrew a communications set and tapped on it. Satisfied, Francis swept back a longish piece of red hair and looked up at Klatk's face. "What do you want to do, Honored Klatk? You have a couple of options as I see them. You can fight, or you can go home. Without a mercenary unit, fighting isn't the smartest choice and without transport home, you'll have to ask the Guild for protection, and the Consortium will own everything you have. We call that a lose-lose on Earth."

Klatk gaped. "Then what would you have us do, Peacemaker?"

Francis grinned. "What does your Council say? I'm sure you have an idea of their views."

"They have requested that I ask you for protection so we can return home."

Francis nodded, her grin swept away like dust on a breeze. "And what do *you* want to do, Honored Klatk?"

Klatk looked over the Peacemaker's head at the colony. Many of her citizens went about their duties, but more than a few of the defenders, still at their posts along the walls, watched intently. Seven years before, the council came together and approached her to lead a colonization mission. All of them wanted nothing more than a fresh start in a new place. There would be challenges, they said, but they would always trust her leadership. The council wanted to leave, but her citizens would not be convinced as easily. Watching them work told her they would not be cowed into an evacuation. With two colonies against them, and a consortium that did not have their best interest at heart, Klatk wanted to run as much as she wanted to fight.

"I haven't made up my mind, Peacemaker," she said.

"Fair enough," Francis said. "But you don't have a lot of time to make a decision, Klatk."

"I am aware of your predicament. 96 hours should be long enough to allow a decision to be made. That's how long you have to reach peace? If the Selroth and the GenSha follow your wishes?"

"Let's hope," Francis said. "How soon can I meet with your council?"

Klatk blinked. "You would step foot in our colony after what my soldier tried to do?"

Francis took a sharp breath. "This is your opportunity to win my trust, Klatk. I think you want to fight, while your council wants to run."

* * * * *

Chapter Ten

Jessica followed Klatk up the dusty hillside from the floodplain to the Altar's colony walls. Nehra, Araf's distant yellow sun, warmed her back as they trudged up the hill. The loose scrabble of rock slowed Jessica's progress and sometimes caused her to slide backward. Klatk practically danced up the slope ahead of her. The colony's walls were a good three meters tall and adorned with parapets and racks of defensive missiles. Looking over her shoulder, Jessica took in the terrain from a strategic perspective and approved. From the high ground, they could see a good distance in every direction save for west where the colony backed up against rough hills. Above her, the *Tchrt One* roared through the sky, turned over the colony and prepared to land by the river below.

You've been assuming a ground fight. What if the mercs have air support?

On the high desert ground, there wasn't much in the way of natural protective cover or concealment she could see. Constructing cover would give them more protection, and hiding some of the weapons systems would help with that, but a dedicated air threat could be deadly. Ensuring the air avenues were defended was the first priority. Ground forces could be channelized and driven where the Altar wanted them to go. The river and the plains to the south were certainly expeditious avenues of approach, and the Altar at least had the presence of mind to mine the river near the Raknar to deter the Selroth. Tactically, the position met her expectations and could be improved upon should the Altar want to fight.

At a defended gate, two Altar stood with laser rifles across their chests. Both snapped to attention, Jessica surmised, as Klatk approached. The soldiers snapped their heads above Jessica's, peering down the hill. After a moment, she heard a voice yelling and recognized it as that of Kenos.

Klatk looked at Jessica. "It appears the Administrator wants another audience, Peacemaker."

Jessica bit the inside of her lip. "He does, it would seem. Would you call me Jessica?"

"Thank you, Jessica."

"Peacemaker!" Kenos shouted. Clamoring up the slope, Kenos skidded and slid backward as he topped the rise and darted toward them waving a slate. "I must protest your action to determine neutral ground. One of these…Altar just tried to kill you! The Consortium has long appointed the key spaceports on our Dream Worlds as the sole place to conduct negotiations. I must insist you move there now."

"You could have said something earlier, Kenos, but my decision is final." Jessica turned to him. "While I appreciate your facilities, my choice is to set up negotiations here so that any future clandestine operations can be dealt with immediately and reported to my Guild as necessary."

Kenos actually sputtered for a second. "But…you can't…that is highly irregular!"

"This situation is irregular, Administrator." Jessica tilted her head conspiratorially toward him. "You said it yourself that you do not trust the colonies to work this out. I cannot trust they will not continue their attacks on the Altar or force the Altar to defend themselves while we play nice around a conference table at D'nart. My negotiation site will be here at the Raknar."

"It will take time to arrange a housing unit and—"

Klatk stepped forward. "The Altar would be happy to provide housing for the Peacemaker. We can modify and move a temporary structure in an hour's time, if that would be satisfactory."

Kenos' mouth curled in a sneer. "Do you know what would be satisfactory, Klatk? If you and your colony gave up your resource claims and moved. The Peacemaker identified a nice spot on the Dorchak Plateau that would be a viable colony site. She wants you to move so she can be done with this negotiation and be granted her full Peacemaker's commission. She's going to find the easiest way so she can get back to Earth and start looking for her missing father."

Jessica's temper flared. "How dare you bring my father into this! My responsibility is to this negotiation, not the whereabouts of my father, Administrator Kenos. You are close to compromising any negotiation with your conduct, which I will report to the Guild immediately. I have not concluded anything about the Altar colony and its placement or needs. Yes, I scouted out a potential area, but that has no bearing on my judgment in this situation. Is that clear?"

Kenos grinned. "The only one compromising the negotiation is you, Peacemaker." He stressed the last word enough that Jessica wanted to punch him in the throat. "Still, the Consortium and all of the parties to this negotiation will uphold your 96-hour information period. If you're not ready to finalize this situation by then, I'm sure the Consortium will resolve it soon after. I'll have a launch standing by to take you back to Earth."

Jessica smiled thinly. *Keep on assuming, asshole.* Instead of saying what came to mind, she simply replied. "You do that, Administrator

Kenos. I'll make my report just the same. If you'll excuse me? I have a meeting with the Altar Council. That is my first priority."

Taemin scrambled up the hillside behind Kenos and stood. Out of breath from the effort, he stared at her impassively and slowly walked forward. "Peacemaker, I believe the Administrator would like to discuss initial terms for the Altar move."

"He just tried." Jessica shook her head and raised an index finger. "No. I am about to speak with the Altar Council, Taemin. That is my first priority, and where I will begin my investigation. As such, I will hear the Administrator's initial terms at the end of the next 48 hours. Is that clear?"

Taemin nodded and said nothing further. Kenos spun on a heel and stomped past Jessica's mediator. For a moment, Taemin looked at her, and she wondered if he would stay for the meeting. He spoke slowly, "I believe you have angered the Administrator, Peacemaker Francis."

Jessica nodded. "Good. Now we really know where he's coming from, don't we?"

Taemin flinched but a small smile appeared on his lips. "Indeed, Peacemaker. It would seem we do."

* * *

The GenSha came down into the tunnel much faster than Bukk expected. Laser rifles firing from platforms attached to their wide backs, the bovine aliens charged into the tight Altar tunnel a minute after the detonation. Bukk and his soldiers weren't there to meet them. The bulk of his group waited 500 meters down the tunnel to the north. Setting the collapsing mines could have been done by any of the lower ranking soldiers. Bukk chose to do it himself. Two hundred meters from the entrance, the detonation sounded muffled like a mid-summer storm on the horizon. As Bukk watched, a wave of smoke rolled down the tight tunnel and filled the air around him with thick, awful scents that pressed against his skin as it moved north.

Bukk moved to a prone position, lying flat on the tunnel floor with a laser rifle sighted into the dark tunnel. Holographic sights off, Bukk used his superior night vision instead. GenSha typically charged into dark spaces with lights and weapons blazing. The darkness was as much a weapon for Bukk as the rifle he cradled. In the distance, he heard the GenSha bellowing as they charged into the tunnel. Bukk waited and let the GenSha form up. He'd instructed his soldiers to dig the tunnel just wide enough for two Altar to pass easily in both directions. Two GenSha would not be able to fit as they made their way into the tunnel. Fifty meters from the blast site, the tunnel narrowed to a single width—an expedient chokepoint. Two GenSha appeared in the tunnel side-by-side, charging forward. They slowed, held up by the pinching rock walls and Bukk opened fire.

Neither GenSha fired back, and their bodies fell into the tunnel and blocked a sizable portion of the entrance. That wasn't enough. As the GenSha bellowed and tried to lay down suppressive fire, Bukk fired five bolts at random into the tunnel to rile them up even further. He rolled to his feet and snatched a detonator from his bandolier, as he moved down the tunnel to the north, counting his steps. When he reached 600, more than 400 meters from where the GenSha found the tunnel's bottleneck, Bukk snapped the trigger and collapsed the tunnel behind him. The closer, second explosion was more intense than the first, but Bukk hardly noticed. He sprinted down the tunnel as fast as his legs would carry him to the rendezvous point.

A thousand meters from the original target, the tunnel made a series of 90-degree turns. As Bukk approached the first, he turned on his slate and sent a low frequency radio transmission to his soldiers on the other side. Thirty seconds passed and he received a single chirp on the same frequency. They were in position. Bukk placed his rifle on safe and slung it over his back before making the first turn. At the second turn, he paused for 30 seconds according to plan, before making the next turn. Again, he sent a single chirp on the frequency and waited for a reply that came in seconds. This repeated twice more before Bukk paused at the last turn as a familiar voice hissed.

"Stop. Identify yourself."

Bukk spoke slowly. "Bukk. I am alone with no one behind me in the tunnel."

"Advance and be recognized."

Bukk turned the corner with his clawed forehands raised. "Alone. No pursuit."

A young engineer stood and slung his own rifle. "We heard the tunnel collapse. Easy, right?"

Bukk should his head. "Nothing is ever easy, Plec. We stopped them for now, but they'll be coming. Have you set the additional charges?"

"Yes, sir. We have the tunnel mined above the turns, and we've mined about a thousand meters on this side. We'll continue to collapse it on the way out."

"Very well," Bukk said. "Let's get going."

"Couldn't have said it better myself." Plec motioned down the tunnel. "After you. I've got rear security."

Bukk moved down the tunnel quickly. The team continued to spread and detonate explosives every thousand meters. It was overkill, to be sure, but the intent was to avoid leaving the GenSha any high-speed avenue of approach. Sixteen charges and 10 kilometers later, Bukk and his team pushed into the light of the colony's walls. Under the command center, he pushed through a series of hatches into the wide, clear passageway. Klatk was there along with a human who pressed a large weapon against the side of his head.

"And who might you be?"

Bukk looked at Klatk who nodded. "Bukk, this is Peacemaker Jessica Francis. Peacemaker, this is my chief scout and offensive force commander, Bukk."

He turned his head after the pistol moved away and drew up on his hind legs. "Well met, Peacemaker."

The human was a female, he saw with a start. Her red hair framed her face above the standard dark blue coveralls of a Peacemaker. Bukk focused on her eyes, though, and saw something he'd not seen in many humans. Experience, especially in a combat environment, left an impression in the lines at the corner of a human eye. The eyes told of hardship and loss, of joy and excitement. In the Peacemaker's eyes were the experiences of combat, tinged with the loss of friends and an unknown deceit. Yet those signs did not trouble him. He saw confidence and competence in her eyes as well, but there was a tinge of anxiety as clear as the morning sky.

The human extended a hand, which he took lightly in his claw. "You're responsible for the central paddock explosion?"

Bukk nodded and glanced at Klatk. "Mission accomplished, yes. They knowingly attacked our brood, Peacemaker. We had no choice but to attack them in the same manner."

The Peacemaker shook her head. "There were more choices than that, Bukk. Your queen and I are about to meet with the Council to discuss those choices going forward. I believe you should be part of the conversation."

Bukk stiffened. "Am I under complaint, Peacemaker? I have simply followed the orders I was given."

"I don't care what you've followed, Bukk. I care about what you've done and what choices all of you make from here on out. You have no mercenaries to defend your colony, and from what I can see you're hopelessly outmatched. While I can't condone what you did to the GenSha, I understand why your leadership undertook the mission. I do not agree with it either, Bukk, but that's a part of my being human." The Peacemaker looked at Klatk then back at him. Her eyes studied him for a moment. "You delayed the explosion to minimize casualties, didn't you?"

Bukk tried to cover his surprise. "We were delayed in the tunnel. The strata were—"

"You waited," the Peacemaker said. "I can see that you did. You did not want to disappoint your queen, but you wanted to complete the mission as ordered, am I right?"

He looked at Klatk and whispered. "That's correct."

Klatk's mandibles twitched. "We will speak of this later, Bukk."

The Peacemaker motioned down the passageway with her head. "Let's go speak with the council. I'm curious just how far they'll want to go, and if they'll balk like you did, Bukk."

"I had my reasons, Peacemaker."

"You showed restraint. That's a good thing, but you may not have that luxury in the future," the Peacemaker said over her shoulder as they walked. Ahead, at the entrance to the council's chamber, a Caroon in a long crimson robe waited by the door. Draped around his neck was a ribbon reserved for special mediators. He nodded at Klatk and the Peacemaker solemnly. He looked at Bukk and the malice in his small, black eyes made Bukk turn away. He glanced back to see the Caroon smile just before he ducked into the council chamber.

* * *

Kenos tapped furiously on the slate until the appropriate channels opened. The screen was blank for secrecy, but he soon heard a distinct click in his ears as the connection propagated. He waited the arranged five seconds before speaking. "Are Alpha and Bravo on this call?"

There was a crackle in the connection before a soft, clipped voice responded. "Alpha is here."

Five seconds later, a distinctive voice replied. "Bravo is present." The "s" sound trailed like a hiss.

"You are both here, and you know who I am. We will start there." Kenos paused. "The Peacemaker engaged a waiting period approximately two hours ago under the articles of colonization. As proxy actors, the articles deem you in the command and control of your respective units and, therefore, you are technically under the Peacemaker's authority. As such, all combat actions must halt during a waiting period for negotiation."

Kenos paused again and fought a smile from curling his lips. The fun part was to come. "Under the auspices of the Consortium, a

Dream World has no particular case or precedent for mercenary operations. Further, a Consortium planet does not technically fall under Union law or the Peacemaker Guild's enforcement until such time as the governing authority, in this case the Consortium, applies for recognition. Araf is an unrecognized planet. Due to technicalities, the application was denied, but you get the idea. As far as the Consortium is concerned, any action that takes place in such a waiting period is, like the rest of your contracts, outside our influence. I'll need an hour to clear the area and ensure any collection assets are disabled for the duration. I expect that will be acceptable to you?"

The crackle returned, and he heard that line terminate on one end. The other hissed, "Thank you," and ended with a click.

Kenos rested his paws on his stomach and settled back into the *Tchrt One's* command chair. Alone on the flight deck, he imagined the ship racing through space as it had in his youth. His mother and father prohibited joining a mercenary force so he started out in the family's business right out of secondary schooling. The urge to pick up a weapon and race into combat faded with time, but his deep-seated desire to fly returned from time to time. Cooler senses prevailed, as usual, and the urge to fly as fast and as far as he could faded with the promise of fortune.

Due to their reprehensible behavior, the Altar colony stood to forfeit their six billion credit deposit for the Dream World. After his expenses, pocketing four billion seemed likely. If he were to cause the forfeiture of another claim, by the loser of a prolonged conflict, then another several billion credits would default into his possession. That would be enough to go to the end of the galaxy, if he wanted. He had a ship and a trustworthy crew. All it took was money. The universe revolved on the power of credits, not the information present in the Aethernet or the trust of species working together for any type of common good. The only common good was profit. If it meant destroying the whole damned "Dream World" concept to let him leave it all behind, so be it.

Kenos sat forward and switched on the multiple Tri-V screens as he enabled the *Tchrt One's* secure communications pod and set to work. Preprogrammed routines ran through the Consortium's servers on Araf, and across the galaxy, to ensure that all monitoring stations switched to ill-timed maintenance failures according to the plan. Certain aspects of the planet's management he allowed to remain functional. Positioning satellites would remain in operation and a few of the more "primitive" communications satellites would continue to function in their decaying orbits. Depending on the outcome, deorbiting them would be an easy, effective way to ensure incriminating data would not find its way off the world.

He hesitated over the execute command for a heartbeat and pressed it. If anyone found out that he let three colonies go to war over something as simple as water rights and the perception of value, the risk to his company would be great. His reputation did not matter. He'd long ago given up hope for any type of familial relationships. What mattered to him was the deep, dark black. His oldest brother died in the void chasing something bigger than himself. Something bigger than the whole Cochkala race could understand. Kenos had been little more than a pup when Tsoc died. *Accidents happen*, his parents had said. Tsoc died in an emergence point collision with a freighter from Earth, far from home. Mercenaries from one of the Four Horsemen companies brought him home in a steel casket, so the family could cremate him and say their goodbyes.

Tsoc wanted nothing more than to stare into the deep black. Kenos would honor his brother's wish by proxy, and damn everyone and everything in his path.

* * * * *

Chapter Eleven

"You're certain the Peacemaker is a human, Qamm?" T'Genn chewed for a moment, his brows wide in surprise. "This is an unusual development."

Qamm stood in front of the GenSha leader's dais with her paws clasped at her waist. Her nose twitched. "I heard her voice myself, and the computer classified it as a North American human female."

"You are gathering information on her, I presume?"

"Administrator Kenos has a shabbily-constructed security system on his Aethernet servers." Qamm smiled. They both knew it was a purposeful lack of security. The Consortium's theory of thick veins of gold deep beneath the Altar colony had far reaching implications. First, there was enough to destabilize the economies of every gold-based system in the galaxy, of which there were more than three thousand. Second, the Consortium's lack of protection included a lack of security forces designed to protect assets discovered on Dream Worlds. Enough gold to finance his own little wars gained T'Genn's full attention.

"We're certain of the target?" T'Genn asked. He knew the answer, but his mercenary commander's valuable opinion backed his critical decisions. "And am I to purposely allow my people to be targeted again?"

Qamm tilted her head to one side. "You have the full backing of your people and your homeworld now. An atmosphere of terror is difficult to manage. By providing a ready-made target, you persuaded the vast majority of your citizens to go war. This is something to appreciate and take further advantage of, T'Genn."

T'Genn stood slowly and stretched his curved, heavy back. He chuffed, "And how do we do that, Qamm?"

"A gesture of mutual goodwill."

"To the Altar? Gods, no!"

Qamm shook her head. "No, to the Selroth."

T'Genn laughed. "They hate us as much as the Altar do, Qamm. Our need to farm the land takes away their precious water. What we use and return to the ecology, to them, is contaminated beyond safe use or consumption for their citizens. What could they possibly want that we could provide?" T'Genn realized the answer before the last words stopped reverberating around his circular office.

Qamm merely smiled. "Two colonies controlling this well-resourced continent. One has the land, one has the sea. Split the gold, fix their climate generator, and then drive the Consortium from the world. I like the sound of that, T'Genn."

T'Genn stroked his broad chin and smirked. "How do we maintain the peace? The Selroth would bring in more forces to take the land from us."

"You have to spend money to make money, to quote a human maxim." Qamm said. She stroked the white fur near her face as if she was thinking. "You'll have the resources to hire the best mercenary forces in the galaxy."

"I thought we'd done that."

Qamm nodded. "There are others who would like to play in this conflict, most certainly. What matters is that they are not here, and the Wandering Death has the proprietary rights to support your claim. We are prepared to execute our contract to support your colony. As your military advisor, I recommend a discussion with the Selroth. We have a certain number of hours to make this happen."

"Kenos expects us to attack. We should not let him down." T'Genn said. The Administrator's disdain for the Altar and their hampering his efforts to produce a sizable shift in the extraction of metals was the cause for most of the hostilities. Part of it was poor political relationships. Colonies on their own in a strange new world tended to approach life as a "snatch and grab" event. Resources of all sizes and shapes were the first to be fought over. Given Araf's failed weather systems and climactic assurances, water was at the top of the list. "Can you repair the weather systems?"

Qamm laughed, clutching her belly with both paws. "No. I doubt the entire Science Guild could get the Consortium's half-witted systems working." Her mirth evaporated under T'Genn's steady gaze. Contracts, after all, were contracts. "My best programmers continue to work on the system, T'Genn. There is nothing they can definitively point to as the cause of the failures, aside from nature itself."

T'Genn snorted. "Civilizations have controlled the weather for hundreds of years. Lengthening the sun-soaked months and adding to the rainy seasons by artificial means is nothing new. The Consortium holds out on us. They've put us in a position where we have to either oust the Altar from their granted lands by violence, or set up mutually assured-to-fail relationships both tenuous and dangerous in nature. The Selroth are not to be trusted." T'Genn knew from experience that the aquatic bastards felt the same way about the GenSha. The Altar would be a mutual enemy, but once they were gone, the Selroth's need for perfectly clean water would force his colony into famine or all-out war.

"I'm not going to argue about the weather, T'Genn. It's pointless and beyond understanding. If the system can be brought under control, my team will do so. Right now, I'm asking for your permission to speak with the Selroth and their mercenary forces."

T'Genn turned his back to the Veetanho leader, and could feel imaginary lasers from her eyes cutting into him as he feigned thinking about her request. The answer was simple, really. Even a mediocre student of tactics knew that there was safety in numbers, and partnering with the Selroth could be beneficial, provided the right precautions were negotiated. "What are you prepared to give them?"

"The river south of your expected dam site with a promise that your emissions from farming will not exceed what is tolerable for the fish species the Selroth harvest downstream. We will install a million acres of wetlands to disperse the water."

T'Genn turned back to her, interrupting the mercenary. "This assumes you get the rest of the climatological system in order, and you've told me you have made no progress toward that."

"The Selroth don't need to know that, T'Genn," Qamm said. "I would speak with them inside of an hour, given your permission. Given the dispersion of their forces, we can jointly attack the Altar by nightfall."

"You know their commander?"

"Leeto? He's a Sidar and a competent commander. He fancies himself more of an air warrior—deploys flyers and levitating gunnery platforms that are somewhat effective. He's a greedy fuck, though, and will gladly play for a chance at the gold. Can you persuade the Selroth leader, Ooren?"

T'Genn sighed. "Unknown. He and I have differed on almost every issue in the last three years. If he reaches out, I will do my best. Perhaps this is best resolved at the mercenary level."

Qamm tittered. "You won't tell Ooren about the gold?"

"Oh, he knows about the gold, Qamm." T'Genn smiled. "His people are quietly mining what they can reach from the water. Given half the chance, he'd love to come inland to get more."

Qamm nodded. "Incentive for another is a good thing until it crosses your personal intent."

T'Genn snorted. "What matters is that all we have to do is dangle the possibility in front of Ooren's gills, and he'll bite. He'll send as many troops as he can to take the Altar's mines from the ocean. There are two viable underground streams where his teams could infiltrate."

"The Altar certainly have them defended. At the very least, they're mined for passive defense."

T'Genn waved it off. "I don't care about the defenses and how many Selroth will die. Tell them to attack the mines and the Raknar from the water, and you'll hit the colony walls from the the land side. Have them bring their flyers in, too. One large attack may be enough for the Altar to cut and run."

Qamm nodded and bowed slightly at her waist. "I will make the arrangements, T'Genn. We will attack two hours before sundown."

T'Genn turned away. Ears intent, he heard the Veetanho mercenary skitter out of his chambers, and he smiled. For a mercenary, Qamm set a new standard for competence, but her lack of vision bothered him. Clearly, the Altar would mine the underground avenues of approach and maintain a layered defense of their mines and the colony itself. Klatk was a tactical genius. The Selroth casualty rates would skyrocket and that would further enrage Ooren. His previous attack on the Raknar obviously failed, undoubtedly killing a selection of his finest troops in the process. Another failure or two would drive him to the point of reckless abandon. When the Selroth over-committed and succumbed to Ooren's mistakes, T'Genn and his forces would be there to clean things up. If Qamm and the opposing Sidar mercenary leader could come to an arrangement, there was a possibility for complete and total victory.

Qamm bore watching, though. After all, she was a mercenary and a damned good one at that. Few Peacemakers would stand a chance against a mercenary like Qamm, much less a human. The Altar would withdraw or be annihilated by the following dawn, of that he was certain. As such, T'Genn walked a familiar path through his chambers as he planned.

* * *

Hak-Chet moved through the Peacemaker Hall silently. The lunar night gave the sky an unparalleled darkness of a new Earth. Countless stars and nebulae shimmered in the distance. He'd seen many of them in his years, and there were many still to see before he joined the sky. Wide marble halls empty, the guild's enclave on Luna felt like a mausoleum. More than 400 of the special halls existed in the galaxy, each laid out exactly as this one. One day, he believed, a statue of himself as Selector would reside in the halls for as long as they stood. Many of his pupils, living and dead, gazed back at him from their permanent positions. Amidst the statuary of the famous and infamous, Hak-Chet made his way to the Guildmaster's chambers. Past the statuary hall and into the observatory with its clear dome a full 20 meters overhead, there was more than enough starlight to navigate by. His eyes followed the astrographs in the floor and an imaginary line back to his home planet, Cielo, and beyond. There was nothing there for him, though, and memory would serve him poorly in its nostalgic lenses.

A voice from one of the deep couches in the center of the room snapped his reverie. "Selector? Won't you join me?"

Hak-Chet stopped and pivoted toward the Guildmaster. "You startled me, Master Rsach."

There was a chuckle. "My apologies, Selector. I merely wanted to enjoy the darkness instead of my chambers. Would you permit our meeting to take place here?"

There wasn't much choice. The Guildmaster always got what he wanted. Still, the confluence of the heavens above them welcomed him more than the stuffy offices in the official chambers. "Certainly, Master Rsach," he hesitated slightly.

"If you're worried about our conversation, old friend, we are alone and not to be disturbed. This conversation takes place outside of official duties. A discussion between a mentor and a friend."

Hak-Chet nodded and weaved through the opulent chairs and lounges. Rsach lay back on a couch, his eyes staring toward Spica. Hak-Chet sat across from him and leaned forward as much because of his age as for comfort. "We've never had a conversation between a mentor and friend, Master Rsach. There is no reason that we would do so now."

Rsach chuckled. "Selector, you are most impressive. Do you ever let your guard down?"

Hak-Chet sighed and let his mouth turn up in a slight grin. "It's been a very long time, Master Rsach. What are we to discuss?"

Rsach half rolled to face him. "The *Victory Twelve*, Selector. Hex Alison in command, with four tanks and twelve CASPers crewed by humans fresh from the Pan-Pacific CASPer pilot's course. Do you happen to recall that?"

"Of course, I do," he said and locked eyes with the Guildmaster. "And you know why I sent them."

Rsach nodded, but he sighed heavily. "We cannot interfere in any test of a Peacemaker, Selector. Even the first human. I understand that Peacemaker Francis earning her commission is a great honor for you, but we cannot—"

"It's not about my honors and distinctions, Rsach! You know as well as anyone that she cannot succeed with any negotiation on Araf because of the Dream World Consortium. There are already two mercenary forces on the ground there supporting two of the three factions. Jessica will ground herself with the Altar and determine her next move."

"Listen to you, Selector," Rsach chuckled. "Jessica will ground herself...you are emotionally involved in this human's attempt to commission."

Hak-Chet rocked back slightly. "I won't deny that I am, Rsach. I am quite fond of her and her abilities. She is one of the best candidates we've seen in decades. Her status as a Peacemaker is vital to Earth's continued position in the Union."

"I don't deny that, Selector." Rsach rolled up to a sitting position and turned to face Hak-Chet's. They were inches apart and the Master's voice was low. "But we cannot interfere. What did you tell Alison?"

Hak-Chet relaxed. He may be in trouble, but the threat from Rsach was low. "He's his father's son, Rsach. He knew what was going on without my telling him a thing. He filed a flight plan to deliver the Peacemaker's ship to her at Araf and enjoy a vacation. What better place for that than a Dream World?"

Rsach snorted and openly laughed. "And the cargo?"

"Simple hauling. I've arranged a dummy transport to meet them at Araf," Hak-Chet said. "This is not the first time I've assisted an operation from afar, Master Rsach. You yourself have benefitted from the Selector's discretion from time to time, have you not?"

Rsach crossed several sets of arms in front of him and growled. "I have, Hak-Chet. You've assisted a great many of our best and brightest. I should have expected nothing different."

"No, you should not have," Hak-Chet said. "Her status as Earth's best candidate ever is beyond reproach, and I know you agree with me despite your sending her to Araf to fail."

Rsach recoiled as if slapped. "How...how did you know that was my intent?"

"You've been interested in her ever since her initial Peacemaker assessments two years ago. You saw them, and you wanted to test her."

"More than just I want her to fail," Rsach said after a moment. "I'm told the Speaker of the Mercenary Guild wants her to fail, too. She has, however, exceeded every test and situation thrown at her since the completion of her academic training. Her mission to bring in Ch'tek and a gods-damned Canavar egg? There was no way I could have imagined she'd bring in the egg unscathed and incriminate Ch'tek in one fell swoop. It was an incredible performance."

"And yet she believes she failed."

Rsach looked up at him. "What do you mean?"

"Remember how she was once a part of Lemieux's Marauders? She knew most of that company by name, and lost several good friends in the process of recovering the egg and completing her mission. She and Hex Alison were the only ones besides Lemieux to escape with their lives. That she accomplished her objective under such circumstances is far more than incredible, Master Rsach. It proved that she has the skills to succeed in an impossible situation."

Rsach leaned back against the couch again and regarded the stars. Hak-Chet studied his eyes and their path from Arcturus to Spica. "How will she handle this, Selector? Will she maintain a diplomatic focus or charge blindly into the situation with her guns blazing?"

"Her guns will be a little way behind her." Hak-Chet grinned. "I expect her to recognize the situation as difficult and to attempt to maintain her presence as a Peacemaker as long as possible, Rsach. I also expect she will recognize the situation is much worse than she was briefed. As long as she maintains a sense of the big picture, the overall situation along the Choote River, she'll see the Consortium and their poor contracts are at fault. To what extent she will charge in with guns blazing, I cannot predict."

"But you suspect?" Rsach chuckled. "You sent her less than a company to fight against two complete mercenary companies—one with air support—and you're expecting her to fight them off."

Hak-Chet shook his head. "No, Master Rsach. I expect her to win."

* * *

"Second squad, move out," Hex snapped over the primary armor frequency. "Demon One, we're crossing your nine o'clock now. Lift and shift fire!"

"Roger, Boss," Tara replied. As one, her four tanks lifted their gun tubes and rocket pods about 10 degrees over the heads of the advancing CASPers as they charged into a nest of Tortantulas with every single cannon blazing.

Hex hadn't seen the ugly things up close and personal, and though this was a simulation event, they made his skin crawl. Even the sight of a terrestrial spider made him want to smack it with the first thing handy. In a CASPer, he'd almost fired his main cannon more than once at the tiniest arachnids. "Alpha Team, prepare to jump. Bravo Team, covering fire!"

The six CASPers to his left grounded and centered a withering mass of fire onto the nest. Bravo Team stowed weapons and prepared to jump.

"Demon One, cease fire! Bravo Team—now!" Hex ordered.

The tanks stopped firing and accelerated forward to cut off any retreat. Bravo Team jumped to max altitude and came down in the center of the nest and scattered the remaining Tortantulas. The little bastards and their Flatar riders managed to run about 200 meters to the south before Tara and her tanks cut them off.

Hex checked the radar and saw no threat icons. "Scope check and hold fire."

"Angel Two, negative and ceasing fire."

"Angel Seven, negative and ceasing fire."

"Demon One, negative contacts, all guns silent," Tara said. "Security posture alpha."

Hex stabbed his radio button with a grin on his face. "Coil up and set the defense. Great job, people!"

The private message light blinked, and he thumbed over to the channel without removing his hands from the CASPer's controls. Tara shouted in his ear, "Did you see that? An almost perfect run."

Hex grinned. "It's a sim, yeah, but they did really well. You did, too."

"Roger, boss," Tara said. "Recommend we end here. Recovery operations for emergence will start in an hour. The kids need a break."

I do, too. Hex sighed.

"Yeah, roger that. We'll have a bit of a party tonight to welcome them into our ranks, so to speak."

Tara didn't say anything for a few seconds. "Do we have ranks, Hex? What are we calling ourselves?"

"I haven't given it much thought," Hex replied. The idea of naming themselves simply for their mission to support Jessica seemed stupid. However, he realized the soldiers needed it. The experienced tankers expected it, and the newbies believed that their first assignments said everything about their abilities. They needed a name. "Have you got any ideas?"

"There are 28 people in this, including us. Maybe they have a few ideas."

Hex nodded to himself as the idea crystalized. He chuckled into the microphone. "Huh."

"What? What did you think of?"

Hex smiled. "My dad. He used to watch old war movies a lot. Said that men could learn a thing or two about others, even from a bad movie. There was one, something with Force Ten in the name.

Had a bunch of people thrown together that had to complete a complicated mission deep in enemy territory. It was actually a good flick, and they called themselves Force Ten. Let's go with Force Two Eight until we come up with something else. We're all in this together, right?"

"And we're only as strong as our weakest member," Tara agreed. "Okay, Force Two Eight it is, Boss. You do like that better than Angel One, right?"

"Not much of an Angel, Tara," Hex laughed. "Bring in Angels Two and Seven before we meet with everyone else. I'd like to spend a few minutes with them."

"And actually learn their names?" Tara asked. The implication was crystal clear, and he knew he was guilty. Treating newbies as numbers, his father said, was necessary.

You didn't get too close to the ones who were going to fuck up and die. If you did, their loss would turn into guilt, and that never ended well. If you couldn't save them, and you believed you could have, then no one could save you either.

This time, Hex realized that outside of Tara's tankers, newbies were all he had. "Yes, Tara. That's why I want to spend time with them. They're part of the team as much as you and I, and they're starting to act like it."

"Boss? Not to sound like an ass, but you're starting to act like a leader, too." There was a hint of a smile in Tara's voice, and it made Hex feel a little better about himself despite his critical self-facing eyes.

"Thanks, Demon One. Boss, out." Hex disconnected the transmission and touched a series of commands to terminate the simulation and place all weapons systems to standby. He opened a channel to the ship. "Lucille? We're standing down from simulations. Set the cargo loading programs to arm all weapons systems."

<<Affirmative. We are 37 minutes from emergence. Timing suggests that the *Tchrt One* has arrived on the planet.>>

Hyperspace, boring as it was, didn't lend itself to news updates. They'd figure out the situation in the transit from the emergence point to orbit. There was much he would not know until they could establish radio contact with Jessica. What he did know was that every weapons system on the *Victory Twelve*, and those in her hold, would be armed and ready to fight just as his father taught him.

"Lucille? Sound boots and saddles. I want Force Two Eight ready to deploy the second we emerge."

* * * * *

Chapter Twelve

Jessica hefted the last of her bags into the temporary living shelter erected by the fallen Raknar's helm. Inside the small, clean space was a twin-sized bed tucked against one wall, a small desk, and an auto galley that looked as if it had never been used. Across from the bed was a chest with wide drawers for her clothes and a small laundry machine. There were no Tri-V screens or media devices that she could see, and that was just as well. The last thing she needed was a distraction.

Unpacking her clothes took only a few minutes, and she set her slate and a collection of manuals on the small desk. She closed her eyes and leaned against the chair, suddenly exhausted. Her mother had called it "a tired coming on." There were times during her adolescence, and especially on her visits home, where they could be deep in a conversation or simply watching a holo-film and her mother would stand up, shuffle toward her bedroom door, and simply say those words. No wishes for a good night, pleasant dreams, or even an "I love you." She was tired and that was that. Jessica rubbed the inside corners of her eyes with one hand and stood there under the weight of her fatigue and the godawful decision she'd made to take the mission in the first place.

One hand found its way into her pockets and the cool, smooth plastic chipset with Snowman etched into the surface. Without withdrawing it from her pocket, she felt the connector spines along one side and tried to recall ever seeing something like it. There was nothing in her memory that could link the chipset to any technology capable of reading it, and Lucille had been unable to do anything in the brief test she'd run on the *Victory Twelve*. She squeezed the chipset carefully. There would be time after the mission to find a way to read it, especially if she failed. She'd have all the time in the world.

Stop thinking like that, Jess.

Brushing the thoughts aside proved easier said than done. In reality, failure to commission as a Peacemaker meant she'd go back into the Mercenary Guild. With her track record, she could easily gain a staff position with any number of companies—perhaps even one of the Four Horsemen. Five years ago, she would have jumped at the chance to do just that. Falling in love with Marc derailed everything, and when she fell out of love with him and had the chance to be the mercenary she'd always wanted to be, things changed.

Being a Peacemaker called to her. On the surface, a Peacemaker was little more than a galactic cop to most of the galaxy. She understood the role better after serving as a mercenary herself. Peacemakers weren't cops any more than they were soldiers. Problem solvers, go-betweens, and strong-willed enforcers that they were, Peacemakers gained instant respect. The notoriety and fame of being Earth's first one would be difficult, she knew, but it called to her. After bringing in Ch'Tek and stopping his crazy scheme to plant a Canavar egg on Earth, the path seemed laid out in front of her, until the Guild questioned her diplomacy—her very methods. With a sigh, she sat down at the table and cradled the chipset in her palms. The last thing she wanted to do was walk outside and face the situation. Taemin, with his smug face, would doubt and demean her decisions at every turn from his position as a mediator.

Whose side was he on?

Does it matter, Bulldog?

Her father's voice in her conscience snapped her back to the present. Jessica stared at the chipset for a minute, thinking of her father so deeply she could almost smell his aftershave. How many times had she imagined walking into any seedy bar in the galaxy and seeing him cradling a cold can of Coors? She'd looked for him everywhere and found nothing.

Get going. There's no time for memories.

Does it matter?

Jessica sighed. Her father's idioms and sayings came back to her at the oddest times, mostly when she needed them. She and Taemin would have a conversation when she was ready to confront him. As it was, her stated intervention phase ticked by. She stood and slipped the chipset into the shoulder pocket of her coveralls, quickly brushed her hair, and tucked it under a dark-brimmed boony hat. After a quick smear of sunscreen across her face, she felt ready to step out into the Araf sun and see just how bad the situation was.

The door snapped open behind her. Startled, Jessica drew her pistol as she half-turned and leveled it at the dark figure in her doorway. Just as quickly, she recognized the mediator, and kept the pistol trained on his narrow chest.

"I can see that you're not ready, Peacemaker." The Caroon smirked at her.

"What the fuck do you think you're doing, Taemin? You can't just enter my quarters and—"

"A mediator can go anywhere in a defined diplomatic area. If you wanted your quarters amended from that list, you should have said something. This merely proves my point, and the point I will make to Klatk and the Altar Council: you are not ready for this negotiation and should be removed as their appointed Peacemaker."

For the briefest of moments, she considered pulling the trigger.

"Let me make this abundantly clear, Taemin," she said slowly. The pistol's barrel never left the center of his sloped forehead. "You are never to open the door to my quarters again. You will knock and wait for an answer. If there is no answer, you will walk away. Any attempt to enter my quarters will result in your getting your face blown off."

Taemin's eyes widened. "You're threatening a mediator in the performance of his duties. This is —"

"Shut up," she said. "You are well aware that a Peacemaker can exact extreme force if threatened, and it would be wise for you to consider your choices. Opening a door on a female from your culture may be acceptable and expected. For a human, it's not. Do you understand, or do I need to make my point another way?"

Taemin's head bowed slightly. "My apologies, Peacemaker. I intended no harm."

Bullshit.

Jessica lowered the pistol, engaged the safety, and holstered the weapon without taking her eyes from Taemin. "You want me removed from this investigation? You make the call."

"That's not the proper procedure. I can only make recommendations. There is no action a mediator can take other than to provide counsel to both sides. I'm telling you that you are not ready for this negotiation and should request an immediate replacement."

"Noted," Jessica said. "I will not be making any such request. As of right now, Mediator, you need to gather more documents for my investigation."

Taemin stammered. "I-I've already fulfilled that requirement onboard the ship."

"Which is precisely my point. Pull the agreement files from the Altar. If there are any inconsistencies, I want them noted as evidence in accordance with Union trade provisions."

"Yes, Peacemaker Francis," Taemin said. The tone of his voice, lower and more serious, threatened to make her smile. She'd managed to rebuke him with his own responsibilities.

"There's more." Jessica stepped out in the warm afternoon. "I want to see the original Dream World contracts and the hydrological and geographic discussion of rights on this property. I also want to see whatever you can find about this Raknar—schematics, capabilities, anything in the Union archives."

Taemin nodded, his eyes bright and interested. "You're looking for something specific?"

"I'm looking for anything specifically missing." They walked toward the small command center, dodging Altar scurrying back and forth to the walls with ammunition, and others moving supplies toward the cavern entrances to the east. Klatk moved across an overhead walkway and dropped effortlessly to the ground in front of them. Taemin flinched backward.

"Honored Klatk."

"Peacemaker," Klatk said, her mandibles flexing in a gesture akin to smiling. "We are preparing for another attack. Ground surveillance radar systems near the GenSha colony have picked up a lot of movement and preparation within their walls. This is something we've seen before, and it's the closest thing we have to early warning."

"What about the Selroth?"

Klatk shrugged. "Their last incursion damaged many of our underwater sensors and we don't have enough spares to adequately cover the river. I'm shifting direct observation there and will use a few of our spare systems for warning purposes, but I am concerned they could use a GenSha attack as a diversion and hit us again."

The very same thought ran through Jessica's mind along with a thousand others in a flash. The first one was the most obvious one. "I need to know how you're laid out to fight, and what your intentions are. We need to look at the terrain and your weapons and attempt to figure out what to do when they attack."

Klatk tilted her head to one side. "I agree, I think we..." She paused, her antennae twitching in silent communication. Klatk turned to the command post and then looked into the sky high above. Jessica did the same, but saw nothing in Zehra's intense glare. "Peacemaker, there is communication traffic on Araf's approach channels referring to you by name. Please come with me."

That sonuvabitch! She whirled to look at Taemin expecting to see a defiant grin on his elongated face. Instead, he looked shocked and surprised.

"Did you make that call, Taemin?"

"No, Peacemaker," Taemin replied. "It is possible that Administrator Kenos did, but the timing does not match the situation."

"No, it doesn't," Jessica said as she turned to follow the Altar queen. She scrambled behind Klatk as they climbed over low walls to the command center—the shortest distance between two points. Klatk paused at the top and looked down in what Jessica thought was horror.

"I'm so sorry, Jessica. I forgot that you can't move like an Altar."

Jessica laughed and pulled herself over the last wall. Sweat stood out on her forehead, and she breathed harder than she wanted to from the exertion. She touched her hand to the Altar's upper shoulder joint. "It's okay, Klatk."

"I won't do that again."

They pushed into the command center, and Klatk pointed to a speaker. The soldier on duty flipped a switch, and the speaker came to life with a very pissed off controller yelling at someone on the other side.

"...I don't care who you're trying to reach, you've entered controlled space without proper authentication. You are ordered to halt in place and prepare for a boarding party from the Consortium's inspection division."

"Araf approach, this is the *Victory Twelve*—"

Hex!

"— Negative on your last request. I am commanding Force Two Eight and we have orders to report to Peacemaker Jessica Francis on the surface within the hour. These orders are signed by a Peacemaker Guildmaster. I recommend you get the Peacemaker on the channel to confirm, over."

Jessica grabbed the microphone. "*Victory Twelve*, this is Peacemaker Francis. Reference check on Foxtrot Two India Kilo priorities, over."

Hex's voice came back. "That's affirmative, ma'am. We are Foxtrot Two India Kilo, over."

Jessica beamed and quickly swallowed the smile. "Araf approach, Peacemaker Francis. I am confirming the *Victory Twelve's* mission and requesting immediate clearance to my location as granted under the Peacemaker Guild statutes. Acknowledge."

There was nothing on the frequency for five seconds. Jessica sucked in a breath to transmit again but didn't need to. "Peacemaker Francis, this is Araf approach. Request acknowledged. *Victory Twelve*, proceed to the following coordinates via data package."

"*Victory Twelve* acknowledges receipt. Peacemaker Francis, our ETA is seventeen minutes to station. Foxtrot Two India Kilo will commence on arrival."

Jessica set the microphone gently on the console and looked at Klatk. "Things just got interesting."

Klatk's antennae twitched. "Our surveillance radars report halted movement from the GenSha compounds. What do you mean by interesting? What is Foxtrot Two India Kilo?"

Jessica smiled and tapped the lone soldier on the shoulder. "Could I have a moment, please?"

The startled soldier looked at Jessica and then at Klatk, who directed him away. As he departed the command center, Jessica stepped closer to Klatk with the intent of hiding their conversation as much as possible.

"The *Victory Twelve* is my personal ship, Klatk. It's in the care of one of my former mercenary brothers. His name is Hex Alison. I don't know what he's doing here, or how he found out where I am. I can assume by his transmissions that the Guild knows, and sent him, but I don't know why. That's where Foxtrot Two India Kilo comes in. It's one of our old codes. It means "Fuck If I Know," and that means Hex knows people are watching, and he doesn't want to let anyone know what he's doing just yet."

"You trust this Hex?" Klatk's mandibles twitched.

"With my life, Klatk. Whatever message he's bringing is important to what's going on here."

"He is a mercenary? Is he bringing a force?"

Jessica shrugged. "I don't know."

"The Altar cannot afford to secure their services. If they are uncontracted and attempt to align with my forces, we are subject to piracy claims from both colonies," Klatk said. "I cannot allow them to land at my colony in such a position, Jessica. You are aware of this, aren't you?"

Jessica nodded, but her mind raced and anger surfaced. Hex brought her ship and gods-knew-what to Altar either in pursuit of a contract or without a clue as to her position and mission – both of which were bad business. An unsubstantiated claim and unfounded action would label him, and by proxy her ship, as pirates. A piracy charge would ruin her chances of being a Peacemaker.

It had to be Hak-Chet. Why would he send Hex and the *Victory Twelve* unless he brought some type of combat power? But what good was that if Hex, and whoever else was onboard, were going to be listed as pirates? It would have been far easier for Hak-Chet to...

Oh shit, Jessica grinned. *I can't believe this.*

She reached for the microphone. "Araf Approach, this is Peacemaker Francis. Please log for the record that the *Victory Twelve* is secured for official mission requirements under the Peacemaker Guild's statutes for property acquisition. Further, acknowledge that the crew of the *Victory Twelve*, and all equipment therein, fall under similar statutes and will be deputized the moment they arrive. Record the current time and date, and forward via GalNet to the Peacemaker Guild immediately on my authority. Acknowledge all parts of this transmission. Over."

This time, a response took more than a minute. There was little doubt in her mind that Araf Approach relayed everything in realtime to the Consortium, which was exactly the intent of her message. Deputizing Hex and whoever was onboard cleared them individually. By acquiring the vessel itself, and all equipment therein, she could employ it to conduct her mission. Hak-Chet's gift could be the key to solving the negotiations simply by giving the Altar an equal footing against the mercenary forces of the GenSha and the Selroth.

The *Victory Twelve's* hold, though, was not big enough for a full mercenary company. Whatever was there would be outnumbered and outgunned. Jessica tried to quell the rising doubt in her mind.

It's a start, Bulldog. Sometimes that's all you need whether you know it or not.

She snorted. *Fuck if I know, Daddy.*

Klatk tapped her on the shoulder. "Are you all right, Jessica?"

"Yes." She dabbed at her left eye with the sleeve of her coveralls. "We're going to be fine, Klatk. We're going to be just fine."

* * *

Kenos sat forward in his seat. "What did you say?"

"The Peacemaker has acquired the vessel *Victory Twelve*, and deputized its crew for her mission requirements, Administrator."

"She can't do that." He looked at a small Tri-V display. "Can she?"

"Yes, she can."

Kenos huffed three deep breaths. "This is most unfortunate."

"It appears she is more resilient than expected."

"You're going to have to do something about it," Kenos barked. "Once combat operations begin, find a way to remove her from the situation."

"Like you attempted to do? Outside our agreement?"

"Excuse me?" Kenos gasped. "What are you talking about?"

"An Altar soldier, one of their underground specialists, pulled a weapon on Peacemaker Francis shortly after she disembarked. Given your position aboard *Tchrt One*, I thought you would have seen it from external cameras."

"I'll have to check," Kenos said trying to maintain the charade. "There's no guarantee our sensors saw anything. Regardless, the Consortium disavows any knowledge of an attempt on the Peacemaker's life. Did she take action against the soldier? Anything unsettling that the Guild would appreciate advanced warning of?"

"Klatk disarmed the soldier and beat him to death, though it appeared he might have tried to engage a self-poisoning device. While a nice touch, your play was very risky to the overall operation, Kenos."

"And what if it had been successful? We could have annihilated the Altar and taken their mines before any of the Guilds noticed. We would have what we want and the situation would have resolved itself." Kenos stroked the side of his face with a claw. "Besides, it's not as if you or your partners have been able to stop this nonsense."

"My actions, and that of my partners, are not your concern. You've made a promise they believe you have no intention of keeping. Perhaps we should let the Peacemaker continue her investigation, Kenos? What else might she find that you're not sharing with our mutual friends?"

"How dare you!" Kenos stood and balled his paws into tight fists. "My part of this deal remains intact, and I have shared every single discovery from Araf. You will find everything I have reported is true."

"I am more concerned about what remains unreported, Kenos. Your research showed promising early data for the presence of a host of precious metals. You've only successfully identified gold. While that helps to devalue lesser quality economies throughout the galaxy, it does little to help our manufacturing requirements. You promised platinum and diamonds in mass quantities, Kenos. None of your other mining ventures have found anything of consequence in terms of tonnage. You promised this mine was the best positioned to produce. Now, you have a colony moving their young underground and slaving power from a fallen Raknar. They're moving in to protect what they've found, Kenos. If you aren't prepared to deal with it, we will—"

"I am doing everything I can!" Kenos closed his eyes in an attempt to quell his rage. "The mercenary forces are in place, and the rest of the plan is ready to implement."

"And the Peacemaker's injunction? How soon will you end it?"

Kenos laughed. "I will do nothing. The agreed upon instructions are in the hands of those who need them. When they choose to act is a product of the situation. While that's been complicated by the arrival of her suspiciously-timed deputy forces, it's of no consequence. Numerical superiority and combat power remain in our favor. Whatever resistance they are capable of generating will be easily defeated—it's simply a matter of time. I hope to gain their order of battle information soon. You will be able to assist?"

There was no response, and the connection terminated in a burst of static. Kenos stared at the speaker for a long moment, and let a smile curl his upper lip as a Tri-V screen flickered to life and a real-time video feed from the Altar colony appeared. A single drop ship appeared in the frame, descending from orbit toward the colony from the southwest. By its design, the drop ship would not be capable of holding more than two tanks or a fire team of CASPers. His smile turned into a laugh. Unless the Peacemaker's friends dropped more ships or made more than 20 descents from orbit, there was no way they could stand up to his previously-made arrangements.

No way at all.

* * * * *

Chapter Thirteen

No sooner had the *Victory Twelve's* skiff, *Molly*, touched down than Hex bounded down the ramp and jogged up the slope to embrace Jessica. She smiled, but he could tell it was strained. When she hugged him, her arms felt like taut steel. She turned her head against his shoulder, and he felt her breath against his neck.

"Are you going to tell me what's going on?" Jessica whispered.

"Fuck if I know," Hex replied. He felt Jessica laugh against his chest. Before they drew apart, he pressed closer to her ear. "Hak-Chet."

He felt her relax against him, and they released the embrace. The lines around her eyes told him she was tired and a little frazzled, though she would never admit it. She held his forearms and smiled at him. "I'm glad to see you, Hex."

"Glad to be here, Bulldog."

Jessica's smile widened slightly, enough that Hex knew it was genuine even as her words thumped his heart. "Those days are long gone, Hex."

"Are they?" Hex cocked an eyebrow at her. "I don't think they are, Jess. You're just not in Bulldog mode, that's all."

"Not everything is a fight, Hex."

Hex shook his head. "My dad used to say a lot of things, you know that. The one that always got me was that everything is a fight, Jess. You might not be able to arm a weapon or put steel downrange, but everything is a fight. You know how to handle yourself in a fight better than anyone I know."

Jessica shook her head. "I don't think this is a fight, Hex. There has to be a peaceful solution."

"That's why I'm here, Jessica. Why we're here."

She squinted. "What's on board?"

"Four tanks, twelve CASPers." Hex said.

Jessica rolled her neck to the sky. She was still holding on to his arms, and he felt almost all her weight on him. "That's not enough."

"For what?" Hex asked. "I thought you said this wasn't a fight?"

Jessica lowered her eyes to his, and he saw a little flicker of life in them. "Lots of hostiles, Hex."

Good, Hex thought. *Get her thinking tactically and not strategically.*

"I need to send the skiff back up. Brought two tanks and four CASPers this trip. We'll need two more trips."

"Who's flying the skiff?"

"My armor commander. Her name's Tara Mason. You'll like her, Jess."

Jessica tilted her head to one side as if studying him, wanting to know if he liked her. He looked away, and Jessica dropped his arms. "Are you doing okay?"

"I'll make it."

Jessica motioned to the Altar nearest her, and the female approached. "This is Klatk. She is the queen of this colony."

Hex bowed ceremonially. "Your Highness."

Klatk chittered a laugh. "Not that kind of queen, Mister Alison. An Altar queen is merely the matriarchal leader of every colony. Our royal family is many light-years away from here and our greatest secret."

Jessica touched his arm again. "You learn something new every day in this business, huh?"

"Yeah," Hex shrugged, embarrassed. "My apologies, Klatk."

Klatk extended a hard claw, which Hex shook awkwardly. "Not necessary. May I call you Hex?"

"Please." Hex grinned. The Altar's warm, almost human mannerisms set him at ease. She was far more practiced in inter-species relations than he was, and it showed.

"You come from an honorable lineage," Klatk said. "Our people are well acquainted with the Alison family and welcome you to our colony, Hex. I wish there was more time to tell you some of the stories, but the time for pleasantries is over. I fear we are in a defensive posture and will need your assistance immediately."

Hex nodded and tapped on his wrist-slate. "*Molly*, this is Boss. Proceed with remaining lifts. Have all crews load their vehicles."

"Roger, Boss," Tara replied over the channel. "What about your CASPer?"

"Bring it on the last run, I'll be fine until then."

"Copy all. *Molly* pulling away." Down the hill, the skiff powered up its lifters, rose effortlessly from the surface, and spun toward the southwest in one smooth movement. Hex watched it ascend for a moment.

"She's a good pilot, I'll give you that," Jessica said at his side. "And she's a tanker?"

"Yeah."

"Did she know Marc?"

Hex shook his head. "Only by reputation. That was enough for me to bring her and her four tanks on board."

"Where did they come from?" Jessica's hand crept to her hips. Hex had to cough and cover a smile. Where the composed Peacemaker had stood, Bulldog slowly emerged. Her old mannerisms were a welcome sight.

"Death on Tracks," Hex said. "I know, not the best tank unit ever fielded, but they have been more successful than the Marauders. If we'd had some of them we might…might have…" His voice trailed off, and his vision swam with a sudden onset of tears that brimmed but did not fall.

Jessica stepped in front of him closely. Her hands found his jaw and raised his eyes to hers. "You did everything you could, Hex."

"It wasn't enough."

"No, it wasn't," Jessica said. "Sometimes that's all you can do. You loved her, and she loved you. That has to be enough for you."

Hex nodded but the pain in his chest told another story. The nightmares wouldn't stop for a long time. More than once he'd heard her voice as clear as day. A single tear leaked down his cheek. "What if it's not?"

Jessica swept the tear away. "You don't have a choice, buddy. That's all you have."

The finality of it caught him by surprise, but Jessica was right. There was nothing more to be had, save for his memories and his regrets. One would be a pleasant experience, and the other would lead to sleepless nights and insanity. The road to closure would not be easy, but he understood it was a choice he could make and, more importantly, could deal with through the help of others. Jessica understood, and she loved Maya as much as anyone, save for himself. If she could function, then so could he.

"I'm okay," he said.

"No, you're not. But you will be," Jessica said. "What do you want to do?"

Hex looked around at the colony and the fallen Raknar. His mind switched on, and he walked up the slope behind them into the colony proper as he looked for the highest point. The small alcove in the center of the colony, he figured, was the command center. He reached it quickly and then scrambled up to stand on its rough adobe slab roof. He could see 360 degrees.

To the south were wide, flat plains that stretched to the horizon 80 kilometers away. He traced the line of the Choote River with his eyes and easily made out the GenSha colony and their expansive agricultural complex. To the west were craggy hills laid out in rough ridge lines that looked like stone dolphins just under the surface of the ocean. To the east, behind the Altar complex, there were more hills, and he could clearly see several cavern entrances. Again following the river to the north, he saw a faint sliver of blue beyond the river's mouth into the sea. The submerged Selroth colony was out of view, but he knew the littoral waters could give the amphibious aliens the element of surprise.

Jessica clambered onto the roof next to him. "What do you see, Hex?"

"Is this a teaching moment, Bulldog? I'm fresh out of quarters." He grinned. As the second in command of the Marauders for several years, she earned a reputation of making the younger mercs learn from their mistakes and the mistakes of others. All of them earned lectures. Some were stern warnings and others were simply bits of shared knowledge and information she thought relevant to them. After one of the latter, Maya walked up and gave Jessica a quarter.

"What's this?" Jessica had asked.

"A lecture like that gets a quarter, Bulldog." The 25-cent lecture series had been born. It was a good memory, one that brought a smile to both of their faces.

Jessica laughed and looked away for a moment. The breeze was up, warm and dry from the east. Araf's late afternoon sun warmed the top of his head, and he ran a hand through his longish blond hair. She wasn't answering, and he knew what she wanted to hear. The answer was an old one, taught by the armies of Earth long before first contact. Like much of that training, mnemonic devices and acronyms taught soldiers how to do the simplest of tasks. A twentieth-century operations order had five paragraphs: Situation, Mission, Execution, Service and Support, and Command and Signal. The device for that was Sergeant Major Eats Sugar Cookies. His father hated that one, as most sergeant majors did.

Identifying terrain, and especially key terrain for defensive operations, was OCOKA. They'd changed the acronym a bunch in the ensuing years, but the original was part of his education by fire, and it stood the test of time just as well as the others. Observation, Cover and Concealment, Obstacles, Key Terrain, and Avenues of Approach assembled a three-dimensional picture of the battle space.

"This is a good, defensible position, Bulldog. We can see both colonies, and the terrain to our backs is difficult to traverse with vehicles and doesn't offer much concealment. We're holding the key terrain, including the Raknar, which we should use to our advantage as much as possible. I'm assuming the river is mined, but we'll need to look at the terrain to the south to see what we can do to move the GenSha into kill zones with obstacles and indirect fire. The Selroth are a wildcard. If we take the river away from them they can still approach easily from the north and not so easily from the west. We'll need obstacles there, too."

He paused as Klatk climbed up to the roof and stood next to them. Hex looked past her and saw the cavern entrances. *The river!*

"Are there any subterranean lakes or streams in your mine system?"

Klatk stiffened. "Why is that important to you?"

"The Selroth. They could approach through a subterranean aquifer. We have to make sure they don't."

"And you want access to our mines?" Klatk's antennae waggled from side to side in irritation. "Absolutely not! Our mines are protected by our agreements with the Consortium and are sacred ground! No one is allowed down there besides my teams under any circumstances."

Jessica brushed hair out of her face and said, "Even if the Selroth attack down there, Klatk? We are at a significant disadvantage without being able to defend the mines properly."

Klatk's mandibles worked side to side. "I cannot allow just anyone down there, Jessica."

"We can't defend you without knowing what's there," Hex said.

"I understand that, Hex." Klatk looked at Jessica. "You, though, aren't just anyone. You are a Peacemaker and bound by your oath to remain impartial. I can send you, Jessica. You can survey what's there and determine a way for my people to best defend it."

Jessica looked at Klatk for a long moment. It wasn't a perfect answer, and she couldn't help thinking that sooner or later they'd have to move people underground to defend the mines. Jessica bit her lip for a second and then spoke. "Okay, Klatk. I'd like to go now."

"I'll get you an escort," Klatk said. She skittered down from the roof and left the two friends alone.

"What's she hiding?" Hex asked.

"Her brood is down there. I'm fairly certain of that. The Altar's contract with the Consortium stipulates that they mine for precious metals. The list is about two thousand minerals long. I think they've either found something not on the list, or they've found enough of something that could destabilize the Trade Guild."

"Like what?" Hex asked and then blinked. "F11?"

"Doubtful. F-11 isn't usually underground like this. It's probably something else. Defending the tunnels is the right way to think, though; I'm proud of you for realizing that. Determining what she's hiding from us, no matter how good her intentions are, is another thing entirely."

"That's why they pay you the big bucks, right?" Hex chuckled.

Jessica shook her head. "I have an injunction on the opposing colonies. We simply don't have time to waste. I need to check out the tunnels. Set the defense."

Hex nodded. "What about the Raknar?"

"Later," Jessica said. "I don't trust anyone in this situation."

"Is that paranoia or fact? Klatk seems to like you."

Jessica frowned. "It's not a matter of being liked, Hex. She respects my position, and that's great, but it doesn't allow me freedom to be myself. One of her soldiers tried to shoot me after I landed."

"Really?" Hex blinked.

"Klatk killed the soldier and has been close by me ever since, but I'm walking around looking over my shoulder constantly."

"What about the mines? You're not going to be safe down there."

"Maybe," Jessica shrugged. "We have to know what's down there."

"You can't tell me that, though. Right?"

Jessica slapped her own forehead comically. "Gods! I forgot all about that."

"Forgot about what?"

She grinned. "Raise your right hand and repeat after me."

* * *

Tara brought down the skiff hauling the final load of CASPers and provisions near the torso of the fallen Raknar. Landing pads down, she thumbed the switch to lower the cargo ramp and consulted the Tri-V screens for the landing checklist. She tapped through the commands quickly, grateful for the concise, clear directions. A few reassuring thumps from the fuselage told her the unloading started without incident. Unloading the last three CASPers and a ton of provisions and fresh water for the unit would be short work for CASPer operators. The skiff powered down, she lingered in the cockpit for a moment looking at the screen menu and the words <HOT START?>.

Tara hesitated to flip off the vehicle's main power switches. Using the throttle-mounted cursor controls, she keyed the hot start option, keeping the vehicle ready for a quick launch and return to orbit under duress. The quiet, busy colony outside belied what she knew to be going on around them. Through the cockpit windows, she saw Hex make his way down the gentle slope toward the river to unload his CASPer. Tara couldn't see where he'd deployed her tanks, but that was okay. She trusted him to make the initial emplacement.

If he'd erred, she could fix it before any fighting started. Being in the defensive position gave them that option.

Tara unstrapped from the command seat and made her way out of the cockpit and into the skiff's cargo hold in the space of a few seconds. Hex stepped aboard just as her boots hit the deck.

"Hey there," he said and smiled. His attempt at charm made her smile as well, even though she knew he'd misunderstand it. "Any issues?"

"No." She put her hands on her hips. "Lucille has the *Victory Twelve* in a good orbit with defensive measures engaged. I didn't see my tanks."

"They're providing security. We've got them dug in and concealed at the four corners of the colony with rockets and indirect fire behind them. Good fields of fire," Hex said. "I'm putting the CASPers between them in concealed positions, too. The Altar dig crazy fast, so it's been easy to get the vehicles in with as little observation time as possible. They're watching us."

"Orbitals or air breathers?"

"High-altitude drones, I think. We get tracks on v-dar, but can't see them any other way," Hex said. "I wish we had air cover."

Tara agreed. Timing had worked against them, and she hadn't been able to secure even one flyer to patrol the sky above them. Velocity detectors on board the CASPers would be their only way of seeing airborne intruders, and they'd have no way of fighting them off if anything up there became hostile and engaged weapons. "We can modify a couple of CASPers and one of the tanks for air defense."

Hex nodded. "I was thinking the same thing. Once you get your gear stowed, I'll show you the layout and brief you on the plan. We're at 50 percent security right now."

Impressed, Tara felt better about what they'd discussed and practiced aboard ship. Fifteen hour days of simulations and training seemed to pay off. Their CASPer operators moved with grace and precision in the 1.08 G environment, and there was a quiet confidence to Hex that hadn't been there when they'd left Earth. His brain appeared ready for the task at hand. His heart was another matter. "You doing okay?"

"Better now." He grinned.

"Stop it." She frowned. "We're here to protect the Peacemaker and get this situation resolved, Hex. You're a nice guy, but I'm not a rebound and neither is anyone else in our group. Got it?"

Hex recoiled. "Yeah...okay, I just—"

Tara stepped closer but did not touch him. "Focus on the mission, Hex. That's what Maya would want you to do, not sportfuck around."

"Sportfuck?" Hex chuckled, but he nodded. The smile on his face slid away exactly as she'd intended. "This isn't the time or the place."

"No, it's not," Tara said. His charm and hovering would have led him nowhere, but he didn't need to know that. Mission accomplished, she changed the subject. "Where's Jessica?"

"Preparing to check out the tunnel complex. If there's a subterranean water source, the Selroth could use it against us. Plus, Jessica thinks the Altar are hiding something down there." Hex shrugged. "No idea what it is, or if there really is anything down there. Something's just not right."

Tara turned and stared over his shoulder at the defensive weapons erected atop the colony walls. "Wouldn't it be easier for them to relocate? This colony is all modular. We could move it in a couple of days at most."

Hex shook his head. "No, they can't. They're slaving power off the Raknar. It's not much, but it's more reliable than the power the wind and solar systems can produce because Araf's weather system is pretty fucked up most of the time."

"The Dream World isn't so dreamy then?" She asked with a smile. Hex returned it, though without the cheesy charm he'd displayed since they left Earth. Maybe she'd gotten through to him after all.

"Just not these three colonies. It's a colossal mess, Tara."

"Are they going to fight? The Altar, I mean."

Hex nodded. "I think so. We won't really know until the colonies and their mercs hit us."

There was a far away look in his eyes, and he kept staring over her head. She turned and looked to the south against the glare of the sun. Dust trails rose along the horizon. "Looks like we won't have to wait long." Tara said. She turned around but Hex was already running to his CASPer.

She tapped her wrist slate and opened a comms channel. "Angels and Demons, stand-to, and lock and load. Enemy mobilizing to the south. Weapons hold. I repeat, weapons hold. If they come into sector, we'll hit them hard, fast, and keep right on hitting."

* * * * *

Chapter Fourteen

The report of enemy vehicles on the horizon stopped Jessica in her tracks. She pulled a small earpiece from her thigh pocket and slipped it into her ear. A few taps on her wrist slate, and Hex's voice came through loud and clear. "Bulldog, we've got enemy vehicles on the horizon. They're moving slowly in this direction. Looks like a patrol or a show of force. Can't say right now."

Jessica frowned. Seeing the tunnel complex and understanding what the Altar were possibly hiding couldn't wait. "Can you estimate a time of arrival, if they keep their current pace?"

"Negative. They've appeared to stop and are doing some type of rehearsal." Hex sounded bored. "We'll keep watching."

"What about the river?" Jessica asked as she climbed a slight hill toward the main cavern entrance. Klatk and another Altar stood on their back legs waiting for her. The new Altar carried a large rucksack brimming with tools. Seven more Altar soldiers waited near the cavern entrance.

"Quiet. I've got two tank crews watching it, and Klatk left an engineer named Plec in charge here. Seems competent enough. He's mining the Raknar's legs again, as we speak."

Jessica replied, "Copy all. You know the litany, right?"

"Waiting for you, Bulldog."

Jessica laughed. Their banter was straight from old Earth tactical manuals. Leaving a set of instructions without the traditional format didn't seem fitting. "Right. I'm going into the tunnels and taking eight Altar with me. Klatk will stay here with you. If you're hit, engage defensively with suppressive fire, and I'll come back as quickly as I can. If I get hit, be prepared to divert an additional Altar platoon and two CASPers to my location. Acknowledge?"

"Good copy, Bulldog. We'll leave a light on for you."

The connection terminated, and Jessica set the communication alarm to key her headset from a beacon set she carried in her backpack. Ultra-high frequency radio signals wouldn't go through solid rock, but with a series of beacons, she'd be able to remain in contact with her defensive forces on the surface. Klatk motioned for her, and Jessica closed the distance quickly.

"Jessica, this is Bukk. His squad volunteered to take you into the tunnel complex."

Jessica's eyebrows rose a fraction. "Does that mean I can trust him and his men?" The unanswered question was whether or not she could trust Klatk and the Altar at all. Since the early attempt on her life, the colonists scurried away from her, and she'd never been alone with anyone other than Klatk, much less a squad of eight.

Bukk spoke first. "Peacemaker, you can trust this squad to protect you and fight alongside you, if required."

Jessica studied the Altar's impassive face. His mandibles, the telltale sign of anxiety or untruth, were steady. His antennae focused toward her in a measure of respect. She didn't like the prospect of it, but there was no other way she could see the tunnels. With a deep breath, she looked up at Klatk. "I don't like this, Klatk. I appreciate Bukk's words, but beyond yourself I've been avoided by your colonists, and my life was threatened by one of your soldiers. I've left specific instructions for my team. If I am killed under suspicious circumstances, they are ordered to evacuate this planet immediately."

"No harm will come to you, Jessica," Klatk said. "It is important that you see what the Consortium wishes to take away from us."

"If it's that important, it will need to be defended, Klatk."

Klatk hesitated for a split-second, Jessica was certain. "If that comes to pass, yes. We believe the enemy will fight us on the surface."

"Is there a way the Selroth could infiltrate the tunnels?"

Bukk's antennae wiggled from side-to-side. "No. The underground aquifer is not deep enough to support them and there is not enough space for them to pass through the chokepoints. There are seven they would have to traverse. We've mined the last two."

"Why not all of them?" Jessica asked.

Klatk shook her head. "Altar cannot swim, Jessica. In those locations, the water is too deep to allow my soldiers to emplace mines or any other defenses. Are you sure you want to do this now? Perhaps waiting would be best."

Jessica turned and looked over her shoulder at the horizon. The GenSha colony lay obscured by dust plumes, but nothing appeared to be moving any further north than before. "No, I need to see it now, before this gets any more out of hand, Klatk."

"There are 90 kilometers of tunnels on seven levels, Jessica. It will not be something you can see in one mission."

She bit the inside of her lower lip and barely resisted the urge to ball her hands into fists. Anger fought reason and almost won. Jessica looked at her feet for a moment, the dusty pea-sized gravel of Araf left them more of a dusty brown than black. The words formed carefully as she raised her head to look at Klatk and let the emotion drain from her face. "Klatk? It's time you level with me. What are you hiding down there?"

"It's best you see it, Jessica," Klatk said. "Bukk? Take her to Levels Two and Seven with all possible speed. I do not like the idea of our Peacemaker being below ground if the enemy attacks."

"Yes, Klatk," Bukk said and turned to his soldiers. Even in the chittering, high-pitched Altar language, she heard the familiar orders of a senior officer to his troops, and it made her smile. Her childhood as a mercenary brat pulled her across the country to more than a dozen former military bases. She really only remembered a few. She had scattered memories of little girls and boys she'd known in the home-schooled classes of the mercenary wives, and playgrounds and kickball games in the mid-summer heat and humidity of Georgia or South Carolina. She'd left all that behind when her father went into interstellar shipping instead of hauling mercs on their missions across the galaxy.

"Jessica?" Klatk's voice cut through the flash of memory.

"I'm ready."

"That's not what I was about to ask." Klatk's antennae and mandibles quivered, suggesting a chuckle. "Are you certain this is what you want?"

The question felt like a slap. "It...it goes back to you telling me the truth. What's down there?"

"Our brood is on Level Two. We are down to our last chance to have a successful cycle and populate the colony or we'll have to return home in shame."

"And what's on Level Seven?"

Klatk leaned closer, and Jessica caught the metallic, dusty scent of the Altar queen in her nose and tried not to flinch. "I do not even want to say it aloud, Jessica. I do not trust this nice, pre-fabricated colony site or its builders."

"They built this for you? The Consortium?"

Klatk nodded. A very human gesture, but on an Altar queen, it looked absurd. "Going into the tunnels will make you their enemy, most assuredly. You will see what they are after and will understand the consequences to your people and many other civilizations."

It has to be F11. The Consortium wants to overthrow the Merchant Guild's leadership, and what better way to do so than with a massive, unknown quantity of the most desired resource in the galaxy.

She took a long, deep breath. *I wish Klatk would just tell me to my face.*

Jessica nodded. "Okay then."

"Be safe. We'll see you in an hour," Klatk said.

Jessica shrugged out of her backpack's straps and removed a handful of metal tubes that were sharpened on one end like stakes. On the other end, she screwed a two-inch cube receiver and paused before locking it in. The Peacemaker's standard issue should work, but the whole idea of being deep underground sounded worse with every passing second. Her gut twisted as much as her hands did as she prepared the beacons.

Finished, she slung her backpack over her shoulders. Beacons gathered in her hands, she walked to the cavern entrance. Bukk and his squad watched her approach. Each cradled a laser rifle and carried a rucksack on their backs. Jessica knelt and pushed the first beacon into the ground.

"What's that?"

Jessica didn't look up at Bukk. "Secure radio beacon. I need to be able to hear what's going on up here, just as you do."

"We communicate the same way. Just hypersonically." Bukk said.

"I know, but that doesn't do me any good."

"We can relay for you." Bukk's voice trailed off. His eyes widened in realization. "Peacemaker, I am sorry if we've—"

Jessica stood and pointed down the cavern entrance. "Are we going, Bukk? I really don't want to waste any more time."

Bukk signaled to the point soldier, and they walked into the cavern. Jessica waited until most of them were in front of her before she followed. Bukk crunched along in the gravel behind her. Jessica tried to distract herself from the sense of danger surrounding her by counting her steps with the goal of placing another beacon 200 meters into the tunnel or at the first junction, whichever came first. Away from the entrance, small horizontal lights gave the cavern enough light for her to see. The five-meter wide tunnel was only about three meters high in the center but it felt larger. She tapped her wrist slate and opened a mapping function to scan the walls and record the data. With a swipe, she raised all of the sensors to their maximum settings. Whatever was down here needed to be verified so she could study it back at her quarters.

Jessica turned and looked past Bukk to the small half-circle of light at the surface longingly. "Hex, we're heading down now. Map function is on. You're in command. Out."

* * *

"Copy your last, Peacemaker. Good luck." Hex locked his CASPer's communications system on the remote beacon and toggled the frequency to listen. The Tri-V mounted in the center of his console separated into two smaller, rectangular feeds. The top one was a roving function from Jessica's slate that mapped and analyzed the cavern as she moved. The bottom one keyed a video feed from Demon One, and he saw Tara's face as she set her vehicle for combat operations. Watching her, he felt a bit like a voyeur and a bit like an asshole for thinking beyond Maya's loss so quickly.

What else am I supposed to do? He snapped the video link off just as Tara looked in the general direction of the camera. *Where is your head, Hex?*

Hex blinked the thought away and looked back at the horizon. The tall dust plumes were moving north. Above the Tri-Vs, a series of lights blinked from red to green. The *Victory Twelve* was overhead and available. "*Victory Twelve*, this is Hex. Do you read? Over."

<<Hex, this is *Victory Twelve*. Read you loud and clear. Am receiving supplementary data feeds from a mapping beacon. Confirm, please. Over.>>

"Roger, Lucille. Jessica set the beacon and is mapping a cavern. Lock onto the frequency profile and download as frequently as you can. Isolate the profile for search and rescue. Over."

<<Are you expecting problems, Hex? My feeds show a sizable contingent of mercenary armored vehicles proceeding north from the GenSha compound. The chances of an attack are 92 percent. Over.">>

Hex closed his eyes. "Roger, Lucille. We're prepared to meet them. Track the beacon and isolate the feed in case of emergency. Out."

"*Victory Twelve* confirms. Out."

Hex reared the CASPer up and moved toward the southern wall of the Altar Colony. Sensors engaged, Hex pushed into a clear area and jumped. Clearing the wall easily, Hex landed with practiced ease and bounded forward from the colony to the south 100 meters before his radio came to life.

"Boss, this is Demon One. What are you doing?"

"Reconnaissance," Hex said. With the colony behind him and slightly higher on the slope, his radar and velocity sensors could sweep the oncoming vehicles and check for any airborne systems. "Moving forward to max engagement range. I can see them better up close."

Tara came back immediately on a private, direct laser channel. "Negative, boss. You've got a platoon of tanks and two squads of CASPers depending on your leadership. What happens when you catch the Golden BB, huh? Get your ass back in line, or fire a drone to see what you need to see. Got it?"

Hex stood with the CASPer's arms at its sides for a moment. Sensors painted a picture of the oncoming attack. Forty vehicles, minimal infantry and no air support. Direct laser ranging put them at a little more than 9,000 meters away. Communications frequencies were quiet, too. The mercs were professionals; that he could tell by sight alone, and it steeled him to action.

"Demon One, Boss. Moving now. Count 40 inbound vehicles, negative on air support. Over."

"Roger, Boss. Get back in position. They'll be in artillery range in 30 seconds, and Altar batteries are prepared to fire, right Plec?"

A new voice came on the frequency. "Command batteries are at your disposal Demon One."

Hex turned and bounded toward the colony using his legs more than his jump jets. As he bounded to the wall and prepared to clear it, he looked down the fallen, rusting torso of the Raknar. A plume of water erupted skyward.

Mines!

"Command! Status report on the river!" Hex yelled into the radio and adjusted his final jump to stay outside the colony walls and changed direction toward the shoreline.

"Enemy contacts at the outer ring," Plec said. "Negative contacts along the Raknar hull."

Bullshit! The mines wouldn't have gone off if—

Hex slid to a stop five meters from the waterline as a second, and then a third, mine exploded. He tapped on the mapping function and saw Jessica proceeding down into the second level. The data feed continued to populate and he saw the word limestone appear and disappear as the feed ran along the raw data. A shiver ran down his spine.

Not mines! They're trying to clear an aquifer! If there was water underground, there had to be a connection between the underground source and the Choote.

A bright flash flared off to the north about a kilometer down the shore line. His visual systems overloaded, and Hex blinked in the sudden darkness of his cockpit as the displays slowly rebooted and came back to life. *Sonuvabitch!* He turned toward the explosion and saw a large cloud of dust and debris continue to rise. Anti-artillery radars in the Altar command center screamed a warning of incoming fire. His external displays came to life to see a barrage of 60 artillery rounds descend on the Altar compound. Defensive weapons engaged them in a hail of bullets and laser fire, but the damage had already been done. He'd let the defense focus solely on the GenSha's attackers and left the river, especially its hidden tributaries, virtually unguarded and undefended.

Of the initial burst, seven rounds made it through the defenses and impacted the colony. As they did, a portion of Hex's Tri-V display winked out. He looked down and froze. The mapping function, and the relay beacon to Jessica, were gone.

* * *

In the cavernous mines, transitioning from Level One to Level Two reminded Jessica of an elementary school field trip to a fire station. As a kid, the highlight was the fireman's pole to get from the sleeping quarters to the garage in the least amount of time possible. On Earth, for humans, it made sense. On Araf, the Altar built their vertical columns and passageways with the electrical conduits hanging down the center to give them the maximum range and clearance to climb up the available sides. Wrapping her arms and legs around a wire system coursing with gods-knew-how many watts of power stolen from the Raknar didn't seem like the best idea. Of course, neither did having to jump a full meter and a half to get to the conduit in the first place.

"You're sure this is safe for me?" Jessica asked Bukk. "Touching it isn't going to kill me right here before we get anywhere with this mission?"

"Is that what you want?"

Jessica shook her head. "Of course not. I just—"

"You want to know you are safe. I understand that a third-level soldier tried to kill you, and that our queen enacted immediate punishment on the guilty party. Do you really think anyone else wants to kill you?" Bukk nodded toward the vertical tunnel, and his soldiers easily shot down the walls to the next level 20 meters below. "Is that why you walk in the rear, so you can see us and plot our deaths in your defense?"

Jessica shook her head. "No, I...you have to see it from my perspective, Bukk."

"I have, Peacemaker. Dishonesty is not something easy to see. You are right to feel insecure because of what happened on the surface. Klatk put my squad in charge of this expedition as a show of respect to you. Your security is paramount, even though you may not believe that."

"There's a human saying, Bukk. Actions speak louder than words. Do you understand?"

Bukk swiveled his head toward her and said nothing for a moment. "I see your point, Peacemaker. Your own actions are key here, too. I've promised your safety and you have no other way down than the conduit in front of you. Will you trust me?"

It's not like I have much of a choice.

Jessica tightened her backpack's straps and attached a small strap between them across her chest. The conduit looked to be the size of a large wound rope, the kind she'd climbed during her VOWs years before. The 20-meter deep tunnel was a full three meters wide and the conduit hung in the exact center. There was no other way to get there than to jump. She shuffled back two steps to gain clearance, took a long, powerful stride forward and leapt into the tunnel. Her hands found the flexible conduit and to her instant relief there was no shock of electricity. To her surprise, the conduit's covering was as slick as a greasy pan, and she slid uncontrollably down until she was able to wrap her legs around it and use friction to slow her down.

She looked up at Bukk and saw his mandibles approximating a chuckle. Under control, she slid down the conduit to the second level.

The air seemed heavier and smelled moist. In several places, water ran down the limestone walls. The tunnel itself was no different than the one above in design, but the dimly lit chambers above paled in comparison to the warm, brightly lit tunnel around her. Against one side of the tunnel rested hexagonal-shaped chambers with 12 internal compartments the size of shoe boxes. The chambers were a meter high and roughly a meter in length as they lay across the tunnel floor. Each unit hummed with electricity and warmed the air in the immediate vicinity.

Jessica put her hand on the first unit and felt the strong vibration. Bukk appeared over her shoulder, and she turned. "How many are down here, Bukk?"

"The brood is over 7,000 in number, Peacemaker."

She pulled her hand away from the incubation unit and looked down the tunnel. "You have a tenth of that on the surface. The number doesn't make sense."

Bukk looked at her for a moment. "We expect to lose 50 percent before the end of the cycle due to complications from power. We will lose another 20 percent to environmental adaptation. We were promised a very different planet, Peacemaker."

"I understand that, Bukk. Why move the brood down here? Your main power sources are on the surface. The solar panels and wind generators. Down here you have to move the power and that affects the wattage available, right?"

Bukk's antennae nodded. "Solar and wind generators are unreliable in this atmosphere. Any significant disruption to the available power current kills our brood. Running power from the Raknar's fuel cells augments what we struggle to pull in from the atmosphere."

"Why not land your ships and slave the power from them?" Jessica's voice trailed off. The look on Bukk's face said it all. "You don't have ships in orbit or parked some place?"

"No. Once placed, an Altar colony either succeeds or fails. In the event of failure, a ship is dispatched to collect the remaining colonists and equipment. The colony queen is executed, and the colonists return home as fourth-class citizens. We would rather die than fail."

Jessica understood. Klatk did not want to fight, but there was no alternative. Diplomacy was not going to work, and with mercenary units involved on both opposing sides, fighting was a last resort as well as an acceptable way to fail—through death. Jessica's stomach churned.

"You're fighting as a way to respectfully fail."

Bukk's pincers quivered. "We fight to protect our brood, Peacemaker."

"But, you sound like you're expecting to fail."

"We do not expect to fail." Bukk said. "We expect—"

The tunnel shook, and a shower of dust fell from the ceiling. Bukk's antennae whipped from side-to-side. Jessica looked at her slate and saw the transmission indicator blink red. "I've lost comms with the surface."

Bukk looked at her. "We are under attack. The Selroth have attempted to gain access to Level Six via an aquifer. They were not successful, but Level Six is flooding. I will not be able to take you there until the pumps engage."

Jessica grabbed her slate and tried to connect to Hex's data feed. There was nothing. "We need to go."

Bukk chittered at his soldiers, and they raced back to the vertical tunnel and disappeared upward. "Come," he said. There was no way she could climb the conduit given the slick coating. She was about to protest when Bukk slung his weapon across his chest and motioned to his back. "Grab on, Peacemaker. I will carry you to the upper level."

For a brief second, her mind thought of ants on Earth carrying more than their body weight, and she decided to trust him, again. Bukk stood against the circular wall and she climbed onto his back. He dug into the wall and immediately slipped, jostling her against his hard back. He dug another claw into the rock and looked over his shoulder. "Would you trust me, Peacemaker?"

Jessica snorted. "It's not like I have much choice. You could easily leave me down here or worse."

"Then we would have no choice but to fail, Peacemaker." Bukk climbed the tunnel in the space of a few heartbeats, safely depositing Jessica at Level One. Bukk's soldiers stood at the ready, rifles raised, pointing toward the cavern entrance. A solitary figure walked toward them in deep silhouette. Bukk stepped forward, in front of Jessica as if to shield her, and challenged, "Who goes there?"

"Mediator Taemin," the figure said. "I understand you were unable to proceed beyond the second level?"

Bukk replied. "We are under attack. The Peacemaker wished to return to the surface to take command of the defense."

"Oh, did she?" Taemin stepped close enough for Jessica to see the sarcastic smile on his elongated face. "I'm sorry, soldier, but the Peacemaker cannot command the defense. She and her...deputies are obligated to take all orders from your commanding officer. Nor can the Peacemaker or her deputies legally suggest a course of action to your commander. They are simply a token to be employed in the event of a military attack."

Bukk looked at her, and she sensed the question before it came out. "Technically, he is correct, Bukk. A Peacemaker cannot be in command of an operation when legal mercenary contracts have been engaged."

Taemin grinned. "I see you did at least read the Union laws you try to step over, Peacemaker."

You prick.

Jessica took a breath and composed herself before she turned to Bukk. "However, in the unique case of a contracted mercenary force opposing a civilian government operating in a peaceful setting, the use of force by one side constitutes a violation of the very same Union law I described."

"Only if the planet is a Union world, Peacemaker. Araf is the property of the Dream World Consortium and is not subject to that law. That is likely why the mercenary forces have attacked." Taemin grinned. The motherfucker actually grinned at her.

"Bukk? Does Klatk report to your homeworld on a frequent basis? Do you operate at their discretion?"

"Yes." His antennae twitched in a tic she knew to be confusion and interest.

"Your colony hardware, the walls and such on the surface, was provided by the Consortium was it not?"

"Yes, except for...except for the command center, Peacemaker."

Jessica smiled and turned to Taemin. "The command center is the property of the Altar government, and Klatk acts as an entity of that government in contract with the Consortium and, therefore, is not subject to them."

"That's a very naive interpretation of the law, Peacemaker."

Jessica looked at Taemin and started walking toward him. At his shoulder, as she passed him and headed to the surface, she said, "A loose interpretation is all I need to wage the defense, Taemin. I do not need your permission to defend this colony from a mercenary force, nor do I need your permission to defend them from the Consortium, the GenSha, the Selroth, or anybody else. If you cannot negotiate a peaceful solution, with my assistance, there is no other way than war."

"Only if you have a death wish, Peacemaker."

Jessica turned to him and shook her head. "These people are prepared to fight, Taemin. As long as they wish to defend what is theirs, I will be at their side and will exploit every advantage we find."

Taemin's mouth opened but nothing came out for a moment. "You intend to use the Raknar."

"Whatever it takes to win."

* * * * *

Chapter Fifteen

Hex vaulted his CASPer down the shoreline and heard Plec call, "Demon One, the waterfront is secure. Deploying depth charges now."

Tara was busy, though. Each of the tanks facing the assaulting GenSha mercenaries maintained a steady rate of fire at maximum distance. With the Selroth meeting significant resistance, the GenSha and their mercenaries inexplicably stayed back from the Altar colony. Given the distraction from the river, it would have been a perfect time for the GenSha to attack. Instead, their artillery harassed the colony's defenses, but did little damage. Any vehicles that treaded deeper into the Altar fields of fire instantly became a target. The result was a long-distance standoff. Hex used the virtual lull to bolster the river defenses and push the Selroth back.

"Plec, Hex. I'm moving your way."

"Acknowledged."

Hex jumped again, the jump jets flawlessly carrying the CASPer down the slope to the shoreline. He turned and ran north. Plec and two Altar soldiers worked at a cart assembling and tossing small depth charges into the river, downstream from the Raknar. The intent was clear. Any survivors of the initial blasts would be destroyed where they hid. Plec hefted a charge into the river, but only maybe 20 meters into the water and it gave Hex an idea.

At the cart, Hex skidded the CASPer to a stop and turned on the external communication system. "Plec, give me six charges."

The Altar worked quickly and loaded three of the depth charges into each of the CASPer's hands. Loaded down, Hex stepped away from them and bounded toward the river as he engaged his external sensor arrays. The sonargraphic image of the shoreline appeared in holographic form and showed that he could bound into the water a good 50 meters and still find footing for the CASPer to land and jump again. Hex leapt into the water and leapt again. At the top of the second jump, he threw the left-hand bombs in a line down stream. As the CASPer slammed into the water and found the bottom again, Hex changed the charges in his right hand to his left, pivoted the CASPer and jumped farther downstream. For a second time, he threw the charges from the top of his jump, watched them arc into the water and erupt in thundering columns of water. As the CASPer descended, he drew the rail gun and watched for a target of opportunity in the river below

"Boss, Demon One."

"SITREP, Tara," Hex said as the CASPer landed on the shore.

She came back a second later. "GenSha forces stalled at maximum effective range. They're starting to withdraw by forward sensor readings, but we haven't seen a visual confirmation."

"Are you in contact with Jessica?"

"Negative. Klatk says they are fine and moving to the surface."

Hex sighed. At least she was still alive. "Got it. Moving to your location now. Maintain 100 percent security until we have confirmation that both the Selroth and GenSha forces have withdrawn."

"Copy, Boss. Demon One, out."

Hex walked down the shoreline to where Plec waited. The Altar cocked his head to one side. "Impressive, Hex."

"Thanks. What are you making those charges with?"

"Whatever we can find," Plec said. "Most of these are not very powerful and some work better than others."

Hex chuckled. "Let's get you hooked up with our ammunition and see what we can do to make them better. We're going to need every advantage we can cook up."

A burst of static erupted in his ears and disappeared as the dampeners kicked in. "Hex, you read me?" Jessica's voice was calm and sure, like always.

"Copy, Bulldog. Looks like you missed the party," he said. "Probing attack, multiple prongs. They're testing our defenses and looking for weaknesses, but their attack was disorganized and clumsy."

"Did they find any weaknesses?" Jessica asked.

"We can tighten up a few things, sure. I'm most worried about the river," Hex said. "Did you get what you wanted?"

"Almost, Hex. Bring your armor commander and your squad leaders to the command center. We need to talk about how we're going to skin the cat."

"Copy, Bulldog. Moving now. Break." Hex released the transmit button and pressed it again. "Demon One, Angel Two, and Angel Seven—get to the command center. Maintain security and surveillance."

"Demon One, roger."

"Angel Two, roger."

"Angel Seven, roger."

Hex turned and headed back in the direction of the colony walls. Up the slope, he watched Angel Seven rocket into the sky, spin on one axis, and descend effortlessly to a thin wall before executing a similar jump in the direction of the command center. All in all, Hex knew that Hak-Chet's attempt to help Jessica could have been an entirely different story. Tara and her combat-proven tank platoon were a no brainer. The fresh cadets in the CASPers were a different variable. He didn't have to flip over to their internal frequencies to know they were excited and believed themselves to be combat veterans. Their exuberance would fade the next time the GenSha and the Selroth attacked. A probe was a probe. The GenSha's mercenaries barely entered the effective range of the Altar's weaponry. For all they knew, the Selroth mercenaries hadn't even deployed.

Wherever they are.

An icy chill ran down his back. "Bulldog, Hex, on private when you can. Over."

He kept bounding back to the colony and decided to go farther up the slope. A probing attack either tested a defense, or emplaced an offensive unit for a future strike by way of diversion. The hard, exposed rock faces of the low hills made scrambling in a CASPer nearly impossible, but doing so saved fuel. As he moved up the slope toward a small escarpment, Hex felt the cooling system kick in to lower his rising body temperature. Sweat dotted his forehead as he reached the escarpment.

"Hex? What are you doing up there?" Jessica called. There was no doubt she could see him trying to get to the top of the ragged ridgeline.

Hex flexed his knees and primed the jump jets for a maximum leap to the top of the three-meter tall escarpment. "Checking our six, Jess. The Selroth mercs didn't probe us."

"Bukk walked me through what the Altar reported. They think they won."

Hex laughed and went ahead with the jump. A gust of wind along the ridge wobbled his CASPer mid-flight, but he compensated easily and landed on a house-sized boulder with a flat enough surface for him to stand. Across the river from the Altar colony, to the south and west, a series of ragged ridge lines rose and fell in craggy poses like dolphins chasing the bow of a ship. Each ridgeline worked progressively higher, with snow-capped mountains dominating the distant horizon. Below, the immediate valley looked arid and empty. Behind him, there was a series of significant rolling hills. Among the scrub brush around the hills, he saw nothing moving. There were too many dead spaces where the mercenaries could be hiding.

The CASPer's onboard sensors were fully engaged, and Hex let them run for a full 30 seconds before replying. "The GenSha and their mercs never passed more than a few hundred meters into the maximum effective range of the Altar rocket defenses. When they did, the Altar fired at them with mixed results. Tara's tanks fired a few rounds and hit their targets. None of the CASPers engaged the GenSha. The Selroth attack failed to get into the underground tunnels, but I'm worried about the damage. If they were simply trying to widen the hole for a future attack, we're going to be fighting on two fronts."

"Roger. What do you see up there?"

"Nothing." Hex turned off the sensor suite. "Given the terrain, if I were their mercs, I wouldn't be in this valley either. There's at least a half dozen others they could use for cover and concealment back here. We really need air support, Bulldog."

"What about *Victory Twelve*? Have Lucille get some imagery for us."

Hex wanted to slap himself. "I didn't think of that."

"Call her up, Hex," Jessica chuckled. "She's your ship."

For the time being, Hex finished for her silently. He smiled. "Roger, Bulldog. As soon as she's in range."

Jessica replied, "We may not have time, Hex. Record it and auto-transmit. We're going to break into the Raknar."

He spun the CASPer and engaged the long-range cameras. Jess and a party of CASPers stood by the fallen Raknar's helm. "Roger, Bulldog. Moving." Hex stabbed the record transmission button. "*Victory Twelve*, this is Boss. Mark position and gather imagery in all spectrums centered on the Altar colony for 30 kilometers. Add multispectral filters and correlate the data. Direct transmit when complete. Boss, out."

Hex scanned down the slope below and identified a landing point. With barely a blink of hesitation, he jumped into the air. Mid-flight, he looked down at the picture of him and Maya mounted in the cockpit and smiled. For the first time in weeks, being alive felt better than the alternative.

* * *

"What was that?" Kenos seethed into the radio connection. "You promised an attack, not a tentative distraction!"

The Sidar hissed. "You promised us a defenseless colony. The Altar have significant artillery, and your Peacemaker's deputized forces seem quite formidable."

"You have numerical superiority and never bothered to deploy your forces!"

"The Altar have a significant terrain advantage." The Veetanho mercenary chimed in. "We understand their layouts now. The Selroth and GenSha remain unconvinced and do not wish to deploy forces in direct combat."

Kenos stroked his jaw. Their apprehension was not unexpected. Having a dedicated and well-funded mercenary force to fight their wars for them made the governments complacent. Unlike the mercenaries, the governments could be manipulated. Mercenaries needed to be paid. "When can I count on your attack?"

"When the time is right," the Sidar hissed. "Reconnaissance is necessary."

"The GenSha have an airstrike package standing by. They want an assurance the Consortium will replace the vehicles lost." He heard the sneer in the Veetanho's voice.

Kenos nodded to himself. Of course they would want their assets replaced. "Let the GenSha know their costs will be covered upon the successful completion of this operation and the agreement they signed." Anger crept into his words, and he closed his eyes for a moment to compose himself. "Ensure the GenSha understand their role."

"Noted, Administrator."

"You agreed not to use my—"

"And you agreed to give us the autonomy to act in our best interests instead of those of our initial contractors. That your contract supersedes theirs strips you of your privacy, Administrator. A keen eye would notice. Perhaps they already have?"

Kenos sat forward. "What do you mean?"

The Sidar hissed, "Suppose the Peacemaker Guild is aware of your plan and they've sent a human to be a sacrificial lamb? Maybe they believe she will be forced to act in a non-Peacemaker way to solve the conflict. You would be defeated, and they could write her failure off as a typical human response. The Guild would feel satisfied about keeping humanity at the fringe. The less they can infiltrate the Galaxy the better."

Kenos laughed. "You're assuming the Peacemakers would want a public relations nightmare. They do not want their precious reputations tarnished, Leeto. Of that, I'm certain. What matters is that the Altar are defeated, and we are in a position to best influence further negotiations."

"The GenSha and the Selroth will not be happy with your actions, Administrator."

Kenos shrugged. The very human gesture looked odd on his Cochkala frame. He caught himself and felt soiled by approximating humans. "I do not care. Have the GenSha launch their airstrike."

"Reconnaissance."

Kenos growled, "No. Strike the Raknar. Render it inoperable, and the Altar will fold. Then, we deal with the Peacemaker and her benefactors."

* * *

Jessica watched Hex run down the shoreline in his CASPer, the late afternoon sun glinting on the mecha's dark, tactical-gray skin. Deep Oogar claw marks remained, and she wondered how long they would stay or if the scars on his heart would fade first. As the CASPer's cockpit opened, she looked at his face and decided he looked better than before. A brief shot of operations cleared the minds of most mercenaries in an instant—they craved the action to make them human. Hex wanted a different life with Maya and with the idea torn asunder, he returned to the most basic rules of mercenary life. Action meant life. Inaction bred demons.

He met her eyes. "Hey Bulldog? I show *Tchrt One* descending from orbit to our position. I'm still waiting for Lucille's information."

She nodded. Kenos would, of course, want to survey the damage firsthand. Taemin seemed all too interested in keeping the administrator abreast of every development in the colony. Kenos would likely attempt to convince Klatk and her colony to fold as he ascertained the situation on the ground. Knowledge was power, after all. "Come on, Hex. We need to talk Phase Two."

He shook his head. There had been no such phase, and he knew it. But making it up as they went was only going to go so far.

Three other humans approached from the colony. Two were women, one with longish blonde hair, and the other with short, black hair. Off to one side, a lanky kid with a buzzcut ambled with a bouncing stride that reminded her of a classmate from high school. She shook off the thought as they approached, and she locked eyes with the blonde woman, first searching and then confirming she'd seen the woman before.

"You're a long way from the bar," Jessica said. She stepped forward and extended a hand. "Jessica Francis."

"Tara Mason." The blonde's hand was warm and dry. "I'm in command of four tanks from Death On Tracks."

Jessica curled a lip under. "You guys were pretty torn up at Essex Five, if memory serves me right."

Tara's eyes grew distant. "I'd rather not talk about it."

"Deal," Jessica said. The relief in the tank commander's eyes was palpable. Bad contracts and shitty combat planning was the death knell of too many human mercenary units. There were some damned good ones, even outside the Four Horsemen, but too many found an early and unfortunate end. Most died as a result of poor leadership and cowardice in the face of the enemy—like Death On Tracks displayed.

Does Hex know?

Jessica turned to the young man and wondered if he was old enough to operate a CASPer. "Jessica Francis."

"Neal Kirkland." The young man's handshake reminded her of shopping for fish in Seattle. He looked at her and immediately beyond her. From his accent, she figured Edinburgh, which matched his pale complexion. The smile that crossed his face looked like that of a child.

She turned to the young Japanese woman who shook her hand tightly. "Kei Howl. It's nice to meet you, Peacemaker."

Behind the three mercenaries, Hex climbed down from his CASPer and jumped about a meter to the dusty ground. He walked up to them, and his eyes looked clearer than in the Luna hangar 10 days before. Jessica closed the distance and hugged him without a word. They separated after a few seconds.

"You've met my team?"

She smiled. "Yeah."

Hex looked at them. "Jessica, I mean Peacemaker Francis, and I go way back."

Jessica nodded. "We do, but we don't have time for embarrassing stories. Even the good ones."

Hex chuckled and crossed his arms. *Gods, he looks like his father.*

She shook off the thought. "Okay. You guys set a good defense earlier, and that's a great start. But, when those bastards come, and I mean both colonies and their mercenaries, what you set won't work. We have to change that. As we do, I'm going into the Raknar. We need every advantage we can leverage."

Tara squinted. "Into the Raknar? What are you expecting to find?"

"I honestly don't know, but that Raknar has power available," Jessica said. "If there's a way to use it without taking anything away from the Altar breeding facility below the surface..."

"Jess? There's no way to use a Raknar," Hex said. "Even if you get it powered up, you don't know how to fight with it unless they taught you in Peacemaker school."

Jessica snorted. "They didn't teach that, Hex. I'm trying to find an advantage, that's all."

"Just shore up our defenses and work the enemy into our killzones," Kirkland said. "That's what they taught us at school. We have better terrain. All we have to do is get them where we want them."

"We do not have the combat power," Kei said. "Channelizing the enemy isn't enough defense. We need dedicated artillery."

Jessica raised her hands. "Listen, people. We don't have time to debate this. Hex? You and Tara set the defense and adjust the Altar stand-off weapons. Keep pinging Lucille for the reconnaissance data we talked about. You two," she pointed to the young CASPer pilots, "I want you to place listening posts on the north and south sides of the colony as soon as night falls. That's when we'll try to get into the Raknar. Set your security at 50 percent and make sure people get chow. We'll—" A flicker of eye movement from Kei meant someone was behind her and approaching rapidly, and surprisingly without a sound.

"Giving orders, Peacemaker?" Taemin's voice came up from behind her.

Not now.

"Offering my consultancy," Jessica said and spun to face him.

"I would hate to think you've asserted any type of command over these forces in direct violation of your oath," Taemin said. "Perhaps we can discuss a replacement when Administrato Kenos arrives? I'm certain your Guild could have another Peacemaker on the ground within a few days at most."

Hex spoke, "Alright, just like I briefed. Let's make it happen." The four humans moved away from her and Taemin. As much as she thought Hex nailed the delivery, being alone with the alien moderator, whom she wasn't exactly sure of in the first place, left her quite unsettled.

"I don't know what you're trying to do, Peacemaker," Taemin sneered, "But, you have failed to do anything to engage the opposing sides in direct dialogue. You promised an audience period after your injunction period ended. Given that the GenSha and the Selroth seem to have dissolved such an arrangement it would be prudent for you to meet them face-to-face, don't you think?"

"Is that why Kenos is on his way here?" Jessica asked and immediately realized it was true. "You've set up a meeting with them, haven't you?"

Taemin smiled, and it turned her stomach. "The Administrator attempted to contact you. His call for negotiations ended the previous incursion. You could have done the same thing if you'd not been chasing useless information underground."

Jessica shook her head. "I received no such transmission, Taemin."

"As I said, Peacemaker, you were underground." The Caroon's tone dripped condescension.

Her throat tightened as she raised a finger to point at his face, a clear affront to the Caroon. "You failed to tell me that when we made contact in the main tunnel. What else are you failing to tell me, Taemin?"

"I assumed you heard the transmission, Peacemaker. My apologies."

You lying sack of shit.

Breathe. Jessica swept hair away from her face with a hand and tried to calm down and maintain her bearing. "Apology accepted, Taemin. We need to discuss what I did see down there. The Altar use the Raknar's power source to stabilize their brood's incubation system. Any attack by the GenSha or the Selroth against the Raknar constitutes a war crime. Children of any species shall not be harmed under any circumstance."

Taemin paused for a moment. "You're saying there is a brood below the surface?"

"That's exactly what I'm saying."

"This certainly changes the situation." The Caroon's thin eyebrows rose comically in surprise.

Jessica felt a surge of power. "You're damned right it does!"

"The Altar are in breach of contract, Peacemaker," Taemin said. "Under the articles of the Dream World Consortium's charter, recolonization efforts, including mass breeding operations, must be declared to the Consortium and approved by unanimous action of the Board of Directors. The clause is under Article Three. Do you not remember it? The only exemption would be for operations intent on providing less than 50 children per breeding cycle. Just how many are down there?"

Jessica frowned. "More than that."

"I see," Taemin said. "Well, as the mediator, it is likely that Kenos will assign me to account for the brood before taking action. It appears that your investigation here is over, Peacemaker. The Consortium can lawfully contract with a third party to remove the Altar from their colony location. Well done."

"And if the Altar don't move, Taemin? Then what?" Jessica's stomach flopped before the mediator could answer. Contracts were the cornerstone of the Union and breaching them in any form tended to end badly.

Taemin blinked. "Then under the auspices of the agreement they can be forcibly moved or exterminated, Peacemaker. Either way, your work here is finished."

* * * *

Chapter Sixteen

Taemin walked away, and Jessica stared at the Caroon's back with a mixture of emotions threatening to burst the dam of her Peacemaker bearing. On one hand, there was fresh rage that he would dare to end her mission. On the other hand, there was an excruciating anger with herself for failing to recognize the importance of a brood to the contract. *How could I miss that?*

"Oh, and Peacemaker?" Taemin turned around and tapped his wrist slate. "Kenos has diverted to D'Nart spaceport. He has requested you go there immediately so you can brief the Peacemaker Guild on your...unpreparedness. He'll send a transport within an hour."

Jessica squinted. "He's not coming here?"

"He'll have to meet with the Board of Directors, of course. This has become a very delicate situation. I suspect he'll send a stand down order for your deputized forces immediately upon arrival. Once you and your forces have been removed from the colony, the Consortium can deal with the problem regarding their contracted agreements."

Jessica nodded, but her brain clicked into gear. Having her and her deputies leave the colony meant the Consortium would act, and act quickly. She glanced at Klatk and saw the colony queen intently watching her. Hex's lower jaw clenched, and the young officers did nothing. Tara wiped away a strand of hair and stared at her. The blonde's eyes narrowed slightly. Jessica turned back to Klatk and curled under one side of her mouth before she looked at Taemin.

In the flash of a millisecond, she thought of her father and his study of the Vietnam War. Everyone else in school called it a conflict, but her father vehemently called it a war. Her great-great-grandfather, John, had been a helicopter pilot. The crazy bastard survived a tour flying Huey gunships. The average life expectancy of a Huey pilot in combat was something like a minute or less, and he'd survived a full year. Twice. Grandpa John managed not to fall into the trap of using drugs or alcohol to deal with his memories, save for the occasional jar of homemade amaretto. He'd lived to be 104 years old, he didn't take any shit from anyone, and he was one hell of an historian.

Jessica's mind flashed to one of Grandpa John's Vietnam stories. The Ia Drang valley was the first meeting between American and North Vietnamese forces, and it was a bloodbath. Throughout the battle, the American higher headquarters kept asking the ground force commander, a Lieutenant Colonel named Moore, to leave his troops and return to brief their headquarters. Moore repeatedly refused and was able to withdraw his men before they were overrun. There was no way in hell she was leaving until the Guild came and made her.

"Fine, Taemin. We'll need at least two hours to collect our gear and load it aboard the *Victory Twelve*. Once that happens, I'll dispatch my deputies home and report to D'Nart for the required meetings," Jessica said. "And I'll plan to make a full report to the Guild as well."

"Of course you will, Peacemaker." Taemin smiled, bowed his head, and continued walking toward the colony walls. "Klatk will provide me a guide immediately."

Klatk looked at Jessica, her mandibles almost imperceptibly twitching. "Yes. Ten minutes."

Watching him, Jessica's mind stayed with Grandpa John for a moment longer. Once, he'd even lied to the authorities, or so her father told her, to protect his grandson from a bullshit traffic citation. Said he'd been driving when his grandson had taken the car out to help a friend gather a buck during deer season. Her grandfather had been fourteen, but he'd been driving farm trucks for years. The cops knew his father wasn't the one behind the wheel, but Grandpa John had been adamant, and he hadn't wavered. Disinformation, he'd chuckled, could be honorable in the right hands.

He'd also never sworn the Peacemaker oath, but he would have been prepared to break it, too.

As Taemin turned into the walls and disappeared, she turned to Hex.

"Quaker cannon."

Hex grinned. "Will take us more than two hours."

"Doesn't matter." Jessica saw questions all over the two young CASPer pilots' faces and a bemused smile on Tara's. She looked at the pilots. "Deception. It's a term that predates World War One. George Patton used it a lot when he was placed in command of a fake Army north of London. They used inflatables, deception, and outright lies to get the Germans so spun up about him that they very nearly left Normandy undefended. Kenos wants us to leave and that's what we're going to make him think. I have no intention of leaving Klatk's colony undefended, and you guys aren't going anywhere."

Tara nodded. "We can hide the CASPers easily. What about the tanks?"

"Up to you. Just get them out of sight."

Kei spoke up. "There are cameras everywhere. We have to assume Kenos is watching all of them."

Jessica nodded. "I have an idea about that. When is the *Victory Twelve* overhead, Hex?"

The young man looked at the slate on his wrist. "Three minutes, ten seconds."

Jessica felt the plan come together in her mind. "Kei and Neal, make a show of unloading the CASPers like you're preparing them for shipment. Stage crew duffels and packaged supplies on the shoreline down there. Don't move everything, just let the cameras track you."

"That copy and replay a video thing never works," Kirkland said. "Or it does only in the vids." He stuffed his hands into his pockets and looked away like a scolded puppy.

"Not doing that, Kirkland," Jessica said. "Kenos and his cameras are designed for complete surveillance and likely compensate for each other. We'll have to take down the entire system. We do have a secret weapon, and if we do it right, we'll kill two birds with one stone."

Hex scratched his chin. "You're going to bring her down here?"

"She can do more than fly a ship, Hex. That's why I confiscated her from Marc in the first place. We'll need the reconnaissance imagery, too. I think those bastards are out there waiting for the signal to attack," Jessica said. She looked up at Klatk. "You know what's going on, right? The minute we leave, two colonies and their mercenary forces would knock down your walls and kill as many of your...citizens as they could. They don't want you here, Klatk. Whatever you've found on Level Seven, and whatever they think is aboard that Raknar, have Kenos, his Consortium, and who knows who else interested. The only thing keeping them from it is you. They want you gone, and they want me gone, too. That's not going to happen."

"After we hide the tanks and the CASPers, what do we do?" Tara asked.

"Prepare to defend the colony against an all-out assault," Jessica said. "While you're doing that, I'm going to buy us as much time as I can. As soon as the sun goes down, though, we're going into that Raknar."

"And your negotiator?" Klatk asked. "Should he receive a scenic tour?"

Jessica grinned. "That's the second bird. When we take out the camera system, the explosion will be so big it will shake the tunnels enough to scare the hell of out him. Don't hurt him, Klatk. But were he to get lost for a few hours…that would be just fine. I'm sure your soldiers know those tunnels better than anyone else. We can stage a rescue after an hour or two. We just need enough time to disrupt the cameras and get into the Raknar."

"He's a Caroon and built for life underground, except in certain scenarios. We will create those and take care of him for you, Peacemaker. Level Three can be quite dark and narrow. We'll ensure he's not hurt and out of your way," Klatk said, "like you're preparing to take care of us."

Jessica glanced at her slate. "Let's go. *Victory Twelve* is coming up over the horizon now. Kenos wants a show. Let's give him one."

Hex chuckled. "One hell of a Quaker cannon coming right up."

Jessica looked at Tara. "Your tanks are direct laser comm-equipped, right?"

"Four channels at one kilowatt," Tara said. "What do you have in mind?"

Jessica chuckled. "Insurance in case we're being jammed, mainly."

Hex nodded. "Multiple port download—makes it faster to get Lucille down here into the command system. That's what you're intending, right, Bulldog?"

"You got it," Jessica said. She glanced at Tara, but the blonde was already moving away at a fast walk. "Hex, I'll need your CASPer in that loop, too. I want you to have an interface with her."

"She said the same thing on the way here." Hex shook his head. "I told her to stay on the ship. I didn't think she could help us down here. I know, I know, you always talked about capabilities and the chance to use them. I just didn't think of it that way."

Jessica checked her watch. One minute and forty seconds. "Go, Hex. You two," she pointed to Howl and Kirkland, "get your squads moving toward the waterfront as though we're planning to jump away. Carry some supplies and establish a debark point. Take it nice and easy, but make it look urgent. I want Kenos to think we're going to leave him an opening."

Howl smiled. "You're going to shut it in his face."

"No," Jessica said. "We are. And we're going to give them something they never expected once we get in that Raknar."

Kirkland exhaled loudly through his nose. "You can't get that thing working, Peacemaker. Only a handful are powered up, and no one has ever started one much less fought in one."

"We don't need to have it stand up and fight, Kirkland. We need one little advantage, that's all. I believe there's a defense system on that Raknar we can engage to help protect the colony."

"They teach you that as a Peacemaker?" Kirkland asked. "How to understand the Dusman and their mechs?"

Jessica shook her head and stuffed her hands into her pockets. The familiar shape of the chipset found its way into the palm of her right hand, and she closed gently around it. "My dad. He hauled out the first teams for recoveries on Jabnah and a few other worlds before the Union discouraged messing with Raknars. The Besquith know a lot about them, and the Canavar, too. Thanks to them, I've picked around the insides of a few other Raknars. I should be able to see what systems might work. From there, Lucille will have to interface with it. It's risky, but I don't see that we have a choice."

* * *

Kenos settled into his chair at the D'Nart spaceport and composed himself. Recording a message was never an easy thing to do. Lying on live camera came easier, for what it was worth, and the Peacemaker Guild would order Jessica Francis to stand down. Humans were so predictable, really. The Altar were stubborn to a fault and would not leave their brood mid-cycle; that was a given. Francis would use all her forces to defend them. Maybe it was a female thing, he mused, that she would direct her forces to protect an unprotectable lot like the Altar in the first place. He'd known they would be her weak point from the minute she'd arrived. So far, her moves were expected and easily countered.

Kenos took a breath, centered himself on the Tri-V camera, and pressed the record control on the screen. "Honored Rsach. I am pained to send this message, but I feel you must know the situation on Araf with Peacemaker Francis has become unsettled. On arrival, Peacemaker Francis took up a forward position with the Altar. Unbeknownst to the Dream World Consortium, the GenSha and Selroth colonies appeared to have contracted mercenary forces. I will need confirmation of this from your Guild. Shortly after our arrival, a ship appeared in orbit and contacted the Peacemaker directly. She immediately, and quite illegally, deputized the forces aboard the ship and placed them in her command structure. She turned her efforts away from peaceful negotiation and attacked GenSha and Selroth parties in neutral grounds established by the Consortium's contracts. However, there is something more egregious that requires your immediate interaction with the Peacemaker."

Kenos cleared his throat, really getting into it. He forced himself not to smile. "I'm afraid Peacemaker Francis has drawn a proverbial line in the sand. I am concerned that she has chosen sides. Her embedded position with the Altar remains unchanged, and I fear that she will not order her forces to leave. Embedding with the Altar, who are clearly the defendants in the eyes of the Dream World Consortium and are guilty of a dozen infractions against their contract, is tantamount to a declaration of her intent. The GenSha and the Selroth have yet to be heard from in her negotiations." He stressed the last word with a hiss. "She has been on the planet for more than six hours and has already threatened the GenSha and their forces acting within their territorial space, and I have it on reasonable authority that the Altar, perhaps with this Peacemaker's permission, mined the free waters of the Choote River in another clear violation. Her actions are unconscionable."

Kenos took a breath and closed his eyes to enunciate carefully. "Therefore, I request an official investigation from the Peacemaker

Guild into the conduct of Candidate Jessica Francis on the planet Araf. Her inability to defuse the situation here has lead three peaceful colonies to the brink of all-out war. If she is allowed to continue, the Dream World project will suffer incalculable losses and open the Peacemaker Guild to an official complaint. I await your response and remain your consulted and honored servant, Kenos."

He snapped off the monitor with a clawed finger and sat back against the couch. The lies were good and effortless, like those of a lifelong diplomat or politician. The Guild would answer, of that he was certain. What mattered was how quickly they received the message. He classified it as urgent, and engaged the diplomatic protocols within the Aethernet, so the message left his planet and flew at the speed of light to the stargate for immediate transmission with the next departing ship. However the protocols functioned, undoubtedly through the inner workings and secret mechanisms of the Cartography Guild, the message would get to the Guildmaster faster than any normal message. It would make a good fallback. As it was, her mediator was preparing to go into the tunnel system, and her CASPers appeared to be loading out for an orbital transport. If all went as planned, the Peacemaker would be dead before her Guild received the message. The dead told no tales.

Kenos flipped the surface camera system to follow Taemin into the main mine entrance. As the Caroon disappeared into the wide hole, Kenos smiled. With any luck, there'd be a cave-in or some other unfortunate incident. As much fun as it would be, he wanted to ensure the Peacemaker was serious about her agreement to a diplomatic meeting. He'd notify the GenSha and the Selroth of course, but they wouldn't particularly care to meet for the sake of meeting. They wanted the Altar gone. Kenos looked across the immaculate office at a credenza below a wide, curved window. His personal weapons were there, and while he didn't want to take a Peacemaker's life, if her death meant he got what he wanted in the tunnels below the Altar colony, then all would work out.

After all, who could possibly care about a human, Peacemaker or not?

He consulted the displays again. Satisfied that all was well, he turned to the refreshment station and poured himself a drink. While humans had considerable failings, they made good corn liquor. Kenos filled a tumbler and twirled the clear, lethal drink in a small crystal glass. He tweaked the cameras to watch the CASPers haul their gear back to the beach with a satisfied smile on his face.

* * *

"You think this is going to work?" Kirkland looked at Kei Howl. Her normally stern face seemed down, depressed. After they'd made love the first time, as cadets four months before, he'd seen the look on her face and knew she thought everything had been a mistake. "You okay?"

Howl nodded. "I'm fine."

"You wanted more of a fight?" He smiled as he asked the question. She would never back down from a conflict and seeing the enemy just out of reach pissed her off. "The Peacemaker thinks they're coming back."

"I know they're coming back, Neal." Howl ran her hand over her stubbly hair. "Keep moving."

"There's only so much shit we can pretend we're carrying," he grinned. She did not return it, and he felt his own face slowly melt together and harden again. She was right. There was a mission to complete. He could think about down time when there was down time to be enjoyed. "I'll go check in on the team. Get those upper fortifications ready and move the other ammunition crates up there for the Altar to use."

"Good plan," she said. He turned to walk away, and he felt her hand snatch his wrist. She squeezed it once and let it go. He looked at her. "You stay clear of that diversion blast, will you?"

He grinned. "My guys already have it set up. Where's the Peacemaker?"

"In her quarters. It's a straight shot from there to the Raknar's helmet area. She's going to move as soon as you detonate the device."

Kirkland checked his slate. "Four minutes and counting."

"Then you should go, Neal," Kei said.

"Can't I just stay a minute longer?"

She took a deep breath and sighed. "It's not that I don't want you to. We have to stay professional. On target."

In school, their instructors loved that phrase—on target. Every task had a start point and an end point. Any deviation from that end target wasn't allowed. In their analogy, some spindrift was built into the task at hand. If they were to assault a bunker, all that mattered was that the bunker was destroyed. How the squad did it wasn't really important, except there were only a few tried and true methods leading to success. Here, success remained undefined. In three minutes and a few seconds, they'd divert the Consortium's attention to allow their de facto commander, a Peacemaker, to enter a war relic and attempt to do the impossible.

"You think she can do it?" Kirkland asked.

"No," Howl said. "There's nothing on that Raknar that works, much less a weapons system that can help us deflect the attack that's going to come." She looked into his eyes for a moment. "Do me a favor, will you?"

"Sure, Kei."

"When the time comes? Hide. Surrender if you have to—don't do something stupid like fighting to the death."

Kirkland blinked. "Why?"

"I'm not sure that any of this is worth it," Howl said. "We don't even know what we're being paid. If we die, what will they tell our families? I'm not saying I won't fight like hell, or tell you not to fight either. Just remember there's going to be a time when it's okay to put up your hands."

In her deep brown eyes, there was the hint of tears gathering. She loved him, he knew. In that moment, he knew the depth of her feeling was much deeper than either of them let on. He touched her cheek with a finger. "I understand, Kei."

She laughed. It was a quick bark, something on the order of a snort except that she smiled and wiped at her face. "You don't, Neal Kirkland. But you will. Maybe here, maybe someplace else. You will."

He frowned. "I wish you'd tell me, Kei."

She shook her head. "When this is over, maybe. Right now, we have to focus on our mission, Neal. Get your CASPers moving, and I'll do the same. You've got three minutes to be in position."

He chuckled. "Two minutes and forty-five seconds."

"Go," she slapped his shoulder with an open palm. Her smile came back and it was genuine. They cared for each other, but there was no indication she had thought any deeper about their future than he had. Their drill sergeants warned them about relationships in combat units. Friends would always be friends but lovers would die slow, agonizing deaths. He had never understood it until he and Kei made love the first time. Losing a friend was terrible, and they'd lost two during training alone. Losing a lover, though, would be worse.

He walked away and waved before he jogged toward the command center and his position for the diversion. She smiled and turned away to climb into her CASPer, but he kept looking. For half a second, he could see her a million light years away, or wherever Earth was from here. Maybe there he could tell her how he would feel if he lost her.

Infinitely worse.

* * * * *

Chapter Seventeen

Victory Twelve's external antenna array locked onto to Jessica's position automatically; locating her owner's transponder took milliseconds at best. *Victory Twelve* readied her cameras to conduct the aerial reconnaissance requested by Hex. Sensors on, the *Victory Twelve* swept up and over the target area. Targets appeared. Processors engaged and relayed their findings in picoseconds to the main computer which triggered Lucille to wake from a sleep state. She—even though a non-gendered program she thought of herself as she—found several messages and quickly made sure the *Victory Twelve* was ready. Reconnaissance pods came first, and she ensured they snapped into position and began recording as directed. Bursts of electromagnetic interference appeared in the target area, and Lucille adjusted the sensors to null out the offending sources and frequencies to take in as much spectrum data as she could.

The second message brought the engines online and adjusted the ship's orbit as if preparing to land or take on the cargo shuttle on the next orbit. The calculations were loose and in Jessica's style. Humans were smart, to a point, but even the brightest threw up their hands in frustration and asked their computers to do the work. Pictures and preparation meant the mission was over. Logic circuits engaged and decided that battle damage assessments should come next per Jessica's standard operating procedure. Even with Hex Alison in command, Lucille knew that Jessica was on the surface and would want to know the situation from orbit.

The imagery target area passed below, within the scope of the sensor suite. Visual imagery was clear of targets. Infrared showed a few possible enemy vehicles in the target area, but nothing conclusive. Multispectral imagery, though, showed a bevy of vehicles had moved through the terrain between the ship's current orbit and the previous imagery pass. Lucille collected the data in milliseconds and packaged the imagery for transmittal.

The third message directed a laser engagement. Lucille found the target, four Conquest Mark Seven tanks used in sequence and locked on. Within two seconds, the chime for connectivity sounded, and Jessica was on the line.

"*Victory Twelve*, Bulldog. How copy, over?"

Lucille checked the signal parameters. "Read you five-by-five, Bulldog."

"Prepare secondary download, full personality."

Lucille readied the batch file system in a 100 milliseconds. The target antennae would accept the download, but she needed a specific target. "Location, please?"

"Mobile three, Lucille. I need you in several places at once," Jessica said.

"I recommended to Commander Alison that specific course of action. He did not feel ready to have my assistance."

The sound Jessica made appeared, at 85 percent accuracy, to be a chuckle. "He's not, Lucille. No one is, really. Set up the *Victory Twelve* for autonomous ops—including combat operations. Emergency comms and jump protocols are still valid."

"Affirmative for all actions. Reporting will commence immediately according to SOP." Lucille marked the time. In precisely 10 minutes, she would report all current functions and back them up to significant file locations. This would continue for 24 hours. In the event of Jessica's death, the ship would automatically jump to Luna and lock down until the Peacemaker Guild came for the reports. "Any further instructions?"

"Download, Lucille. Bulldog, out."

Lucille checked the systems aboard the *Victory Twelve* again and commenced the download. At 500GB per second across four channels, her multi-petabyte system would download in a matter of minutes. The transmission window would hold. Lucille checked the surrounding orbits and the ground below for threats and found nothing. Accelerating the download, Lucille moved back to her list of tasks as the *Victory Twelve* raced across the fallen Raknar.

Sensors indicated a radiation leak, small but steady, from a vent on the Raknar's upper left shoulder. Lucille classified it as a minor Class Three leak and decided to report it on the next pass. There was more important information to transfer and way too little time to process it all.

* * *

Hex moved slowly toward the command center. Keeping up the act was vital. Bouncing around like he was ready for combat operations would not work. The surveillance systems would give their efforts away. Head down, hands at his sides, he tried to mope through the colony and avoided all eye contact with the Altar and the other humans. In his earpiece, he heard Lucille's download commence and listened to Jessica give the *Victory Twelve* orders in case of trouble. He moved north along the main corridor and up a series of wide, flat steps built for the Altar but definitely not for humans without a CASPer.

At the top of the stairs, he ducked past two Altar guards and into the command center. Klatk stood there looking to the south at the GenSha colony and a rising, unexpected storm surging over the distant mountains.

"Looks like rain," he said. Klatk did not turn around.

"The rainy season isn't for two more months. That's another example of the Consortium's failure to deliver on their promises."

Hex shrugged. "You can't control the weather."

"They said they could and we took them at their word, Hex." She turned and looked at him, her black eyes cool and distant as they studied him and moved back to the storm. "The GenSha would be wise to attack in a storm. They are better prepared for that fight than we are."

"You think they're coming?"

Klatk's antenna wavered. "They would be stupid not to. Any advantage they can press is one to pursue, regardless."

Hex was about to answer when Jessica's voice clicked on the frequency. "Lucille is down. Angel One, you're cleared to engage at your discretion."

"Bulldog, Angel One, 30 seconds."

Hex looked at Klatk again. "Where is our party downstairs?"

Klatk cocked her head. "Level Five and proceeding to Level Six. Taemin has counted the brood and is pushing hard to get to the lower levels. He is uninterested in the precious metals we mine."

"What's he trying to find, Klatk?"

Klatk spoke slowly. "Something that's not there, Hex."

"F11? Oil?" Hex looked to the south at the coming storm. Something in the sky glinted against the clouds and disappeared. Hex strained to see it again, then dismissed it as a bird on a reflection of twilight.

"Ten seconds," Kei called over the secure laser comms.

"I hope this works," Hex said and casually grabbed the consoles in front of him as if looking at the sensor displays. Up the hill, near the cave entrances, the colony's pre-manufactured solar power station connected to a series of Consortium servers monitoring all critical systems in the main complex. The whole shooting match came down to whether a new CASPer pilot could trip on command.

* * *

Kei carried one too many boxes in her CASPer's arms, and they'd made sure more weight rested on one side of the armload to help tip her balance. That had been the easy part. CASPers could balance in almost any situation with a good pilot at the controls. Convincing the CASPer to remove all safety protocols and keep her right arm rail cannon loaded and capable of firing in a loss of balance situation was another entirely. Disengaging accelerometers and keeping the targeting system online at the same time took sheer wizardry, but it had been doable. All she had to do now was trip in the right place, fall on her right arm and blast the server bank to hell.

Up the slope, she worked the CASPer easily into position. A series of cables snaked across the terrain. The probability that a CASPer would trip and fall there had to be a few hundred thousand to one. While she'd trained for her VOWs all through school, Kei enjoyed stage performances and excelled in the most physical. Comedy was the hardest of all, and the pratfall bordered on insane. How some of the professional actors could get up from some of them seemed impossible, yet she'd learned. Doing one in a full combat-equipped CASPer, with a live railgun on her arm, felt an awful lot like suicide.

She spotted her mark. Carrying boxes for an hour provided several chances to practice the whole charade and time her approach carefully. "Ten seconds," she called. No one responded, and it was just as well. Focused on her steps, Kei counted out the approach.

Left. Right. Left. Stagger slide right. Left—quick and unbalanced. Right foot under the cable trunk and...

She fell. A quick shove sent the boxes in the opposite direction. She whirled as if to catch them and kept falling toward her right shoulder. In the chaos, she sighted the rifle at the periphery of her vision. From five meters away, she wasn't going to miss the servers, but she wanted to make sure the camera banks would fail. Kei sighted the weapon precisely and used her pinplants to move the selector switch from safe to fire as she fell. As planned, nothing was in her field of fire as the CASPer tumbled forward. Her shoulder impacted the ground and she squeezed her palm with her fingers. The railgun lit off with a single soda can sized round at 5,000 miles per hour.

The server bank, and the cameras it powered, never stood a chance. It was the last thing she saw.

* * *

Safety disengagements for the rail gun left an open conduit in the system's power supply. The trigger squeeze fired the weapon effortlessly. In the picosecond after ignition of the rail, the conduit failed and unleashed an electrical wave that crashed through the disengaged safety barriers, through the insulation of the gun, and into Kei's armor where it found a weak spot and punched through. Tearing through the armor, 20,000 volts of electricity overcame the protections of her haptic suit before her body fully hit the ground. Kei died a millisecond later, well before the rampant electricity overcame the last safeties on the CASPer's hydrogen-powered engine and exploded, taking down everything and everyone within a 200-meter circle.

* * *

The force of the blast froze Jessica at the Raknar's abdomen. Up the hill, behind the command center, a large fireball rose and turned black in the evening wind. Something was wrong. A simple railgun shell wouldn't have detonated a server complex like that. Either there was something else in the target, or something terribly wrong had happened. Stomach knotted in fear, Jessica started for the command complex, forgetting the Raknar. "Hex! Report!"

"Bulldog? What the hell—"

She sped up, breaking into a run. "Hex! What happened up there?"

"Cameras are down, Bulldog. I've got no contact with Angel Two. Nothing. Four other CASPers down. Altar reporting mass casualties," Hex said. "Moving to investigate now."

Jessica grunted, "Hex, I'm on my way. We'll get eyes on the—"

"Bulldog! No!" Hex said. "Cameras are down. Get to the Raknar and get inside."

Jessica skidded to a stop along the inner colony wall. She heard skittered screeches from the injured Altar at the site. Her own slate showed five of the twelve CASPers at her disposal were offline, and one tank was partially damaged. She needed to help them, to do something. A Peacemaker's job was to be first on the scene, but Hex was right. There wasn't going to be another chance to get into the Raknar's control segment without resistance. Hex could handle the situation and assess the damage. She should get into the Raknar and try to make a difference. "Hex, get a handle on things. Figure out what happened and keep me informed."

"Get going! That explosion had to trigger Consortium orbital assets, Bulldog. Get in the Raknar now! You're not going to make it if you don't go now!"

<<Affirmative.>> Lucille called in her headset. <<Your window for passage is 43 seconds and counting.>>

Jessica spun and ran down the steps, jigged around a 90-degree corner, and sprinted down the hill to the control segment of the fallen Raknar. A cacophony of voices sounded in her ears, and she twitched her head to clear the channels one by one, leaving only Lucille's toneless, urgent voice.

<<Thirty seconds.>>

On the beach, Jessica slowed down in the soft, yellow sand. Legs burning, she pushed forward with her eyes on the Raknar's central control segment. External lights lit her path to the Raknar and up its torso. She'd planned the route earlier, looking at each piece of the climb like she'd done a few years before in Utah. Twenty-four hours of leave was all she could manage, and a rock climbing class was the perfect way to avoid the crowds at the bars and get a workout in before the next mission. They'd climbed all day, but only three or four good pitches. The rest of the time was preparatory. Studying the rock, as her guide said.

Every chance she'd had since landing, she'd walked past the Raknar and studied the route she'd take when the time came. From the moment she touched the rusting hull, she had a plan for every movement—where her feet would go and what her hands would grab. There were cracks and gouges in the Raknar's hull that she could use to her advantage. Jessica slowed her pace as she reached her planned starting point and began to climb.

Her right foot found a space in the Raknar's armor, and she used it to vault onto the hull. Her hands grabbed a maintenance handhold and her left foot found the same space as her right. Jessica moved up the hull quickly and easily. The Raknar's control segment loosely resembled a human cockpit. It opened the same way as the clamshell of a CASPer, but the interior space was big enough for at least three humans. As she grabbed the cockpit rail, Lucille barked at her.

<<Five seconds. Consortium command and control satellites are in range and preparing to image the colony.>>

Gods!

Jessica vaulted into the exposed space and promptly struck her head on the partially open hatch. She winced, pulled her legs into the space at the top of the cockpit's rail, and rolled backward into thin air.

Shit!

The thought and the impact on the side wall of the Raknar's cockpit came simultaneously. Her right hip hurt and she pressed a hand to the top of her head. There was no blood, it just hurt like a sonuvabitch. She tapped her earpiece. "Lucille, do you read?"

<<Affirmative.>>

Jessica exhaled sharply in relief. "Relay to Hex that I'm inside the cockpit and beginning my assessment. Have him get me a SITREP as soon as he can."

<<Message relayed.>>

"Notify me if Hex or Klatk want to contact me. For everyone else, I'm unavailable until further notice. Code me in emergency mode." Jessica reached into the left thigh pocket of her coveralls, withdrew a small, bright flashlight, and snapped it on. Lucille replied, but Jessica didn't pay much attention. Unlike the last Raknar she'd seen up close, the cockpit was a mangled mess of cables, roosting sites for a few dozen skittish lizard-things, and strange, furry carcasses. The surrounding stench nearly overpowered her. Stomach roiling, Jessica pushed herself to a standing position and fought disorientation. Walking on walls would take serious effort to keep her sense of orientation. After a minute or two, and some deep breathing that nearly made her retch, Jessica used the flashlight to orient herself to the cockpit, recalling her Raknar training from her Besquith instructors.

A standard Raknar cockpit held one Dusman, so it was much like a super-sized CASPer, but there were variants. Given the space, this was a variant and, likely, the heavy experimental model the Besquith instructors told fantastic stories about over drinks in the bar. There were three positions: control, weapons, and systems. Control, a vaguely humanoid-shaped space where the Dusman in command of the Raknar would have sat, rested in the middle and slightly forward. The three-sided console sat at Jessica's eye level as if hanging there.

Weapons was to the right and well down from Jessica's position on the wall. She'd finish there, with any luck. Weapons required power, and the only place she could see what the Raknar could do was the other console. The system position was tucked about a meter above and a meter or so behind the control station.

"Well, shit," She laughed. "This isn't going to be easy."

Her earpiece clicked. "Bulldog, Hex. Over."

"Go ahead, Hex."

There was a pause. "It's bad. Kei is dead along with three other Angels. I mean, we're assuming she's dead. We can't find a body. It's like her CASPer detonated instead of the camera system. There's at least 40 Altar dead, maybe more. The server compound is gone. It shouldn't have detonated like that. I don't…no idea, Jess."

Jessica paused. She needed to calm him down. "Hex? What about Altar casualties?"

"Um…yeah, there's about a 100 wounded and the central air defense system was damaged. Klatk is getting a damage report now."

"I need you to take charge up there."

Hex sighed. "How am I supposed to do that?"

Jessica shook her head. "Find out what happened, Hex. What's the situation down below?"

"Klatk lost contact with her team. There's been a cave-in on at least one of the lower levels. I'll send a team down there as soon as I can."

"Gotcha. Keep security up and don't let your guard down."

"Roger, Jess."

She studied the control console and decided it was worth trying to climb. "Keep the faith, Hex."

"Roger, Bulldog. Will advise of changes. Out."

Jessica turned and looked around the slightly curving wall with the light for anything usable. She snapped the light's cylindrical shaft into a 90-degree bend and nested it into a bunch of cables and wires so it pointed up at the target console. Wiping her hands on her coveralls, she reached out to an open panel on the control console and found a solid handhold for both hands. Swinging her left leg up as she vaulted to the console, she found purchase on the side of the control station, pulled her full weight up, and scrambled for a higher grip. Right foot placed on her initial handhold, Jessica tested her weight on the console and found it stable. Able to rest, she looked up into the cockpit at the systems station and froze. One entire panel was gone, revealing the inner workings and board systems within. The interior gold board reflected the flashlight and showed row upon row of silver connections and black chipsets. Most of them were square, but a few were round. In the depth of the console, there was a board of rectangular shaped ones just like...

Oh, shit!

An icy bolt of electricity shot down her spine and she reached into her pocket—

WHAMM!

<<Airstrike!>> Lucille called. Jessica bent over the control console and grabbed for anything as the Raknar shook around her. <<The Raknar has been hit by incoming aircraft.>>

No shit!

The Raknar bucked from side to side as multiple detonations hit the mech's body. From the feel of it, several hit the Raknar's back, and the vibrations threatened to throw her off the console completely. Whole body frantically grabbing the console, Jessica barked at her earpiece. "Hex! Report!"

Outside, she heard the Altar batteries open fire with a deafening whoosh. "Returning fire on red air. Six bandits. They're making another run. Hang on, Jess!"

A series of detonations rippled along the spine of the Raknar. The first few were lower down, near the Raknar's hips. They traveled up the imaginary spine of the beast, and Jessica realized it wasn't any type of collateral damage. The Raknar, and she, were the targets. This wasn't about the Altar colony at all. The Raknar and whatever was below the surface were the problems. *What if it's all connected? Klatk's people are simply in the way and—*

Jessica didn't have time to finish that train of thought. A large explosion threw her from the control console and toward the cockpit door. Pain shot through her for a millisecond before her head glanced off the cockpit rail. She slid down the wall and came to rest in a pile of cables and filth as the cockpit door clanged shut above her.

* * * * *

Chapter Eighteen

Hex bounded into his CASPer at the first siren. Adrenaline pushed him up the mecha's body without a crew ladder, and he barely noticed the strain in his limbs as he climbed. Hex fell into the cockpit and felt for the leg openings with his feet. Haptic cables engaged by feel, he connected the CASPer to his suit. "Close canopy; weapons power on. Sensors to maximum and cleared for combat movement."

Across the heads-up display, green lights flickered to life. The sensor package immediately picked up the circling flyers and selected the closest one as a primary target. A red box appeared around the target. Darkness made a visual confirmation impossible. Hex flipped the sights to infrared and immediately saw the faint targets turning nose-on for another pass.

"Klatk, all weapons to active. Bandits approaching from bearing two one zero at an altitude of 1,500 meters. Speed is two five zero."

The CASPer's canopy sealed and Hex bounded down the hill toward the Raknar. He broke away to the south of the massive, fallen mecha to set up a firing position. One CASPer, though, wasn't going to do much against six fully-armed flyers.

"Demon One, I need some assistance."

Tara's voice came back immediately. "Roger, Boss. Two bandits converging on your position. Arrival in 30 seconds."

Hex shook his head. "I don't have 30 seconds, Tara. Engage at maximum effective range and knock those fuckers down."

"Copy all. Watch yourself out there." Tara replied and the channel fell silent.

Hex kept running down the shoreline. The CASPer's heavy footfalls were muted in the loose sand along the Choote's bank. Hex looked back over his shoulder and saw another CASPer closing on him from his seven o'clock. The icon read Angel Seven and the bastard closed the distance faster than Hex could have imagined.

"Angel Seven, turn around and get back to the colony for defense."

"Negative," he heard Kirkland sniffling in the transmission. "There's no way in hell I'm going back there, Boss."

"That's an order, Kirkland."

Angel Seven continued to bound forward, firing his jumpjets to accelerate beyond Hex's position and move further down the shoreline. "I'll take this mission, Boss."

"Get back to the colony!"

Kirkland laughed over the connection. "You're not the only one who'd rather die now, Hex."

Hex slid the CASPer to a stop. His eyes fell to the picture of him and Maya along the instrument panel. *Drawing fire away from Jessica wasn't suicide, was it?* Six flyers versus one CASPer were decent odds for him, if he weren't the commander of the mission. "This isn't about dying, Kirkland."

"Really? Tara says all you want to do is die, that your last mission was a shitstorm worse than hers," Kirkland replied. "You lost everything, and you can't fight like you did or should. I understand that now. Let me handle this, Hex."

Kei.

Hex blinked and it all fit together. *How could I have missed the two of them?* They'd been careful and private, but there were lingering moments when they'd worked on a problem or stood too close together while they did CASPer maintenance. They were a lot like he and Maya had been in the early days of their relationship. Just as he knew how much losing Maya hurt, he knew that Kirkland's age and inexperience fueled his rage. Hex understood it all too well.

Suddenly, being two kilometers away from the colony, facing six incoming flyers, seemed like a bad idea. "Angel Seven, return to base. I'm right behind you."

"Negative." Kirkland's CASPer closed the remaining distance and stopped a good 200 meters away. Both arms came up and the supplementary rocket pods deployed. "It's a good day to die, Boss."

Hex smirked and brought his weapons online. "Neither of us are gonna die today, Kirkland. Maximum spread—missiles first and cannons to standby. Save the rail guns for later."

"Bringing them in close, huh?" Kirkland chuckled. "Roger, Boss. I'm locked on the trailing three."

Hex selected the lead three flyers with his fingers and cued the visual targeting system to the missile pods on his CASPer's shoulders. A low, warbling tone in his ears said the missiles were online and tracking. In a matter of seconds, the warbling tone became a constant growl, and he saw the LOCKED icon flash on his screen. "Locked on the lead three. Fifteen seconds to intercept."

A new voice entered the conversation. "Hex? We have targets acquired and are prepared to engage once you've fired upon them." Klatk's voice was measured and calm. "I have negative contact with Peacemaker Francis and the subterranean patrol."

Hex nodded to no one. "Long distance contacts?"

"Surveillance radars report nothing. This appears to be an aerial strike and nothing more," Klatk replied.

"Then let's send them to hell." Hex adjusted the sights and watched the ducted-fan flyers spread into a double wedge formation. Not mercenaries, he realized. The GenSha were trying something direct for a change. Their mercenary forces were unmoving and quiet, at least it appeared that way. His range indicator flashed green, and Hex loosed three missiles and bounded directly toward the incoming flyers, closing the distance as he did. The flyers tossed out flares to evade the heat-seeking missiles and swerved across his view. His second and third salvos were ready. The lead flyer broke away and dove toward the ground, accelerating in the general direction of the Raknar. Hex didn't take the bait. As Kirkland unleashed on the trailing vehicles, Hex fired multiple missiles at the two flyers not on the leader's path. Both went down spectacularly. Hex bounded toward the shoreline, his eyes and sensors on the leader, as the flyer raced along the water's surface at 300 knots. Closing the distance, Hex selected a spot on the wide, central sandbar and engaged his jumpjets at maximum power and range. The CASPer shot into the air effortlessly.

"Splash one," Kirkland reported.

Three to go.

Hex brought his rail gun online and snapped the CASPer's right arm up to engage the leader. "Lead the target," he said and the suit's optics and cannon worked as one, positioning the barrel so the projectile would intercept the flyer. Before Hex could fire, the flyer banked sharply toward him and Kirkland. Hex cut his jets and spun in mid-air. Landing on the sandbar, he looked across the river toward Kirkland and saw the CASPer with both arms up, spraying fire into the sky. Two flyers descended on the young man's position, cannons firing. A cloud of dust and debris erupted around him.

"Angel Seven, jump!"

Kirkland stood his ground, weapons firing. One of the enemy flyers sparked under fire. The ducted fans on the starboard side shuddered and stopped. The flyer rolled violently to the left and spun into the ground not more than 500 meters from Kirkland's position. Hex looked over his shoulder. The lead flyer was nose-down and accelerating toward them. There were seconds to act, maybe less. The CASPer's feet hit the sandbar, and Hex reflex-jumped to maximum altitude on an arc toward Kirkland. He keyed his weapons systems mid-jump and fired twice. The missiles shot out and descended to slightly above the surface as they raced down the Choote River toward the accelerating target. The first missile reported an overshoot warning and self-destructed harmlessly 3,000 meters from the flyer. The second missile made the proper correction and shot down the riverbed toward the flyer as it banked and tried to cut across the missile's path. A flash creased Hex's vision.

<<Missile warning.>> The voice was Lucille's and not the CASPer's interface protocol. <<Break left.>>

Hex cut the jets short and smacked into the shallow river. Jets at maximum, he jumped low and hard to the left. The missile passed him closely enough for him to see three yellow stripes along its fuselage. Unable to follow through the turn, the missile detonated and showered Hex with debris. The CASPer's caution and warning system lit up with a series of warnings. He scanned them and saw nothing critical, but his CASPer wasn't going to fight or fly as it should.

The lead flyer pivoted and swung around to face him. For a moment, he and the flyer did not move and while Hex couldn't see the pilot's eyes, he knew they were thinking the same thing. The first one to move would dictate the fight. Hex didn't hesitate and fired two missiles from his left pod. He jumped left, toward the sandbar in the middle of the Choote and crashed into the water again. With water at the base of his cockpit, Hex watched the flyer dart to its right and swing across Hex's field of vision with the missiles in pursuit. He raised the railgun, "Compensate."

The gun tracked with a snap hard enough to jolt him in the cockpit. Hex squeezed his fingers to his palms and the railgun fired six high-velocity rounds. After the second one, the flyer ceased to exist.

That's four. Two to go.

Hex spun and sighted Kirkland on the beach. The kid was still up and firing, even though his CASPer broadcast a steady litany of failures and emergency action requests. One of the remaining flyers hovered and continued to fire. Hex raised the rail gun again and the ballistic computer locked. He fired and instinctively looked for the remaining flyer even before his target detonated spectacularly in midair. The little bastard swung around from the north at scrub bush level, almost too low to see. Altar guns from the colony walls fired a barrage of tracer rounds that didn't find their marks. Hex brought up his weapons as the flyer came at him nose on and fired.

A missile tracked into the fight and closed the distance to the flyer. There was a small, proximity detonation and the flyer hit the river at 200 miles per hour, shattering into a million flaming pieces. Hex looked up into the dark sky and saw nothing else, but he waited for his sensors to confirm it. The sky was quiet again. He jumped from the river toward the shoreline and Kirkland's torn up CASPer.

"Nice shot, Seven."

"Thanks, sir."

Hex landed on the riverbank and forced himself to relax at the controls. There was no indication of additional attacks from either force. Their target had clearly been the Raknar and not the Altar colony, itself. Hex turned back to the Raknar and saw a half-dozen small fires burning along its gigantic, rusting hull. A small explosion shot a fountain of bright blue sparks into the sky like fireworks. He pressed the transmit button. "Bulldog, do you read me?"

There was nothing but a hiss of static.

Hex tried again. "Bulldog, this is Hex, do you read?"

Again, nothing.

Hex clenched his jaw, but relaxed it immediately. There was another information source he could try. "Lucille, this is Hex on standard frequency alpha. Do you read?"

<<Acknowledged.>>

"I need a SITREP on Bulldog."

<<Life signs are stable, but communications are down. I am unable to reach her. Her vital signs point to unconsciousness.>>

Hex engaged the jumpjets, squatted down for power, and leapt into the sky toward the bank of the Choote. He looked back over his shoulder. "Angel Seven, you have command of the forward defense while I check on Bulldog. Get a listening post out here immediately. How copy?"

"Roger, breaking for Demon One."

Hex flipped to the Altar command frequency. "—Urgent, I say again, urgent. Hex, this is Klatk, please get to the command complex."

His stomach knotted. "Klatk, is it Bulldog?"

Klatk's voice came back. "Negative, Hex. We're still unable to reach her. That puts you in command of the Peacemaker's mission."

"Roger, I'm moving there now. Have your forces muster, Klatk."

"Negative, Mister Alison," a new voice replied. "This is Mediator Taemin. Your mission is over. You will direct me to the Peacemaker's location. If she is dead, you will identify the body. Is that clear?"

* * *

"You're certain of this?" The last syllable drug out in a hiss that grated Qamm's last nerve.

She rubbed the soft fur at the interior corners of her eyes. "Confirmed. They have a handful of CASPers and four tanks. That's it."

"And the explosion?" Leeto asked. "The Selroth have given us no information other than strength of the explosion and location. Something happened in the Altar colony, and your aircraft couldn't assess what happened."

Qamm took a breath. "We know their security and communications connections to the Consortium have been severed. We know there are multiple casualties, both Altar and human. And, we know the strength of the mercenary force that's there at the Peacemaker's request. I believe that's enough to act upon, hence this conversation, Leeto."

There was silence on the line. "My source at D'nart tells me that Kenos is not leaving the spaceport to investigate until morning. When are you proposing this...action? First light?"

"How quaint and very human of you," Qamm smirked. "The Peacemaker would expect that, and I'm not prepared to give her the advantage. I propose we attack now. Tonight."

"I think not," Leeto replied. Before Qamm's anger flashed to words, he continued, "For the value you've theorized, I'd prefer to wait until the Administrator is on the ground, himself. The dead cannot prosecute those who breach contracts, which is exactly what you've proposed. Doing so would mean I would need enough credits to protect my entire force from litigation and so would you. We will never work as mercenaries again, Qamm. Forced retirement requires more than adequate compensation to fend off my enemies."

Qamm paused. Eliminating Kenos went well above defrauding the Dream World Consortium's contracts and their own individual contracts with the colonies employing them. "You're proposing we attack and grab as much as we can and flee? I'd rather slowly defraud unknowing colonists than a galactic Consortium."

"The payout would be greater, Qamm."

It would be by at least 20 million credits. Money wasn't a motivator in her world. Money would only help her run. The Veetanho would disavow her. Spending the rest of her life looking over a shoulder, even with a lot of money in her pockets, wasn't an option. "This isn't about money, Leeto. You can run anonymously for the rest of your life. I cannot."

Leeto laughed, making her seethe. "You forget how big this galaxy is, Qamm. Even your species can hide from each other in distant worlds."

"I don't want to hide in the distant worlds!" Qamm barked. "Skimming on a contract is one thing, Leeto. You're talking a complete breach, not to mention murder."

"It's not murder if it's a horrendous accident, Qamm. Without their surveillance system, we can stage an attack to be anything we want."

Leeto's words stole her breath. As maniacal as it seemed, the Sidar was right. All she had to do was insure that Leeto or his forces pulled the trigger on Kenos. She could retain her honor and the credits. "You're proposing we wait until the Administrator lands? Your forces are much closer, are they not?"

"We are repositioning further to the west. I believe we were imaged by the Peacemaker's ship," Leeto said. "A few kilometers distance and better cover should be enough displacement. I imagine, though, they'll be too busy cleaning up whatever happened to notice."

Qamm's subconscious mind clicked over from doubt and self preservation to the task at hand. Her worries fell aside as she considered the dual-pronged attack. "Will you be able to commit the Selroth to the river and the aquifers?"

"Undoubtedly," Leeto said. "The bigger question is can you commit the GenSha? They're not terribly bright, but will they attack across open ground?"

"Of course not. They're not humans," Qamm said. "We'll escort them into the fight. With enough infantry, they'll provide a solid distraction to allow your forces to cross in from the west. Timing is critical."

"Do not worry about timing, Qamm. Deliver your artillery and follow the plan. We will kill two targets with one strike."

The line clicked off, and Qamm stared at the console for a solid 30 seconds before nodding to herself. There was no way Leeto would stick to his own plan. She considered his actions and decided there were a few possibilities. Leeto was no fool. He'd likely pin any action directly against Kenos on her forces. Nulling out the ability to target the Cochkala administrator would be easy enough—like most administrators, Kenos wore pinplants. Her communications specialists could identify their isolated frequency pattern, and she could feed that to her weapons. Easy.

The other two possibilities were more troubling. Leeto and the Selroth could double cross her forces by getting to the lower levels of the Altar mines before them, if the aquifer network could be opened and not risk flooding the mine. The Peacemaker would know there was a subterranean avenue of approach and would defend it. Depending on the damage, and what weapons the Selroth used, their bounty could be contaminated not to mention harder to extract. Time would be of the essence, and the more time they spent removing what they hoped to find, the shorter their escape window would be. Lastly, Leeto could easily fail to get the Altar defense to commit to his attack. Their superior stand-off weaponry would decimate the GenSha attack and leave her forces vulnerable. Without any air support, her best plan was to use her own indigenous artillery to soften the Altar defenses. The minute she opened fire, though, they'd be able to counter it and lay waste to the GenSha infantry heavy forces.

Qamm cued the video footage from her drone gunships on the night attack. In the infrared band, she clearly noted the positions of the tanks on the four corners of the colony complex. Should they remain in place, targeting such defined points would be easy. All that mattered was the right type of round, the right fuse, and the right impact point on the weaker top armor.

It could be done. Qamm hated herself for thinking it, for even considering a plan that would lead to the death of an administrator and a breach of contract. Kenos wanted them to eliminate the Altar and pocket a hefty sum, but he'd clearly hidden his agenda. The Selroth believed the tunnels hid something of tremendous value. Kenos and his Consortium had brought in the Altar to mine it. Whatever it was, the Altar believed it best left alone. Their inability to bring it up ruled out the obvious, F11. Altar tended to believe that precious metals and crystals belonged to the dirt they lay inside, but they would extract it in their slow, almost religious method and sell it. No, what lay beneath the surface was something they knew to be problematic and valuable.

With that thought, Qamm called for a council of war and set about planning the defeat of all their collective enemies at once.

* * * * *

Chapter Nineteen

Something licked her face. In the funk of a throbbing headache and the semi-peacefulness of where she lay, Jessica first thought it was a cat. *Mittens, maybe. Or was it Squeak? The one that loved to sleep in the bathroom sink or the one that shit all over her bedroom?* She couldn't remember. The lick came again, and she roused enough to stick a hand out and touch something warm and scaly.

Fuck!

Jessica woke and shook off whatever it was with flailing arms and legs. The thing squealed, flew across the cockpit section, and disappeared into the shadows. Her light had fallen over, but still lit half the space. She crawled through the detritus and shit along the curved wall and reached the light. The side of her head throbbed, and she pressed a hand against it, feeling for swelling or blood. There was neither. Her earpiece was missing, though, and she snatched the light from the mess on the floor of the cockpit and swung it around. Whatever had licked her was gone or simply hiding in the shadows. A slight, acrid haze filled the upper portion of the cockpit and turned the directed light from her flashlight into a beam of sorts. For the first time, realized the Raknar's cockpit doors were closed and she sucked in a panicked breath. The total darkness of the cockpit closed in around her, so she closed her eyes and exhaled slowly.

The scent in the cockpit no longer nauseated her, which was good considering she sat in who-knew-what among torn bundles of cables and other trash. Across the way, three meters farther around, a blinking red light caught her eye. She moved slowly toward it, recognizing her earpiece. As her fingertips closed around it, a clang from behind startled her a split second before fresh, moist air rushed into the confined space. The cockpit door opened fully against the bright Araf sunlight. She could see a CASPer's arm holding it up. A silhouetted figure climbed up the arm and stepped into the space.

"Jess?" Hex asked.

"Down here," she said and stood slowly. Hands raised to block the bright white light, she stepped toward him. "What happened?"

"Are you okay?"

"I'm fine. What happened?"

Hex's face contorted as a shadow's movement caught his eye and he looked past her into the open door. He frowned and lowered his eyes to hers. "Let me check your head. Looks like you whacked it pretty well."

As he leaned closer, she whispered, "Where's Taemin?"

"Right behind you," Hex mouthed.

Shit. Jessica winced as Hex prodded her head. "You can stop, Hex. I'm okay."

"I'm delighted to hear that," Taemin spoke from behind her. She made no effort to turn and face him. "Your mission is complete, Peacemaker."

Jessica shook her head. "You've said that before."

"The Altar brood numbers slightly more than seven thousand, well outside the approved range. I've taken the liberty of letting the administrator know. He will be here in the morning to investigate. I'll be disconnecting the slaved power supplies with your deputies' assistance."

Jessica spun and faced him. Balancing was difficult, but she raised herself up to her full height and stared at him. "Over my dead body, Taemin."

"Your duties are over, Peacemaker." He stressed the word with utter condescension. Jessica curled her fingers into fists but did not move forward. "Though I doubt you'll have that title by the end of this abysmal mission."

Jessica squared her shoulders to him and ignored the pulsing throb in her head. "Those power cables run the incubators below ground. Disconnecting them will kill the Altar brood."

"To end this conflict, I will unplug them all right now. The Altar are in violation of their contract." Taemin smiled at her, and it made her blood run cold.

Jessica stepped forward. "This mission is over when I say it is, Taemin. Your position as a mediator grants you some leeway, but you crossed the line. Nobody unplugs that brood while I'm still standing. I don't give a damn about you, the Consortium, or my own Guild. That brood gets a chance to live. The Altar have scraped by on a planet that did not meet the contract documents' guarantees. The Dream World program, at least on Araf, is null and void."

"And your degree in judicial affairs tells you that? Oh, wait. You're a failed mercenary the Peacemaker Guild took pity on, aren't you? Your first assignment was busting your own ex-husband, was it not? Could you have chosen an easier mission?" Taemin snorted and shook his head. "No matter. I've also sent a message to your Guild. I'm afraid I cannot recommend you for a commission."

Her earpiece vibrated in her palm. She instinctively put it into her right ear without taking her eyes from Taemin. Lucille's voice came over the frequency immediately. <<I am monitoring your communica-

tions. There have been no outbound transmissions to the Guild's coded channels of any type from your location. The mediator is lying or has some clandestine means of communication I cannot track.>>

Jessica's anger smoldered rather than burned. The brief shot of calm from Lucille's transmission washed over her, but she made no move. "Fine. Tell them what you want, Taemin. We aren't leaving this location. We will defend the Altar colony at all costs. Until my Guild comes to take my powers and authority in person, I remain a Peacemaker. That means you do exactly what I say, is that clear?"

The Caroon's brow furrowed. "Of course, Peacemaker. What would you like me to do?"

Go fuck yourself.

She snorted but did not smile. "Get out of this Raknar and stay out of it. You are also banned from the tunnel system and will remain under guard at all times."

"I hardly think that's—"

Jessica raised a finger and pointed at his face, knowing it would anger him. "You threatened 7,000 lives, Taemin. Remember? You would unplug them to end this conflict? That's a threat. You will do exactly what I say, is that clear?"

A ripple of fury crossed his normally passive face. "Perfectly, Peacemaker Francis. Though, in my professional opinion, you are making a terrible mistake."

"Opinions are like assholes, Taemin. Everybody has one. Get out of this Raknar. This is officially Peacemaker property, and you are not welcome."

Taemin nodded solemnly, and she saw the hidden laughter on his face as easily as if her flashlight pointed it out. The little bastard thought he knew everything. Well, he didn't, and she decided it was high time he understood that. She'd had more than enough. "By your leave, Peacemaker."

Get out. She couldn't make herself say it, yet. There would be a time to give the Mediator what wrath she could muster, but it needed to wait. She knew her face didn't betray her thoughts. She'd mastered the effect of a direct, burning stare as well as her mother wielded it. The Mediator turned and made his way to the cockpit opening. Jessica watched him all the way out the door and down the CASPer's legs before she turned to Hex.

The younger man looked around the cockpit, poorly concealing a smile on his face. She waited until Taemin was gone before she asked, "What are you smiling about?"

"It's about time the real Bulldog showed up." Hex grinned. "You find anything in here?"

"Maybe," Jessica said. She could feel the damned chipset in her pocket calling to her. His words similarly resonated. It was time to be herself and not a tactical robot. The Peacemaker Guild didn't need any more of them, after all. "Help me get back up to the systems console. Where's the fire?"

"On the hull. A couple of spots. I have the remaining CASPers from Alpha Team putting them out right now," Hex said. "Tara and Kirkland have command of the defense."

"What happened?" Jessica moved to the control console and climbed as she'd done before to reach the systems station. "Did Kei take out the server system?"

"Yeah," Hex sighed. "But something happened with her CASPer. In order to trip convincingly, she disengaged the safeties. The railgun shit the bed, we think. It fired and took out the system, but the damned thing fried her electrical system, and the engine exploded. Took out a huge chunk of the colony's east side."

"Holy shit," Jessica blinked. Through the shock, she compartmentalized the loss easily. There would be time to honor absent companions and consider what happened to her as a lesson learned. "What was the damage, besides Kei?"

The jovial look on Hex's face faded. "We lost Angels Three and Four along with Kei. They were outside their suits helping feed the loading illusion when Kei's suit detonated. Angel Five has a concussion, but is mission capable."

"I need their names, Hex," she said, "for my report and my conscience, as much as yours."

"I'll get them." He ran a hand through his hair. "Klatk lost 82 Altar and more than 200 were wounded."

Gods. Jessica shook her head. "All of that from a CASPer detonation? Are we sure there wasn't some anti-tampering device in the complex?"

"Maybe. We just don't know. The hydrogen fuel kit technically has the power profile matching the explosion, but I've never seen one fail on a CASPer because of a simple fall."

"Me either," Jessica said. She stepped onto the control console and prepared to scramble up. "Have you checked all of them?"

"Working on that now," Hex said. "Tara is checking them out."

Jessica sighed. Now was as good a time as any. "How did she do?"

"Checking the CASPers?"

"In the fight, Hex."

He shrugged. "Fine, as far as I could tell. Do you know something I don't? What happened to her old unit?"

"We know what happened to her old unit, Hex. Death On Tracks was overrun by Jivool on Essex Five. They were outnumbered five-to-one. What we don't know is why Tara and her platoon ran."

"No," Hex said. He met her eyes. "She's squared away. Tara says her platoon never dropped. What you're saying doesn't make any sense. Her tanks are literally the cornerstones of our defense, Jessica. They're not going anywhere."

Jessica climbed atop the control console and reached up to the shattered remains of the systems console. "Hand me my light, will you?"

"She's not going to run, Bulldog."

"I heard you the first time, Hex. We don't know that she won't run. You met her hours after the last mission ended, and you ended up here because of Hak-Chet. I realize he may have seen something in her, too, and as much as she's done so far, her history stands against her. I will not suffer deserters."

"She didn't desert," Hex said with a sigh. "I know she won't let us down when those bastards come back."

"Everyone fights when they're behind a wall, Hex. Your father taught you that much. We haven't seen a real attack or anything approaching the real strength of those we're facing. You and I both know it's coming."

"What are you looking for?" His question changed the subject, but not her mind. Tara and her crewmen performed well, which was good. The last thing Jessica had time for was watching her friends instead of her enemies. Being a mercenary taught her that.

"An active power line or a way to find one," she replied. Nothing in the panel appeared operational, yet her eyes drifted up to the board of rectangular chipsets. "Lost cause. There's nothing live in here any—"

A single LED bulb the size of the half-moon on her pinkie fingernail winked to dull purple life on the chipset panel. Jessica froze.

"What is it?"

Jessica realized she was holding her breath and forced it out of her lungs. Had she imagined the flash? She forced her eyes to remain open. Tears threatened to well up from the strain as the light blinked again. "Got something, I think."

"What is it?"

"Not a clue, but there's power. That's a start." She looked over her shoulder. "You have a spare combat slate in your CASPer?"

"Yeah, what do you need?"

She smiled. "Lucille."

Hex shook his head. "I'll have to download her."

"No, you don't have to. She's already there."

Hex put a hand to his forehead. "I am such an idiot."

Jessica smiled. "Why?"

He chuckled. "I thought I heard her when those flyers came in. I should've put two and two together. Let me go get that slate. You need anything else?"

Standing still, her leg muscles tense from the effort of holding her position, she realized how sore she was. You got any CASPer candy?" In training, CASPer pilots tended to eat analgesics such as acetaminophen like candy, and the name stuck.

"Always," Hex said. "Be right back."

Jessica looked up into the console at the chipset board. She could reach the bottom of the board with the rectangular chips. The dusty, black chips looked very much like the one in her pocket with her father's name scratched on the surface. Jessica reached up and grasped one by the edges and pulled it out of the board. A shower of dust fell into her face, and she closed her eyes and tried not to sneeze. As she wiped her face with the left sleeve of her coveralls, she could clearly see a second purple light in the space where the chip had been. She slipped the chip into the opposite thigh pocket and looked up again, trying to make sense of the mess of cabling she found. Dusman numerical figures were the only markings visible. The ports were numbered, which helped, but without any written description she would never be able to decipher them on her own.

"Here you go." Hex stepped into the cockpit section and handed Jessica a combat slate. The reinforced carbon fiber devices were hardened against everything short of a thermonuclear blast and had a more powerful processor and battery than commercial slates. Jessica rummaged in a shoulder pocket for a connector cable, one with a vice-like grip, and attached it to the cable port on the slate. She plugged the vice-grip into the space where the old chip had been and found connectivity.

"Lucille, trace the power conduits of this system. Expedited full scan."

<<Acknowledged. Processing.>>

Jessica saw the counter start moving forward. "Relay system progress to my slate, updating every hour until complete."

<<Confirmed.>>

"You really think you're going to find something we can use to protect the Altar?" Hex asked. "I don't think we've got that kind of time, Jess."

She agreed with him. "You're right, we don't. I'm not betting we can get the weapons or anything else to work. That's not the point. You guys set the stage for the Quaker cannon, right?"

"Yeah," Hex replied slowly. "But that's really what you're doing here, aren't you? You're forcing their hands."

"That's right," Jessica said. "Right now, Kenos is having kittens trying to figure out what I'm doing. Taemin's told him what he thinks I'm doing, so I'm guessing they're convinced we're going to use this Raknar to defend the Altar colony using some kind of Peacemaker mojo. Kenos will come in tomorrow and follow Taemin's advice. He'll attempt to boot the Altar out by force, and we won't leave. He'll have to come up with something else."

"And he's going to have the GenSha and the Selroth do it for him." Hex rubbed his eyes. "You really think he'll do that?"

"He wants them off this terrain. There are only two answers why—this Raknar, or what's in the bottom of those mines. He's willing to do anything, including starting a war, because it's the only way to get what he wants."

"I know what I want," Hex said. "Chow…and maybe some sleep."

Jessica chuckled. "We can do that. Set security to 50 percent with two-hour watches. Get everyone fed who hasn't already eaten. Hold off on any fresher tablets, though. We may need them for operations tomorrow. I'd rather see how many of our folks can sleep a little and eat a good meal." Alertness via artificial chemicals had certain advantages, but Jessica wanted to avoid it, if possible.

Her stomach rumbled in response. Confident she'd done as much as she could in the Raknar, Jessica led Hex to the cockpit door and crawled out into the cooling Araf afternoon. Clouds obscured the sun, but they were too light and high to produce rain. Waiting for Hex to climb down the CASPer's outstretched arms, she stared into this particular sky and closed her eyes like a little girl. The ritual had been the same almost every day she could remember. Some days, particularly those when she was on missions or under fire, she forgot or simply did not have the time. Others, she would stare into the heavens for hours thinking the same thing over and over again. On rare occasions, she whispered the words to the wind. Under an unfamiliar sky, so far away from home, it seemed appropriate.

"Where are you, Daddy?"

* * *

"The Peacemaker is up to something, and I have no idea what it could be."

"She wants to help those she sees as weak without knowing the power they have to wield," Kenos said. "No matter. I will personally verify the size of the brood in the morning and will file an injunction against her and the entire Peacemaker Guild before mid-morning. Once that is in place, we can move forward on Araf."

"Your forces are in place?"

"Assembled and ready." Kenos stroked his chin. "All they need is my signal to proceed."

"You are aware of what happened in the colony?"

Kenos snorted. "A human CASPer fell and destroyed our telemetry and surveillance package. It's irrelevant. We no longer need it. We know what they're hiding underground."

"Only on one occupied level. You still believe there is something deeper?"

"Of course. Why else would they stay?" Kenos said. "They're protective to a fault. Believing they should protect it by hampering legal extraction is what they've done across the galaxy for hundreds of years. They want to mitigate risk and hold onto the fragile peace the Union provides. This is a single colony we're facing, and they've put a stop to development long enough. A simple act of war tomorrow will push this conflict over the edge."

"You place too much faith in your combatants."

"They are handsomely paid to do what I want them to do. They will be in position and ready to act. Do not forget your end of this arrangement. I expect a proper opening sequence to our, shall we say, dance." The connection terminated abruptly. Kenos grinned in the dark office. The opulent D'Nart spaceport spread below him in all directions. There would be a new gem in the Consortium's crown once the Altar colony and that gods-damned Raknar were razed, and the bounty hauled from the mines. Terraforming had one goal—resources. On rare occasions, the resources created far exceeded the cost of the overall project. In the event of an exceptional rarity, something that could destabilize a healthy portion of the Union's economy, opportunities were not to be wasted.

* * * * *

Chapter Twenty

An hour before dawn, Hex rubbed dirt and sleep from the corners of his eyes. His bedroll stretched out under the early morning skies at the feet of his CASPer. He looked up into the galaxy for a long time. Months before, he and Maya slept on the beaches of Kaua'i looking up at the swirling arm of the Milky Way. They'd talked, made love, and talked some more. Their future laid out in front of them, they'd looked past the next mission and into uncertain possibilities. Hammer promised them an easy mission, one that would not only fund their wedding and honeymoon, but leave enough so they could plan the rest of their lives. Retirement by age 35 was possible. Granted, they could have left the Mercenary Guild at any time and lived off the pension from Hex's father's considerable funds, but he'd wanted none of it. His brothers and sisters would squabble over their inheritance with their lawyers for years. Hex preferred to earn his own and keep his finances separate from his family. In Maya, he'd found the partner of a lifetime, but everything changed in the blink of an eye.

There are no easy missions, son.

His father was a legend in the mercenary community, having served in Cartwright's Cavaliers before moving on to other opportunities. Hex knew a part of that legacy could be his, but he'd struck out on his own. With Maya, he'd believed it was possible to leave it all behind and find a secluded beach somewhere to watch the world turn. His father's insistent presence, the constant flow of lessons learned and experienced, kept coming back. Maybe it was time to admit that he'd never be anything but a mercenary, much like his father.

Footsteps crunched closer in the loose gravel. He turned and saw Tara walking toward him with two steaming, steel mugs. "Want some coffee?"

He unzipped his sleeping bag and moved to a sitting position. The coffee smelled strong and bitter, exactly the way he liked it. "Thanks," he said, taking a mug. For a split second, he wondered how someone so squared away, so professionally competent, could be lying about everything.

"You're welcome," Tara said. "Security is ramping up to 100 percent. The Altar are moving to the walls and readying their systems in case of an attack at first light. We'll be ready in about 10 minutes."

Hex nodded. It had been their plan all along. "Everything quiet out there?"

"So far," Tara said. She looked to the west and the craggy ridge lines. "Nothing moving on surveillance radars, and everything we can see is calm. The reconnaissance images from over there don't really show anything. A couple of possibles, but I can't make anything out."

Hex sipped the coffee. He'd studied the same images before going to sleep. "Yeah, I'm not an analyst either. Something's out there, though. They're just better at cover and concealment than we are."

Tara snorted. "We're out here in broad daylight, by comparison."

The position wasn't great, but it held the key terrain, and that mattered. High ground provided an advantage in both weapon ranges and observation. What they could see, they could kill at a sizable distance. "It's a good position."

"Yeah," Tara said sounding unconvinced.

Hex turned and looked at her. "What is it?"

"Good positions aren't everything," she replied, sipping from her mug. "History hasn't always been kind to those fighting from good positions. Relying solely on our advantages leaves us at risk. We have to be flexible and keep the initiative no matter what."

"Have an escape plan, huh?" Hex said before he could stop. The effect was a sarcastic inflection which only made it worse.

"What's that supposed to mean?" Tara said. "I didn't imply anything about an escape plan, I said we needed to be flexible."

Hex cradled the mug in his lap, deciding after a half second of consideration to just get it over with. "Flexibility is one thing. Living to fight another day is something else. My Dad always said a mercenary shouldn't ever think about the next day, only the one they have and never, absolutely never, the past. I've done way too much of that in the past couple of weeks, Tara. I think you have, too."

"You have no idea what you're talking about, Hex."

"Then what happened to Death On Tracks, Tara?"

Her face contorted in rage. "You sonuvabitch! How dare you bring them up!"

"Did you run or not?"

Her fingers tightened around the mug in her hands, and her arms shook from the tension. All vestiges of composure disappeared, as barely controlled anger took over. She seethed back at him, "I didn't run."

"Your word? Or the official report?"

"Both," Tara said. "Gods, Hex. Why would you bring this up now? "

"Jessica told me. Frankly, I should have asked before now, and that's my fault as a shitty commander. Before we get started today, I need to know the truth, Tara. I need to know if you're going to have my six or if I'm going to have to watch for you to cut away when the shit hits the fan."

Tara looked at the horizon for a few seconds and wiped away a tear Hex didn't see fall. She sniffled and sat down on the ground next to him. "We were on Essex Five, going after a mercenary force called the Wandering Death. The Jivool on the planet contracted them to secure key terrain at any cost. Commander Schwartz put us into a defensive position solid enough to hold off an attack for days. We had artillery support on all our obstacles, we had the advantage for our direct fire systems, and we had air support out the ass. All we had to do was hold, and we did until the bastards charged us from short range with a full company of heavy armor and about a thousand Jivool infantry. They hit one spot with everything they had, sucked all our direct fire assets onto it, and hit us with artillery and aerial strikes to disrupt command and control. Schwartz died in the first wave, and the command post went dead fucking silent. All communications were jammed or down. We couldn't call in our transports. We had orders to withdraw from the jammed environment and save ourselves if that happened. I followed those orders with my four tanks. No one else made it out."

She took a breath and wiped her nose with one sleeve. Hex asked, "Then why did you lie about not dropping? And why do people think you ran?"

Tara snorted. "We were a mostly human unit, and I was the junior platoon commander. Not to mention being a woman, Hex. It was easy for people to assume I ran instead of doing my job. I'd rather have died there than run. The official report clears us of wrong doing and paints a very accurate picture of what happened. But I've got fifteen other folks who can't find work either."

Hex squinted. "What about the Guild?"

"The Guild takes no official position on what happened at Essex Five." She looked at him, and he knew there was much more to the story. Mercenary forces fighting one another, even under proper contracts, was a dirty part of the business no one liked to acknowledge.

"What did Hak-Chet offer you? It had to be more than a job."

Tara sipped from her coffee mug, obviously putting the words together carefully. "Call it redemption, if you want, but he offered a recommendation for me and my soldiers for future employers. That's why we're here, Hex. My troopers and I are going to do everything we can to make this mission succeed. You have my word on that."

Hex reached out a hand and touched her elbow. "I'm sorry. I needed to know."

Tara nodded her head but did not look in his direction. "There's a lot of shitty things we have to say and do in this business."

"There's also nothing more important than trust, Tara. I have yours and you have mine."

She looked at him, her eyes still bright from tears. "This is about a lot more than trust, Hex. My troopers and I are at your disposal. I wouldn't say that to a shitty commander."

Hex laughed and saw her smile. "Everybody is getting ready?"

"Just as you requested, Boss," she said. "You want to wake up the Peacemaker?"

Hex shrugged. "It can wait a few minutes. My father used to tell me that the best things he learned about those he fought with came from eating chow or drinking coffee with them. I seem to have at least a half a mug of coffee left, and a few minutes to enjoy it. Care to stay?"

* * *

Beep.

Jessica assumed the beep was part of her dream of the wide, blue Mediterranean off the eastern coast of Spain. The air was warm and caressed her face as she stood overlooking the old Spanish castle town of Tossa De Mar.

Beep.

The noise wasn't part of her dream. She clawed up from sleep wondering what it was. None of her own technology was programmed with an alarm that beeped. She hated the damned things. Why she would have set a beep as an alarm on her slate made no sense.

It's not my slate. It's Hex's calling mine.

Lucille!

Jessica rolled up from her bunk and grabbed for the slate. She dispatched the alarm with a keystroke, and Lucille's voice sounded from the built-in speakers. <<Good morning, Peacemaker. Progress on my survey stopped at 14%. Communications arrays are missing a processing unit from the main board. Did you find anything on the floor or in the area that could be returned?>>

Jessica blinked and rubbed her eyes. "I've got it, Lucille. I'll bring it down and get it reinstalled. Can you continue with the other systems?"

<<Affirmative.>>

In the cool morning, she padded across the small housing unit in a t-shirt and underwear to her coveralls. The two nearly identical chipsets were in the left thigh pocket. She pulled them out and snapped on a light that made her wince. The Raknar's chip was three times as thick as the one with her father's callsign on it. They had a similar connection pattern, but the materials were very different. She'd forgotten to compare them after leaving the Raknar in exhaustion. Even Klatk commented that she needed sleep, and she barely managed to get to her housing unit, peel out of her uniform, and fall into bed.

A glance at her watch and some early morning math confirmed she'd slept a little more than five hours. Her alarm was set to go off in 30 more minutes, so going back to bed made exactly zero sense. The ache in her head was still there, so she collected more CASPer candy from her coveralls and dry swallowed two before tugging herself into her uniform.

As she sat down to strap on her boots, she studied the two chips and chastised herself for getting her hopes up about a silly idea that a chip from Earth would fit a gods-damned Raknar. Boots on, she strapped her armor and laser pistol to her body, slipped the chips into her pocket, and fumbled around in her hip pocket for a bottle of water. The tepid water woke up her insides and kicked her brain into full waking mode. Some coffee would be in order, and then she could get the chip reinstalled, provided the two mercenary forces and their colonial supporters weren't charging across the plains at them.

"Lucille? Is Hex awake yet?"

<<I am unable to determine. His communications unit has not been engaged.>>

Let him sleep. No doubt one of the tankers has coffee ready. She smiled at the thought of her father telling her mother that no son or daughter of his would ever be a dumb-assed tanker. As a result, she'd never considered it and neither had her brothers. Still, though, the tankers would have coffee, and while it would never be as good as what the starship crews had, it would be enough to get her working.

Gear in place, Jessica opened the door of the unit and looked out into a calm, dark night. Above her on the slope, she could see the muted red lights of the Altar colony. A few shadows moved along the walls, suggesting the early plan was in motion. She reached down, grabbed her laser rifle and slung it over her right shoulder with the barrel pointing down, across her body. With a deep breath, she closed the door and headed for the tanks and the promise of a cup of coffee.

Sure enough, the tankers were awake. She approached Demon One from the front, casually and without really thinking. There was the click-clack of a large caliber machine gun from the vehicle, and she froze.

"Halt. Who goes there?" a familiar voice called.

"Peacemaker Francis."

"Advance and be recognized."

"Permission to come aboard?" For some reason, tankers referred to their vehicles the same way sailors referred to their ships. They also used similar terms such as cupolas, sponson boxes, turrets, hulls, and who knew what else. They loved the permission to come aboard thing, too.

"Granted."

Jessica climbed aboard, approached the turret and found the business end of a large caliber pistol in the hands of Tara Mason.

The young woman smiled and pulled the weapon back, holstering it quickly. "Hex said you'd come looking for coffee."

"He's already awake, too?"

"Yep," Tara said. She ducked into the turret and the smell of strong, freshly brewed coffee came up from the open hatch, making Jessica's mouth water. "I hope you don't take cream or sugar. We're fresh out."

"It's fine, thanks."

Tara passed her a large steaming cup. "That's all I have left. If you'd like more, I can brew it."

Jessica shook her head. "This is great. Any more than this, and I'll either vibrate or spend the morning in the latrine."

Tara laughed. "I think we'll be busier than that, Peacemaker."

Her tone was all business and confident, any trace of doubt or cowardice either buried or non-existent. Jessica hoped for the second. "You've done your morning procedures?"

"We had stand-to 30 minutes ago." Tara sipped coffee of her own. "All vehicles are manned at 100 percent and security is active around the colony. The Altar have established their own security. I have Angels Eight and Nine manning a listening post to the west at the ridgelines. Surveillance radars are quiet, but I'm expecting the enemy to come rolling around by daybreak."

Jessica chewed the inside of her bottom lip. "We can't expect anything specific. I'm not sure they'll attack today, much less at daybreak. These are alien mercenary forces we're dealing with—not human ones. Their application of surprise differs a lot from ours."

Tara didn't say anything.

Jessica blushed. "I'm not trying to lecture you, Tara. I'm just stating that though we're prepared to fight, they won't come when we want or expect them to. That's all. I'm sorry if I came across badly."

"Like I'm a coward?"

Jessica flinched. "I didn't say that."

"Hex said you told him all about what you think happened to Death On Tracks. You were misinformed, Peacemaker. The official report clears my troopers and me of any wrongdoing."

"But you're guilty in the word of public opinion, aren't you?" Jessica asked. "Is that why you're here? You signed on to this mission thinking you'd find a way to clear your names in the eyes of the Guild?"

"Hak-Chet promised us an official recommendation upon completion of this mission. He told us you were his most promising student and, with your situation here, you would need particular assistance. That's why we're here, Peacemaker. We're going to support you or die trying."

Jessica took a lingering sip of the hot drink. Tara was telling the truth, she believed. "Okay, then. I'm glad to have you and your troopers. Let's hope it doesn't come to dying today or any other day."

Tara nodded. "Hex is up with Klatk discussing another trip into the tunnels. He's worried the Selroth will use the aquifer. He thinks their first bombs were supposed to open it enough that they could get through and attack us from underground. He wants to take a CASPer down there to check it out."

"It would take one hell of a pilot to maneuver one of those things down there," she said and sucked in a breath of realization. "That means him, doesn't it?"

"I'll command the defense while he checks it out. He wants to go as soon as Klatk can muster a team," Tara said. "You want me to tell him you're on your way?"

Jessica looked at the horizon now clearly visible in the distance. Before Morning Nautical Twilight was the first time the horizon was visible and was a harbinger of dawn, usually 30 to 40 minutes later. "I have to get back into the Raknar. My system scanner hit a snag. Once I'm done with that, I'll go to the command center. Tell Hex to go if Klatk is ready before then."

"Copy that," Tara said. She met Jessica's eyes for a long moment. "We're a long way from buying you that drink, huh?"

"I did finish it before I left."

Tara smiled. Her teeth were visible in the waxing light. "Maybe when we're done I'll get another chance?"

Jessica nodded. "Deal. I'm going to get going. Keep your eyes peeled."

"My what?"

Jessica chuckled. "Something my father always said. Keep your eyes open? Your head on a swivel? Same thing, but older. He was a character like that."

"You'll have to tell me more about him."

"I might," Jessica said. "We have to get that drink first."

"I'm holding you to that, Peacemaker."

Jessica reached over to the open hatch and extended a hand, which Tara shook. "Jessica. My name is Jessica."

"Well met, then."

A piece of memory flickered to life and Jessica laughed. "That's funny."

"What?"

"Something I haven't thought about since high school. The play Julius Caesar—something about meeting again and smiling, and if not, then the parting was well made."

"Brutus and Cassius before battle," Tara grinned. "We must have had the same teachers."

"At least ones that appreciated Shakespeare," Jessica said.

"I'll take that," Tara said with a laugh. "All things considered."

Jessica looked, again, at the first tinges of sunlight touching the horizon. The high, thin clouds glowed red. If she believed in omens, it would have been a bad sign. Still, it wasn't something she wanted to see, much less acknowledge as anything symbolic. But she had to. The young woman sitting with her and her soldiers, along with the Altar colony and Hex, were counting on her best effort. That meant understanding every possible piece of information and taking it at face value. Even bad omens.

"Going to be a long day, I think," she said and stood up on the tank's upper deck, stretching her back as she did. The rifle's strap cut into her neck, and she straightened it out, her hand lingering on the cold barrel. "A very long day."

* * * * *

Chapter Twenty-One

Hex stomped up the slope to the mine entrance in his CASPer. All systems green and cannons loaded, he made his way across the loose gravel, dodging Altar soldiers as they readied the colony's defenses. He glanced down at the Tri-V displays and saw that ground surveillance radars in the GenSha area were picking up too much movement to be simple morning chores. He punched up the radio. "Angel Seven, Boss. Wake up out there."

"Not sleeping, boss. Too much going on."

"What're you hearing, Kirkland?" Hex replied and kept moving up the slope.

"Vehicles, mainly. Some armor and a few lighter skiffs. No flyers or ducted fans that we can break out," Kirkland replied. "Things are busy to the west, too. No visuals, but plenty of noise."

Hex smirked. *Well, we knew they had to be there.*

"Relay that to Demon One, Angel Seven. Will try to get eyes on. You two be ready to un-ass that position, copy?"

"Loud and clear, Boss." The connection terminated, and Hex looked again at the mine entrance to see Klatk standing there on her hind legs waiting for him.

He stopped the CASPer a few meters away and opened the cockpit, but made no effort to disconnect any of the haptic connections or to leave the vehicle. He took off his earpiece and looked eye-to-eye at the two-meter-tall alien. "Honored Klatk."

"Where do you think you are going, Hex?"

Hex pointed at the mine entrance. "The Selroth are going to come through the aquifer on Level Six or Seven, Klatk. We have to seal it off."

Klatk's mandibles twitched. "Doing so will threaten both the brood and the aquifer. If we breach the aquifer, it will contaminate the mines and the river, itself."

"We don't have much choice." Hex shook his head. "They've already attempted it once. We have to get down there and plug the breach before they get through. What's the water going to contaminate if it gets through? What's down there, Klatk?"

Her antennae stiffened for a moment, and she leaned forward. "The water will be contaminated, Hex. Level Seven has a natural vent for raw crude oil. We sealed it off six months ago, but the wall structure is weak in many places." The aquifer would be contaminated and that would threaten the lower river and the Selroth colony, not to mention the bay and all the life there.

"Wait, do the Selroth want the oil?" Hex blinked. An aquatic species wouldn't want anything that would hurt them. He glanced up at Klatk. "There's more, isn't there? This isn't about oil. What's down there?"

Klatk's antennae swayed side to side. "When we dug the mine, we uncovered an enormous vein of gold running from Level Six to a much greater depth. We believe it's the largest vein ever found on a Dream World. Given the instability of the ground, mining it is nearly impossible. Having the Selroth detonating a bunch of explosives carelessly risks breaching the aquifer and opening the oil vent, as well as collapsing the whole mine."

For a moment, Hex thought that driving the Selroth away with the oil might be a good solution, but he understood. "Can we close that off, too? Say we close off both levels? Maybe everything below the brood?"

Another Altar scrambled up. "Yes. It's possible, but we'll have to plant a significant number of charges, and I'm not sure we have the time to haul them all down there."

Klatk nodded at the other Altar. "You've met my chief engineer?"

Hex waved. "Load me up, Plec. We can get down there now, seal off the mine below your brood and keep the Selroth out."

"It's not without significant risk, Hex," the engineer said.

"Then it's worth doing." Hex grinned. The Altar's mandibles vibrated in an equal response. "Can I fit down there?"

Plec studied the CASPer for a moment. "Can you walk with the legs bent more?"

Hex maneuvered the hips and knees of the CASPer to a more bent position. "Will this do? It won't be fast, but I can manage it."

"Our explosives are on Level Three. We should get them before we head down," Plec said, looking at Klatk.

"I'll send two squads of soldiers with you," Klatk said. "They can defend the aquifer and assist in laying the devices before you collapse the mine. I wish there were another way to do this."

Hex stared at her for a moment. "All we can do now is save your brood and cut off the Selroth's avenue of approach. If we can force them onto land, we stand a better chance of defeating them."

Klatk nodded. "I understand. I think you humans have a saying…good luck?"

Hex grinned. "We'll take it, but we need time and explosives first. Right, Plec?"

The engineer's antennae shook as he turned around and headed toward the entrance of the mine with Hex in tow. Either he was scared or ridiculously excited, Hex could not tell. He pushed the transmitter. "Bulldog, Hex. Over."

"Morning. What's your plan?"

"We're going to collapse the mine below Level Three. I'm taking their chief engineer and a couple of squads," Hex said. "Going to private Kilo One."

Hex flipped over to a scrambled standard frequency he knew Jessica would still have loaded on her slate. "What is it, Hex?"

"Level Seven is gold, Jess. The largest vein of gold ever discovered on a Dream World and maybe any other planet. There's a shit ton of it. But there's a significant risk of oil contamination, too."

He heard Jessica sigh. "Well, now we know why they're hiding it. Earth's economy, and more than a few other worlds', would spiral out of control with that discovery. Kenos and his asshole company must know about it, too."

"Or they strongly suspect there is something of value and are willing to kill for it," Hex said.

"This whole thing stinks," Jessica said. "They brought me out here to negotiate something they had no intent of negotiating, in order to make me look like an idiot and undermine the Guild, too."

"Well, let's stop them," Hex said. "I mean, Kenos has to come and verify what's in the mine, right? If he gets here, and I've collapsed the lower levels, he can't verify anything."

Jessica paused. "It opens up the Altar for lawsuits, Hex."

"Isn't that better than killing their brood and all of Klatk's colonists?"

"You have a point there." Jessica realized that settling a serious dispute in a Union courtroom, in this particular case, was a much better idea than all-out war.

Hex paused at the mine entrance and lowered the CASPer to its duckwalking position. "I'm going in, Bulldog. You'll feel it when we bring the mine down."

"Don't be in there when it comes down, Hex. I don't want to bury another Alison."

Hex chuckled with gallows humor. "If this doesn't go well, I'll have spared you the effort by burying myself, Jess."

"Be careful, Hex. I'm heading to the Raknar. By the way, you were right about Tara. Thank you."

Hex released a deep breath. "I'm glad you talked it out, Bulldog. She's almost as tough as you are. Hex, out." Hex opened up the CASPer's arms and accepted two crates of explosives from Plec and the gathered soldiers. At the entrance, he flipped on the rear camera and looked at the intense red sunrise along the horizon, imagining he could feel this planet's sun on his skin. He'd watched a sunrise with his father once, atop a craggy peak in New Mexico when he was barely a teenager. If he weren't meant to survive the day, his last memory of life on the surface was as poignant as his father's arm around his shoulders so many years and light-years distant.

"Let's go, Plec. Lead the way."

* * *

Qamm woke to urgent knocking on the door of her private quarters. "What is it?"

"Leader Qamm, there is a suborbital transport leaving D'Nart matching the description of *Tchrt One*. It's turning on a course that will bring it to the Altar Colony."

Her brain spun off the webs of sleep in an instant. "Estimated time of arrival?"

"Seventeen minutes," her aide said from the other side of the door.

"Wake the unit and have them ready to move in five minutes."

There was no reply, but she could hear the young Cochkala running away through the loose gravel outside her door. She leaned over to her slate and tapped in an access code. The communications application opened. She augmented it for security and pressed the last transmission button to re-engage in voice mode only.

"What is it, Qamm?"

"Kenos is enroute, Leeto. Are your forces ready?"

The Sidar chuckled. "My forces are ready. Unfortunately, the Selroth are not. I hope they can attack when we are ready to commit forces into the Altar zone."

Liar.

"Roust them, Leeto. Kenos will be on the ground in 17 minutes, and I want to push our forces forward the moment he sets down and starts raining confusion on the colony and its forces."

"You have too much faith in his abilities, Qamm," Leeto snickered.

She smiled in return. "He is a buffoon, incapable of handling a crisis with tact or focus. Our window will open within an hour, and we must be ready to strike."

"My forces are ready to move now. I will engage the Selroth and have them ready as soon as I am able."

Qamm fought the urge to roll her eyes, like a human, in disgust. "You do that, Leeto. The Darkness, out."

She disabled the connection and quickly donned her battle armor. The Veetanho prided themselves on near constant readiness for combat. She eschewed food or water and let her body chemistry warm up to the idea of combat. The "blood lust" effect of her pheromones would doubly affect those of her species in her employ. Their rage would be the crashing wave she and the rest of her forces would ride through the Altar defenses. Weapons in their holsters at her muscular hip joints, Qamm pushed through the door and found her vehicle moving towards her. Fully manned with four external laser gunners, the rolling platform could hold an entire battalion of forces at bay for a few minutes on its own. The twin 80mm recoilless rifles and quad laser cannons fired from the central gunner's position were overkill. She stepped aboard and clambered to her position atop the platform behind a dual mounted machine-gun. Despite her disdain of humans, their weapons of war, particularly the older, more lethal ones, had a special attraction for her. She charged the .50 caliber machine guns and tugged her combat helmet on.

"Darkness, this is Leader Qamm. Combat readiness check. Go."

One by one, her small hemispherical displays filled with vehicle icons that snapped to life as red boxes and transitioned to green diamonds as they readied for combat. In one minute, all her vehicles were prepared and ready to move. She tapped her console with a clawed hand. "Combat drones, prepare for launch on planned tracks."

Four icons flickered, and smaller icons that looked like a mixture of arrows and crosses hovered over the GenSha colony and moved out to create a forward position at 500 meters. The drones would look for obstacles and disrupt communications of anything in their path.

Qamm's radio crackled to life. "Qamm? What is happening?"

The GenSha leader's wavering voice made her smile. Fear was an incredible motivator, and the worthless politician was scared shitless. "Get your forces ready to attack as described in the plan, T'Genn. Move them north on my command by regiments. They are to continue the attack until I tell them to stop. Is that clear?"

"Yes, Qamm. But, I am concerned that—"

Qamm had just terminated the connection and changed her radio back to the command frequency when her fingers froze. A secure message on the agreed frequency blinked to life. *Do not target the Raknar. Acknowledge.*

She typed a message. *Acknowledged.*

For the briefest of moments, she paused at the controls. *Why would Kenos ask her not to target the Raknar? Had he or the Peacemaker discovered something useful?*

Qamm hesitated with a claw hanging in space above the transmit button. *Does it matter?*

Decision made, she jabbed the button. "Forward elements, move out. All units standby for consolidation. Targeting orders to follow."

With a swipe and a series of furious taps, she sent the information to her units telling them to avoid directly targeting the Raknar. One entire section of her forces undoubtedly sighed and whined to themselves as soldiers always did when things changed at the last minute. Most of them wanted to set the Raknar aflame simply so they could brag about it for the rest of their careers, no matter how long or short. The icons on her command ring formed up into their movement groups. Her first units, the reconnaissance team, moved out in a group of four-wheeled vehicles creeping forward slowly with all the sensor packages in full collection mode.

She'd let them get a kilometer or two ahead of the next unit before adjusting the movement plan based on what they found. The first 500 meters, there was nothing. Exactly as she expected, but there was nothing complacent about the approach her mercenaries took. At 1,000 meters out, there was a faint gathering of electrical component noise. Fifteen hundred meters out, there was a probability warning exceeding 60 percent for some type of enemy equipment on the battlefield. Weapons charged and ready, the reconnaissance team accelerated.

Two human CASPers jumped quickly in the direction of the Altar colony, loosing a spread of folding-fin aerial rockets to cover their escape.

"Let them go," Qamm transmitted. "Slow down to Gear Three. Forward strike teams, forward. Recon team take up the screen to the west and protect the riverbed. We'll draw their attention away from our friends."

She turned to her artillery officer, a young Sidar with leathery yellowish scales. "Hob? Set our first missions on preplanned points one through four. Standby for targets six and eight."

Less than five seconds passed. "Cannons are ready and targeted, commander. We're prepared to fire at any point along the attack corridor."

Qamm smiled. The temptation to start unleashing hell itself on the Altar and their human saviors almost prodded her to action, but she waited. The Wandering Death needed to get their attack together. Once they were in position, she'd certainly rain fire down on the colony and reduce the Altar infantry to pieces. The humans in their CASPers and tanks would be another story, but they were Leeto's problem. He wanted to get close enough to kill Kenos while wiping out the Altar completely.

He could deal with them while she did exactly what her contract stipulated. The icons for the forward strike teams, all four of them, moved out from the colony in a line abreast, separated by a few hundred meters. As they progressed north, the four groups of six vehicles would space themselves out further to confuse the Altar's visual sensors. Each of the sections possessed at least one vehicle capable of generating smoke on the battlefield that would spread and conceal the actual number of vehicles in the ruse. Had she not wasted her flyers at the urging of Leeto and Kenos, she would have positioned them in between each of the sections to broadcast false signatures of more than 100 vehicles each in the hopes of triggering a massive fusillade of defensive gunfire at very small targets. Whatever the enemy spent now, they could not spend later.

Qamm watched her reconnaissance team pass more than 2,000 meters out from her main unit with the forward strike teams close behind. It was time. She powered up her vehicle and its turrets and gestured to the driver to move out. As she did, she pressed her transmit button.

"Full complement forward! Attack!"

* * *

Taemin heard the commotion outside his temporary quarters a full two hours before sunrise. He rose and spent a half hour in silent meditation on the floor of the unit before he dressed and took his time with a sparse breakfast. As the level of noise rose to include the occasional stomp of CASPer units, he looked outside for a few moments and observed the activities in a clinical, detached manner.

Jessica Francis obviously thought her enemies would strike at first light—a popular human notion reinforced by countless poor holo-videos and Tri-V shows that had been around since the beginning of time. Administrator Kenos would arrive early, that was certain, but she knew nothing beyond what she might have felt in her gut during the planning process with her own *deputies* and the Altar colony leadership. They were awake and preparing for war, that was certain. Whether it would come, they did not know, but they did not wish to be surprised.

Taemin understood that reasoning. He spent a few minutes watching the humans moving around, and occasionally glanced at the Peacemaker's quarters. Her interior light wasn't on, and it appeared that no one wanted to wake her. He grinned. Another poor human trait was the notion that leaders needed their rest while those expected to follow them were exhausted by the lunch hour. Their guilt at waking their precious leader made him smile in pity. He watched her quarters for a full 15 minutes expecting her to emerge, but she did not.

He considered walking over and waking her, himself, just to see the exasperation on her face. She'd banned him from the Raknar, and whatever she was trying to do there, but the reality was that her mission was over the moment Kenos arrived and verified the presence of a brood exceeding contracted stipulations. She knew that, too, but she didn't trust the overall situation. He could write that off as paranoia in his final opinion, and it wouldn't change his recommendation. Should Jessica Francis survive the day, she would not be recommended for a Peacemaker's commission. Nor would any human, if Taemin had his way.

A shadowed figure walked between his quarters and hers, and in a split second of recognition, he knew it was the Peacemaker. Surprised, he checked the clock imprinted on his retina via neural connections. She'd been up for some time and was already moving quickly toward the Raknar to continue her work. She wouldn't find anything usable, of that Taemin was certain, as he had conducted his own investigations when others weren't looking the day before. None of that mattered. Kenos, if he kept to his schedule, was on his way to put an end to this charade of a mission. And yet, Taemin had to smile.

Kenos would certainly disrupt the Peacemaker's plan to save the Altar. But even on his best day of planning, and after his years of carefully executed manipulations, Kenos wouldn't expect to see anything like what he would find upon his arrival. Humans and Altar working together to protect a colony with a deep, expensive secret, facing annihilation from two very well-trained and experienced mercenary forces and their complicit colonial leaders was not in his thoughts.

It was all by Kenos' design, but the Administrator lacked the vision for truly enjoying the spoils of war. Manipulation was a key, but unspoken, tool of a mediator. Combined with vision and understanding, it would be easy to let the Administrator feel his plan was successful until the mercenaries converged upon him. The trap had been easy to set. The Peacemaker and her forces would be no match for the combined strength of the Wandering Death and the Darkness. Add in a few thousand Selroth and the herd mentality of the GenSha, and the battlefield would become a teeming storm of chaos and destruction that would both resolve the tense situation along the Choote River and make him a very rich mediator. He'd laid it out perfectly, and with Kenos on final approach to the Altar colony, there would be no stopping it.

All Taemin needed to do was find a place to watch the fireworks from and maybe force the Peacemaker to join him. He slipped a pistol under his robes and left his comfortable quarters for the Raknar's cockpit.

What better place to tie up all the loose ends?

* * * * *

Chapter Twenty-Two

Jessica reached the Raknar's crumpled form as the sun broke over Araf's eastern horizon. The craggy hills exploded in a shower of gold that slowed her steps and caught her attention for a moment. In the hills, deep oranges and reds showed from the exposed faces of the rocks in layers of varying thickness. Bright against the still dark skies, the mountains glowed like a stunning beacon; something she'd never seen the likes of on Earth. Above them, a bright white dot appeared and seemed to slow. There was no doubt who it could be, and it spurred Jessica's legs to action again.

One of the now crewless CASPers replaced Hex's as the holder of the cockpit door. The brand-new Mark VIII was a sleek machine. Realizing the need for munitions, Hex had stripped the heavier cannons and missile systems from the chassis before using it as a makeshift door stopper. A rocket launcher and two smaller machine guns remained on the vehicle's arms. She climbed up the built-in combat ladder on the vehicle's left leg and stepped into the open cockpit, placing a foot on the rail. From there, transferring further into the Raknar's cockpit section was a simple step. Jessica dug in her pocket and brought out two flashlights. One she positioned to shine up into the open system console and the second she put in her mouth. The climb was easier now. After several successful iterations, she knew where to put her feet and where to grab with her hands. She reached the control console in barely a minute, as the screeching sound of the *Tchrt One's* engines spooled down after landing.

She removed the flashlight from her mouth and slipped it into the system console, where it shone on Hex's combat slate and the panel with the missing chip. Jessica swiped the slate's screen. "Lucille? I'm replacing the chip now."

<<Affirmative. Systems check is now at 47 percent with negligible success. I was able to identify and open a bilge pump in the lower leg, but all other systems appear inoperative.>>

Figures. Jessica grimaced and looked up at the components. "Is there another panel I should try to engage?"

<<The central computing panel appears to be the third panel to the right from where I am connected. I recommend disengaging a chipset from there to achieve the connection.>>

"All right." Jessica reached over to the board filled with circular and semi-circular chipsets and carefully removed one. "Will that work?"

<<I need to be disconnected and plugged in,>> Lucille responded. <<A connection test will take approximately 120 seconds.>>

"Disconnecting you now." Jessica removed the clips connecting Hex's combat slate to the missing chip's position. She brought the clips to the new panel and attached them the same way. A flashing icon on the combat slate showed that a connection attempt was in progress.

Killing time, she looked into the console again and tried to discern the numerical system the Dusman used for identification. It should have been simple, but without the time to solve it and reverse engineer the Raknar's instrumentation there was nothing she could do but let Lucille evaluate the internal controls and try to find something, anything, they could use to their advantage.

"Peacemaker!"

Jessica whirled at Kenos' voice. It sounded as though he was climbing the CASPer from the proximity and volume of the call. She glanced at the slate and saw no change in the status. The realization that she should get down shot through her like a bolt of electricity. She reached into her pocket, found the missing rectangular chip and reached up to slip it into place with one hand while she tucked the combat slate out of view with the other. Satisfied, she grabbed the flashlight from the panel and climbed down the control console again. A clawed hand appeared on the cockpit door railing as she rose to her full height and placed her hands on her hips. Kenos wasn't tall enough to make the step from the last ladder rung to the CASPer's cockpit and over. That bought her just enough time to pick up the second flashlight, crouch below the control console and point her flashlight at the weapons console.

"What are you doing?" Kenos screeched as he crossed into the cockpit and stood on the curving wall above and behind her.

"Looking for an advantage," she said over her shoulder, without meeting his eyes. "What are you doing here?"

"Ending this charade of an investigation," Kenos huffed. "Your Mediator communicated to me that the Altar queen has been hiding a brood far exceeding the limits of the contractual agreement. I've come to verify his findings and remove the colony from Araf once and for all, by force if I have to."

Jessica looked over her shoulder again and turned just enough to see his face. "And did he also tell you that I'm not leaving? That you're not forcing anyone off a planet they colonized under your own false promises?"

Kenos sputtered, "You can't do that! The Peacemaker Guild cannot usurp the authority of a commercial venture."

"All decisions by a Peacemaker must be followed until vetted by the Guild, even those under duress. If you'd like to have my conduct vetted, I recommend you leave now and register a complaint with the Guild in the nearest system."

"How dare you!" Kenos screeched. "You are undermining the wishes of the Dream World Consortium! The Trading Guild will most certainly know that you have precluded their lawful pursuit of resources from this planet."

Jessica stood and turned. Kenos clasped his short arms across his chest. There was no weapon she could see. Standing higher on the wall, he had the advantage in a hand-to-hand fight. She had a laser rifle over her shoulder and a pistol on her hip. She might not get it out of the holster before he moved, but she could deflect him. Simple combat tactics were the best. Jessica slowly crossed her arms across her abdomen. "Just what resources are we talking about, Kenos? You're under contract for precious metals and other unexpected discoveries according to your contracts. They found something they are unwilling to extract, and you decided you want it. So, what is it? What do you hope to grab by setting three colonies to war?"

Kenos smiled and almost nodded. "If I knew that, I wouldn't be here, Peacemaker. My efforts to get into the mine, including the use of your mediator as an unbiased observer, have failed. With his discovery of their brood, I have the legal right to see what's in that mine. Once it's identified, the Consortium will declare first right of extraction under the auspices of the original contract. The Altar forfeit all claims to territory and equipment. They must leave and you have no grounds to protect them."

Jessica shook her head. "I have 7,000 reasons to protect them. Loss of life, especially of a species attempting a mass breeding effort to preserve colonization, is inherently protected by the Union."

Kenos waved her comment away with a laugh. "Not in our contracts, Peacemaker. Legally, our rights preclude their need for procreation. Besides, they are a barely sentient species. When they send a colony off, they have guidelines for return. The only reason Klatk and her citizens attempted this was to avoid disgrace."

"They did it to better meet their contract, Kenos. You knew that, and that's why you stopped purchasing what they extracted at the proper rates. You sold them everything from the company store and kept them from flourishing because they wouldn't do your dirty work. The minute you started manipulating their deliveries, they knew. Having more workers to produce would mean your supply would exceed your ability to sell it. That would lower the Consortium's ability to charge for whatever they found. You've been after them for a long time, Kenos. Now that they have something they will never willingly surrender, you're forced to enact a poorly worded contract and have mercenaries fight your war by proxy. It's fairly pathetic."

Kenos shook his head. "All I have to do is say the word and—"

The smile on his face faltered. His mouth worked soundless and he staggered forward. A trickle of blood, violet in the low light of the cockpit, spilled from the corner of his mouth, and he turned to the cockpit door and crumpled to the floor. Taemin rested an arm with a laser pistol on the railing and looked over it at her. Smoldering

Cochkala fur filled the cockpit with a noxious odor that made Jessica want to retch, but she held her ground and her stomach.

"Make no sudden move, Peacemaker," Taemin said. "If you'll be so kind, remove your laser rifle from your back and throw it to me."

Jessica felt for the strap without breaking eye contact with him. "It wasn't Kenos at all, was it?"

"Oh, he served a purpose, but he exceeded his usefulness." As Taemin finished there was a crumpling sound from outside, the familiar sound of artillery cannons. Detonations vibrated the Raknar's hull. "My friends have arrived with impeccable timing."

Jessica held out the rifle. "You sonuvabitch."

"Throw it out of the cockpit, Peacemaker." Taemin smiled as she did what he ordered. "I figured you deserved a good seat to watch the end of the Altar colony. All I forgot was your awful popped corn and syrupy drinks." He chuckled.

She slowly unbuttoned her holster and wondered, for a split second, if she could draw fast enough to get off a shot.

"I know what you're thinking. I can't recommend that course of action." Taemin chuckled. "Of course, it would make my task easier and faster. Either way, you'll have your name inscribed in the Guild's halls around the galaxy—the human peacemaker who almost was."

Jessica removed the pistol and hung it from the trigger assembly on her index finger. Taemin motioned with his head to throw it through the open cockpit, and she did. "Now what, Taemin?"

Another large explosion, much closer, rocked the Raknar. Taemin smiled over the pistol in his hands. "The Selroth are about to make things interesting. We're just in time to watch the festivities."

* * *

Leeto checked the readings relayed from the Selroth underwater team. "Honored Ooren, were you successful?"

"Negative on the first charge. We're deploying the remainder now. Will need cover for three minutes."

He pressed the radio transmission button on the control console for his skiff and said, "Darkness—attack by formations!"

Immediately, the different vehicles and complements of his combat teams accelerated from cover in the mountain valley. He led them from the front, using the large ballooned tires on his vehicle to bounce effortlessly over the rugged ground as he accelerated into the open Choote valley. To the south, immense dust columns rose as the Wandering Death and the GenSha infantry charged across open ground toward the Altar colony. Leeto smiled as he primed and tested his forward cannons. Action was everything and all too often under-appreciated. His 3,000 strong force roared forward into the quiet Altar flank.

After a moment, the Altar's defenses pivoted and fired volley after volley at his forces with some effect. He saw a bright flash as an enemy tank bolt roared into his formation and detonated on one of his large artillery pieces. The secondary explosion flipped 10 vehicles and disrupted the march of a full third of his forces for a few seconds.

"Enemy armor! Corner of the colony!" he roared into the radio. "Evasive maneuvers authorized!" Another bolt tore into the attack, and another. Each round hit its target with spectacular results.

Leeto changed frequencies and roared at Qamm, "Where is your gods-damned artillery! Their armor is on the corners of the colony!"

Qamm's voice came back in a staccato chuckle. "Reaching firing range now."

He glanced back to the south and saw a torrent of rocket-propelled shells arc up from the advancing mercenary forces. Leeto followed their arc, then lost the rounds as their engines cut off for the terminal guidance phase. The colony wall nearest him erupted in a series of explosions. Altar defenses, though, did not stop firing and two more tank bolts raced just past his vehicle to create more havoc behind him.

"Hit them again!"

"Do not tell me what to do!" Qamm screeched. Another round of rocket-assisted projectiles arced up from the advancing mercenaries, along with a fusillade of directed energy weapons that devastated the southwestern corner of the colony. A tremendous secondary explosion demolished much of the Altar colony's corner structure.

"That's one," Leeto said. Using a joystick, he toggled a targeting laser to the northwestern corner of the colony and transmitted it to his units. "Indirect fire engage at my command!"

A message scrolled across his heads-up display causing his fingers to freeze above the command console for a good five seconds.

—Primary target neutralized. Render colony to ashes.—

"Fire," he managed to say. As 100 rockets leapt up from his lead vehicle section toward the Altar colony, Leeto frantically wrapped his mind around the situation. With Administrator Kenos dead, the race would be for the resources in the Altar mines. Leeto looked away from the battle and scanned his displays for a layout of his forces and their intended targets. They were spread to provide maximum firepower on the colony, which was ideal given their position, but would not work for exploitation. "Infantry forces to the northwestern corner and converge on the mine entrance to assume primary mission. Acknowledge and move out immediately!"

The radio checks came in fast, but he hardly paid attention. The infantry icons moved where he wanted them to go, and he followed in their midst. Arrival at the mine entrance before Qamm's forces meant a greater claim to the resources below, providing they could eliminate the Altar completely and manage to hold off Qamm, the GenSha, and the Selroth until a settlement could be reached. That meant getting there first and getting the best position possible.

Leeto accelerated forward as his infantry converged on the main mine entrance against heavy resistance. The thousands of rounds exchanged shifted as the Altar broke and streamed toward the entrance, themselves. Leeto grinned. Gathering in a tight space would make it easier for his forces to eliminate them all. "Forward across the front. Maintain your rate of fire and target anything that moves. Double bonuses for all kills recorded."

The whoops over the radio let him know his troops weren't about to let a single target go unprosecuted. Leeto glanced at the colony and found the structure he believed to be the command center. He fired a handful of rockets at it and increased speed. His forward troops were two minutes away from the mine, and he was not going to let them enter it without him.

* * *

Hex hoisted the CASPer up the narrow tunnel from Level Six to Level Five without a care for the central conduit. As the power failed below him, Hex shuffled the CASPer out of the hole and ensured the Altar squads were far enough away to trigger the lower level collapse.

"Hex?"

He turned to see Plec moving his way. "We're almost out of explosives. We're going to need to go back to the surface for another load."

"I don't think we have that kind of time, Plec," Hex said. "We've got the aquifer plugged down there. Lay what you have here, and we'll collapse everything down there before we go."

Plec's antenna waved and hesitated. "There is another possibility we haven't considered."

Hex frowned, glad that Plec could not see his face inside the CASPer. "What?"

"There are other potential connections from the cavern aquifers to the river. The water table in this area is exceptionally high. Any avenue the Selroth can exploit, they will."

"And there's a place they can exploit?"

Plec almost shrugged in a very human way. "Level Three at the extreme northern end. There is a tributary of the river, an intermittent surface stream, that flows within a few meters of the aquifer's upper level. An explosive device placed there would be more successful than the locations they attempted before."

"You think they'll find it, Plec?"

"Yes. I believe they're finding it as we speak," Plec said. "They can use the sound waves from the explosions to find weaknesses as effectively as you humans use sonar."

Hex watched Plec's teams continue to work. The lower levels would collapse effectively, but Level Four really had no purpose other than to provide a stair-step approach from the surface. "Don't lay any more explosives. Tie these off to the ones below. Take everything else we have to Level Three."

"It won't be enough to close off that level, Hex," Plec said.

Hex worked the CASPer backward to the Level Three transition tunnel. He reached up with the vehicle's arms and yanked the conduit out of place to give him room to move. "Can we create an obstacle for the Selroth? Something to slow them down if they come through that aquifer?"

Plec's antennae waved, and Hex watched most of his team stand and move toward the vertical tunnel structure. "We can try, Hex. Once they breach there, incoming water will rapidly fill the tunnels below. We'll need to detonate them before we move up."

"Do it," Hex said. "We have to stop the Selroth on Level Three or they'll get to the brood and come in behind our flank on the surface."

Plec motioned silently to his soldiers, and they scrambled past the CASPer, up toward Level Three. The Altar engineer stepped up to Hex and held out a slate. "You can initiate the detonation sequence."

Hex squinted. "Why? I trust that you'll do it the second we're up there, Plec."

Plec nodded in a very human way. "Thank you, Hex. It is important for us to have your trust."

The mission timer caught Hex's eye. "Get up the tunnel. The second I'm clear, set it off and we'll move north to stop those bastards."

Plec scrambled up the tunnel leaving him alone in the near darkness of the defunct level. Hex checked his communications functions and found nothing that would get a message through to the surface. With a grunt, he reached up into the tunnel, dug the CASPer's articulated hands into the rough-hewn walls and climbed. Sending a message wasn't necessary, he realized. At the top of the tunnel, Hex shifted the CASPer clear of the vertical tube as Plec detonated the lower four levels in a series of explosions that sifted dust from the tunnel walls, causing it to rain down on them like a fine, gray snow.

Hex grinned. Jessica would know they'd done the first part of their task as clearly as any message he could transmit. The rest, though, was up to him, Plec, and two dozen Altar soldiers. The Altar scurried ahead of the CASPer to the northern end of the tunnel with laser rifles held at the ready. Hex duckwalked the CASPer after them and ensured his weapons systems were online and ready to fire. No matter how the Selroth came through the tunnel walls, they were in for one helluva surprise.

* * * * *

Chapter Twenty-Three

"Gunner! Fire and adjust!" Tara called to her gunner and relinquished command of the main gun tube. The hefty 150mm railgun tube swung from target to target. Belching out a little more than eight rounds per minute, her tank held the northwest corner of the Altar colony firm. "External machine guns to guided manual."

She flipped a switch and hefted the tank's heavy commander's hatch to a vertical, locked position. Tara stood on the back of her chair and engaged the twin .50 caliber machine guns hanging above her station. The mercenary forces from the south, combined with a tremendous number of GenSha infantry forces, flowed in giant waves toward her position and the main entrance to the mines. The teeming dark bands of infantry tried to use what cover and concealment they could, but the last 1,000 meters of their sprint carried them over open ground and left them vulnerable. Thumbs on the dual trigger, Tara disengaged the locking mechanism and swung the machine guns toward the forward elements of infantry. Leading the faster vehicles, she laid down a line of protective fire that sent the mercenaries who survived her initial barrage diving for cover. Finding none, they either fired in response or scrambled helplessly. Either way, her machine guns tore bloody swathes through them.

The Altar along the walls watched her for a moment, then turned their laser rifles the same way. A wall of ammunition stopped the infantry cold, but there were more coming. Artillery warnings screamed along the colony walls, again, and Tara dropped into the tank as a thundering assault of rounds dropped around the tank and the colony walls. She pushed up through the hatch, again, and took in the sight. More infantry rushed the position.

They're making for the mine.

She jabbed her radio transmit button. "Demon Three, Demon One. Disengage your position and get over here. Now."

Demon Three sat on the adjacent corner of the colony, facing southeast. The Selroth, if they were coming, were staying in the protective cover of the river. A perfectly good tank was sitting idle when she needed more fire on the enemy.

"Demon One, moving."

She went back to the guns and tore another broad swath through the mercenaries and more of the GenSha infantry forces. Artillery warnings screamed, and she dropped into the tank, again. In the cacophony of hell outside, dirt and rocks poured through the open hatch as a round narrowly missed the top of the tank.

Thank Gods they're firing dumb rounds.

Tara swung up and saw that the advancing infantry were moving out of sight toward the high ground at the mine's entrance. Demon Three showed up on her flank and laid fire on what it could see, but there were mercenaries in their rear area.

"Demon Three, you're in charge. Protect the mine entrance, that's their target. Standby for instructions. Break." She looked back at the northeast corner of the colony. "Demon Two, prepare for a full-frontal assault. Divert all Altar weapons to hold them off. Demon One is dismounting. My crew will continue to fight taking orders from Demon Three. Good hunting. Out."

She reached into the turret and unplugged her helmet from the tank by feel. Her rifle lay in its strapped position above the communications panel. After a second of hesitation, she grabbed it. As Tara vaulted up from the hatch, she brought the rifle to a ready position and made sure it was charged and active. The assaulting infantry's shots pinged off the colony walls near her with greater accuracy. Once they reached a good firing range, they would pick off Altar soldiers and defenses. Off the back of the still firing tank, she found one of Klatk's lieutenants.

"Bukk! Hit that infantry column with as much artillery as you can from this side of the colony. We've got them pinned down, but it's not going to last."

Bukk's antenna twitched animatedly. "More are approaching from the river. The Selroth are inbound. We have to stop them, too."

She changed tactics. "There's at least 50, maybe 100, that got through and are moving toward the mine. We have to stop them."

"Move one of your CASPers!" Bukk moved away to command the defensive effort from the nearest wall. Tara flinched as the idea struck her, followed by a thousand potential negatives.

I can't drive one of those things! I'm not a trained pilot.

You can't stop them with just this rifle and your charms, sweetheart.

The voice of an old drill sergeant broke through. *Why the hell not?*

Since Kei's inadvertent explosion, the unclaimed CASPers from her team sat in the middle of the Altar compound below the command center. Tara sprinted across the complex, feeling momentarily relieved as the amount of fire hitting around her shrunk to nothing. Artillery warnings came to life again and she dove for cover behind a series of containers that rocked and shook with every impact. Debris choked the air and she coughed and tried to move forward. As the dust cleared, she saw the command center still standing, but smoldering from several direct hits.

Not much time.

The CASPer they'd named Angel Three was open, attached to external power, and fully loaded as a backup. She reached the three-meter beast, climbed nimbly up the ladder and backed into the cockpit like she'd seen every CASPer pilot she'd ever known do. Once her legs were in their positions and the arms were down their interfaces, she wondered what the hell she was doing. There was no way this was going to work.

"I can't even close the gods-damned hatch!"

<<Hatch closing.>> A woman's voice came from the speakers mounted on the forward shield above her temples. The heavy cockpit shield swung closed and pressurized with a quick whoosh of air.

With only the safety lights on, a dim red glow surrounded her. *How the hell do I do this?*

"Cockpit lights?"

The interior white lights flickered to life. The Tri-V screens and the external camera displays were still off so all she could see besides the instrument panel was the inside of the cockpit door about six inches in front of her face. "Well, that's a start."

<<Confirm vehicle start?>>

"Confirm vehicle start," she said slowly. The master vehicle power controls snapped on one-by-one and her displays came online.

<<Full operational capacity in 30 seconds.>>

Tara blinked. "CASPers don't talk, and I don't have pin plants. How in the world are you doing this, Lucille?"

<<Peacemaker Francis wanted better command and control during combat operations, so she allowed me to download to a vehicle as necessary. Given that you are not a trained CASPer operator, yet inside a CASPer, produced a logic error. I compute a 90 percent probability that you are intending to deploy this CASPer to prevent the Darkness from entering the mine complex. Your chances of survival are low given your lack of training and experience with this vehicle. In this capacity, I can maneuver this vehicle based on your inputs and your verbal commands.>>

"Like a co-pilot?"

<<That is a satisfactory definition. I'll have to use accelerometers in the vehicle's limbs to approximate your movements, or I can take mobile control, if you wish.>>

"Will the accelerometers work accurately—say if I'm trying to walk, can you make it walk?"

<<There is an eight percent chance I will be able to accurately read your leg movements. The arms are significantly better at 71 percent because of their fine motor dampening system. Walking under your own power is not possible or recommended.>>

"Can you help me make this thing walk?"

<<Affirmative. Walking is little more than mastering balance. What you do with your inner ear, I can do with accelerometers and faster microprocessors.>>

Tara laughed. Everything sounded so easy from intelligent computers. Still, without Lucille's assistance, she was a sitting duck in a CASPer and unable to stop the assaulting infantry. Altar soldiers could hold them off for a bit, but their lack of firepower would be grossly overmatched by the mercenaries. Any force worth their salt hit the ground running with as much manpower and as many weapons multipliers as they could afford. The good forces, like what she'd seen so far, would eradicate the Altar in minutes.

The master vehicle power console was fully green. All external displays came on line and she could see the battle space through the heads-up display. A large command skiff pushed past Demon One and brought multiple cannons to bear on Demon Three. The tank's more open position left them vulnerable. The two vehicles traded three bolts a piece before Demon Three detonated. The enemy command stiff skidded to a halt. A Sidar opened a top hatch and waved its leathery arms wildly. About 50 infantry stood up from cover and moved ahead of the skiff. The leader closed the hatch and set to engaging more targets that Tara couldn't see, but it was clear where they were headed.

"Get us to the mine entrance, Lucille. As fast as you think you can go. Bring all weapons online and tie me back into the command net."

<<Affirmative. Weapons online, and you are active in the network.>>

The CASPer reared up on its legs and began to move with Tara as a passenger. For a second, it was like being in a horse costume. She moved the front quarters and Lucille moved the rear. Uncoordinated and clumsy, it could still get the job done.

"This is Demon One Actual in a CASPer, callsign is now Angel Two, moving to the main mine entrance. SITREP, over?"

A massive explosion nearby shook the CASPer. Demon One's icon winked out. Demon Two called over the radio. "Ma'am, we've got Selroth advancing out of the river. Request permission to pull back the defense. Over."

Dammit. Tara pressed the transmit button. "Supplementary positions authorized. Get the Altar to —"

WHAMM!

Artillery rounds exploded around her and knocked the CASPer off its tenuous legs. "Lucille!"

<<Systems nominal. Restoring movement now.>> The vehicle stood upright again and moved up the hill. She came around the last external revetment of the colony and found the mercenary infantry pinned down by Altar fire.

"Hold up here, Lucille." She pulled up on the arms and the twin cannons rose. The charged icons clicked from red to green as the safety disengaged. There were more than a dozen icons just on the other side of the wall. Tara took a deep breath and got ready to step around the corner. "Get ready to fire, Lucille. If there's something I can't hit, but you can—take the shot."

<<Just once or for all engagements?>>

"Every time."

* * *

As she stood in the hatch to clear a jammed weapon, Qamm looked over the battlefield and saw the mechanized portion of Leeto's forces were precisely where they should have been. The 200 collected skiffs and wheeled vehicles laid down an impressive rate of direct fire on the southern wall of the Altar colony. Yet, something was wrong. It took Qamm a few seconds to put it together. The infantry had moved to the north and flanked the colony. Given the position of both the Altar defensive weapons and the Peacemaker's tank forces, it was suicide.

Unless it wasn't. She cleared the mechanism, reloaded the old, reliable machine gun and dropped into her hatch, reaching for the radio before her haunches came to rest in her command chair. "Leeto, you've deviated from the plan."

"Kenos is dead, Qamm. Our unofficial arrangement is off, and my forces will secure the mines and eradicate the colony while your forces attrit the enemy for us. Pleasure doing business with you!"

The line terminated, and she slapped the side of the console in anger. Kenos dying had been part of the plan in the first place. Something had happened at the colony to give Leeto an advantage for flanking the infantry. She reached over and fired a ballistic drone on a maximum arc trajectory. As it leapt from its tube and accelerated to several hundred miles per hour and an altitude of 3,000 feet, she mashed the transmit button. "All forces, guns to maximum and charge on plan bravo. I repeat, charge on plan bravo. Make those bastards pay!"

Half of her combat forces broke for the Altar compound walls at full speed with their cannons blazing. Altar defenses sprang to life but quickly fell silent under withering fire. The other half of her forces charged directly across the open plain at Leeto's mechanized vehicles and the Selroth's deployed artillery pieces. Immediate results were similar. The mercenary units returned fire and attempted to maneuver to attack or withdraw before Qamm's vehicles overwhelmed them. The Selroth moved like fish out of water in a blind panic to the north. Her claw hovered over the transmit button for a lingering second as she considered the carnage her soldiers would expend on the hapless Selroth. They, like Leeto, would be taught a lesson. Her forces continued their bloody pursuit as she swung the vehicle back to the Altar colony and centered her weapons on what she believed to be the command complex. "Match my target and fire—all available cannons!"

She fired a stream of guided missiles at the structure and saw similar streaks erupt from different cannons across the battlefield. Without a commander, the Altar would panic. All defenses along the walls would cease, and she would be able to better direct her forces to both undercut Leeto's infantry and see what resources she could acquire. The ballistic drone reached its peak altitude and deployed wings and sensor packages. Immediately, a clear picture of the Altar colony came into view. Three of the four human tanks were gone. The one remaining was badly damaged and firing only from its secondary loader's machine-gun. As she watched, two of her vehicles dispatched it in a dual cannon crossfire.

Leeto's infantry streamed toward the mine entrance, but the Altar defenses were impressively coordinated and holding them mostly at bay. A command vehicle and two platoons of mercenaries appeared to have breached the colony walls and worked their way through the complex toward the entrance. The Altar defensive ring appeared decidedly soft with their backs toward the colony complex. The other side of the ring was six or eight soldiers deep compared to a line of troops three deep securing the colony exits and logistics area. Soft targets were Leeto's speciality. There was no doubt that he, personally, led the attack.

Qamm pushed the vehicle to its maximum speed and jostled inside the cockpit as it bounced over the roughening terrain near the quiet colony walls. A look back at the drone's display showed a single human CASPer still moving toward the mine entrance. One vehicle against that many soldiers and a command vehicle wasn't very good odds. As she studied the screen, something appeared near the fallen

Raknar. She zoomed the camera in and released the accelerator controls.

The Raknar's cockpit section sat ajar, held open by the frozen arms of an unmanned CASPer. Inside the cockpit were two figures. One was the human Peacemaker. The other appeared to be a Caroon wearing long robes despite the rising heat. Interestingly, the Caroon held a pistol on the Peacemaker.

Qamm slammed the brakes on her vehicle and cut back across the colony walls, making for the Raknar at all possible speed. Kenos was dead. The Peacemaker and her forces had been effectively neutralized. Leeto charged the mines against significant resistance and carelessly left a loose end. Whoever the Caroon holding a weapon on the Peacemaker was, he was more important to the situation than Kenos had ever been.

And someone with whom she could discuss terms.

* * *

Klatk turned back to look at the destroyed command post, as more weapons slammed into the collapsed roof and flattened it into the rock from which it came. Her antennae twitched with thousands of pheromone-carried messages. The injured called for assistance. Commanders rallied their troops. Damage control teams reported the loss of the colony walls and defenses. Markers for the dead, both human and Altar, also filled the air. She caught the scent of the Peacemaker, alive and well, on the wind from the river, along with the dead-fish stink of the Selroth as they came up from the water and surrounded the Raknar but kept their distance from shore. There weren't more than 100 of them, which meant they were waiting to come ashore until their infantry pushed through the mines from below.

Klatk sifted through the data in the air. There was nothing from Plec or any of the teams below ground. She'd have to send a runner to establish contact. It was time to consolidate the defenses and protect the brood.

She rushed into the wide circle around the mine entrance and screeched for her commanders. "On me! Consolidate the defenses on Levels One and Two. Protect the brood!"

Bukk rushed past with his squad, and she grabbed him by the arm. "My Queen?"

"Get a message below, as far as you can. Protect the brood and consolidate all defensive positions. We fight to the last Altar."

Bukk met her eyes. She could see and taste his fear. "I understand. Protect the brood."

"It's the only chance we have, Bukk." She tapped his shoulder with a claw and noticed his wounds. He'd been injured several times, many of the ragged holes in his carapace slowly leaking thick, dark blood. The young warrior hadn't quit, though. She knew he would get the message to Plec. "Do it well."

"I am honored," he said and jogged away to the mine entrance. She watched him go for a moment as the circle tightened inward, and more of her troops flowed to the mouth of the cavern to take their final defensive positions. Klatk reached down to the ground, collected a laser rifle and slung it over her shoulder. A few meters away, she picked up a second, and then a third. One she placed over her other shoulder, the other she loaded and carried to the edge of the circle.

The commander there, a young female soldier named Chart glanced over her shoulder and stiffened in recognition. "Queen Klatk! How can we—"

"Let me pass," Klatk said. She nodded down the embankment toward the river. "The Peacemaker is in trouble and as long as she lives, there is a chance we succeed."

Chart stammered. "Let-let us come with you. You will need our protection."

Klatk snorted. "Their approaching guns are silent. They believe they've won, save for the final battle they expect here. You must give them that battle, Chart."

The young warrior's mandibles quivered in fear, but she bowed her head. "We will not let you down, Klatk."

"Nor I you," Klatk said. "Covering fire on my mark. Keep the infantry to our right pinned down, and let me get to the top of the containers there. I will vault to the colony roof and get out of their sights."

Chart's antenna waggled. "We will give you a clear path to the Peacemaker, Klatk."

Klatk nodded. She didn't need to go that far, but once she got down to the colony, she could move to the Raknar without being seen. "Our enemies on the plains are more concerned about each other, Chart. Stop these infiltrators and give the Peacemaker time to deal with their leaders, and we will see another day."

Chart's mandibles stiffened, and she turned to her soldiers. "Covering fire!"

Twenty laser rifles came to life in a pulsating wave of fire. Klatk hesitated barely a second before she ran toward the containers, effortlessly climbed them, and sprang into the open air across a wide passageway. She glanced down and saw mercenaries moving toward the security perimeter and heard a vehicle approaching behind the near corner. Landing on the roof of the far structure, she turned back and caught a different scent in the breeze.

Tara was still alive and in a CASPer, moving to stop the clandestine attack. She looked at the Raknar in the distance and ran. Tara could hold her own in a fight, much like the Altar soldiers at the mines. They knew their task and what must be done, and they didn't need her to command them.

Klatk, like most Altar, didn't believe in a higher power or presence like God. Nor did she believe that things in the universe were random occurrences. Fate and karma were familiar concepts, but outside of the Altar lexicon. What mattered to them was action. Rather than wait for Tara to stop the mercenaries, or for Hex and his team to detonate the lower mine levels, or sit and watch the enemy get closer and her own soldiers die, there was something she could do for a young human that needed her help. Klatk moved across the colony as fast as her legs would carry her. Jessica Francis could still end the conflict if the mercenaries didn't get to the brood first.

If Hex and Plec failed in their quest to detonate the lower levels, and the Selroth and mercenaries reached Level Two, the slaughter would not stop. Committed to the last soldier, Klatk wished for another result but knew that, ultimately, action was the only way forward. Her eyes on the Raknar and Jessica standing in the open cockpit door, Klatk ran.

* * * * *

Chapter Twenty-Four

On the edge of the Raknar cockpit's tilted view of the world, Jessica crossed her arms and spoke over her shoulder. "You must be pretty proud of yourself, Taemin. Most mediators never amount to much more than overpaid, self-indulgent barristers in the Union courts. You've managed murder, proxy aggression, and undermining a civilian government within, what, two years of graduation from the legal academy?" She snorted and let it become a throaty laugh. "That must be some kind of record."

Taemin said nothing. His silence surprised her as much as his inaction did. He obviously wasn't going to kill her, at least not yet. He wasn't capable of it, and she was sure he wanted someone else to do the job. Whether it was a mercenary or a different colonist, he would have someone else do the deed. Deep down, he was a fucking coward who didn't have the balls to own up to his plan in the end. She shook her head silently. Taemin would have been a perfect fit for the planetary military units—all pomp and circumstance without the ability to fight their way out of a wet paper sack. His bravado and cunning, she had to admit, were stellar qualities, but he lacked the follow-through to really get anything done. This whole colony versus colony business was simple proxy aggression. He'd made promises to all sides to facilitate his own endgame, and he needed Jessica alive in case it all went south. If the battle ended the way he intended, then he could easily have one of his paid associates pull the trigger. As long as the Altar fought off their attackers, Jessica was fine. She knew the defensive structure Klatk would use, and it kept anxiety from rearing its ugly head and panic from overtaking her thoughts.

She listened for several heartbeats and could hear a steady thumping of weapons fire from the area near the mine entrance. The fight continued, and that gave her the most precious resource possible: time.

Think, Jess.

Taemin spoke softly. "How does it feel to see it all slip away? You could have had the easiest mission any Peacemaker ever undertook, but your sense of duty got in the way. The Altar have been defeated. All you gave them were a few extra hours, at best."

"They're still fighting, Taemin. As long as there is one Altar with a weapon, it won't end." She walked closer to the edge of the cockpit and looked outside. Fewer attackers than she imagined surrounded the two colony walls that she could see. "Your forces took a beating. There's barely a regiment at the walls."

"They couldn't keep from fighting each other." Taemin laughed. "Given that they think there's something of value to their home worlds buried in that mine, you could almost say it was destiny for one of them to try and take it. What is it you humans say? To the winner goes the prize? Something like that?"

"To the victor go the spoils." Jessica relaxed her arms, placed her hands on her hips, and glanced down. The sandy shoreline was no more than three meters away; she could make the jump easily. Both of her weapons were close enough to grab once she hit the sand. The fall would be simple. She'd learned enough in basic parachutist school to handle the fall and the landing. Technique wouldn't be a problem. Her footing would be the issue. Snap or roll an ankle, and any escape would be impossible. She'd be enough of a stricken target that even Taemin could finish her.

"Don't think about jumping, Peacemaker."

"I'm thinking about the landing and wondering if it's worth the chance." She looked over her shoulder. Taemin stood up and kept the pistol leveled at her.

"There's nothing stopping me from shooting you right now."

She half-whirled on him. "Then do it, Taemin. You've orchestrated this whole thing. You killed Kenos in cold blood and set three peaceful colonies to war. Killing me should be the easiest thing you have to do."

He raised the pistol. Her mind flashed that he was really going to do it. She dropped her arms to her sides and brought the palms up quickly. She staggered backward once, then again, her feet searching for purchase along the cockpit's railing system. "You don't want to do that, Taemin. My neural recorders are active and—"

Taemin barked laughter in a staccato measure that made her queasy. "You don't have pinplants, much less a neural network, Peacemaker."

Look away, even for half a second you piece of shit. Just look away and—

Inside the cockpit, a click reverberated through the floor and an immediate, deep thrum came up through the floor/wall. Taemin flinched and looked up at the systems console. Jessica jumped feet first through the open cockpit hatch. As she fell to the sand, she heard Taemin gasp.

"What have you done?"

Jessica hit the sand in a textbook parachute landing—feet and knees together—rolled to one side and kept moving under the protective curve of the Raknar's Control section. As she scrambled to safety, she grabbed the laser rifle and decided in a split second that the pistol was too far away to sensibly reach. Under cover, she cleared and function-checked the rifle, and selected burst. There were 40 rounds available in the battery. It wasn't going to take that many.

She tapped her earpiece. "Lucille? Report."

There was no response.

Jessica watched the motionless CASPer's legs looking for Taemin to climb down. Nothing happened. After 90 more seconds of watching, she moved along the curvature of the Raknar's helm section to find a better vantage point. Fresh explosions rippled down from the colony. A large secondary explosion detonated into a sweeping, high rolling cloud tinged with blue flames.

More gunfire rippled along the higher ridgeline. Klatk's forces were almost in their final defensive positions. As long as they could get to the mine entrance and seal it, they would be okay. A piece of the Raknar's fuselage hooked the leg of her coveralls and she knelt to remove the snag, watching the CASPer for any sign of Taemin. The ragged tear in the Raknar's armor looked just large enough to hold her. She shimmied into the space and managed to keep a clear vision of the field in front of her. If Taemin came down to find her, there was just enough room for her to sight and fire the rifle.

It only takes one, Bulldog. Her father's voice was calm and little more than a whisper. They'd been hunting ducks on the family's property with her first rifle. There was no way she was going to hit anything with a .22 rifle, but hunting wasn't always about hitting targets. She'd fired until her bony shoulder was tired and sore, each time learning a little more from her father's whispers and corrections. Every time she looked at the sight picture of a weapon, she could hear him in her head as clearly as if he were there.

From her VOWs right through the Peacemaker Academy, she'd qualified as an expert on every weapon system she trained on. Shooting was as easy as breathing, but it was not something cavalierly done. By edict, a Peacemaker only used a weapon when all diplomacy and decency failed. As a cadet, she'd argued with her instructors about the use of force, suggesting that common practices like rules of engagement only served to escalate conflict. They refused to budge on her assertion that a weapon in a holster or on a sling was just as powerful as a weapon at the ready in the face of an enemy. Honoring the threat went beyond believing the enemy should only see a weapon in the worst situations. When a Peacemaker's weapon was drawn, it was the end of diplomacy and the beginning of the end for their opponents. With nothing to lose, and colonists needing what protection she could deliver, she had more than enough reason to fight back.

* * *

Level Three resembled hell. The tight corridors were filled with thick, acrid smoke. Hex used the CASPer's thermal view system to see into the distance as marauders from the Wandering Death assaulted from a closed-off, unstable mine entrance far to the northwest of the colony. Fifteen to twenty of them came into the main tunnel complex, quickly established a defensive position and produced a withering rate of fire.

Another explosion rumbled through the mine from the northeastern side as the Selroth worked on the tight aquifer to gain passage into the complex. His radio buzzed to life. "Hex? They're through the aquifer."

The two tunnels to the north branched out, and Hex saw lights in the distance in the northeastern one. For a moment, the firing from the defensive position halted as they likely tried to see what was happening in the other tunnel. The lights grew closer and came with a familiar buzzing hiss.

Selroth.

He watched them approach and expected the mercenaries to open fire. A scream like a gods-damned rebel yell rang out in the cavern. The Altar squads at his command did not need orders or encouragement. They rose as one from their defensive positions and returned fire. Hex hoisted the CASPer up from its defilade position and brought both cannons to bear on the advancing forces. The Selroth numbered at least 100, maybe more. They poured through the northeast passageway and into the main tunnel. The mercenaries lifted their fire and allowed the Selroth to move up and find positions. A crew-served weapon on a tripod appeared.

"Not this time," Hex said and fired his left railgun at the piece. It exploded and took out a circle of Selroth five meters wide. The advancing humanoids and their hissing rebreathers kept coming.

"First squad is 30 percent effective," Plec called from his position. "Second squad is 15. We have to blow this whole level now!"

Hex walked the CASPer forward. What felt like thousands of rounds impacted the sturdy metal frame. He brought his cannons up, noted they both had less than 3,000 rounds remaining, and opened fire. Tracers let him see the rounds and walk them over the Selroth positions. As the machine guns fired, he rippled off a half-dozen missiles into both tunnels to create confusion.

"Fire in the hole!" Plec called and mashed the detonator. Under their feet, the mine groaned and rippled as the ceiling partially collapsed. Rock fell from the ceiling in small showers everywhere Hex could see. The mercenaries and Selroth howled in rage and came up firing.

It's not enough!

"Covering fire!" Hex yelled and tried to walk the CASPer into a protected position. There was nowhere to go. The caution and warning system flashed a dozen critical warnings at once. He brought the missile pods online and fired them on semiautomatic, in rapid succession, to give the engineer time to formulate a plan.

WHAMM!

Plec's volume of fire ended in a violent explosion. Hex turned the CASPer and saw another tripod weapon scanning toward him. The left railgun dispatched it. There was nothing he could do for Plec or the others.

<<Critical ammunition warning!>> The onboard system called along with a litany of failures Hex barely heard. He looked around and saw the Altar around him were dead. Mercenaries of various species rallied together with the Selroth and advanced on him.

The servo motors on the left leg seized and braced him in an awkward position, but Hex continued to fire. Seven hundred rounds per gun remained.

Shit.

He looked down, firing blindly outside, at the picture of him and Maya just a few months before, smiling, happy, with the rest of their lives ahead of them—together. They'd never imagined this. Both cannons spun into empty chambers. The mercenaries and Selroth continued to fire for a moment, and then ceased. A taller, older Selroth with black on the tips of his facial tentacles stepped forward into the smoke barely 50 meters away. None of the crowd behind him moved.

"They're waiting for me to surrender." Hex whispered.

Hex laughed and checked the vehicle stores. He was out of rockets and cannon ammunition. His laser might fire, or it might not, because of damage.

I might collapse this whole level and take out a whole bunch of those fuckers if I blow up like Kei did.

Hex froze. The thought ran over his mind like ice-cold electricity and made every hair on his body stand up straight. Most of the suit stood on the edge of failure at any second. All he had to do was disengage everything except the reactor safeties and it would be easy.

But the reactor would be a bigger boom.

"Disengage all safety protocols." Hex chuckled and shook his head. "My father always said, 'Go big or go home.'"

Using his cursors, Hex disabled the safeties one by one until only the reactor safety remained. With the right railgun's power spooling up, he'd need to replicate what happened to Kei in order to jolt the system into electrical failure. The CASPer strained to move, but Hex brought the left leg around as if squaring to the crowd eagerly awaiting his surrender. He raised the right arm, with the hand open, methodically slowly. The railgun showed a power reading of 104% and climbing.

"Adios, motherfuckers," Hex called over the CASPer's external speakers. The Selroth didn't move. A few of the mercenaries, the ones who obviously understood English or had watched enough bad movies to recognize the saying, backed away wide-eyed. Hex pushed off the CASPer's half-frozen left leg and drove the right arm into the cavern wall. The impact jostled him, but nothing happened.

109%.

114%

Hex staggered back to the left and tried again. The Selroth howled and brought up their weapons. His external cameras failed under the onslaught. Again, he slammed the cannon into the wall, but nothing happened.

127%

At 150%, the generator would overload and shut down the entire CASPer system—the one failsafe he could not disarm.

134%

A series of heavy impacts staggered the CASPer backward, and Hex nearly fell over. The gaping tunnel to Level Four was back there somewhere. If the cannon wouldn't fail, he'd try to rupture the reactor shell. That would be enough. He lunged at the wall again, but nothing happened. He looked down into the cockpit and panicked. The picture of him and Maya had fallen away. Hex scanned for it and saw nothing.

"No!" He grunted and shook himself inside the cockpit from side to side. "Gods-damnit!"

A cool breeze tickled his forehead. Logic told him it was a sputtering cockpit fan trying to cool down the system, but for a moment it was a seabreeze as clear and fresh as it had been several months before and conjured a memory that Hex allowed to stay. The quiet bungalows of Barking Sands glowed yellow in the setting sun as he and Maya lay there listening to the quiet surf. They'd made love there in the afternoon as the private beach was deserted and empty most of the time. Maya curled against his chest, with an elbow across him.

The smile on her lips grew wider with every passing second. Her tanned skin shone with sweat from their lovemaking and the last remnants of sunscreen many hours old. Black, curly hair hung down by her face in waving tendrils that tickled his face and neck with every breeze. A fingernail traced his bare chest as she looked him in the eyes.

"Just one more?"

He grinned up at her. "You're insatiable."

"I know what I want" she said and leaned down to kiss his lips gently. "I want you. With me. Forever."

"So not just one more, then."

She squeezed him with her elbows. "One more is all we need for now."

Hex opened his eyes.

146%

I love you, Maya.

He pushed to the right with everything he had. The CASPer crunched into the wall, but there was no bright flash of light. No detonation. The braying sounds of his failing suit filled his ears. The left leg froze, and he stumbled backward, into open space. Falling down the vertical connecting shaft, his back toward the rapidly approaching ground, Hex tried to pull the memory back but it would not come. He'd failed. There was nothing anyone could do now. In the moment, all he wanted was that scrap of memory—like after waking from a dream and desperately wanting to somehow, in some way, get back inside—to feel her as if she were there once more.

Eyes squeezed shut, tears erupted under his eyelashes. "C'mon! Just once!"

White light blossomed behind his eyelids. Amidst the sudden heat, he heard Maya playfully call, "Just one—"

* * *

The empty outer defensive walls of the Altar colony felt eerie and strange as Qamm made her way down the hill toward the fallen Raknar. Occasional missiles ripped through the open sky above her, and coupled with the sporadic laser fire, gave the impression of an early morning on a training range instead of the end of a pitched battle. Nearer to the Choote River, the air cooled and felt moister than at the higher levels. She peered around every corner as she crept quickly through the defensive revetments. Dead Altar lay everywhere. In places, their bodies lay entwined with human soldiers and their smoking, destroyed CASPers. At the last corner, the gentle breeze swept a choking smog of burning fuel, ammunition, and human remains from a smoldering main battle tank.

Qamm shuddered. The idea of dying in battle was nothing new to her, but dying without a chance of escape in a cramped and dangerous space like a tank sickened her. She glanced at the fire only once before turning into the passageway that opened to a gentle slope all the way down to the Raknar. In the placid river, she saw several Selroth raiding parties keeping their distance from the shore.

What are they waiting for?

She answered her own question almost immediately with a snort that became a silent sneer on her face. "For someone else to do their job," she said to the breeze.

A ripple of explosions shook the upper portion of the colony enough that she felt the vibrations in the lower revetments. There were no forces in the space between her and the Raknar, but she did not want unnecessary trouble. She fingered a small button on her combat vest and pressed it—alerting friendly forces to her position as she ran down the slope, angling toward the back of the Raknar's helm. From there, she could creep around to the open cockpit.

The sprint took only 40 seconds, and she pressed her back against the cool Raknar's hull. Making her way around the helm took a minute, mainly because she checked every direction she could see, looking for the Peacemaker or whomever held her captive.

At the crest of the helm, Qamm glanced around the curving surface just as the Peacemaker fell from the open cockpit, rolled to her feet and scrambled into the cover the fallen mecha's body provided. If she could capture the Peacemaker, she could have an advantage. She readied herself to move by holstering her laser pistol and removing a large serrated-edge combat knife. Up close, the blade proved to be a far better motivator than a pistol.

Hands pressed against the Raknar, she inched toward the rounded edge one last time to survey the scene when the ground buckled violently, throwing her into the Raknar's hull, then to the ground like a doll.

KA-WHAMM!

Dust rose up from the ground and curled in an invisible gale rushing down from the Altar mines. More ripples came across the sandy soil, streaking toward her in a groaning, seething mass. The Raknar's hull squealed and flopped.

She touched her earpiece and heard nothing. The entire command network was silent. As she looked back toward the colony, there was nothing there but dust gently billowing up from everything. A series of smaller ripples raced across the ground and were gone. Qamm stared at the silent destruction.

What did they do?

* * * * *

Chapter Twenty-Five

Tara strained to see anything in the CASPer's forward quarter even with the thermal imaging system engaged. Thick clouds of dust swept down the colony passageways obscuring everything in front of her.

<<The command vehicle is moving again.>>

"I can't see it, Lucille."

<<Radar lock. Fifty meters and moving this direction. Weapons online and prepared to fire.>>

Tara waited. Her position in concealment, aided by the swirling clouds of dust and rock, gave her an advantage. "I'm going to let him pass. Have you established contact with Klatk or Hex?"

<<Negative. All communications channels appear to be offline.>>

"What the hell happened?" Tara asked without expecting an answer.

<<Assessment is 75% probability of a medium-yield nuclear detonation below the surface.>>

Tara blinked. "How much of a yield?"

<<Consistent with the capability of a CASPer engine.>>

Her stomach knotted up and flipped in one motion. She mashed her eyes shut and forced herself to focus on the task at hand. They didn't know what had happened and even if Lucille was right, it didn't mean that Hex and the others hadn't survived.

"Where's the command vehicle?"

<<Thirty meters.>>

Tara tried to relax and formulate a plan. Most combat vehicles possessed thick armor on the fronts and sides to repel as much potential damage as possible. That typically left both the rear and the top of the vehicle vulnerable to direct fire, especially from short range. "Lucille, when I tell you, we're going to get behind that thing and jump onto the rear deck—have the guns set to short range, and we'll tear them a new ass."

<<Acknowledged. Fifteen meters. Sensors detected—going silent.>> On the console, a red light blinked signaling her to not speak, sneeze, or make any unnecessary sound as the enemy's sensor suite swept the area.

At the far-left edge of her vision, Tara saw the dust swirl up and away from the ground suddenly. An air-supported armored vehicle slowly moved past not more than two meters away. As its self-contained fan units blew the dust around, Tara identified the vehicle as a Sidar-made command skiff. With a crew of six, the four gunners worked multiple remote-controlled cannons on top of the vehicle, while the driver and vehicle commander monitored the outside situation. She'd seen one like it before—bearing a large red diamond with a Grim Reaper on the rear—the one that'd routed her old unit and left her marked as a coward.

The light turned green. "Lucille, can we jam their communications? Their internal gun control systems?"

<<Unknown,>> Lucille answered after a few seconds. <<Recommend those platforms are the primary targets—railgun loaded and ready.>>

Tara approved but said nothing. The rear end of the skiff appeared along with a familiar emblem that made her blood run cold.

Sonuvabitch!

"Lucille, it's the Darkness."

<<Affirmative. Are you prepared for this?>>

Tara took a deep breath. As many times as she'd seen that emblem in her nightmares, she should have been scared. Instead, there was only rage. "I'm ready when you are."

Lucille didn't respond for a half second. Before Tara could say anything, the CASPer stood up tall, stepped forward twice and fired its jump jets. On the screen, four targeting icons appeared on the skiff's remote gun platforms. As the CASPer jumped, Tara sighted the railgun and squeezed her fingers to her palms on both hands. The first two gun platforms detonated as she reached the apex of the jump about five meters above what looked like a bustle rack on the skiff's rear end.

Time slowed. The two remaining guns pivoted in her direction as her own cannons came up and centered. She squeezed again, this time holding her palms long enough that multiple rounds tore up each cannon mount and ripped into the weak upper surface armor. Each of the slugs created a gaping hand-sized hole as it tore through armor, critical systems, and flesh. Lucille cut in the jump jets to slow their descent and landed squarely on the skiff's central command pedestal, crushing an external weapon pod and ammunition crates as the CASPer settled to the roof. The propulsion system apparently undamaged, the skiff accelerated and Lucille braced the mecha automatically with an arm on a camera system that pivoted in her direction. Tara squeezed the CASPer's hand together shattering the camera lens.

<<Proximity warning.>>

Tara turned the CASPer's torso and saw a Sidar emerge from a cockpit hatch. She brought the left arm up to fire, and the Sidar threw a grenade that impacted the outstretched arm and adhered to the metal skin. An instant later, the device detonated.

<<Electronic attack weapon detonation. Partial power loss. Left arm malfunction. Left hip and leg malfunction.>>

Tara brought the right arm up and across her body. Only her fist mounted, small caliber machine gun could reach the target. She squeezed off a burst and the Sidar ducked it easily by jumping down into the cockpit again. Through the external microphones, Tara heard a squawking sound as the skiff's speakers came to life.

"Pathetic human."

Her CASPer lurched as the skiff shot forward and accelerated madly down the narrow passageway. With the good arm, she dug into the skiff's light armor and tried to maintain her grip. Satisfied, she studied the caution and warning system. "Lucille? Status?"

<<Rebooting the left servo control systems. Ten seconds.>>

The skiff lurched around a 90-degree turn. Tara felt the CASPer sliding and the left side came back online. Lucille whipped the arm out to catch the remains of a gun turret and easily maintained the mecha's balance on the speeding skiff. The right arm let go of its temporary hold, and Tara felt it return completely to her control.

"Give me the railgun, Lucille. Full automatic."

<<Engaged. Target is lit.>>

On the CASPer's heads-up display, a targeting reticle appeared on a thick portion of the skiff's armor. "Confirm cockpit location?"

<<Confirmed.>>

Fuck it. Tara brought up the right arm, centered her fist on the targeting reticle and squeezed her palm. Sixteen rounds exited the barrel of the railgun. The first three plowed into the armor and failed to punch through. The next four made it through the ceramic armor and splintered the inside plating enough to create a deadly field of shrapnel around the Sidar leader. He was dead before the eighth and ninth rounds passed through his chest cavity and continued into the seat behind him. The next six rounds punctured the interior titanium turret and left the internal wall molten enough for the last round to pass through and into the reactor fuel storage tank. As the materials mixed uncontrollably, the skiff detonated in spectacular fashion.

<<Blast—>>

Tara heard nothing else. In the white light and violent explosion, the CASPer systems failed in unison, and the mecha twisted as it flew and slammed her unprotected head into the helmet mount on the right side. Her world went black.

* * *

Qamm remained on her hands and knees long after the final ripple ran down from the Altar mines. All radio frequencies were silent, and there was nothing she could see in the mess around her. She suspected the Altar detonated their colony and the mine entrance in one fell swoop. The thought of her lost mercenaries, and the millions of credits in lost equipment, enraged her. With Kenos dead, there was no viable pay source. The Peacemaker Guild would only reimburse the cost up to a certain percentage based on the situation. Given what happened, and what their representative on the planet knew, they might not pay anything at all. Qamm picked up her knife and snuck around the curving helm of the Raknar toward where the Peacemaker landed.

The Peacemaker had to die for Qamm to be paid. The dead could not refute the claims of the living. It was reason enough for Qamm to leave cover and concealment. She moved quickly through the loose sand. Scanning the ground in front of her, she looked away to the river and noticed the Selroth had retreated. Twisting for a better glance, she contemplated the changing situation as a laser bolt tore through the exterior of her combat vest just below her sternum and passed harmlessly underneath her arm pit. She made for the legs of the stationary CASPer, slid the knife into her sheath and drew the pistol. Another bolt impacted the titanium alloy legs as she knelt for cover behind them. The shooter was up against the Raknar and well hidden. Qamm pressed her back into the thick armor of the CASPer and looked over her left shoulder.

"It's over, Peacemaker! Put down the weapon and come out!" she yelled and heard an echo of her voice in the distance. There was no response.

Her back against the CASPer leg, Qamm pushed herself into a standing position and brought the pistol to her chest. "Peacemaker! Put down that weapon! I'm here to help you!"

The lie came easily and as much as Qamm believed gullible human nature would take effect, it did not. She looked around the leg expecting a shot, but there was none.

Maybe she believes me?

Qamm decided to press the advantage. "That's right, Peacemaker. I know what's happening, and I can help you. You have to put down your weapon. Let me approach, and we'll get out of here together."

There was no response again. Qamm came out of her position and held up her own pistol, barrel up and away from the general vicinity of the Peacemaker. Still nothing. Emboldened, Qamm shuffled forward, portraying a weary and tired commander. "Look, I want this over. You can help me end it."

Fresh rifle and cannon fire filled the air behind her. Qamm turned and pointed. "See? The mercenaries and the colonists are killing each other. Kenos and his promises are dead. There is nothing that can stop peace."

"Quite right," a voice called from behind her. Pain in her back followed a split second later. The smell of dead fish caught her nose and Qamm looked down at a smoldering exit wound on her chest about three centimeters below the right shoulder. She turned slowly toward the voice and tried to bring up the pistol in her right hand, but found it would not respond. The pistol clunked into the sand. A Selroth, his rebreather-hidden face twisted in a smirk, held a pistol on her but kept his eyes on the Raknar hull. "Leader Qamm. You should have stayed with your forces."

Qamm blinked in pain and sudden realization. "Ooren? You killed Kenos?"

"No, but it's just as well he's dead. He was a figurehead and, frankly, in the way of my benefactor." The Selroth smiled. "It's perfect that you've come along just as I am tying up loose ends."

The knife on her left thigh called to her. She could try for it and perhaps draw it as she closed the distance. Selroth, especially those bred for the boring duties of leadership, reacted poorly in a combat situation. This one looked like he'd never held a gun, much less used it. A distraction, even for a few seconds, would work.

"What of Leeto and the Wandering Death?"

The Selroth laughed. "He's dead. Along with scores of Altar and almost all of the humans our Peacemaker brought with her." He stressed the words loudly enough for the Peacemaker to hear, but there was no response from the human.

Is she too scared to move? Qamm thought and dismissed it immediately. Peacemakers were too well trained to be scared in any situation. There had to be something the human waited for. Something that would give her an advantage. "She's not here," Qamm said. "I think she ran toward the colony."

"She did not." Ooren stepped forward, leveling his pistol at her chest. He was three meters away and easily within striking distance. He froze and looked into the sky above them, and the pistol's aim moved away. Qamm snatched the knife from its sheath and lunged forward. She grasped at the Selroth's throat and plunged the knife into his chest. The Selroth gurgled and tried to wrap his arms around her as life drained out of his body. She pushed away, letting him fall, and stood. Her body quivered for a moment before a massive weight hit her from above and drove her right shoulder hard into the sand. Her left leg twisted grotesquely, popping as it failed. The smell hit her nostrils as sharply as the pain along her spine. *An Altar!*

"Get off me," she wheezed. The damned thing could not hear her, but her mercenaries could, and the radio filled with chatter instantly. The weight above her shifted painfully and then lessened as the Altar stood on its legs. Qamm looked up to see it render the Selroth's head from his body with a snap of its powerful mandibles. Black blood spilled across the tan, dusty sand as Qamm struggled upright. Her leg would not work properly as she tried to get it under her.

Her headset squealed to life. "Leader Qamm! Orders? The Altar have retreated into their mine, and the other mercenaries refuse to retreat. What are your orders?"

Qamm stood in agony. She screamed and looked directly into the sun as she did. Legs wobbling in pain, she pressed a clawed finger to her headset and snarled in her native tongue. "Kill everything that isn't ours. Let the Darkness fall!"

She lowered her head and saw the Altar, their queen no less, staring at her. The big ant-like alien's mandibles quivered. "You must experience justice for what you've done."

Qamm laughed through her tears of pain. "Just kill me, Klatk."

The Altar did nothing, and Qamm saw her eyes move a fraction to the left. Qamm tried to turn, but her shattered leg would not comply, and she collapsed into the sand. The Peacemaker approached from her cover and made her way toward the Selroth's corpse with a rifle in her hand. She fired once, at the Selroth's head for insurance, and closed the distance rapidly.

The Altar spoke. "This is Qamm. She is the leader of the Wandering Death."

The human stared, but said nothing for a moment. "Your forces are engaged in genocide, Leader Qamm."

She chuckled. "My forces are fulfilling a contract with Administrator Kenos and the Dream World Consortium, Peacemaker. As it is a valid contract, there is nothing you can do."

The human looked up the hill behind Qamm for a moment. Cannon fire continued. "You ordered your forces to kill everything that wasn't yours. That exceeds your contract guidelines."

"Other incidents as required," Qamm said. Her knife was a full meter away and beyond a quick reach. Any move would clearly show hostile intent, and that would end badly for her, without the chance of at least wounding the human. "The contract is quite clear that negotiated positions change with the situation. Arrest me if you wish, but your charges will not stand in a court of law."

"My charges are born out by the weight of evidence, Leader Qamm, as stipulated by the guidelines of the Peacemaker Guild," the human said. She drew her weapon and pointed it at Qamm's head. "I have no intention of arresting you or your forces."

Qamm snarled. "No Peacemaker would ever execute an unarmed suspect, regardless of the crime."

"It's a good thing I don't have to," the human said as she stepped back and holstered her weapon,

By the time Qamm reached for her weapon, she realized the Altar queen was moving toward her, mandibles open, with a speed she'd never seen much less believed possible. She reached up helplessly, "Please! We can talk this through. We can—"

* * *

Jessica turned her head as Klatk fell upon the screaming Veetanho mercenary. Under the false awning of the fallen Raknar, she looked up at the cockpit section expecting to see Taemin readying himself to shoot them both or awkwardly climbing down the CASPer's legs. There was nothing. Grotesque, wet noises ended the mercenary's screams and screeches. A bone jarring crunch almost caught Jessica's attention enough for her to turn her head, and then there was silence. As she waited for Klatk to finish, Jessica collected her pistol, performed a quick function check, and holstered it against her thigh.

"Is it done?" Jessica asked.

"Yes," Klatk said. "Why would you let me kill when you should have arrested her? I do not understand."

"There is a battle going on, Klatk. I don't have the time, nor the personnel, to handle a prisoner," Jessica said. "Move back from where Taemin can see you."

Klatk glanced up and shuffled forward. "Are you okay?"

The question took her aback. Klatk stood there drenched in the blood of a mercenary she'd violently killed and asked her if she was okay. She frowned and nodded. "I'm fine. What are we going to do now?"

Klatk pointed up at the cockpit section. "This mercenary arrived here without being seen. So, there must be a way to escape Taemin's sight. From there we can get to the battle and salvage what's left."

"What's happened?"

Klatk stood silent for a full five seconds. "Hex detonated the mines and likely his own CASPer to save the brood. My entire team that was with him is dead. None of your tanks survived the initial attack. Only one CASPer remained operational, but it has since gone offline. My people retreated inside the mine and are securing the other entrances. About 400 mercenaries remain engaged and are trying to breach our defenses."

Jessica considered the odds and found them lacking. "We have weapons, though? There are unused CASPers in the compound and more ammunition. You really need to move."

Klatk's mandibles wobbled, the equivalent of a human shrug. "Given their proximity to the command center, they may have been destroyed. Your computer is trying to—"

A large laser bolt tore down through Klatk's chest and the Altar queen crumpled to the ground in front of Jessica. Jessica whirled, tracing the line of the shot, and froze. Taemin stood atop the motionless CASPer with one of the mecha's small laser cannons cradled in his arms.

How in the hell? She gaped. Either he'd studied a lot of CASPer mechanical engineering or something was more than it seemed. Jessica squared her shoulders to him. The breeze picked up and swept her hair across her eyes, but she didn't move.

"You're not a mediator, are you?" she yelled up at him.

The Caroon smiled. "I am in this iteration of life," he said. "Before this life, I did many things the council expunged from all records. Wars for hire. Disputes solved with disreputable tools. All the things you hate. Being a mediator allowed me the opportunity to study disputes and determine where my services could be best used."

"For your own gain," Jessica raised her palms up, showing him her hands were empty, and pulled her hair back over her ear just enough to brush against the on switch for her earpiece. The device rebooted with a series of chimes. "You've managed to kill all of the parties involved, haven't you?"

"Almost. The major players are dead and these simple colonists will feed from their fear long enough to render their colonies incapable of survival. The nuclear detonation below does not change anything, either. I can decontaminate the gold and secure the oil for good measure before the Consortium mounts any type of legal resistance. When they do, I won't be here. My work," he adjusted the heavy rifle's barrel in his arms to point at her chest, "is nearly done."

Jessica laughed and brought a hand to her mouth in surprise. He meant to kill her, and there should be nothing funny about that, but he'd found a way to fool nearly everyone in his life including her—despite her top scores at the Academy in reading others and judging character. That was funny. A fresh breeze came up and blew her hair again, giving her another chance to touch the earpiece and whisper, "Lucille, foxtrot tango."

"What did you say, Peacemaker? Something to your precious computer?" Taemin jutted his chin up at the cockpit section, the meaning clear. "I disassembled that damned thing the moment the power came on in the consoles. I don't know what you were trying to do, but it only managed to work for about 90 seconds. This beast isn't going to fight for you or anyone else. You humans haven't learned how to make others fight your wars for you, just yet. Pity, really. Until you do, you're nothing more than cannon fodder disguised as a worthwhile distraction for most of the Union worlds. I can stop part of that right now. There won't be another human peacemaker for a very long time."

Jessica looked down at the sandy soil as if hiding tears. In reality, she was double-checking that the safety strap on her holster was open, and it was. She cautiously flexed the fingers on her right hand and prepared to draw. She froze. Under her feet, the top grains of sand around her footprints vibrated and pulsed away from the Raknar in shimmering, dancing waves. More followed as the vibration came up through the ground and filled the air. A shriek from above caught her attention and she looked up to see twelve, red-tipped missiles streak over the Raknar from the southwest. They detonated on the high ground around the Altar mine entrances.

More missiles came, followed by four green-camouflaged ducted fan aircraft unlike anything she'd ever seen outside of history books. Their sleek noses, hump-backed fuselages, and small tail sections gave them a sleek, porpoise-like appearance. Under their wings was a bevy of ordnance and twin cannons blazed from their noses.

She looked at Taemin, "Friends of yours?"

He lowered his eyes to her and hefted the barrel again. "What did you do? In the Raknar?"

Jessica shrugged. "Plugged a slate into the console to run a system check. Why?"

"The whole console came alive," Taemin said. "I disabled it, but not fast enough."

What does that mean? These ships came because of the Raknar?

Jessica squinted. "These aren't your friends?"

"No," Taemin said and raised the rifle's barrel up slowly. Another ducted fan aircraft shot over the Raknar, no more than 50 meters overhead, and pivoted sharply to bring its nose onto them. Taemin looked away, and that was just enough time.

Jessica drew her laser pistol without looking, pulling it smoothly from the holster and feeling the touch sensors accept her handprint with a barely perceptible click before the pistol reached her waist. Her arms came up smoothly, left hand reaching across to stablize her right hand under the pistol's grip. As her arms came up, she sighted the pistol on Taemin's narrow chest and fired three quick shots. His face upturned to the flyer, he never saw a thing. The rounds impacted him in a four-centimeter area tearing apart his chest and leaving his back shrouded in a crimson mist. He contorted, fingers squeezing the trigger of the laser rifle as he fell forward from his perch on the Raknar. A green bolt passed harmlessly over her shoulder. Taemin hit the ground with a thud and Jessica shuffled forward, pistol down. The mediator's eyes were open and unfocused. She knelt and checked for a pulse, and the body flinched one last time and settled into the sand.

"You bastard," Jessica said as she stood.

Movement to her right caught her attention, and she knelt an instant before a laser bolt ripped through the air over her head. She spun toward the river, the pistol coming up in her hands. A squad of five Selroth emerged from the still water focused on her. The closest howled in rage, an awful choking sound through its rebreather. Jessica centered the pistol on its chest and pulled the trigger. As it crumpled to the surface of the water, she moved the pistol to the right and found her next target.

Center mass. Squeeze.

Again, she found her target. She whirled to the third Selroth, an enormous tentacle-headed thing, just as it fired a laser bolt that grazed her left shoulder. Jessica winced and went instinctively down to one knee, firing five quick shots as she did. The third Selroth fell into the water. The two others closed the distance to her quickly. She fired again, knocking down the fourth Selroth as the pistol's power failed. The last one came up from the water and charged.

Jessica dropped the pistol and dove for the laser rifle lying in the sand next to Taemin's body. She grabbed it and rolled in one smooth motion, bringing the rifle up in both hands. The Selroth slammed a two-meter long trident towards her face, which Jessica blocked. Jessica swung out her legs, catching the Selroth offguard, and tripped it backward. She rolled up from the sand, rifle at the ready as the Selroth staggered three steps away and turned to face her.

From her position, Jessica realized she could still see the tops of the Selroth's feet, which from her basic combatives class meant that she was out of its striking distance. She raised the rifle to her shoulder. The damned thing was heavier than it looked. "It's over."

The Selroth squatted into a fighting stance, its trident lance at an angle, prepared to attack. The breeze freshened from behind her and swept her hair into her eyes. Jessica shook her head to clear her vision and saw the Selroth snarl at her.

"Now you die." Jessica realized the Selroth would attack her regardless, and the heaviness of the CASPer machine gun in her arms would render her unable to keep it aimed much longer.

"Not today."

Jessica pulled the trigger once and that was enough.

She turned and saw one of the camouflage-painted aircraft hovering over the river not 100 meters away. Jessica studied the ducted flyer for a long moment and felt its pilot's eyes and sensors on her. For a moment, it was a comical standoff and then it was over as the flyer spun and descended on the mine entrance with its cannons firing. She dropped the rifle into the sand and wiped her hands on her coveralls. "Guess y'all are friendlies then."

She tapped her earpiece and scrolled for all active frequencies. There was nothing on the frequency for 10 seconds. She tapped a button to transmit her beacon and authorization code to allow for instant translation. Nothing happened for another 10 seconds.

Fuck it.

"Any station, any station, this is Peacemaker Jessica Francis broadcasting position and authentication. Please respond."

She bit the inside of her lip. After three seconds, there was a click on the frequency, and a human voice with a terrible southern drawl came through the radio. After the first word, she wasn't really listening. Tears filled her eyes in a flash of recognition that stole the air from her lungs and left a lump in her throat.

"Bulldog, this is Snowman. It's about damned time, honey."

* * * * *

Chapter Twenty-Six

Jessica made her way to the Altar colony under the cover of a dozen gunships and a very large drop ship that hovered like a cloud in the morning sunlight. Her earpiece beeped and squawked as she neared a CASPer sprawled across the top of a wall.

Ba-dum. The command frequency connected. "Lucille? Are you out there?"

<<Affirmative. Angel Two has weak but stable life signs.>>

"Who is in Angel Two? Berger was killed."

<<Commander Mason. She attempted, with my considerable assistance, to take on a platoon of mercenary infantry and the command skiff of the Wandering Death. We were successful, but she is unconscious and in need of medical attention.>>

Jessica climbed up onto the wall and onto the front of the CASPer with little difficulty. On the broad surface, she found the emergency crew extraction handle and pulled it. A series of beeps gave her time to step back from the CASPer and down onto the retaining wall, and then the canopy blew off.

"Peacemaker!"

Jessica turned and recognized Bukk moving toward her. "Bukk, I need your help."

The Altar lieutenant scrambled onto the CASPer and helped Jessica to do the same. She worked the straps and released Tara.

"Grab her." Jessica gestured to Bukk, and he grabbed Tara's shoulders. "You have a better reach to pull her forward and up. I'll get her legs."

"I understand," Bukk replied and did exactly what she'd asked. As Tara's legs came free, Jessica grabbed them and lifted up.

"Now, bring her this way and we'll get her flipped around."

Bukk turned his head and Jessica saw his antennae waving from side to side. "I have a better idea."

Three more Altar ran to them and positioned themselves under the CASPer's shoulders, on the opposite side from Jessica. They took Tara's limp body without effort and lowered her to the ground. Jessica climbed down and knelt beside her.

Tara's skin was cold and clammy, and her pupils barely registered light, but her breathing was steady and rhythmic. The right side of her head was puffy and swollen and her hair was matted with half-dried blood. A quick check of her pulse gave Jessica hope; it was strong. Jessica patted Tara's coverall legs and found what she was looking for in the left inner thigh pocket. The medkit injector would heal Tara or place her in a medical coma until better medical care could be arranged. Shaped like a large permanent marker, it was designed to be quickly jabbed into the wounded person so the pressurized needle would fire into the skin. Jessica opened the protective cap and slammed it into Tara's still leg. The injector beeped when complete. She removed it from Tara's leg and tossed it aside.

Bukk looked down at her. "Who came to our rescue?"

Jessica blinked. "I don't really know who they are, Bukk."

"You talked to them, though. On the frequency. We heard you. Who is Snowman? He called you Bulldog, the same as Hex did."

Jessica raised a palm to him so he'd stop asking questions, and she could clear her head. "Snowman was my father's callsign. I don't even know if it's really him, okay?" Tears filled her eyes, and she wiped at them and shook her head. "I screwed up trying to get a complete system scan on the Raknar."

"I do not understand how you could have screwed up and brought in reinforcements."

She dug into her pocket and withdrew the chipset. "This is from the Raknar's System console. It's a long story, Bukk, but my father left me one that looks a lot like this. When Kenos came to find me, I wasn't paying attention. I stuffed my father's chip into the Raknar's board. It should not have worked..." She trailed off and shook her head. "Or maybe it should have. I don't know. I'd engaged a combat slate to run a system check, too. Maybe that did it. I just don't know who they are and how they got here."

Bukk looked over the colony. "Queen Klatk would be pleased, regardless."

"She came for me and protected me from the mercenaries," Jessica said. "I could not protect her from Taemin."

"We owe a debt to Hex that we will never be able to repay," Bukk said. "They closed the mines and managed to protect the brood at the same time. We may never really know what happened down there, but I am resolved to investigate."

Jessica stood up and looked at him. Absent a queen, he would be the colony leader. As such, certain protocols had to be followed. "Do you wish to maintain a protected status?"

Bukk looked at her. "Yes, Peacemaker. We want a full investigation into what happened here. I will alert our home world, the Trade Guild, and the Peacemaker Guild that we intend to file measures against the Dream World Consortium and all other parties discovered in the course of an investigation. We are hopeful that the Peacemaker Guild will assign you for the investigation."

Jessica nodded. "Thank you, Bukk, but we both know that won't happen. I am involved in this situation as much as any other party. They'll want to speak with everyone. Who knows? I might not even be a Peacemaker after everything is reviewed and settled."

"You have little faith in yourself, Jessica," Bukk said. "All of the Altar and humans who died to protect the colony did so because of your leadership. They placed great faith in you, as did Klatk, and so do I."

Jessica sighed and could not help but feel a small surge of pride through the malaise and hurt that conflicted her emotions and twisted her stomach. In the space of weeks, she'd forced the retirement of her ex-husband, completed her Peacemaker training, and lost a host of soldiers. No losses hurt more than Hex and Maya, though. The young lovers were as close to friends as she had in the galaxy. Without them, her personal life would be emptier than it had been before. So much of her life before Peacemaker training was gone now. Over the years, the only people close enough to be her friends had died on missions big and small. There were fewer and fewer people she'd be able to call on for help, the ones she'd be willing to give up her life for, as they would do for her.

Yet, there was a new development that could change everything. Jessica looked up at the twin-rectangular hulled ship hanging a couple of thousand meters overhead. Bristling with cannons and hangar doors, it obviously wasn't a trade vessel, and she'd never seen anything like it under the command of a mercenary force. A sleek flyer descended from an open hangar door. Built in the same manner as the smaller ones she'd seen raining missiles onto the mercenaries, it was clearly larger and could also carry cargo.

"How many mercenaries are alive up there, Bukk?"

"None, Peacemaker. The Selroth and GenSha retreated to their colonies along with some of the mercenaries."

Jessica knew the mercenaries would find a way to run. The colonies, all three of them, could be forced to the negotiating table if the mercenary threats were completely neutralized. She tapped her earpiece again. A chime sounded that Lucille was listening as she radioed the man who might be her father.

"Snowman, this is Bulldog. I need to make sure any mercenary stragglers don't get off this planet until the Guild arrives for a full review. Do you have any resources that could do that?"

The voice came back immediately. "I've got flyers patrolling both colonies now and we've got enough stuff in orbit to make sure nobody leaves until you say so. I've even got the station commander at D'nart ready to relay any message you have, honey."

"Are you coming down here?" she asked and forced herself to bite off the "Dad" at the end before it leaked out of her mouth.

"I'm on my way right now." The descending ship came straight down toward them on a course for the shoreline where she'd housed the drop ship from *Victory Twelve* two days before.

Jessica looked at Bukk. "I need to go meet that ship."

"I have a colony to reconstitute," he said. "We both have great tasks in front of us."

The Altar lieutenant moved away slowly, taking all but one soldier with him. The younger Altar stayed by Tara's side and monitored her vital signs with a combat slate. She was in good enough hands that Jessica felt okay leaving her.

<<Communications update. All frequencies out of the colony are now clear for broadcast. I have a relay signal from D'nart good for the entire planet.>>

"Record this message and send. Ready?" Jessica paused. There was a beep in her ear and she spoke slowly. "This is Peacemaker Jessica Francis. The planet of Araf is locked down to departures until further notice. Under Article 42 of the Galactic Code of Military Justice, I am notifying the Peacemaker Guild of an official investigation into this world and all its parties. Discussion is encouraged and will only be accepted at a time and location of my choosing—which I will announce in the next 24 hours. Many citizens have died needlessly and there will be no more bloodshed on my watch. Make no attempt to flee. Peacemaker Francis, out."

<<Message transmitted and relayed to the planetary communication system.>>

"Notify the Guild, too; priority alpha."

<<Acknowledged.>>

Jessica watched the descending flyer for a few seconds before she started walking through the colony passageways, avoiding small fires and the sprawled bodies of the Altar who'd died defending it. She caught the smell of burning rubber from one of the lost tanks. They would need to be remembered. "Lucille?"

<<Yes, Peacemaker?>>

"I want the complete files of everyone brought out here on the *Victory Twelve*. I know you got a full manifest, but I need to know more about them. Some of them were just kids."

<<Acknowledged. I have the file for your access at any time.>>

She would still have to face it at some point. Writing letters to their families about what had happened, and how their loved ones had died, would come later. Jessica stepped through the main colony wall and headed across open ground. "Have you tried to engage any systems from our new friends?"

<<I am blocked and unable to access their servers. This is something I've never experienced.>>

"You learn something new every day," Jessica said. About the size of a small exo-jet liner on Earth, the flyer settled at the river's edge with barely a sound. She kept walking, realizing it was harder and harder to see through misting eyes. A million emotions cascaded down on her. For more than 20 years, she'd imagined this moment again and again during almost any time of the day. Seeing children and their fathers turned from adolescent longing to teen anger to adult sadness. She'd imagined herself running into his arms like a child on the playground. Sometimes she slapped his face with everything she had and walked away. Other times it was a long, awkward silence that ended in ugly tears. Some ended with her crying alone. Again.

None of them prepared her for the well of emotion that opened in her soul. A million questions, a million fears, a million reasons and excuses to run, none of them prepared her to face him. Her mother's pain bubbled up through Jessica's memory. On her death bed, she'd asked for Jimmy several times as tears spilled down her cheeks. Her mother hadn't remembered anything in the end, but she remembered her husband.

Jessica felt a tear cascade down her left cheek and she swiped it away. The dark gray outer cockpit door slid open and a small, three-rung ladder deployed under it. The clear, protective glass inner door slid open and Jessica sobbed. A white-haired man with a familiar grin looked out at her. His shoulders were a little more rounded than she remembered. He stepped down from the cockpit and walked toward her, and there was no doubt it was him. His eyes glistened, and a sob came up that made his broad chest heave.

Her feet moved without prompting from her brain. Tears blinded her as she stepped forward. Her arms came out without warning. She caught the scent of Old Spice on the breeze, and any shred of emotional control failed her. She wrapped her arms around him and let 25 years of tears come.

It was a long embrace.

* * *

Two days later, peace grew between the colonies, and they worked together to clean up the detritus of war. Given full access to the Dream World systems, Lucille diagnosed and corrected the climate control system in less than nine hours. Kenos had never attempted to fix it. Weather patterns shifted almost immediately and brought rain to the starved Choote valley. Cooler weather made the arduous tasks easier and left time in the evenings for rest. Jessica and her father spent as much time as they could just talking. Bukk and his citizens worked through the first night to get their colony power and water systems online. Burying the dead and clearing debris would take many more long days. As the sun set, Jessica and her father left the colony to continue getting to know each other all over again.

They sat on a group of rocks overlooking the Choote. Jessica's bare feet dangled in the cold water as they shared a bottle of beer from her father's ship. The colony cleanup continued behind them, with representatives from the Selroth and GenSha colonies working alongside the Altar. A fair and equitable solution would come soon and she would go home.

"I don't know if they're going to commission me."

Her father took a sip from the bottle and handed it to her. "Why would you say that, Jess?"

She snorted. "Look around, Dad. I'm pretty sure this is a failure. Even though you did manage to sweep in at the last minute to save my ass, the Guild won't be happy with me."

He patted her leg. "The Guild might surprise you. They've handled far worse than this with far worse results."

"I'm just a candidate, Dad. They can wipe me off the books before I ever get started."

He smiled at her like he'd done the first time she tied a square knot. "I think you'll be surprised. They do things very differently."

She chuckled. "You say that like you know them pretty well, Dad."

He reached for the beer bottle and she let him have it. "I've known a few Peacemakers, Jess. None like you though."

She blushed with the compliment as it filled her from head to toe. As it washed over her, a question came along that she hadn't asked. They'd talked about their lives, Jessica's mother, and why he'd never returned. Turns out that he couldn't because of his work. Her mother went to her grave acting as if she never knew why, though she'd been in on the ruse the entire time. James Francis, one of the most respected long-distance haulers, had been a mercenary from day one. In the days after the First Contracts and the return of the Four Horsemen, his hauling service became a mercenary force in its own right, but one that no one really knew. That was his plan all along.

Intergalactic Haulers, Incorporated, was his creation. Originally formed to gather the remains of human mercenary units across the galaxy for reconstitution in the original Four Horseman companies and, eventually other units, the Haulers operated as a half-dozen hauling companies with a very serious level of ammunition and capability hiding in plain sight. If a mercenary unit became overwhelmed and lost a contract along with their forces, and the Haulers were nearby, they'd find a safe place and transport them home. Return with honor was their motto. They'd brought tens of thousands of mercenaries back to Earth and other worlds around the galaxy. Finding him should have been easy, but there was more to the story than she knew, and it didn't answer the toughest question.

"How did you find me?"

Her father laughed. "I knew the minute you got Elly that you'd figure out something was inside it. From there, it would only be a matter of time."

"I meant how did you get the signal? Once I plugged the wrong chip into the Raknar I—"

"I got your initial signal before you left Luna, Jess."

Jessica startled. "Taemin said the Systems console came online before he disabled the slate I left in there. I figured it was the chipset."

"It did something in the Raknar? Hell, it is a Dusman chipset, but I never thought about you plugging it into a mech, Bulldog. We should check it out before your Guild gets here." He patted her leg. "Honey, that's not how I found you. You tested the chip with Lucille aboard the *Victory Twelve* and triggered it to report. That's when I got the first signal, Jess. We got your ship's information and jump profile. I came as fast as I could. We got into the system and saw what was going on, and I knew it was you." He laughed. "Only my daughter would get into the middle of a war between pissed off colonies and a crooked tourism company about their broken planet."

Jessica squinted at him. "Again, it sounds like you know way more than you should."

"You stay out here as long as I have, you pick things up." He looked into the sunset for a long moment. He spoke softly. "There wasn't a day that went by that I didn't miss you, Bulldog. I didn't think it would take so long for you to get Elly, especially after your mother died."

"It's been a long, strange trip, Dad."

He wrapped an arm around her shoulders. The scent of Old Spice came with the one-armed hug, and it made her smile. "Would you do me a favor?"

"Anything, Dad."

"Let an old man pin on that shiny new platinum badge?"

She grinned through fresh tears. "It's not mercenary rank. Are you going to be okay with that?"

There were tears in his eyes, too. One trailed down his cheek, and she wiped it away. He pulled her into a tight embrace. "You're damned right your Daddy is, Peacemaker. Besides, honey, we've got a lot to do."

# # # # #

ABOUT THE AUTHOR

Kevin's head has been in the clouds since he was old enough to read. Ask him and he'll tell you that he still wants to be an astronaut. A retired Army officer, Kevin has a diverse background in space and space science education. A former manager of the world-renowned U.S. Space Camp program in Huntsville, Alabama and a former executive of two Challenger Learning Centers, Kevin works with space every day and lives in Colorado with his family.

Kevin's bestselling debut science fiction novel, **Sleeper Protocol**, was released by Red Adept Publishing in January 2016 and was a Finalist for the 2017 Colorado Book Award. Publisher's Weekly called it "an emotionally powerful debut." The sequel, **Vendetta Protocol**, is due for release in September 2017. His military science fiction novel **Runs In The Family** was released by Strigidae Publishing in January 2016.

Kevin is an Active Member of the Science Fiction Writers of America and he is member of Pikes Peak Writers and the Rocky Mountain Fiction Writers. He is an alumna of the Superstars Writing Seminar.

Titles by Kevin Ikenberry

"Sleeper Protocol" – Available Now

"A Fistful of Credits" – Available Now

"Runs in the Family" – Available Now

"Vendetta Protocol" – Coming Soon

* * * * *

The following is an

Excerpt from Book One of the Revelations Cycle:

Cartwright's Cavaliers

Mark Wandrey

Available Now from Seventh Seal Press

eBook, Paperback, and Audio Book

Excerpt from "Cartwright's Cavaliers:"

The last two operational tanks were trapped on their chosen path. Faced with destroyed vehicles front and back, they cut sideways to the edge of the dry river bed they'd been moving along and found several large boulders to maneuver around that allowed them to present a hull-down defensive position. Their troopers rallied on that position. It was starting to look like they'd dig in when Phoenix 1 screamed over and strafed them with dual streams of railgun rounds. A split second later, Phoenix 2 followed on a parallel path. Jim was just cheering the air attack when he saw it. The sixth damned tank, and it was a heavy.

"I got that last tank," Jim said over the command net.

"Observe and stand by," Murdock said.

"We'll have these in hand shortly," Buddha agreed, his transmission interspersed with the thudding of his CASPer firing its magnet accelerator. "We can be there in a few minutes."

Jim examined his battlespace. The tank was massive. It had to be one of the fusion-powered beasts he'd read about. Which meant shields and energy weapons. It was heading down the same gap the APC had taken, so it was heading toward Second Squad, and fast.

"Shit," he said.

"Jim," Hargrave said, "we're in position. What are you doing?"

"Leading," Jim said as he jumped out from the rock wall.

* * * * *

The following is an
Excerpt from Book One of The Kin Wars Saga:

Wraithkin

Jason Cordova

Available Now from Theogony Books

eBook, Paperback, and (soon) Audio Book

Excerpt from "Wraithkin:"

Prologue

The lifeless body of his fellow agent on the bed confirmed the undercover operation was thoroughly busted.

"Crap," Agent Andrew Espinoza, Dominion Intelligence Bureau, said as he stepped fully into the dimly lit room and carefully made his way to the filthy bed in which his fellow agent lay. He turned away from the ruined body of his friend and scanned the room for any sign of danger. Seeing none, he quickly walked back out of the room to where the slaves he had rescued earlier were waiting.

"Okay, let's keep quiet now," he reminded them. "I'll go first, and you follow me. I don't think there are any more slavers in the warehouse. Understand?"

They all nodded. He offered them a smile of confidence, though he had lied. He knew there was one more slaver in the warehouse, hiding near the side exit they were about to use. He had a plan to deal with that person, however. First he had to get the slaves to safety.

He led the way, his pistol up and ready as he guided the women through the dank and musty halls of the old, rundown building. It had been abandoned years before, and the slaver ring had managed to get it for a song. In fact, they had even qualified for a tax-exempt purchase due to the condition of the neighborhood around it. The local constable had wanted the property sold, and the slaver ring had stepped in and offered him a cut if he gave it to them. The constable had readily agreed, and the slavers had turned the warehouse into the processing plant for the sex slaves they sold throughout the Dominion. Andrew knew all this because he had been the one to help set up the purchase in the first place.

Now, though, he wished he had chosen another locale.

He stopped the following slaves as he came to the opening which led into one of the warehouse's spacious storage areas. Beyond that lay their final destination, and he was dreading the confrontation with the last slaver. He checked his gun and grunted in surprise as he saw he had two fewer rounds left than he had thought. He shook his head and charged the pistol.

"Stay here and wait for my signal," he told the rescued slaves. They nodded in unison.

He took a deep, calming breath. No matter what happened, he had to get the slaves to safety. He owed them that much. His sworn duty was to protect the Dominion from people like the slavers, and someone along the way had failed these poor women. He exhaled slowly, crossed himself and prayed to God, the Emperor and any other person who might have been paying attention.

He charged into the room, his footsteps loud on the concrete flooring. He had his gun up as he ducked behind a small, empty crate. He peeked over the top and snarled; he had been hoping against hope the slaver was facing the other direction.

Apparently Murphy is still a stronger presence in my life than God, he thought as he locked eyes with the last slaver. The woman's eyes widened in recognition and shock, and he knew he would only have one chance before she killed them all.

He dove to the right of the crate and rolled, letting his momentum drag him out of the slaver's immediate line of fire. He struggled to his feet as her gun swung up and began to track him, but he was already moving, sprinting back to the left while closing in on her. She fired twice, both shots ricocheting off the floor and embedding themselves in the wall behind him.

Andrew skid to a stop and took careful aim. It was a race, the slaver bringing her gun around as his own came to bear upon her. The muzzles of both guns flashed simultaneously, and Andrew grunted as pain flared in his shoulder.

A second shot punched him in the gut and he fell, shocked the woman had managed to get him. He lifted his head and saw that while he had hit her, her wound wasn't nearly as bad as his. He had merely clipped her collarbone and, while it would smart, it was in no way fatal. She took aim on him and smiled coldly.

Andrew swiftly brought his gun up with his working arm and fired one final time. The round struck true, burrowing itself right between the slaver's eyes. She fell backwards and lay still, dead. He groaned and dropped the gun, pain blossoming in his stomach. He rolled onto his back and stared at the old warehouse's ceiling.

That sucked, he groused. He closed his eyes and let out a long, painful breath.

* * * * *

Find out more about Mark Wandrey and Jason Cordova at: http://chriskennedypublishing.com/

* * * * *

Acknowledgements

First and foremost, this novel wouldn't exist without the Four Horsemen Universe (4HU) created by Chris Kennedy and Mark H. Wandrey. I'm very thankful to have been asked to play twice now in the 4HU and I hope to have more opportunities in the future. I'd like to see where Earth's First Peacemaker goes from here, too. Thank you, gents. It's been a blast.

I also have to thank my friend Chuck Gannon for introducing me to Chris and Mark after he advance-read my novel Vendetta Protocol (coming in late 2017). I'm in your debt, Chuck, and I look forward to more late-night conversations and projects in the near future.

In the process of writing this book, I reached out to my friend and talented editor Mia Kleve to help me take a rough story and fine tune it into the novel you've hopefully enjoyed. I couldn't have done it without your quick and poignant feedback.

Special thanks go to Beth Agejew, my editor, for pointing out the little things and helping me get this book ready for publication. A keen eye always helps see the things we writers seem to miss.

Lastly, as always, I have to thank my girls. Hopefully our little ones will grow up seeing Jessica, and other strong female characters (like their Mommy, too), as examples to follow as they blaze their own path across history.

Colorado Springs, Colorado
July 8, 2017

Made in the USA
Middletown, DE
19 August 2019